Paula Chase

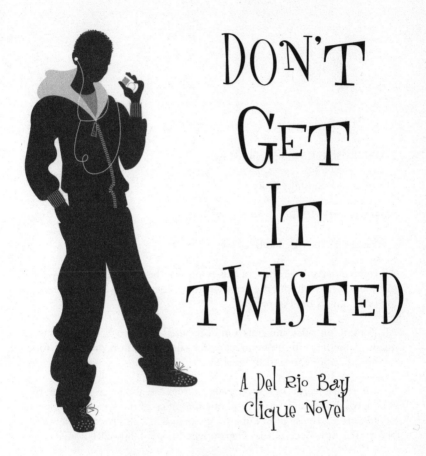

DON'T GET IT TWISTED

A Del Rio Bay Clique Novel

DAFINA BOOKS FOR YOUNG READERS
KENSINGTON PUBLISHING CORP.
http://www.kensingtonbooks.com

For my parents

Acknowledgments

Always, always, thank you to my husband, Ted, and my girls who know the real deal about living with a temperamental "artist" (the moods, the abrupt disappearances into the office midconversation). Your support helps me through. Love you guys. Being forced to put thanks in ink makes you realize just how many people you may leave out once you start . . . so, thank you everyone who has touched me, boosted me along, picked me up, made me laugh or cry and otherwise kept me sane as I lead my double life.

"New York, Cacalacki and Compton check it, check it, check it out."
—A Tribe Called Quest, "Scenario"

The Frenzy

"Shorty, I want you to be my entourage."
—Omarion, "Entourage"

R *U down?*

Mina Mooney stood, hunched over the back of the chair at her desk, staring at the three words on her monitor. Her stomach rumbled. From hunger or anxiety, Mina wasn't sure.

Two seconds ago, it was definitely hunger.

Sick of leftover turkey, mashed potatoes and all the other food they'd eaten on Thanksgiving and all yesterday, she'd been ravenous at the thought of sinking her teeth into something that wasn't stuffed or covered in gravy. When her mom burst into the room and plopped down on the bed, rousing Mina from a sound sleep with a tickle to the neck and a proposal that they cook a very un-Thanksgiving family breakfast, Mina had eagerly shaken off the early—if you could call ten-thirty A.M. early—morning haze fogging her head.

That was five minutes ago. Now . . .

She wanted to be sure that she understood Craig Simpson's words correctly. He *was* asking her out. Wasn't he?

Mina swiveled the chair with her knee and let her butt hover over the seat in a half-sitting, half-standing stance. She scrolled the screen and read the short exchange again.

Bluedevils33: Ay what up?
BubbliMi: Nuthin' ready to go eat
Bluedevils33: O. U know 'bout the Frenzy?

Mina knew. It was all JZ had talked about the last two weeks since football season had ended. It was the big bash Coach Banner held for the varsity football team at his McMansion in Folger's Way, Del Rio Bay's ritziest neighborhood, to celebrate the season.

BubbliMi: yeah. heard they had strippers last year
Bluedevils33: LOL. whatever. people b x-ageratin! It's not that bad
BubbliMi: I figured . . . but u never know! Y'all ballers can get out of control—ha ha
Bluedevils33: tru dat. But naw it ain't nothin' like that.
BubbliMi: I'll have 2 take ur word 4 it
Bluedevils33: No u can see 4 urself. u want 2 go w/me to the party?

And that was when Mina had shut down, unable to move, type, blink or breathe. It was while she was trying to come back to her senses that the last message came in . . .

Bluedevils33: R U down?

Mina stared at the screen, letting the words sink in. She wanted to type "seriously?" but figured that sounded stupid.

She rested a knee on the chair, a big grin on her brown sugar face. Craig was finally asking her out. Exactly four weeks ago they had spent the night bumping, grinding and getting their dance on at a party Mina had given for her best friend, Lizzie. Since then she and Craig talked more at school than they had before and IM'ed when they were on-line at the same time, but nothing drastic had changed between them.

Now, he was asking her out. And not just any date—no movies or grabbing a slice at Rio's 'Ria, the hot hangout spot in Del Rio Bay. Craig was asking her to go with him to the annual Blue Devils' Football Frenzy. She ignored the images the word "frenzy" brought to mind and instead tried to picture the forty-member football team playing rowdy rounds of spades, Madden football or checkers.

Yeah, right.

JZ had already given her and the clique an earful about the Frenzy. Board games and Playstation were never mentioned.

JZ and a few other select junior varsity football players, those who were definitely making varsity next year, were invited to the Frenzy. JZ was the main reason the JV football team had gone on to win the county championship. The invite to the Frenzy was a not so subtle acknowledgment that next year's tryouts were only a formality. JZ's future place on the varsity food chain was set.

The only reason JZ wasn't on varsity football this season, as a freshman, was because of his father. He wanted sports second on JZ's priority list. But JZ was a die-hard athlete—football in the fall, basketball in the winter and track in spring to stay in shape. He trained like a pro, running several miles a day and lifting weights several times a week. Even if sports were second on JZ's schedule because Mr. Zimms said so, football and basketball were first in his every thought.

And being on JV had actually brightened JZ's star, not dulled it. The minute he'd stepped on the field in September, it was obvious to the coaches he was varsity material. They'd been drooling over the thought of having him move up ever since.

Now the varsity basketball coaches were going to get the chance the football team hadn't had, because when football season ended,

JZ's dad had relented and agreed to let him try out for varsity. JZ made the team easily. The only "catch," if JZ's grades suffered even a little, his father was going hardcore and making JZ cut out the sports until next season. So all JZ talked about, lately, were basketball and the Frenzy.

According to JZ, the Frenzy was wild. Coach Banner basically let his "boys" have the run of the house for the night, no chaperons. JZ also mentioned nude foolishness in the hot tub and drinking, *Real World* high school edition.

Other than pointing out to JZ that she thought the details of the party were probably rumors or overexaggerated, Mina hadn't given the Frenzy much thought. Until now. Now she had an invitation from a varsity football hottie.

Was she down?

Mina wanted to type YES, all caps just so Craig would know how down she was.

She couldn't believe that only three letters stood between her and her first date with the guy she'd crushed on for months. Her first date, period.

It wasn't even eleven A.M. and this day was quickly moving toward best-day-ever status.

And to think, in her haste to throw down on some pancakes and bacon, she'd almost walked right by her computer without as much as a glance.

Thank goodness she'd logged on to see if Kelly had sent a message confirming whether she could come over later and hang over at JZ's with the rest of the clique. Mina was anxious for the six of them to get together. They'd squeezed in only a few IMs and phone calls over the weeklong break. Mina didn't mind family time, but five straight days of it was enough. She was ready to kick it with her friends, especially now that she had something more interesting to share than an account of her family's insanely competitive game of Trivial Pursuit on Thanksgiving night.

Mina's head turned toward the loud clanging of pots and pans coming from downstairs, her attention slipping, just for a second, from the three words on the screen. She tipped over to her bedroom door, leaned her head out of the room and waited on her mother's call asking for (requiring) help cooking breakfast. When it didn't come, Mina scurried back over to the desk and sat down, her heart pounding and her hunger completely forgotten.

The loud tinkle of another IM from Craig rang out.

Bluedevils33: Yo, Mina u there?
BubbliMi: Sorry! Listening out 4 my mom . . . I'm supposed to be downstairs cooking
Bluedevils33: Word. I let u go if u answer me. U down w/the Frenzy?

This time Mina didn't think. She typed, quickly.

BubbliMi: Mos' def!!
Bluedevils33: Cool. U be @ the Ria tonite?
BubbliMi: Trying to be. Not sure tho'
Bluedevils33: I can give u a ride if u want

The thought of being in the car with Craig made Mina's heart race. Everything was moving so fast.

BubbliMi: Naw I'm cool. If I go it'll be w/my girls. I see u there if we go.
Bluedevils33: Aight. Later
BubbliMi: C U

Mina stared at the conversation on the screen, reading over it quickly again and again. It felt like a dream. If her heart wasn't practically beating out of her chest, she would swear she was still sleeping.

"Mi–naaa!" her mother called from downstairs. "What's taking you so long?"

"Coming, Ma!"

Smiling like an idiot, Mina closed out the IM box and signed off. She stood up and jogged down the hall to the bathroom. If Craig could see her now, bed head and stank morning breath, he'd run screaming in the other direction. She laughed out loud at her fuzzy-headed image in the bathroom mirror.

Stank breath and all, she had a date!

She had a DATE . . . and one problem. Her parents didn't allow her to date yet.

Mariah and Jackson Mooney's Guide to Dating

"There's no need to argue, parents just don't understand."
—Lil Romeo, Nick Cannon & 3LW, "Parents Just Don't Understand"

Thoughts of her parents' dating rules wouldn't dampen Mina's excitement. And her parents had plenty of rules.

Mariah and Jackson Mooney's Guide to Dating included the following little lovelies:

❀ First and foremost, no solo dating until age fifteen.
(That was going to be a tough one to battle.)

❀ For group dates, there must be at least six other people going. As far as Mina was concerned, going to the movies with six or eight other people wasn't a date but a field trip.

❀ Mariah and Jack must KNOW the parents of each person on the date.

❀ This was Mina's favorite; absolutely no car dating until age fifteen, i.e., parental drop-offs only. (It was why

Mina had quickly turned down Craig's offer for a ride to Rio's 'Ria.)

✻ If the "date" takes place at a party, the 'rents must first speak to someone who is chaperoning the party before giving approval.

Mina bounced happily down the stairs, the rules swirling in her head. As she walked into the kitchen, Mina convinced herself she had a solid argument against each one:

First, this wasn't a solo date because JZ would be there (even if the last thing on his mind, that night, would be keeping up with Mina).

It was a group date, sort of. Couldn't she count the forty other people and their dates (if they brought any) as a group? She was sure to know a few other girls there.

Okay, so she couldn't do squat about her parents knowing everyone else's parents. That rule was just ridiculous. Not that she was going to tell them that, but . . .

As far as car dating, at this point, if her parents let her go, she didn't care if they dropped her off. Maybe she could get them to drop her off down the street from the house or over at Kelly's and she'd walk to Coach Banner's house. Mina didn't know how far Kelly lived from the coach, but they lived in the same neighborhood.

Talking to the chaperons . . . Well, if it came to it, she'd have her parents talk to Coach Banner. Not sure how. It wasn't as though she had his number or anything. But where there's a will there's a way and all that jazz.

Mina's resolve wilted a little. Maybe the arguments against the rules weren't so solid . . . but they were all she had.

"Morning, Mom," Mina chirped. She stood by her mom's side at the stove. A mix of hickory and seasoned salt floated toward her nose, making her stomach growl. "Still need help?"

Mariah Mooney looked up from flipping a pancake, her large round eyes narrowed in mock anger. She put her hand on her hip. "I thought we were fixing this breakfast *together?*"

Mina giggled. "Sorry. I was checking to see if Kelly was coming over today. I'll help."

She put her hand out, and her mom quickly relinquished her pancake-flipping duties, then moved on to the grill where bacon popped quietly.

"Where's Daddy?" Mina scooped a pancake, peeking at its underside to test its brownness. The pancake needed a few more seconds.

Mina's mom paced between the bacon and a pan of fried potatoes. She shook her head. "Still in the bed." She grabbed another spatula from a nearby drawer and stirred the potatoes around. "If I had known a Mooney un-Thanksgiving breakfast meant me cooking by my lonesome, I would have never suggested it."

Mina leaned over and kissed her mom's cheek. "Forgive me?"

Mariah smiled. "No. But thanks for gracing me with your presence, Miss Social Butterfly. So can Kelly join you guys today?"

Mina frowned. In all the excitement of Craig IM'ing her, as far as she'd gotten was opening the inbox. She'd never actually looked at the new messages.

"Probably," Mina said, rushing on and ignoring her mom's perplexed expression. "Hey, Ma, remember Craig Simpson?"

Mariah chuckled. "Oh, you mean the boy you refused to introduce to me and Daddy at your party?"

A slice of regret cut through Mina. Now she wished she had been more assertive about introducing Craig to her parents. They were sticklers for "knowing" her friends. Even though her mom had heard Craig's name mentioned a few times since the school year started, when he showed up at the party for Lizzie, Mina hadn't

wanted Craig to think she was singling him out for a grand intro-
duction. It had felt too formal. Instead, she'd flipped the whole
"group" concept on her parents and waited until Craig and a few
other guys from the football team were upstairs getting a drink before introducing all of them to her parents. It had seemed like a
good idea at the time.

"I didn't refuse," Mina reminded her mom. She flipped two pancakes and took a step back from the stove so she could face her
mom. "I just didn't want Craig thinking that I was going all girlfriend on him. I did finally introduce y'all."

"Un-huh. To him and about four other guys." Mariah shrugged.
"For the few minutes I talked to him he seemed like a nice guy."

"I couldn't risk Daddy asking him a million questions. It would
have been too embarrassing," Mina said. Her face grew hot just
thinking about it.

"Oh, Lord, Mina." Mariah rolled her eyes. "God forbid, your dad
asks the guy's last name, where he lives, who his parents are . . ."

"Exactly!" Mina shook her head. "We were dancing together not
running off to Vegas."

Mina's mother laughed hard. "Girl, where do you get all that
drama from?" She smiled, lighting up her golden brown face, but
tried to sound serious. "Alright. Well, what about him?" She moved
the pan of potatoes off the burner and covered them before moving
back to the bacon.

"Well . . ." Mina stepped back over to the pancakes, slipping
them out of the pan and onto a plate.

"Hold on, sweetie," her mom said. She peeked around the cor-
ner of the kitchen and called out, "Jack! Breakfast is almost ready!"
She popped back around and faced Mina. "Sorry. Now, what about
Craig?"

Mina's words rushed out in a stream. "Heaskedmeout."

Mina watched her mom's eyes crinkle the way they did when
she was happy. Maybe she had a chance.

"Really?" Mariah smiled.

"Yes," Mina gushed. "Ma, Craig is like . . . Do you know how many girls would love to go out with him?! And he asked me. I mean, I was hoping he would. I thought he would after the party. But he didn't. He—"

"Slow down, baby girl." Mariah chuckled. She slid the bacon onto a plate, tore a paper towel off a roll and dabbed at the grease on each slice. "Okay, I get it. You really like this guy, even though you didn't want to introduce him. Guess you're ashamed of the parental units."

Mina rolled her eyes. "Ma, parental units? Okay, please come back to the new millennium."

Mariah carried a bottle of syrup and tub of butter over to the table. "Sorr-eee." She leaned against the counter, arms folded, smile still tugging at her mouth. "Just teasing. I'm glad he asked you out. It's exciting, huh?"

Mina's head nodded in an eager bobble.

"First dates are exciting. And he's nice looking from what I remember," her mom said.

"Understatement of the year," Mina said. She turned the stove off and dropped the pan into the sink, which had water waiting. The pan sizzled as she exclaimed, "Mom, he's FINE!"

Mariah's voice turned serious and professional. "Un-huh. Well, where is this date? And when would it be?"

Mina knew that voice. It meant the preliminary nice-nice chitchat was out of the way and the rules were coming. Scared her mother would see the worry on her face, Mina focused on the dishwater as she washed out the pan.

"It's a um . . . party," she said. "The varsity football team's annual end-of-the-season party. It's in two weeks."

"Well, you know how Daddy and I feel about—"

"It wouldn't just be me and Craig, Ma. JZ will be there," Mina sputtered. She rinsed the pan, dropped it on the rack to dry and wiped her hands on a towel.

"Okay. Anyone else we know? And how were you planning to get there?" Her mother's questions poured nonstop. "Who throws this party? It's a team party, which means lots of people you don't know. Who else besides Craig and JZ do you know? I mean really know?"

"Coach Banner has the party for the team," Mina mumbled. She fiddled with the towel, for once wishing she had another dish to wash to keep herself from looking at her mom. "You and Daddy could drop me off or I could ride with JZ. And I'm sure I'll know other girls there."

"Do parents chaperon?"

"I'm not sure. I mean, Craig didn't go into all that," Mina said.

"I have to be honest, Mina." Mina's mother walked over and stood behind her at the sink. "A team party? I'm not comfortable with that as a first date. How can you and Craig enjoy a date around a bunch of guys blowing off steam from the football season? How is that giving you both a chance to get to know each other?"

"It's just dancing and stuff," Mina said, her heart galloping. "And we already know each other. I see him every day in school."

She could feel any chance of approval slipping away fast. Her stomach fell as her mother went from gathering information on the party to explaining why it wasn't going to happen.

"You know Daddy and I both agreed you wouldn't officially date until next year." Mina's mom put her hand up to stop Mina from interrupting. "Now, there's some wiggle room in there for going out. We don't expect you to stay in your room every week-end," Mariah said. She went to a cabinet and took out plates. "But we don't know Craig well enough. And even if we did, a team party isn't an ideal first date."

Mina pleaded. "But you've met him. You said he's a nice guy—"

Her mom interrupted. "I said he *seems* like a nice guy. I don't know him."

"Well, what am I supposed to do to help you know him better?" Mina asked anxiously, thinking she found a loophole in the denial.

Her mom chuckled as she walked over to the table. "We'll get to know him over time, Mina." She glanced over at her daughter's exaggerated pout. "I think you knew what the answer would be when you asked. Hanging out in a big group is fine and totally acceptable—"

"We *will* be in a group," Mina said.

"A group of football players, not a group of your friends," her mom said sternly. "Being around your other girlfriends would at least help take some of the pressure off the date. You're moving too fast. Especially with someone who—"

"You don't know," Mina mocked, making a face.

Mariah's gaze was stony. "Don't be smart," she warned. "You're not going out on a date with this boy." She walked back over and patted Mina's shoulder in gentle apology, sealing the deal in a soft but firm final-word voice. "At least not to this party."

A tear fell down Mina's face. She swiped at it angrily. She'd fully expected her parents to at least consider letting her go out with Craig. Even as her mother attempted to make sense of the decision, Mina couldn't see any good reason for them to squash the date.

She sulked. "So, now I'll look like a total baby when I call to tell him I can't go."

"I'm sure he'll understand," her mom said absently, checking to make sure all of the stove burners were off.

Mina began to rant. "Yeah, right. Hundreds of girls in school would kill to date Craig and he asks me out. Me! Now he'll probably regret going after the . . . the girl with the curfew and the parents with all the rules!"

Mina's mom rolled her eyes and spoke in a tone that made it clear she was nearing the end of her patience. "Cut the drama, Amina! If he liked you before, he'll like you now . . . rules and all. All we're saying is take it slowly. Hang out with Craig with your friends and learn to be comfortable with one another that way. What's the rush on the solo date?"

"It's not a rush. But he asked me out, and now I'll look like a lit-tle girl saying I can't go because my mommy won't let me."

"Well, then that's what you'll look like, honey. The answer is no," her mom replied matter-of-factly, then added gently, "At least it's no for this party, anyway."

Mina stomped off, her mother's warning at her back. "Un-ah, no you're not stomping, Ms. Thing!"

Mina eased her steps, but nearly collided with her father at the top of the stairway.

"Morning, baby," Jackson Mooney said. He stood in the middle of the landing, a tall, broad-shouldered sentry preventing the petite Mina from getting past.

"Morning," Mina mumbled, her head down. The hot, steamy tears came faster as her father played referee.

"Uh-oh. What did I sleep through?" he asked, raising his deep voice so his wife could hear the question as well.

"Your daughter's just being a drama queen," Mariah answered, not unkindly. She raised an eyebrow. "What else is new?"

Jackson put his arm around Mina, and she buried her face into his chest.

"What's the matter?" her dad asked.

"Mom said . . . I can't . . ." Mina's voice, thick from crying, hitched as she talked through the tears. "Craig asked me out . . . and Mom said I can't go . . . because you two don't . . . know him."

Jackson looked over Mina's head at Mariah, who stood at the foot of the stairs, shaking her head. Her jaw was firm but her eyes were soft. He got the message—*Don't take sides, not right now.*

"Well, come back down and we'll talk about it. Let me hear the whole story," Jackson said.

Mina's head shook no furiously.

"Breakfast is ready," her mom said.

I'M NOT HUNGRY! Mina shouted to herself. But she kept her voice quietly in check as she responded. "I don't feel like eating."

Mariah threw her hands up in frustration and walked back to the kitchen muttering, "So much for a big family breakfast."

Jackson whispered down to Mina. "We'll talk about it later. Okay?"

"I know the answer will still be no." Mina wiped at the tears. She poured on a little extra poutiness. "Mommy seemed like she was speaking for both of you."

Mina looked up at her dad, searching for mercy on his handsome face, dark like maple syrup, hope in her glossy eyes. *Please say she wasn't*, they pleaded.

But Jackson knew better than to disagree with his wife until he knew all of the facts. He changed course. "Well, you know our rules. But I can't weigh in on it without knowing the whole story." He tugged Mina down a step. "Come on and eat."

Mina's body went rigid. She refused to move. "I'm seriously not hungry, Daddy."

Leaving her father standing on the stairway, she walked up the stairs and down the hall to her room. She shut her bedroom door quietly, then threw herself violently onto her bed, letting the tears stream down her face. As much as she wanted to go out with Craig, not being able to go wasn't the truly bad part. The embarrassment of telling him she couldn't go was the worst!

Her head pounded from the good, hard cry, but Mina ignored the throbbing.

Fine, I'll just stay here in this room until I'm old enough to date him.

She threw a pillow over her head and listened to the pulse in her temples beat. The house telephone bleated beside her, vibrating against her pulsing head.

"Mina, telephone," her mom called. "It's Michael."

Mina reached her hand up to her nightstand and grabbed the phone, taking it under the pillow with her. She snapped at her mom through the phone, "I got it!"

Daddy's Girl

"Some you win and some you lose."
—B2K, "Baby Girl"

Minutes after talking to Michael, who was already at JZ's when he called, *"Where ya at, Deev?"* Mina pulled on a pair of soft corduroy flood pants with her new three-quarter-length heel boots. They weren't the best choice for the ten-minute walk to JZ's. But they were hella cute. She'd been dying to wear them since nabbing them off the rack on Black Friday. She hadn't even had to beg her mom for them . . . very long.

Even thoughts of Michael's inevitable teasing about barely getting the new smell out of the shoes before throwing them on didn't discourage her.

Usually, Mina heeded Michael's know-it-all fashion advice. Most times it was on point. So much so, he'd landed a gig as assistant costume designer for Bay Dra-da, Del Rio Bay High's drama and dance troupe.

But the black boots were too cute to hold until Monday.

Her heels clacked against the hardwood as, face stoic, Mina eased down the stairs and made a chilly exit through the sunroom, where her parents sat. Her mom peeked up from a book, but said nothing.

"Gone to JZ's?" her father asked, muting the TV.

Afraid the anger in her eyes was lethal, Mina couldn't even look at her parents. She nodded and mumbled, "Um-hmm."

"I thought the girls were meeting you here?" her mother asked.

Forced to address her mom directly, Mina stood as far across the room as possible, ducking into the closet to grab a jacket as she answered. "I called and told them to just meet down at JZ's."

Her mother slammed the book shut. "Mina, I don't know why you have an atti—"

Jackson Mooney touched his wife's wrist softly, stopping her. "Do you want a ride? Those boots don't look like they're made for walking." He chuckled.

Mina managed a smile. She walked over and stood behind the sofa between her parents, hoping the words of her tee shirt, "Daddy's Girl," shone brightly at her mom. The irony was Mariah had bought Mina the pink and black baby doll tee shirt over the summer. As cute as Mina thought it was, she'd refused to wear it. She was a daddy's girl, but she wasn't about to wear a tee shirt claiming it . . . until now.

Layered over a white long-sleeved tee, the shirt's message dialed right into Mina's feelings. As long as she thought she had at least one of her parents on her side, she wasn't against playing them against each other.

"No, I'm fine. I've gotta break them in anyway." Mina bent down and gave her dad's cheek a peck.

Still leaning over her dad, Mina glanced at her mother. Their eyes met for a second, before Mariah's went back to her book. Mina sidestepped slowly over to her mom's side.

"Oh, no, don't go doing me any favors," her mom said, hurt in her voice.

Mina leaned in and brushed her lips across her mom's cheek.

"Okay. I'm gone," Mina chirped.

She spun on her heels, nearly toppling over as the smooth hardwood and the slickness of the boot's heel connected in a momentary slide, then made a beeline for the front door. So much for making a powerful exit.

As Mina opened the door, she heard her mom whisper in frustration, "Now, why am I the only one getting the Ice Princess treatment?"

The door slammed on her father's response. Mina hoped her plan to evoke sympathy from him was working.

At the top of the cul-de-sac, Jacinta stood, arms folded, waiting. She tapped her foot, just in case Mina couldn't read her impatience, bringing attention to her brown boots with the cute pockets on the sides.

"Why couldn't I just meet you at your house?" Jacinta pouted. "It's cold out here."

Mina waved it off. "Sorry, I didn't mean to take so long." She kept walking as she glanced down at Jacinta's boots. "Those boots are hot. Remind me to borrow 'em one day."

"Dag, wait up. I'm already chilled to the bone. What you rushing for now?" Jacinta fell in beside Mina's quick steps.

"Craig invited me to the Frenzy and my parents . . ." She rolled her eyes to the sky, hands waving as she ranted. "My *mother* said I can't go."

Jacinta squinted. "Your father said you could?"

"Not exactly." Mina frowned.

Jacinta laughed. "Momma drama. I love it." She elbowed Mina. "You just find it easier to be mad at your moms. You know pops not gon' let you get your freak on either."

Mina cracked a smile but felt guilty for complaining. It wasn't the first time she'd regretted being so passionate about her problems around Cinny. No matter what Mina complained about, it always seemed stupid and trivial once she said it out loud to Jacinta.

Jacinta lived with her aunt Jacqi in The Woods, Mina's ultra-suburban nabe, one of many middle- and upper-middle-class subdivisions in the county. But she came from Pirates Cove, a low-income project in the city of Del Rio Bay. She had a recovering crackhead mom, in rehab, whom she wasn't very close to, a best friend who was a drug dealer and three sibs back in The Cove being raised by their dad.

Mina had never once heard Jacinta complain about any of those things. The closest she'd ever come was the time she said that Mina's issues weren't exactly problems in the "real" world. Jacinta hadn't harped on the subject and hadn't said it since that first time, but Mina couldn't help wondering if Jacinta was thinking it right now as she chuckled, adjusting a pair of brown earmuffs over her ears.

Jacinta's honey golden complexion and blond highlighted naturally curly hair against the brown muffs, plus the brown-washed denim jeans, snug (as usual) against her apple bottom, was a good look. She looked like an ad for Gap's autumn collection. Mina half expected her to start singing and dancing like they did in the commercials.

She teased Jacinta about it, to take attention off her own pouting.

"Is Sexy Chocolate part of the new line at Abercrombie or something?"

"Shoot, you know I'm bringing sexy back," Jacinta said. Her laugh echoed in the cold quiet of their community. Most people were still comatose from overeating.

Mina laughed along, her anger on hold.

Jacinta glanced at Mina from the corner of her eye. "Alright, I'm gonna deny this if you repeat it . . ." She paused, smiling as though she had a secret. The sounds of their boots echoed off the bare trees as they quick-stepped down Dogwood Street. "But, I'm glad to get back over here in bobble-head 'burbville."

Mina locked arms with Jacinta, squeezing. "Awww. You missed us over Turkey Day?"

Jacinta shrugged, letting her arm rest comfortably in the crook of Mina's. "Missed might be a strong word." She side-glanced over at Mina, hoping Mina knew she was only playing. Sometimes Mina and the rest didn't seem to get her jokes. Jacinta always felt as if she had to double-check to see if they got her. But Mina was listening quietly—for once. Jacinta talked on through the rare second of silence. "I'm saying, though . . . I haven't been around my brothers and sister for an entire week since summer. Here it's so much more . . ." She fell silent, letting the words form in her head before admitting them aloud.

She always struggled where staying "loyal" to her clique and her reputation as a hard chick in her old hood, The Cove, were concerned. No doubt, she was more mellow here hanging with Mina than at home where she had to make sure people didn't take her for being soft. But if the girls in The Cove could see her walking arm in arm with Mina, they would say she was acting "cute."

Not that Jacinta cared what they thought. It wasn't as if they'd ever know that going back and forth between The Cove and The Woods was like going into two different worlds. Whenever she was home, for the weekend, it felt as though she'd just traveled seven hundred miles instead of only seven miles over the DRB Bridge. The Cove had so much going on—people on the basketball court, hanging out on the front stoops, walking up and down the main road that ran throughout the twenty buildings of row homes. The Woods was like a cemetery in comparison.

Still, being back in The Woods and over at Aunt Jacqi's where she had her own room, her own bathroom and lots of peace was like . . . a sigh of relief.

It seemed wrong to feel that way. But she did.

"Girl needed some peace and quiet after a while," Jacinta said finally, choosing to be honest but without bashing her old nabe.

"What did you and Raheem do all week . . . ?" Mina's eyes did a sly roll over at Cinny. "Or should I even ask?"

She was sure Jacinta's holiday was far spicier than her own. Spending a whole week at home with the dude you've been dating for two years (especially now that they didn't get to see each other much) had spice written all over it. Mina couldn't top that unless . . .

No, Mina couldn't top that. The most excitement she'd had the entire week was slipping on her new fly boots.

Which were already pinching her toes seven minutes into the walk.

True, she was only speculating that Cinny and Raheem hooked up on the regular—helped by Raheem's swagger, which screamed that handholding and canoodling were only the warm-up when he and Cinny were alone. The truth was, she and Cinny were close but not "Hey, so how's that whole having sex with your boyfriend going? Alright? Working for ya?" close.

Mina still had a hard time getting used to the fact Jacinta had had the same boyfriend since she was twelve.

She couldn't imagine having *any* boyfriend at twelve years old.

Hello, she could barely get one now thanks to Momma and Poppa Bear Mooney.

So, she and Jacinta talked around the subject. No details, no questions.

With a coy smile and spiked eyebrow as if to say "What do you think," Jacinta kept the mystery alive with a vanilla answer.

"He hung out a lot with me and my brothers and sister. Just chilling, watching TV and playing on the Playstation." Jacinta snorted. "But by the end of the week I was sick of him, too."

"How come?" Mina asked.

Jacinta skittered to a stop. Her arm fell away from their conjoined link as Mina pulled forward.

Mina back-stepped. "What?"

"Don't tell Kelly I said anything . . ."

Mina nodded.

"Naw. Say it." Jacinta folded her arms. "I know you, Mina."

Mina rolled her eyes. "What?"

Jacinta waited.

"Dag." Mina sucked her teeth. "Alright, I won't say anything!"

Jacinta smiled. "I know you. You'll get all excited, and your mouth will bring it up before your head tells you to shut up. At least if you say you promise, you *might* hold this to yourself."

Mina put her hands on her hips. "Why does everybody think they know me?"

"'Cause we do, Mouthy Mi." Jacinta gave her an elbow poke and started walking again. She kept her pace slow. They were almost to JZ's.

"Angel and Kelly started talking over the break," she said.

"What? Oh, my God! Why didn't she say something when we were IM'ing?" Mina said, too shocked to be annoyed that Kelly hadn't shared.

Angel was Jacinta's friend who was a drug dealer. He'd eyed Kelly the moment they all met him that night over at Jacinta's. It shocked all of them when Kelly gave Angel her phone number. Ever since, Kelly had lived in fear of her grandmother picking up the phone to find Angel on the other end—but Angel had never called.

Mina assumed he'd gone on to the next chick, too smooth to waste his time with Kelly. Not such a bad thing in Mina's opinion.

He and Kelly would make a cutie caramel couple if they ever decided to take it there. But they were about as mismatched as they came—Kelly was quiet, sheltered and rich; Angel was a slick-talking hustler from the projects, an extreme of the opposites-attract theory of dating.

If there was ever a perfect opportunity to try the phone-relationship thing—calling each other every day but never kicking it live in person—this was it. Mina had suggested it to Kelly, who seemed curious but petrified by the mere thought of Angel.

Go, Kell, Mina thought, taking supreme pleasure that Kelly had taken the advice.

"So how did you know he called?" Mina asked. Her eyebrows furrowed. "She didn't call and only tell you, did she?"

"Alright, slow your roll, princess. She didn't violate any friend rules," Jacinta said, only half joking. "Angel got me to call for him on Tuesday."

"Why?" Mina grinned. "Was he scared to call her?"

"Pssh, please. No." Jacinta snorted. "I told him a long time ago that Kelly's grandmoms might trip if he called. So he finally got on my nerves enough and got me to call for him. I called her Tuesday and Wednesday."

"Wait . . . So what does this have to do with Raheem getting on your nerves?" Mina asked.

Jacinta's words picked up speed as they walked down JZ's drive-way. "Because Raheem kept saying Kelly is being boogee for not letting Angel call the house. And how, if she my girl, I need to let her know what's up."

"Okay, I guess you need to tell me what's up, too." Mina laughed. "What did he mean?"

"Just that he thinks Kelly playing Angel with her shy act." Jacinta waved the thought away, rolling her eyes. "He was just looking out for his boy. It got on my nerves, though."

"Well, did you let Raheem know that Kelly probably has no idea what playing some dude is even like?"

Their laughter carried over the naked trees and into JZ's foyer as Mrs. Zimms opened the door.

Putting the Student in Student Athlete

"Hot as ever, I ain't lost no step."
—Bow Wow, "Fresh Azimiz"

Comments flew as everyone offered their two cents. Loud, rowdy and excited to be around one another, their constant whoops of laughter and cracks filled JZ's game room, a boy's fantasy spot— huge pool table in the center of the room, a wall lined with retro arcade games, a bar that the Zimmses kept stocked with soda and juices, and a thirty-six-inch plasma that was perpetually connected to some sort of gaming console. When JZ wasn't hosting pool parties and last minute tournaments on his NBA-sized basketball court, he was down here entertaining.

Mina hovered near the pool table, jumping in and out of the way of JZ and Michael's game, pestering them because she could. Kelly sat on the leather sofa, in the middle of the room, following as many pieces of the banter as she could.

"It sounds like you're scared to me." Mina taunted JZ with her eyes, a smile tugging at her mouth. She loved giving him grief.

Check that, they loved giving each other grief.

One thing Mina had learned from having two boy best friends was how to hang when the disses started flying, especially any coming from JZ. She'd been on the wrong end of his brash boyish humor since they were kids and had learned from the best. She knew how to let 'em fly and push the right (or wrong) buttons.

There was a collective "oooohh" from Lizzie and Jacinta at the Pac Man machine, confirming Mina had dropped a good one that time. She grinned a "take that" smile at JZ.

"She calling you out, son," Michael instigated.

JZ leaned against the pool table. He made his voice loud enough to shush the rest of them. "Yeah, you got jokes." He poked his pool stick at Mina, sending her running to hide behind Kelly. "But even Saint Mother Mina, patron saint of the good girls, is not gonna make me feel bad for worrying about my shine. My pops letting me play varsity and I need to prove that I'm not just hype." He pounded his chest. "Who's the Freshman Phenom?"

Mina and Kelly sang, "You arrrrre," in a sarcastically sweet tune before high-fiving and laughing.

"That's right," JZ muttered.

"So, kid is that bad?" Michael asked. He rammed his pool stick back and whacked at the red ball. Three striped balls fell into the upper left-hand pocket.

JZ sucked his teeth at the triumphant grin on Michael's dark chocolate face before going back to his lecture. He was buzzing, irritated and excited all at the same time, about this new guy, Brian James (no relation to Michael), on the basketball team.

Mina wondered what bothered JZ more, that Brian was his new next-door neighbor (talk about keeping your competition close) or that Brian's hardwood skills were fire with the potential to make JZ's flame burn a little lower in the eyes of the Blue Devils fans—who now currently worshipped his football skill. She had never seen him so agitated. His entire body was in motion as he talked, playing an imaginary game of ball—hands miming shooting a basket, annoying the girls by pretending to block their shots or hip bumping and throwing bows.

He was all over the place. And his pool game was suffering for it.

"Son, dude is that bad plus some." JZ bent over to take a shot. His stick glided toward a ball and connected, sending the red ball close but not into the pocket. "Tryouts were almost over when he showed up. He only made the last day and still scored twenty points in the scrimmage. And at practice . . . shoot, he be tearing up the court."

"Oh, my God, Jay." Mina pretended to faint onto the sofa. Leaning on her elbow, she peeked over the back of it at JZ. "Is that admiration in your voice?"

"I can't lie. He got crazy skills." JZ snorted, shaking his head as if he couldn't believe he was admitting it himself. "And he seems cool. We kicked it after practice twice. But I'm saying, I gotta keep my eye on him."

What JZ left out was that Brian was only half his problem when it came to starting. His Algebra II grade was the other half. The bigger one.

He didn't want to admit, in front of everyone, just how bad things were. The interim grades report, sent home right before the Thanksgiving holiday, stated clearly that JZ was in danger of earning a "D," something his father wasn't having. The mandate was loud and clear, get his head out of the sports page and off the court to focus on schoolwork or basketball was hist. If he brought home one low grade, homework, quiz, whatever, it was lights out for the season. Period.

JZ had no one but himself to blame. He'd been doing fine in class during football season. As a matter of fact, the better he did on the field, the higher his grades. The week the *Blue Devil Bugle,* the school newspaper, coined him the Freshman Phenom in their sports articles, he'd gotten an "A" on every homework and quiz for two weeks—golden on and off the field.

But two weeks before b-ball tryouts, the buzz about Brian James started, first among the guys trying out, then in the hallways as excited students got wind that the team was about to be twice as good. Everyone was talking about how the kid's father was a former NBA baller, and Brian's skills were supposedly just as smooth.

JZ could have ignored the hype if the coaches hadn't been so excited, too. But once he overheard Coach Ewing say that having an upperclassman like Brian as point guard would add solid leadership to the team, he'd been distracted to the point of ignoring his Algebra II homework to get all the 4-1-1 on Brian he could.

He'd Googled Brian's name and found a crazy amount of press in the *Washington Post, Washington Times* and the regional *Sports Examiner.* After he saw Brian for himself during tryouts, things hit rock bottom. He scored two "D"s, a "C" and an incomplete and went from coasting to drowning in ten days. The only reason Mr. Collins didn't call his parents was because JZ begged the football coach, Coach Banner, to talk to him before he could.

JZ could still see Mr. Collins's twitchy mustache frowning down at him after school that day.

"Mr. Banner, I do not believe in giving student athletes a break simply because of their athletic prowess," Mr. Collins said in that prissy, nasal voice JZ hated. It didn't escape JZ's attention that he'd called Coach mister instead of coach.

Everybody in the world referred to the coaches as Coach, even if they weren't athletes. It didn't surprise JZ that Mr. Collins didn't. More like refused to. You could tell by the way he emphasized the words "mister" and "athletes" that he had a special dislike for anything associated with sports.

Of all classes, why did he have to let his Algebra II grade fall?

Mr. Collins was also the director of Bay Dra-da. He was always theatrical—talking with his hands, making faces as he spoke. JZ spent more time than he'd ever admit to, wondering how Mr. Collins ended up a math teacher instead of English where his love of long-winded lectures would have been right at home.

Before he could launch into one that day, Coach Banner had cut him to the quick, his voice softly reasoning. "Now, Walt, he's a good student and you know it."

Mr. Collins pursed his lips, visibly biting his tongue.

"His parents are advocates of emphasizing the student in student athlete," Coach Banner continued. He placed a hand on Mr. Collins's shoulder, looking him in the eye. "This is Jason's first time falling into a bad spot. Just give him a chance to pull the grade up."

"Chip, if he fails, his parents will be highly upset, and rightfully so, that they weren't informed in time to intervene," Mr. Collins said. He glanced over at JZ, who sat alone in the classroom, pretending to be engrossed in his homework.

"The fact that I'm asking you to keep it from them shows you how much confidence I have in his ability to bring the grade up," Coach Banner said.

"You realize it's too late for me to strike this from his interim?" Mr. Collins said, a glint in his eye as if he'd just realized this himself.

Damned if he not happy about it, JZ thought bitterly, his cinnamon brown face on fire.

"Of course, Walt, and I never said anything about withholding this from his interim report." Coach Banner feigned offense. "I'm saying, by the time report cards go home, Jason will have had time to bring up his homework and quiz grades . . . you know, a good faith effort on his part."

Mr. Collins rolled his eyes. He shook his head. "Jason," he said, folding his arms.

JZ looked up, the proper amount of respect in his eyes. "Yes, sir."

"I won't call your parents." Mr. Collins looked from JZ to Coach Banner, his twitchy mustache frogging up and down as he spoke. "But do not ever ask Mr. Banner or any of your other coaches to intervene on your behalf. Keep your grades on point. We have a long year ahead of us. It's up to you how easy or hard it will be."

Ever since that day, JZ felt as though Mr. Collins was just waiting for his grades to slip. He probably had JZ's phone number on speed dial.

JZ managed to eke out "B"s (barely) on the last few homework assignments. But there was a big test coming up on Friday. If he didn't pass . . . lights out.

He could pretend that he was going to pull himself up by the boot straps, buckle down and yadda yadda. But the first game was also Saturday, and it was against the number one school in the county, DRB High School's biggest rival—the Samuel–Wellesly Trojans. JZ's mind was on the Sam–Well game all the time. He needed reinforcements in Algebra II and knew just who to ask . . . when the clique wasn't around.

A Favor Between Friends

"Let me know if you're wit' it."
—Musiq, "B.U.D.D.Y."

Hours later after Kelly's grandmother had sounded the two-minute warning—she was on her way, be ready—and then pulled up in her GL450 Benz SUV, whisking Kelly away amid a chorus of the girls' "goodbye," and the guys' hasty "see you," the clique walked Jacinta home and then stood outside of Mina's house, talking in the cold, dark night.

"Are y'all coming in?" Mina asked. She shivered against the cold, hoping this was one of the nights the guys were anxious to go and do . . . guy stuff. All she wanted to do was throw on a pair of fleece pajama bottoms and talk out Frenzy plans with Lizzie. To Mina, being able to go their separate ways and do the guys-only/girls-only thing was one of the perks of their friendship.

Michael shook his head. "Not me. I've gotta finish this design for Mr. Collins."

Right on cue, at the mention of his Algebra II teacher, JZ said, "Oh, Lizzie, I need a solid."

Secretly, he'd been waiting for the moment to ask for Lizzie's help. But he didn't want anyone else to know. Having all of his friends in on certain problems just made them worse because once the clique knew your business, advice—good, bad, whatever—went flying all over the place. He wanted this kept on the low.

"What?" Mina asked in typical nosy fashion.

JZ palmed her forehead. "I said Lizzie." He took Lizzie by the elbow and walked her a few yards away.

"Fine, it's not like Lizzie's not gonna tell me anyway," Mina yelled down at them before turning her attention to Michael.

"What's up?" Lizzie peered up at JZ through the shadow cast by the single streetlight. He swayed slightly, rocking from one long leg to the other in a nervous fidget.

"Mr. Collins is seriously on my ass," JZ admitted. "If I don't pass the test on Friday, I'm out for Saturday's game against Sam–Well—" He let out a loud breath, then admitted, "I'd be out for the season."

"Are you failing?" Lizzie asked, alarmed. It took flunking multiple classes to get kicked out of any sport or extracurricular activity. The last time she and JZ had talked about their math grades he had a solid "B" and was doing fine elsewhere as far as she knew.

"No, not failing. But I was getting a 'D' at interims. I think it's back to a 'C,' at least." He sucked his teeth. "Man, Mr. Collins can't stand me."

Lizzie chuckled. "No, Mr. Collins isn't fond of any athlete . . . not just you."

"Yeah well, look, this test is like half our grade. If I pass it, I'm cool. If I don't . . ." He jammed his hands in his pockets and shrugged. "I gotta pass it, Liz. I mean, like with a 'B', not a 'C'."

"Your dad?" Lizzie asked, already knowing the answer. Books first and always, the Zimms's student-athlete policy. They all knew Mr. Zimms was hardcore about JZ's grades.

JZ's GPA would have to fall below a 2.0 before the school kicked him off the team. It didn't surprise Lizzie at all that JZ's dad's punishment was ten times more strict. She'd heard a few of Mr. Zimms's stories about being an all-American college player. He always talked about how enough of his teammates were used up by the school for their talent, shuttled through college classes whether they attended regularly or not, then dumped when their eligibility ran out.

"My pops is mad serious about this," JZ said, growing agitated. His shoulders hitched as he talked. "He's already talked to Mr. Collins about it and got him to agree to grade my test Friday afternoon so he'd know then and there whether I could play in the first game." His voice was hopeful as he said, "But if you can tutor a brother up, I might be alright."

Lizzie frowned. "How much tutoring up do you need? The test is on everything we've learned since school started." Her eyes widened. "Jay, please tell me you don't expect me to teach you our entire marking period in four days!"

"Naw, nothing like that." JZ looked up at the dark sky as he thought back on the last time the algebraic equations didn't look like a foreign language to him. "Probably only the last month I'm blanking on."

"Only?" Lizzie shouted. "That's still like two major components."

JZ winced. "Dag, Liz, I don't need everybody knowing my business." He lowered his voice, pleading. "Look, if you can't help me, nobody can. Seriously."

"And you didn't think to call so I could have helped over Thanksgiving break?" Lizzie said, unable to resist lecturing.

"We had basketball practice every day, Liz," he said before apologizing. "I know, my bad. But I know you da girl when it comes to tutoring."

Lizzie snorted. "Really? Ask Mina about her French grade from two years ago."

"I'm a quick study," he promised. "You'll have my total attention. Please?"

Lizzie knew it took a lot to make JZ beg. And she'd never seen him that worried. If theater meant the world to her, sports meant the universe to JZ. As long as she'd known him he'd been an athlete.

Still, trying to cover a month's worth of algebra in four days wasn't just a favor; it was a part-time job. But she agreed.

"I'll help you." Lizzie tugged on JZ's jacket sleeve. "But I need a favor, too."

"Anything if you can help me out. On the real," JZ said, relief all over his eager face.

"Help me run lines, Friday," Lizzie said. "I never get enough rehearsal, and it's always better when you're prompted by somebody else."

"That's a bet," he said, happy once again. He slapped his hands together and rubbed them. "I'm your line boy for life."

"Don't make promises you can't keep." Lizzie laughed. She had both *The Wiz* and a production of *Once Upon a Mattress* with the Del Rio Bay Children's Theater to prepare for. She could keep JZ busy into spring. "Meet me at the library after rehearsal tomorrow. We have a lot to cover."

JZ put his arm around her neck in a headlock as they walked back to Mina and Michael.

"Did I ever tell you I love you?" he asked, his playful mood up a notch now that his plan was in action.

Lizzie chuckled. "Hold on to that thought. You haven't passed the test yet."

Getting to the Frenzy

"I'll be your connection to the party line."
—Pink, "Get This Party Started"

"Oh, my God. I've got it!" Mina yelled. She swiveled her chair around and leapt up and onto the bed next to Lizzie. "Liz, I've got it. I've got it. I've got it."

"Well, don't give it to me." Lizzie smiled at her wry joke. She went back to looking at her magazine.

"Ha, ha," Mina said. She stretched out beside Lizzie, head on her elbow. "I know how I can get to the Frenzy."

Lizzie's face, still sun-kissed golden thanks to many shameless summer days tanning, blanched. Her stomach took a tiny dive. It always did when Mina's hooks got into something. Mina was the most determined person Lizzie knew. And it was both endearing (Mina would have your back in a hailstorm of enflamed bows and arrows if you asked her) and scary (Lizzie refused to speak of the Ty DeJesus debacle).

All summer the clique had been forced to endure how Mina was going to make it into the café, also known as the fishbowl, the beautiful people's section of the cafeteria. It was an obsession times two with Mina. Everything was the café this, the café that. If it hadn't been for the fact that Jessica Johnson, Mina's number one enemy and second in command of the Glam clique, sat in the café during their lunch period, Mina would probably still be obsessing. Thankfully, she'd decided life could go on if she didn't get an invite to the café until next semester—when hopefully Jess would have a different lunch period, increasing Mina's chance of moving up DRB High's social ladder.

Just when Lizzie had gotten used to things coasting along, a new plan was in the works. She took a deep breath and tried to ignore the tingling in her belly. "Okay, how?" she asked, knowing somehow she'd just started down a long road of no return.

"Let's get a chat room open with Cinny and Kelly." Mina hopped up. "I need Kelly for this."

Mina logged on and pumped her fist when she saw Jacinta and Kelly were both on. She typed off a quick message as she talked to Lizzie.

BubbliMi: Hey girlies . . . got a sec?

"We'll do a sleepover at Kelly's next weekend. That way we can just walk down to Coach Banner's house," Mina said.

K-Lo: Hey Mi. just checkin 2 see when Jingle Jam in town
BubbliMi: Ooooo . . . it's New Years Eve. Already sold out tho ☹
CinnyBon: 'sup? My aunt Jacqi tried to get me tix but if u didn't camp out for 'em u didn't get 'em

Lizzie sat on the corner of the desk, bending forward so she could follow the conversation. "Ask Kelly if she can get us tickets."

"I'm not going there." Mina frowned. Kelly probably could get the hookup. Her stepfather was a successful music producer. But one thing she'd learned about Kelly during the soc project—Kelly didn't have many friends mainly because the one time she had any she found out they were all just using her to try and get concert tickets or to meet some celeb. So she'd cut off all the pretenders and then cut herself off from making new friends until she'd met Mina and Jacinta. As bad as Mina wanted to see the Jam with Chris Brown, Pretty Ricky, Mario and Ne-Yo . . . she'd let Kelly bring it up.

> K-Lo: don't hold ur breath but . . . I might b able to get us some tix

Lizzie and Mina began yelling, clapping and jumping up and down.

"Yes, we're going to the Jingle Jam!" Lizzie high-fived Mina.

She jumped when Mina's mom stuck her head in the door. "Girls," Mariah bellowed, frowning. "How can the two of you manage to sound like ten people up here?"

"Sorry, Mom." Mina put her finger to her lips.

Lizzie did the same. Mariah shook her head, gave them the all-purpose stare that the girls could take to mean "don't make me come up here again," "quiet down," or "next time that's your tail," before closing the door.

They quietly giggled as Mina went back to typing.

> CinnyBon: seriously Kelly?
> K-Lo: I'll let u know. But I think so yeah
> BubbliMi: OK nothing is more important than going 2 see my husband, Chris Brown but . . . figged out a way 2 hit the Frenzy and need my girls 2 do it esp u Kell
> K-Lo: Y me?
> BubbliMi: Coach Banner lives in ur nabe. Can u have us over 4 a S.O. that weekend so I can go 2 the party frm ur house?
> CinnyBon: what is she gon' tell her grandmother?
> K-Lo: & what r me, Cinny and Liz going 2 do while ur there?
> BubbliMi: no one ever says no 2 inviting more girls 2 a party . . . y'all coming w/

At that, Lizzie's green eyes bugged. Mina sneaking to the party was one thing. Both of them doing it, she hadn't bargained for. She shook her head. "Mina, you know how bad I am at lying," she said, unable to take her eyes off the conversation.

Mina gave Lizzie's knee a firm squeeze. "We can do this, Liz. My parents have already said no. I don't even think they know Coach Banner lives in Folger's." She thought about it, then confirmed for herself. "They won't see anything strange about us doing a sleepover at Kelly's."

CinnyBon: Look @ u all scheming and plottin LOL
BubbliMi: just doing what I gotta do. Kell what do u think?
K-Lo: I don't know . . .
CinnyBon: HELLO how r we getting out da house that night?

"Yeah, exactly," Lizzie muttered, secretly hoping for loopholes in the plan.

"Please, Kelly's house is huge. We could be there and her grand-mother wouldn't even know it," Mina said as she typed.

BubbliMi: we could hang out in the studio or something. Not like she gon' come looking 4 us
K-Lo: u know . . . there's a teen night at the Folger's Country Club every Fri. Grand has always encouraged me 2 go

"Perfect." Mina squealed.

Lizzie groaned. "You know you're ruining this girl, don't you," she said, only half joking.

Mina chuckled.

BubbliMi: Kell that's perfect! And b/c Lizzie is over here having labor pains about it—we'll go 2 da teen night for a little while and bam . . . no lie

Lizzie's shoulders slumped as her last loophole closed. She should have known Mina was going to talk this out until it worked.

"Liz, trust me. We'll only stay at the Frenzy for an hour," Mina said.

CinnyBon: well if I don't go home I'm in. gotta see the Boogee Princess drink from the bad girl cup LMAO

BubbliMi: w/e. we'll just stay an hour no more. promise

K-Lo: it can work. She'll be happy I'm going, esp w/u guys. She thinks u guys are so nice

CinnyBon: Poor granny she don't know how much her little nenesita is enjoying life these days. Thuggin and now this.

K-Lo: w/e w/e w/e

CinnyBon: just jokes. Y'all my girls.

BubbliMi: cool. Thx Kell . . . owe ya big. Gotta go pick Liz up off da floor. TTYL

She logged off.

Beside her, Lizzie's leg jumped nervously, and she chewed on her bottom lip.

"Are we really going to do this, Mi?" she asked.

"What's got you freaked? The lie or getting caught at the party?" Mina talked soft and rational as if she were a therapist helping a patient. She needed Lizzie to be okay with this or it could backfire on them.

"How about everything," Lizzie said. She hopped up from the desk, paced Mina's room. "Lying to your parents is like lying to mine. And . . ."

"Technically it's not a lie as long as we go to the teen night for a little while," Mina reminded her.

"I know. But I'm so bad at lying. I think it's like only child syndrome or something, not having anyone else to blame stuff on." Lizzie sat on the bed with a bounce and began unraveling her

French braid. Taking the blonde tendrils out, piece by piece, calmed her. She repeated the plan out loud. "We're going to Kelly's so we can go to the Folger's Country Club Teen Night."

Mina nodded, joining her on the bed.

"That's exactly what we're doing. It's more a half-truth than a lie."

It was no use pointing out that if they were caught sneaking to the Frenzy, trying that whole half-truth thing on their parents would hands down be the world's worst argument.

Keeping It Real

"This thing ain't been no walk in the park for us."
—Chris Brown, "Say Goodbye"

Jacinta felt as if she was at a fashion show. Sitting on the couch at her aunt Jacqi's beside Mina and Lizzie, they oohed and aahed over each design that Michael pulled out. All of them were really good. Not that Jacinta had the least bit of expert knowledge on what made a good or bad design. If she liked an outfit, it was hot to her. She didn't need a magazine or television show to tell her so.

But Michael's designs were definitely hot.

Looking at the detail in each 5 X 7 sample he held up, it was clear that Michael had a gift.

"*Project Runway* here you come," she teased him.

Michael kept his face blandly cool. But the compliments felt good.

He was an artist. He didn't paint (though he could if he wanted), and he didn't sculpt (he wouldn't know what to do with a hunk of clay). But he could put an outfit together that would turn heads. Better yet, he could draw an outfit that existed only in his mind and make people wish the outfit were real.

The hip-hop themed costumes he'd helped design for *The Wiz* had drawn him some shine when the local paper did a story on Bay Dra-da's upcoming winter production. The *Bay Times* called him a "surefire bet to one day take the fashion world by storm."

He'd had that little nugget laminated and framed before putting it on his wall.

He pulled out the last sample for the dress he was creating for the new finale of *The Wiz*. Mr. Collins called the new strange ending of Dorothy marrying the Scarecrow "creative license." No doubt, the scene would probably be controversial. Whoever heard of Dorothy hooking up with one of her Oz clique?

No matter to Michael. Whether the scene got noticed for being a good addition or a bad one, Michael wanted Lizzie to be fierce in the fantasyland dress.

He glanced at the last 5 X 7 card and was filled with an odd mix of concern and confidence. He felt it whenever he showed someone his drawings.

One more glance . . .

No worries, this was good. This was the one. He felt it. This would be the costume everyone would love. He was sure of it. He'd stayed up half the night finishing it. The detail was insane.

This was the one.

"Come on, Mike, show it already," Jacinta heckled him.

Lizzie and Mina fidgeted in restless agreement.

Michael whipped the card out dramatically and thrust it in their faces, the smile on his dark chocolate face wide as if he were revealing the world's latest, greatest invention. He pointed out what was what, helping to bring the pencil drawing to life.

Mina took the card from him and admired the design up close.

Even in colored pencil, the dress was dazzling. It was more in your face than the other samples, covered in frills and very Oz-like. Ribbon, the color of the infamous Yellow Brick Road, was woven into the tight bodice, giving it a very sleek, young, prom queen look. Hundreds of pearls dotted the dress's top, sparkling against the gold ribbon. In contrast, the bottom was very Cinderella, with its big, bouffant skirt.

Even though sleek, form-fitting wedding dresses were the in

thing now, Mina thought Michael's design would be blazing in the new milleny, too.

"Dag, Mike, I never thought yellow or gold could look good on a wedding dress . . ." She stared at the design. "But this is hot."

"It's nice," Jacinta agreed. "I like how it's tight up top but not on the bottom."

"When I get married, people are going to be like, who designed your gown?" Mina pretended to model a dress. "And I'll be like, Oh, Mr. Michael of Del Rio Bay."

The girls laughed as Michael grinned, proud but also embarrassed by the compliments.

Lizzie plucked the card from Mina's hand. "So this is for little old me?" She giggled and batted her eyelashes. "Okay, I'm totally not a girly girl. But this is gorgeous."

Michael clucked, satisfied. Until *The Wiz* auditions, Lizzie had been a strict tee shirt and jeans chick. You couldn't blast her out of them. But she was superstitious like most theater heads, and since he and Mina had convinced her to rock a mini with fencing boots for her audition, and she'd gotten the part, Lizzie felt the new look was good luck. She'd started mixing up her look ever since then—wearing more minis and wearing her hair down out of the French braid more often. If he could transform her, he could make anybody look good.

Forget *Project Runway*, he was ready for Paris.

He took the drawing back from Lizzie. "I kind of figured this was the one." Michael's eyes swept over his work. "You're lucky, you my girl . . . I don't know if I would go through all this if someone else was the lead."

"Liar." Mina laughed. "You're obsessed with your designs."

"I know, right." Michael chuckled.

The tinny ring of the phone broke up the preview.

Jacinta sprang to her feet. "Hello," she sang into the phone. "Ay, it's Heem."

"Hey, Boo. Hold on," Jacinta gushed. She turned to Mina, Michael and Lizzie. "Y'all cool? I need to take this."

Mina waved her away. "Yeah, go ahead. We're alright."

"Okay. Hang it up for me when I yell down." She ran up the stairs.

Mina picked up the phone. "Hey, Raheem. It's Mina. Looks like you made Cinny's day. She's grinning like she lost her mind."

"Girl, shut up!" Jacinta yelled through the phone.

Mina laughed. "My bad, I didn't know you had it already."

"Alright, Mina, see you later." Raheem laughed. He teased Jacinta. "Oh, so you grinning, huh?"

Jacinta's laugh was soft and flirty. "Yup. You know I miss my Boo." She hopped up onto her bed, hugged a fat body pillow and settled in. Even though he'd gotten on her nerves over the break, she really did miss him already. It was like that a lot lately. They'd be together and she'd start wishing she were back in The Woods. But then she'd get to Aunt Jacqi's and want to be with him. Hearing his voice was like wearing a favorite tee shirt—deliciously comfortable. She purred into the phone. "What's up?"

"Nothing. Just busy with ballin'. We play y'all this weekend."

"Yeah, I know."

Jacinta rolled her eyes toward the ceiling. Boy, did she know! The first home game of the season, Del Rio Bay High vs. Samuel–Wellesly was on the tip of every tongue.

Only seven miles apart, the two schools were polar opposites in their flavor and swagger.

Sam–Well, fifteen hundred students strong and located in the heart of Del Rio Bay, was the "black" school. While Del Rio Bay High's over two thousand students, nestled in the middle of the 'burbs, was eighty percent white. Rivalry between students in everything from who was more hip to athletics was fierce. Anytime the two schools met in a matchup, ownership of the "Best High School in the DRB" was on the line.

Raheem sneered in mock disgust. "And now you one of them, a Del Rio Bay gray girl."

"I don't know about all that," Jacinta lectured, then softened her voice to innocent little girl level, "But you know I'll cheer when you score."

She'd never attended Sam–Well High, but having grown up in The Cove, she knew everyone expected her to remain loyal to the Trojans. Del Rio Bay High was feeling more like home now, but Raheem was Sam–Well's star player. Of course she would root for him.

He made fun of her compromise. "Oh, you walking that fence?"

"Mos' def!" Jacinta declared.

Raheem's chuckle was low and throaty. "Right, right. Ay, Angel wants to know what's up with your girl Kelly. Like when she coming to visit him."

"Is he there with you?" Jacinta whispered. She shot up as if someone had pinched her.

Raheem snickered. "Naw, he ain't here."

Jacinta reclined back onto the body pillow, scowling. "Now, why would she come to The Cove if she not with me?"

"Well, that's what he saying. He wanna know when you gon' bring her to visit him."

Jacinta frowned. "Heem, look, I don't feel like wasting our time talking about them two. Who knows what's up with Kelly."

"Shoot, she must be down. She told him to call her tonight," Raheem said.

Jacinta pulled the phone back from her ear as she yelled, "What? When did she do all that?"

"You ain't know? She texted him and told him to call."

"When?" Jacinta couldn't believe it.

"Yesterday. I was over at his crib when it came through." Raheem laughed. "He was like, 'Yeah, see, I told you it was only a matter of time.'"

Jacinta wondered why Kelly didn't tell them. Then changed her mind. *I don't care. That's on her*, she told herself. Still, she couldn't push the questions out of her head. Was Kelly ready? Or had she called Angel only because Jacinta had pressed her? Did she really like Angel like that? What?

Even as it nagged at her she feigned nonchalance. "Umph, well, like I said, I don't feel like talking about them two."

"Well, tell your girl Angel said he be calling about seven," Raheem said.

Jacinta sucked her teeth. This was another reason she did not need them together. Now they expected her to play message girl. She wasn't ten minutes into her conversation with Raheem and all they had talked about was Angel and Kelly. The topic wore her out.

"Whatever, Heem," Jacinta said.

Raheem's voice was gruff. "Why you getting mad?"

"Because . . ." Jacinta sat up and pulled the pillow on her lap. She wanted to get Raheem on the same page with her and promise that they would stay out of any matchmaking for Kelly and Angel. She approached it with caution. "Alright, can I be straight?"

"Yeah," he said.

"I think this is a bad idea."

"What's a bad idea?" Raheem barked.

Jacinta picked nervously at the pillow. In her mind, she could see Raheem's thick eyebrows raised practically to his cornrows, challenging her. The anger in his voice made her want to stop, but there was no turning back now. She pushed on. "This thing between Kelly and Angel is . . ."

"I don't get it. What *thing?*" Raheem exploded. "He just trying to holler. You act like it's some complicated business deal or something. Damn, do they have some sort of application process in the 'burbs when it come to getting with somebody?"

Jacinta swallowed a frustrated sigh. Raheem didn't have to go there, making it about The Cove versus the 'burbs. But she wasn't about to say so. Then he'd really start in about whose "side" she was on. She took a deep breath and forced her voice to be patient.

"Look, Kelly's cool. She just shy. I think Angel . . ." *Easy, Cinny, easy,* she thought as she said delicately, "Is too hood for someone as good girly as her." Jacinta shrugged. "Shoot, it's not like Angel won't be on to the next shorty by the weekend."

Raheem sat silent, refusing to admit Cinny was right about that. Shoot, Angel had been hugged up with Charisse right before Kelly texted him. But he'd gotten all happy when he got Kelly's message. Raheem was baffled. He didn't get why Angel, who hadn't chased after a girl since he and Raheem had been hollering at shorties, was so stuck on Kelly.

Raheem agreed the chick was cute, thick wavy hair, heart-shaped, caramel-complected face with big wide eyes. A little thin for Raheem's taste—she didn't have no ass to speak of—but all in all she was worth putting your mack down. But there were plenty of honeys just as cute to choose from at Sam–Well.

"Heem?" Jacinta's soft voice called out, bringing him back to their argument.

He shook his head and sighed noisily into the phone, tired of everybody tripping, Angel and Cinny. "What?" he barked.

"Look, I don't want this to be our issue. This is between Kelly and Angel."

"Angel my boy," Raheem said, an edge to his voice. "If some chicken head trying to play him, then I'm gon' let him know!"

Jacinta's voice rose again. "She not no chicken head!"

"How you know? You've known Angel since you were five and you've known this girl since September."

His words chilled Jacinta. He was doing the same thing she'd done to herself, question her fierce loyalty to a person that she'd met barely three months ago. She shot back anyway. "I still know she not a chicken head. Why it gotta be all that just 'cause I said she's afraid to get with Angel?"

Raheem pressed. "Why are you so bent on keeping 'em apart?"

Jacinta sucked her teeth and pounded the bed.

Why was *he* so bent on getting them together?

Angel never hurt for a girlfriend. Most times, he juggled several at once. Now all of a sudden Kelly was a fixation? Whatever.

Her voice was flat when she finally answered. "You know what? I don't care. I'm out of this! That's on you if you wanna play the dating game."

Raheem didn't answer.

Jacinta raised up and hollered into the phone. "Hello?!"

"Yeah, alright. I'm out of it, too," he said, too calm for Jacinta.

She was afraid to push but wanted to be clear where they stood. "Is this gon' be cause for drama between us?"

"Naw, it's squashed," Raheem said.

This time she pressed. "It don't sound like it. It sounds like you mad."

"I ain't mad. Look, I gotta bounce," he said in a rush.

Jacinta fumed on the other end of the line.

"You hear me?" Raheem asked.

"Yeah, you gotta bounce. Bye," she spat.

"Alright then . . ." he said, without hanging up.

There was silence on both ends. Jacinta sat back against the wall, defeated. She didn't want to end their conversation this way. But she didn't know what else to say.

Her voice was hollow. "Bye, Raheem."

She heard the phone click.

Hot, angry tears stung Jacinta's eyes. Squeezing them tight to fight the flow, she flopped back onto the bed. She considered the disastrous exchange just one more among a growing list of how difficult holding her relationship with Raheem together had become since moving to The Woods.

First, it was the "distance." The Cove wasn't walking distance, and the city bus didn't pick up near The Woods. It wasn't like she could see him whenever she wanted. But since school started, all she ever heard was how they didn't spend enough time together; something Raheem knew was out of her control.

Her father made it clear that she was not coming home every single weekend. Jacinta was in The Woods *living* with Aunt Jacqi, not visiting, he often lectured, and he wanted her to make friends there (she had)—maybe even carve out a new path (she was).

And that was why she had a new problem. Every step she took down the path, making new friends, settling into life as a Del Rio Blue Devil, pushed her two steps away from Raheem and life as a Sam–Well Trojan. Being lonely without a friend on either side was starting to look really good.

Jacinta pulled the pillow over her face and let the tears flow, bitter and cleansing.

Romantic Thugs and Good Girlies

"So tell your friends you in love with a straight thug."
—Mariah Carey ft. Jay-Z and Young Jeezy,
"Shake It Off (Remix)"

One of the reasons Kelly had given in to Mina's request to sneak out from her house was she honestly couldn't imagine getting into trouble for it. She'd never been punished or spanked as a kid a day in her life. If her grandmother punished her for this—an innocent romp to a party a few streets away *and* Kelly's first time doing wrong . . .

Nah, Kelly couldn't see it.

After being a good girl for so long, content reading at her window seat for hours and hanging out with her grandmother and younger brother when most girls were doing double sleepovers and skate parties, she was ready to take the good (the excitement of the unknown) with the bad (the consequences of being busted). A tiny voice in the back of her mind whispered she'd get a pass if they were caught . . . this time.

But Kelly wasn't thinking about that right now. She was thinking about "the call." While in the car on the way home the night before, Kelly had quickly texted Angel "Call me 2morrow" before easing into conversation with Grand about how her afternoon with her friends had gone.

Kelly's heart had skipped just punching the message into the phone.

For her, this was a big step.

Now, she paced her suite. She walked from the window seat to the sitting room. From the sitting room to her study to the bed.

Why hadn't she told Angel what time to call?

This being spontaneous thing already wasn't working for her.

Her stomach growled, reprimanding her for picking over dinner that night. But she'd had no appetite. As good as the southwestern pork chops had smelled while Carmelita, their chef, had cooked them, once Kelly sat down to eat, the thought of putting anything in her stomach became a very bad idea.

Kelly moved from the window seat in her bedroom to the pink princess chair in her sitting room—and jumped straight up and out of the chair when the phone rang, running to it. She picked up before the second ring finished its bothersome jingle. Her ten-year-old brother, Kevin, was already on the other end.

"Kevin." Her usual quiet voice was painted with restrained patience. "I'm expecting a call."

"So?" he shot back in the universal snotty voice of younger siblings.

Kelly rolled her eyes. "If someone tries to beep through, can you please at least answer it?"

"Get off the phone, Kell!"

Kelly tossed the phone down and sat on her bed with a thud.
Little brat.

Minutes later, the phone rang again. She scrambled, picking up on the first ring, and still she wasn't the first to get it.

"Hello?" She heard her grandmother ask in her proper school-teacher's voice.

Kelly waited, barely breathing on the other end, her heart in her throat.

Be anyone but Angel. Seriously, anyone.

But Angel's romantic thug lilt (that was what Kelly called how he switched from talking cocky and sure to gentle and polite in one breath) reached out from the phone, "Ay, may I speak to Kelly, please?" making Kelly very glad she'd passed on the pork chops. Her stomach dropped to her feet.

"I have it, Grand," Kelly blurted.

Her grandmother hung up quietly.

Kelly waited a beat to make sure the phone had been put down before stammering, "Hel . . . hello."

Angel's voice was low with a hint of a Puerto Rican accent. "Ay, girl, it's Angel."

Kelly's legs went rubbery. "Hey," she whispered.

"What's wrong?"

"Noth . . . nothing," she stuttered, trying to get her voice under control. She scurried over to the door, peeked down the long hall for any sign of her grandmother, then quietly closed the bedroom door. She continued in a more normal tone. "Hey. I was waiting for my grandmother to walk away."

There was silence on the other end for a few seconds before Angel said softly, "So what's up, Mami?" There was a hard cackle on the other end before he said, "What? You finally realize what time it is? That's why you letting me call your crib?"

There it was again.

Tough and sweet in one sentence.

It made Kelly dizzy. Listening to his voice's highs and lows glued her to the phone. She found herself silently introducing the two personalities as they talked. She slid onto the floor in front of the bedroom door, her knees bunched up to her chest, anxiously tucking her hair as she laughed, wondering how to answer the trash talker.

"I'm not sure why I'm letting you call. I almost had a heart attack when the phone rang," she finally admitted, figuring being honest with the trash talker was best. Otherwise he'd only brag more, teasing truthful answers out of her the more flustered she got.

"'Cause you digging your man, that's why," Angel bragged playfully. "On the real, my boy think you playing me."

A worried crease ran down Kelly's forehead. "Who, Raheem? What does he mean I'm *playing* you?"

"He said you making a brotha work with your hard-to-get teasing."

The thought of playing hard to get had never crossed her mind, and she told Angel so. "Well, you can tell Raheem it's not that." She laughed softly. "My grandmother . . ." She considered the best way to put it and went as close to the truth as she dared. "Doesn't know about you. And since we're just . . . friends, I'm taking the friendship one step at a time."

Angel laughed long and hard. "So you really are that good girly, huh? That's what Cinny calls you."

Kelly frowned. Was that an insult or a compliment? She wanted to ask but didn't.

"Well, how a brotha go from friend to something a little bit more?" he softly questioned.

Kelly laid her head back on the door. Suddenly, advice JZ had given her the day before felt invaluable. "Of course he gonna want to know the road going somewhere." So here they were, walking down the road.

Was Kelly going to stop and thank him for a nice evening or go around the block a little more?

She had no idea.

"What's up, you still there?" Angel asked.

"Yeah, I am."

"So, what? You scared to see me?" Angel pressed.

Not scared to see you, scared of being alone with you, Kelly thought. Now, what did the Good Girl Book of Etiquette say about that? Was there a nice way to say that?

Oh, hey, I like you but I'm terrified of spending one second alone with you.

Now there was a great way to start a friendship . . . relationship . . . whatever this was becoming. She finally dove in and answered, "I'm not scared to see you . . . but, my grandmother is old school." Kelly stretched her legs out, then bunched them back up. Something about sitting in the cozy ball helped her feel comfortable. She lowered her voice. "If you call the house a lot, my grandmother will want to meet you and . . ."

"You not down with that, huh?" Angel snickered.

No, no and . . . no, Kelly thought. But she let her silence speak for her, bracing for Angel to blast her or hang up. She was shocked when Mr. Tender showed up instead.

"So do I gotta meet your grandmoms just to see you at the game on Saturday?" Angel asked.

"You still want to see me?" Kelly asked. It's wasn't every day you told a guy you were ashamed to have him near your family and he was okay with that. She assumed. Being that Angel was the closest to a boyfriend she'd ever gotten, she was winging all the theories and etiquette.

Maybe she'd ask Mina. Sometimes the way Mina talked about stuff you'd swear there was a real live book out there with rules, regulations and tips on navigating the rough waters of just about anything.

"The question is do you want to see me?" Angel said so tenderly it made Kelly's insides warm.

She answered eagerly at first. "I do." But hearing her excitement, she tried to tone it down. "It would be nice to hang out with you."

"Alright, so then Saturday we gon' kick it." His trash-talking voice, husky and hard, came back. "Too bad the first time we hang out you gonna be crying."

"Crying?" Kelly looked at the phone as if it had spoken instead of Angel.

"That's right. 'Cause Trojans gon' kick that ass." He laughed, but then turned on Mr. Tender again. "Alright, nenesita. I holler later."

Kelly hung up and set the phone on her lap. Her head spun from keeping up with the many faces of Angel. She tried to imagine keeping up with him without the benefit of hiding behind the phone.

Hottie Jedi Mind Tricks

"What's your name? 'Cause I'm impressed."
—Missy Elliott, "Hot Boyz"

Monday morning brought the first real cold of the Del Rio Bay fall. Thanksgiving had been mild during the day and cold at night. Now, cold settled in, bringing with it wind, signaling that winter and the holidays were around the corner.

Layered in scarves, mufflers and hats, Mina, Jacinta and Michael met at the top of Michael's cul-de-sac and trekked down to JZ's bus stop, just to keep moving in the bitter morning. The icy layer of frost on the grass made Mina think about snow, and snow made her think about Christmas (though she'd never seen a white Christmas before) and Christmas made her think about things she wanted; one of them was Craig, the other was tickets to the Jingle Jam and the last was a big fat break from school and having to see Jess every day in soc.

Since the tickets had been sold out since minute one and if all went well with her plan she would get Craig, she focused on the impending holiday—something she'd get for sure no matter what.

She lifted her face, letting the warm scarf drop below her chin. "Just three more weeks until Christmas break," she announced to no one in particular, before burying her mouth back into the toasty cotton.

"Let's just hope these three weeks go by fast," Michael said. Usually he ignored Mina's countdowns. She'd rushed the entire summer counting down to the first day of school, and he'd been against it. Summer didn't last long enough. But this countdown, he could get with. He slowed his stride so Mina and Jacinta's shorter legs wouldn't have to scurry.

"Yeah, fast until the break gets here, then it can slow down . . . a lot," Jacinta said.

Mina and Michael nodded in vigorous agreement.

"You know, these boots are hottie tottie . . ." Mina's muffled voice said. She looked down at her new shoes, scowling as if they'd betrayed her. "But my dogs are barking. Note to self: new boots, cold air and walking down long-ass Dogwood don't mix."

"That's what you get for sporting 'em all early," Michael lectured. "Those boots shouldn't have made their debut until at least the end of this week."

Mina waved him off with one gloved hand. "First rule of fashion, if you got it, flaunt it."

Michael snorted. "No. The first rule of fashion is rock it fierce. And you can't rock those boots walking like Frankenstein."

"I know that's right." Jacinta howled, giving Michael some dap with her gloved hand.

"I am not walking like Frankenstein." Mina stood a little straighter and tried letting her feet hit the ground more naturally, just in case she was. The combination of the cold and the boot's heel (a little higher than she was used to) sent her foot into a dive to the front of the shoe, pinching her toes.

A blue Explorer stopped slowly beside them. Jacinta and Mina kept walking, but Michael stopped.

The passenger side window came down, and JZ's cinnamon brown face smiled from inside the truck.

"What's up? Y'all want a ride?" he asked.

Realizing Michael had stopped, the girls slowly backtracked. Michael's arm was withdrawing from the window as he finished giving JZ and the driver a pound.

Mina and Jacinta stood at the window, gaping.

"Brian, this is my girl Mina, and this is Cinny," JZ said, bright-eyed and all smiles as usual.

JZ was an early riser. When everybody else was turning over begging the sleep gods for one more hour, JZ was up sweating it out in his home gym (sometimes with his dad) at five A.M. every morning.

"Hi," the girls chorused.

"How y'all doing?" Brian said. He rested his arm on the middle console, waiting patiently while JZ explained to the clique that it was too cold to be waiting on the bus.

An orange Atlanta baseball hat hid the top half of Brian's head, but Mina could see enough of his face, a smooth toffee complexion, to see him openly ogling first Jacinta then her. His eyes scanned her body—what he could see from where he was—taking her in slowly from head to shoulders.

Even though her heart did a little quick step, never one to hate attention from a cutie, Mina stared back, daring him to keep looking even though he was busted, figuring he'd look away like people did when they were caught staring at someone. But his eyes lingered, rolling from her eyes to her neckline wrapped in the colorful scarf.

She pulled the scarf down from over her mouth. "Did I pass?" Mina asked, mixing a little flirting in with her sarcasm.

"Maybe." Brian grinned, and Mina's quick step went up a notch. "Y'all want a ride?"

Michael had already opened the door in answer.

Jacinta stepped in and slid over behind the driver's seat. Mina scooted to the middle as the door slammed shut behind them.

"So this is the infamous Brian James," Mina said, reaching up to shove the back of JZ's head.

"Don't even start," JZ warned.

"Oh, so you know about me?" Brian asked. He turned around in the seat and flashed a smile. His eyelashes were full and curly, brightening his soft brown eyes. They seemed to smile at Mina.

"Only what JZ told us. That you're the newbie on the team with him," she said, choosing not to out JZ's open man-crush on Brian's basketball skills. He'd owe her one for not going there, because she totally could have.

JZ's shoulders relaxed, and Mina bit back a giggle. So he'd thought she was going to out him, too.

"Yeah, that's me. But you left out one part," Brian said.

He waited for Mina to ask what, the truck unmoving, his body still turned to the backseat.

First Mina said nothing, playing her own waiting game. If she waited long enough, he'd finish. But after a few seconds, when it was obvious the next line was hers, she asked, "What's that?"

Brian snorted smugly, satisfied his will had been followed. "I'm the newbie that's gon' help us bring home a championship." He put his fist out, and JZ gave it a pound.

"Ya heard?" JZ said.

Mina shook her head as Brian gunned the engine and the Explorer pulled off.

Michael, JZ and Brian fell into a comfortable conversation about sports. Mina let the conversation drift over her head, feeling the truck's warmth melt the ice from her toes.

She didn't get it.

Had JZ not spent half of Saturday fretting about Brian stealing his thunder? Yet he was riding shotgun, and he and Michael were talking to Brian in the tongue of guy friends, world over, calling one another son, kid and man as if hanging out were the norm.

She didn't get it.

Why was it that as long as guys had one thing in common—it could be that they both wore a size-ten shoe—they could get along? Not necessarily become friends, but at least exist in the same space without drama. As long as they could always go back to talking about their size-ten shoe, it was all swazy.

She didn't get it!

She'd tried to have that same philosophy, finding something in common to get along, even if getting along meant having to deal with that person for only a class period (Jess!). But it had failed horribly during the soc project. She'd come out hating Jess more than she had before. And that should have been impossible.

Guys had it easy. JZ was clearly threatened by/in awe of Brian. But a person spying on them now wouldn't know they weren't boys from way back.

Now that the car was moving, Mina took the chance to do some of her own eyeballing. Her eyes took inventory of Brian through his rearview mirror. Tufts of large black curls poked out of the back of the ATL hat. Brian's cologne, a nutty, rustic scent, filled her nose.

No wonder JZ was so agitated. Brian had a definite hottie thing going on. It wasn't just on the court JZ would be competing with him, but off, too, when it came to hollering at the honeys.

If it wasn't for Craig, Mina might—

"Mina, Jason told me that you're a cheerleader," Brian said, checking her in his rearview, bursting into her thoughts.

For a second, her eyes looked away from the rearview guiltily. How long had Brian been looking at her looking at him?

She quickly regrouped. "Oh, so *you've* heard about me."

"You could say that. So you gonna have my back at the games, huh? Cheering us on?" Brian asked.

"Oh, no. I mean, I will but not like that. I'm on JV," Mina said.

"Not in the big leagues yet, huh?" He chuckled.

Mina rolled her eyes. No he didn't go there. "Trust, not because I lack the skill."

"Then why?" He glanced from her to the road.

His eyes, smiling and friendly, teased whenever he spoke.

JZ's body shook with silent laughter. Mina reached up and smacked him in the back of the head, hard.

"What?" he said, body still jiggling.

Mina's voice went from flirting to defensive lecture. She raised up, leaning forward as she fussed. "Coach Em doesn't believe in putting freshmen on varsity."

Stupidest rule ever.

She sat back in the seat with a thump, her arms folded tight against her body.

She had no idea why she was explaining this to him. She couldn't help being on JV. But it stung that Brian would think she didn't have the skill to make varsity, because she did. A burning desire to make him stop the truck so she could do a cheer and back handspring torched the competitor in her.

"It's cool. We'll still let you cheer us on from the stands," Brian said.

"Oh, gee, can I?" Mina pleaded sarcastically.

Jacinta and Michael laughed quietly beside her.

"It's not even that funny," Mina whispered at them as Brian pulled the truck into the light morning traffic.

The Explorer rolled through the sleepy main street lined with boutiques, bistros and eateries. Mina stared ahead at the creeping cars. From the corner of her eye she could see Brian peeping glances at her in his mirror.

She took her fair share of peeks whenever he looked back at the road. She didn't like that crack about her not playing in the big leagues, but part of her liked how Brian jumped right in, not shy about joking on her.

Amazing what having a (almost) boyfriend did for your confidence levels. Mina would have never come off so cool with Brian if it wasn't for Craig. She knew it. Would never admit it to anyone, but she knew it. Because otherwise, Brian had some serious hottie Jedi mind tricks going. He was cute, outgoing . . . smelled good.

If Mina didn't have a (almost) boyfriend, she'd be totally tongue-tied around Brian. Hottie Jedis did that to a girl. Made you forget your name if you didn't focus hard enough against their powers.

But his hotness would come in handy, Mina thought.

Brian was a good diversion. For every girl that went loopy over him, there was one less chick she had to worry about being in Craig's face. All she had to do was stay as far away from Brian as possible . . . you know, just in case that Jedi mind trick thing melted the BF shield.

Cheese!

"I love me some you."
—Ciara, "C.R.U.S.H."

Turned out, staying far away from Brian was going to be trickier than Mina thought. Based on the conversation during the rest of the short ride to school, which thankfully no longer revolved around Mina's ability to bring it on, she discovered Brian had the same lunch period as the clique. But his good looks (and smell) were quickly forgotten when later that morning, Craig's voice whispered from behind her, "How come you don't have any pictures of me in there?"

Mina's heart raced. A huge grin spread across her face as she stuck the last of her books on the top shelf of the locker, buying time to get the smile to acceptable width, before turning around. He was only inches away from her, looking delish in a pair of Phat Farm khakis, Timbs and a creamy yellow Polo that looked good up against his caramel complexion. Just one step closer and she could kiss him.

The thought set her ears on fire.

The corridor was packed. Lockers up and down the hall slammed and opened. Mina's neighbors to her right and left appeared, shuffling items in and out of their lockers, closing Mina in between Craig and the locker bay.

"Hey," Mina said in her best flirty soft voice. Being so close made her grin shoot back up to idiotic, crazy-girl crushing levels.

As people spoke to him, Craig held his fist out for pounds and nodded "What's up?" but never turned away from Mina. Each time he exchanged dap or a handshake it pushed him closer. Finally, he took a baby step forward on his own.

Mina sucked in her breath. Was he going to kiss her right there in the hall?

He leaned in and pointed to a picture of her on JZ's back, hugging his neck, her face smushed against his, clowning.

"I thought you and Jason were just homies," Craig said.

Mina let the breath she'd been holding slowly blow out of her nose. She turned back to the locker, scowling, pretending not to know which picture he was pointing to. "We are. Which pic makes you think otherwise?" She needed a second to calm her heart and her frustration that Craig hadn't laid a big old smooch on her.

Craig lifted the picture off the door, one of dozens of photos Mina had plastered in the cramped storage tin of a locker. They were mostly of her and the clique, but she also had pictures of teammates, cousins and miscellaneous school friends among a spirit pom, an M&M candy wrapper (an inside joke from the clique) and other tidbits better suited for a scrapbook. Mina's locker was a shrine to anything even vaguely near and dear to her.

"I don't know . . . y'all looking kind of close." Craig narrowed his already slanted eyes.

Mina snorted. "Oh. Naw, we've been friends forever." She laughed. "JZ bucked me right off his back as soon as Lizzie snapped the picture."

As Craig scanned the full length of the locker, his breath was on Mina's neck, giving her goose bumps. She sniffed quietly and couldn't help noticing that where Brian's cologne was nutty and outdoorsy, Craig had a crisp, clean fresh scent . . . familiar.

Suddenly it hit her why it was familiar. It was Downy . . . or

Cheer or Tide. Something like that. Having him all up on her was like being snuggled inside a freshly washed sweatshirt. Mina wished he'd close his arms around her so she could soak it all in.

As if reading her mind, Craig laid one arm across her shoulder. "So I guess I need to give you a picture of me for your locker gallery, huh?"

Mina giggled. "Here, I'll take one now."

She dug into her purse and pulled out her cellie. Craig stepped back into the swell of students pulsing through the hallway and smiled wide. People skittered around him.

"Naw, get in it with me." He tugged Mina's wrist, pulling her toward him.

"How can I get both of us?" Mina said, face and ears blazing from Craig's attention. She took pleasure in the envious stares of a couple passing girls.

That's right, girls, Mina's in the house, she thought with giddy satisfaction.

She and Craig quickly became a human speed bump to the hall crawlers. Some brushed against them in the limited space. Some stared as they sidestepped them. Others paid it no more mind than it took to avoid colliding with them. PDA in the hallway was about as unusual as people gathering their books from a locker.

Craig twirled Mina around, hugging her to him from the back. Placing his hands on her arms, he turned the phone toward them and lifted the camera to the right angle. "Smile," he said.

Like he had to tell her twice.

Cheesing, Mina snapped the picture.

She was happy when Craig didn't step away, but stayed there with her leaning up against him. She eagerly flipped the phone open to see her masterpiece.

"Almost," she laughed.

She held the camera up so Craig could see the photo of them with her head practically cut off.

Craig chuckled. "Okay, let me try. Hold still."

He took the camera into his hands, raised it, lowered it, then placed it square in the middle of their faces so it captured both of them. As soon as the camera's exaggerated "ch-chink" sounded, Craig flipped the phone open. "See, there we go."

He grinned as he showed Mina the finished product, a perfect photo of their big heads mugging.

"So I'm gonna see that in your locker tomorrow, right?" Craig said.

Her locker, MySpace, her screensaver . . . Mina smiled at the thought. "Yup."

Finally, Craig took a step back. He was still close, but no longer touching Mina. "So are we on for the Frenzy?"

"Oh, yeah," Mina found herself saying confidently. She wasn't about to ruin this moment with a long-winded story about how she was going to have to tell a lie or two to get there. Shoot, she'd cross that bridge when it was burning and crumbling all around her.

The bell rang.

"Okay then . . ." Craig eased away.

"Hold up," Mina said. She closed the locker and fell into step beside him, heading the opposite direction she needed to go.

No big deal. It was only lunch. She had planned to be late to lunch anyway. She had to stop and see Ms. Dunkirk, the advisor of the school's newspaper, the *Blue Devil Bugle*.

Mina couldn't lie to herself. At this point, as high as she was flying, she'd even risk being late to class.

"What's up?" Craig said. He took long, unhurried strides. Still, Mina's short legs had to take two to his one to keep up.

"Are you going to the game Saturday?"

"No doubt," Craig said. "We gon' take it to those punks at Sam—Well."

Mina nodded. You would think a championship was on the line instead of this being the first home game of the season. Everybody was pumped. Without a second thought, she swallowed her fear and jumped right into the next question. "So, do you want to hang out at the 'Ria afterward?"

She risked a nervous glance over at him.

"That'll work." He nodded.

Mina grinned, not caring how wide her smile was this time. A girl could only play it so cool.

Craig stopped in front of his classroom just as the second bell rang. "Hit me up later."

He flashed one more toe-curling smile before disappearing into the classroom.

Pop Life

> "Except that fame is the worst drug known to man."
> —Jay-Z, "Lost One"

Panting, Mina raced from Craig's second-floor classroom to the stairway. The halls were empty, giving her a free pass to run full blast. If the track coach could see her now, she'd make the team without a tryout. Even with a backpack thumping on her back, Mina effortlessly skimmed the stairs and sprinted down the hall as if toward a finish line. Ms. Dunkirk had instructed Mina to be there at ten. It was now seven minutes after ten.

This wasn't a good way to make a first impression. And Mina doubted Ms. Dunkirk would take "I was flirting with my crush" as a good excuse.

Getting on the staff of the *Bugle* was important to Mina, even though she'd just blown off the one person who could control that, just to be with Craig. She dug in deeper and pushed past the cafeteria, where the usual stench of institutional cuisine escaped the room and wafted through the hallway.

It wasn't the best smell in the world, but the scent of something edible (semiedible) made Mina's stomach growl. She'd skipped breakfast and would probably miss most of lunch. Cheer practice would be unbearable if she didn't get something in her. But she couldn't think of that now.

"The *Bugle*, think about making the *Bugle*," she told herself as the classroom came into view.

At first, Mina had been on the fence about being on the newspaper staff. Ironically, she had Jessica Johnson, her archrival, to thank for pushing her off.

Jessica had no idea, of course.

Archrivals was the best phrase to describe Mina and Jessica's relationship. Just like in comic books, Jessica was an over-the-top villain who begged to be hated. After spending four grueling weekends with her during the soc project, Mina now had confirmation that Jessica enjoyed being hated. The only love she craved was from anybody who came from a wealthy nabe, like Folger's Way. Jessica saw Mina as a wannabe and had a level of dislike (okay, hatred) for Mina that Mina still didn't totally understand.

It was a post, about Jessica, Mina had written in her supersecret blog, *Teen Pop Star*, that ultimately prompted her to seriously consider joining the *Bugle*.

Only the clique knew about *Teen Pop Star*, Mina's tell-all take on DRB's pop life. Even though she changed the names to hide the innocent and not so innocent, anyone with enough time and information on their hands could probably decipher who was who in each wild tale. The funny thing was she'd exaggerated only some of the details. Most of the insanity of each post was hilariously true. Wit and humor were Mina's only contributions to the outrageousness.

The clique had been begging Mina to go live with the blog and let others read it. The plan was they'd leak the URL and drum up traffic. But Mina was afraid people would find out she was the author. She had some way juicy stuff on there, including the truth about how the Glams, the stuck-up rich clique, had once fed Jessica, one of their own, to the wolves.

Jessica wasn't rich but she was way stuck-up, which was all the requirement needed, apparently, because she was second in command of the snooty crew of girls.

At Jessica's soc sleepover, Mina had finally found out the truth about how Jessica's own clique had let her take the fall for something they were all to blame. Mina had had a good time with that "story" on *Teen Pop Star*. Even though most people suspected all along that Jessica had been the fall girl, Mina felt as though the details she gave in *Teen Pop Star* would make it obvious she was the author of the blog.

She wasn't comfortable outing herself and had begged the clique not to buzz the blog, yet.

The blog entry about Jess, aka Queen B, had given her an idea for *Pop Life*, a new column for the *Bugle* that would cover people on the rise among the student body. Mina's idea was to feature the already popular and those aspiring to be.

Right before Thanksgiving break she'd written Ms. Dunkirk an e-mail outlining her idea and was walking on clouds when Ms. Dunkirk e-mailed back and asked Mina to stop by on the last day before vacation.

Ms. Dunkirk had been low-key when Mina walked in. She sat behind her desk, never getting up to greet Mina, only saying a quiet hello and piercing Mina with her brown eyes.

"Amina, your column proposal was interesting," Ms. Dunkirk said.

Mina had forced herself not to check for boogies or eye crust as Ms. Dunkirk's gaze swept over her, taking inventory.

"However . . . ," the teacher continued, purposely pausing, drawing out the torture, "I'm concerned that a regular feature like this will divide the student body. Popularity is subjective." She said "subjective" as if it were an accusation, finally moving her eyes back to Mina's gaze.

"It's not like that at all, Ms. D." Mina squirmed. She felt like she was on trial. But she was ready to fight for the column. "The whole point is to also put the shine on some people who are usually over-looked."

Ms. Dunkirk nodded, waiting for Mina to go on.

Believing it was her only opportunity to prove the column's worth, Mina went full steam ahead. "It's like . . . okay, you know how people automatically assume that certain people are popular?" Ms. Dunkirk nodded softly, encouraging Mina to continue. "Well, *Pop Life* could cover some of those people, especially if they really are doing their thing and aren't just hype. But it will also cover people like Shane Mohr."

She waited for and got Ms. Dunkirk to say, "Who is Shane Mohr?"

Mina grinned as she explained. "Shane is this quiet junior. He always keeps to himself, but he's also like a junior lightweight boxing champion. Hardly anyone knows because in school Shane barely says two words to anyone. And he's kind of skinny, or at least he looks skinny in the baggy clothes he wears."

Ms. Dunkirk's eyes brightened. Mina could see she was hooked. She grew animated as she gave other examples. "Or Julie Bradlow. She's a classically trained dancer, and she's going to be in a Missy Elliot video. And Marlon Case is supposed to be getting early acceptance to Harvard."

Ms. Dunkirk allowed herself a smile. She swept her sandy brown shoulder-length hair back into a ponytail, making her look five years younger, as she finally moved from behind the desk. "So who are your sources, Ms. Mooney?"

She began placing books and papers into a leather messenger bag.

Mina chuckled. "A good reporter never tells."

Ms. Dunkirk nodded, but the piercing gaze was back for a quick second as she looked at Mina over her shoulder. "She tells the editor in chief when asked." She laughed softly. "You seem to know a lot about your peers."

Mina nodded. "I'm obsessed with people watching. I know every clique in our school and could name the top of the food chain for each," Mina said, without bragging. She didn't bother to share that as long as she had Michael, Lizzie and JZ, she would always have the 4-1-1 on jocks, smarties, the artsy kids and fashionistas.

"I tell you what, let me think about it over break," Ms. Dunkirk said. Seeing Mina's face fall, she added quickly, "I still believe this has to be approached just right so it won't . . . further alienate students from one another. But I like where you're going with it."

Mina's heart soared until Ms. Dunkirk said, "Making the *Bugle* is very competitive. You have a good idea, and based on your e-mail, I suspect you're a decent writer . . ."

"But?" Mina asked.

"But, no one just walks onto the *Bugle* staff. We'll talk about that after break." Ms. Dunkirk placed the bag on her shoulder. "Come on, I'll walk you out."

Like that, the meeting had concluded. Mina was disappointed that she wasn't offered the position point-blank, but figured Ms. Dunkirk was following procedure. She had no doubt she had the position on lock. It was her column idea, after all.

Now Mina skidded to a stop just inside Ms. Dunkirk's classroom, her heart swishing in her ears. It felt as if it were ready to leap out of her mouth. She took a few calming breaths, then walked in.

Coach Ewing, the varsity basketball coach, and Ms. Dunkirk turned as Mina walked into the room.

"There you are." Ms. Dunkirk smiled. She glanced over at the wall clock. "You're late."

"Sorry, I . . ."

Ms. Dunkirk waved off the explanation. "Amina, do you know Coach Ewing?"

"Yes. Hello," Mina said to the coach's curt nod.

"The coach was telling me about a basketball player who has quite a background. And I was telling him about our new column," Ms. Dunkirk said.

Mina grinned, in spite of herself, at the mention of the new column. So it was official.

Her head bobbed excitedly as Ms. Dunkirk said, "I think this new player might make a really good first profile for *Pop Life*."

"A splashy feature on one of our players would really help give a boost to the team, help 'em start the season off right," Coach Ewing said, his big hands clapping and rubbing at the thought of pumping up his team.

Ms. Dunkirk laughed, her head bobbed side to side. "I don't know how splashy it will be. The *Bugle* is still only a high school newspaper. Award-winning but still high school."

Mina smirked. Ms. Dunkirk was definitely flirting with the coach. Mina liked the way she had eased that "award-winning" in there to let Coach know she had some skills, too.

Well you go, Ms. D. Down with the swirl, Mina thought.

She could see why. Coach Ewing was easy on the eyes. He had a basketball player's body, tall, lean and broad across the chest. His low-cut caesar was full of waves, and his facial hair was always trimmed handsomely, framing his milk chocolate face. Unlike a lot of the teacher/coaches, Coach Ewing wore more than Starter athletic gear. If it weren't for the little bit of gray popping up in his caesar, he would look like a student today, all prepped out in well-ironed khaki's and a button-down shirt with French cuffs.

Coach Ewing chuckled. "Well, with your award-winning paper and my talented players, I think we make a hot combo."

At mention of the paper, Ms. Dunkirk seemed to remember that Mina was standing there witnessing her shameless flirting. She added a little sigh at the end of her chuckle and cleared her throat. "Amina, what I've decided to do is have you write the feature."

"Sweet," Mina said. She knew writing it couldn't be too hard. She suspected the student Coach was talking about was JZ. Mina could write that article with one hand tied behind her back.

"But I've told you that the *Bugle* is a very competitive paper," Ms. Dunkirk said, all business again. "The last opening on the staff has come down to you and Miles Stevens."

Mina's stomach dropped. She wobbled back a step and bumped into a desk.

"You alright?" Coach Ewing said, extending a hand to steady her.

Mina could only nod.

"Both you and Miles will write the profile, and the best article wins one of you a spot on the *Bugle* staff as *Pop Life* columnist," Ms. Dunkirk said.

"But . . . but . . . *Pop Life* was my idea," Mina sputtered.

"Yes, and it's a great idea. You've proven you can generate great ideas; now I need to see your writing in action, under pressure like it would be on a regular basis as a staffer," Ms. Dunkirk said. She patted Mina's shoulder. "Look, I know it would be hard to see someone else write your column. But I only have one slot open."

Mina was horrified to feel tears stinging her eyes. She didn't want to cry in front of the coach. She hastily wiped at her eyes with the back of her hand.

"But it was my idea," she said weakly.

"Mina, if you're as good a writer as you are an idea person, you'll snag the position easily," Ms. Dunkirk assured her. "But it's got to be this way."

Ms. Dunkirk walked over to her desk. In the pencil skirt, narrow in the hips, only small steps were possible. She tipped lightly, her butt switching as she made her way across the room. The coach watched her from the corner of his eye. It would have been funny if Mina wasn't devastated.

Picking up a packet, Ms. Dunkirk motioned to Mina. "Here's an outline of the assignment. It's due next Monday."

Mina took the envelope reluctantly. She wasn't sure she even wanted to do this anymore. Trying out for her own column idea? It seemed unfair. She was seconds away from throwing a complete fit, demanding to know how Ms. Dunkirk could just steal her idea and give it to someone else.

As if sensing her thoughts, Ms. Dunkirk said, "You're a good student and a smart young lady. Don't let the fact that you have to compete for the spot freak you out. Just give it one hundred percent."

Mina nodded.

An eerie feeling of being an imposter set in. What made her think she could do this? Writing on the blog was one thing. She took things that happened around her and dressed them up as a soap opera. There were no interviewing or reporting skills involved.

This would be her first time having to pay attention to what someone said to her, get the details from the horse's mouth onto paper and make sure the information was accurate.

This was insane. She couldn't do this.

Then it hit her. *It's just JZ. Yes, you can.* The only person who knew JZ better than her was Michael. As long as she came correct with her writing, this would be easy.

Mina stuffed the envelope in her backpack, letting the confidence nibble away at her fear. She could do this.

"Okay, I'll do my best," Mina said. And since butt kissing was sometimes in order, she added, "Thanks for giving me this chance, Ms. D."

She hefted her bag onto her back and headed toward the exit.

Ms. Dunkirk sat back on the edge of the desk and crossed her feet. "Hold on, Amina. Coach Ewing, what was the name of the player again?"

The coach joined them at the desk. "Brian. Brian James."

National Kick the Crap out of Mina Day

> "How long 'til the music drowns you out?"
> —Ashlee Simpson, "Boyfriend"

Mina dragged into the cafeteria. She had all of fifteen minutes to eat. But her hunger had been bumped out of the way by anxiety. She took her time joining the clique at their regular table, a sweet spot right in front of the large pane glass with a perfect view of the café, as she sorted through the facts:

She had to try out for her own column.

The article was due in seven days.

She was going up against Miles Stevens, a fellow frosh who had been the editor of the *Galley*, the DRB middle school yearbook.

Alone, each fact made her brain sizzle. Together, her head felt like it was about to start smoking from trying to compute.

She knew Miles well. They were on the *Galley*'s staff together. Miles because he seemed to genuinely love it—telling stories with pictures was his "thing"—Mina only because the school's newspaper was run by the Frumps, a group of geeks who on their own were harmless but in packs were as vicious as the snootiest Glam. The thought of having someone like Silvy Cohen, the pimpletastic wonder and the perfect example of why miniskirts aren't for every body (the rolls, the rolls, they're burning my eyes), correct Mina or worse, tell her what article she could or couldn't write was on Mina's Top Ten Things That's Never Gonna Happen list. Right up there with spending more than two hours at a time with Jessica Johnson ever again and eating sushi (cold rice, seaweed, octopus surprise . . . uh, no thanks).

And since when did Miles have an interest in newspaper writing anyway?

She recalled him mentioning photojournalism. How he would probably "pursue that career path." Being that the only thing Mina was interested in "pursuing" at the time was the recreation division title at the Extreme Nationals (cheerleading consumed her) and she'd had no friggin' idea what photojournalism was until she Googled it, she'd just nodded, smiled and said the right things, "Really? That's cool." And it was, actually. She'd felt a little silly when she'd found out it meant telling stories with pictures. Duh!

So Miles was more than perfect for it.

She didn't know why he wasn't trying out for the *Pitchfork*, the high school's yearbook. If he did, *Pop Life* was hers, no drama. She had a mind to whack Miles over the head with last year's *Galley*, little college-application-building brown noser. She knew that was all the slot on the *Bugle* was to him, trying to make his college apps look good.

It meant more to her. It should be hers for that reason alone . . . and because it was *her* baby, anyway.

Grrr . . . her head was on fire. She half expected to see smoke pouring out of her ears, like in cartoons. But it was what it was.

The only thing standing between her and *her* column (besides Miles) was getting to know Brian. Not a horrible task.

Still, she didn't relish the thought of telling JZ that the *Bugle* was going to cover Brian, not him, for a feature on rising stars. At Coach Ewing's request.

No matter how good JZ and Brian were getting along, there was no way JZ was going to blow that off as if he didn't care. Shine was his middle name, and he needed lots of it.

Wrapped up in thoughts of how she was going to tell JZ (and

her revenge on Miles, which involved a huge X on the ground, Miles in that spot, one of those big old machines with a hugantic shovel and a box full of old *Breeze* copies) she was too late to skid to a stop when Jessica supermodeled her way in front of Mina. As Jessica struck a pose, legs wide open, hands on her hips (mandatory hair toss), Mina collided with her, unable to swerve.

Jessica held her ground, her hazel (contacts) eyes frowning their usual disapproval for Mina's mere existence, as Mina bounced off her.

"Sorry," Mina mumbled, though she didn't mean it. Why the heck was Jessica standing in the middle of the walkway?

Not knowing, but also knowing this was no chance meeting, Mina sighed and waited for Jessica to say her piece.

Jessica said nothing, just stood there, looking like a wacked-out supermodel crossing guard. All she needed was a whistle and a big old stop sign to hold out.

The image made Mina smile.

Seeing that Jessica was waiting to be addressed, Mina shook her head and played along. "What is it, Jess?"

Her stomach roiled, letting her know that even if she wanted to eat, her appetite had pretty much gone out to lunch, pun intended. Word to the wise: send any food this way and the chances of it being returned to sender were very high.

Jessica whipped her long, wavy weave in a head toss toward Mina's table. "Trapped another pop guy in your web, I see."

"Huh?"

Mina looked toward the table. Lizzie, Michael and Kelly sat talking as they finished off their lunches. Michael smashed into what was left of a burger, Lizzie popped chips (baked, no doubt) into her mouth and Kelly was eating grapes.

What was Jess talking about?

What popular guy was sitting with her? She knew she couldn't mean Michael. All Jess ever called him was "that bald-headed dude you're always with." And JZ wasn't there. Besides, Jess had said, "another."

Mina knew her place when it came to Jess. Real talk, they hated each other. But Jessica was an Upper. Let her tell it, she was the "head" black chick at DRB High. Mina didn't know about all that—there was Cara Jordan (junior, track star), Melina Bryce (senior, cheerleader) and Suki Oh (senior and possible class valedictorian), who was really mixed Korean and black but still . . . Point was, Jess wasn't the "only" black chick rolling with the Uppers. True, there weren't many, but what are ya gonna do? Nature of the beast and all that jazz. Jessica was just the only one who seemed to care if Mina joined their ranks.

It was Jessica's official/unofficial ranking that kept Mina standing here talking (half listening) to Jessica go on about whatever crime Mina had now committed, besides getting up and coming to school.

"Brian James, the new hot baller." Jessica sniffed. "Why he's sitting with you guys and not outside with the rest of the varsity ballers is a mystery. But I know he lives in your nabe, so I figured you must have spun some of your 'look at me, I'm such a nice girl,' magic on him."

Mina's back arched slightly, her shoulders pulling back a smidge as she sighed within—not an easy task, but one she'd mastered over the four weekends she'd spent (served time) with Jessica. The internal sigh, the only way to hide that you were breathing out an extreme amount of air in an effort to not strangle the person in front of you.

"Okay, whatever, Jess." Mina took another glance at the table. Brian still wasn't there. She took a step toward the table, uninterested in debating whether she "deserved" for Brian to sit with her or not.

It was the boy's first day of school and already the Uppers had claimed him.

Just waltz right into the popular pack, why don't you? she thought bitterly. *Be my friggin' guest as I stand by for my turn, waiting until Jessica whisks off on her broom back to whatever coven she's from or next semester when I won't (hope) have her lunch period . . . whichever comes first.*

That was some wacked shiggity for you.

Mina threw it on top of the log of gripes she had for the day. She was in for one truly splendid bonfire tonight. Poor Liz (or Cinny or Kelly), whoever got to her first on-line was going to get an earful . . . wordful.

"You know, Mina," Jessica said. Her back had to be tired from standing so straight. Tyra Banks would be proud. Mina shook her head and lightly, real lightly—almost undetectable—breathed another internal sigh, waiting for Jessica to spew her venom.

Jessica cracked a smile, one of those scary "I'm smiling because I can't bitch slap you" looks, and lowered her voice. Not that anyone was listening. "I don't care how many Uppers you make friends with"—she snorted, then glanced back over to Mina's table, still empty of Brian—"or how many Uppers you *do*. If I can help it, you will always remain on the outside of the fishbowl."

The heat from Mina's brain oozed into her stomach. She could feel first her eyes, then throat burn. The hot anger, embarrassment, frustration spread to her chest, taking her heart from a steady, patient thump to a skittery trot before it settled heavily in the pit of her stomach. There it stayed, churning her insides like a pan of boiled-over rice.

"Got it?" Jessica asked. She rolled her eyes. "Of course you do."

She sashayed off, heading to the café. No matter how chilly or cold it was, the Uppers kept their grip on the fishbowl.

Finally able to exhale in a huge gulp, Mina's shoulders sagged as the air came out of her like a busted tire. She made it to the table and pulled out the empty seat between Lizzie and Kelly, ready to vent about the "tryout" (Jessica, the fact that life in general today sucked big *Fear Factor* cow balls) when Michael blasted her. "Mina, you dead wrong for making Kelly lie to her grandmother."

WTF?!

Was this National Kick the Crap out of Mina Day?

Mina gave Kelly, then Lizzie, a look as she took out her lunch, a fruit bar and a bottle of apple juice.

Kelly popped another grape, her face revealing nothing, yet telling. *You missed more than the dried-out burger today, chick,* it said.

Conversation at the lunch table had been hot, obviously.

Lizzie's face confirmed it. She had the pinched nervous look of someone who realized too late she'd said the wrong thing. It was obvious who had spilled the beans.

Mina had purposely not shared her plan with Michael. Michael loved Mina's parents, and the last time Mina had put him in a position to lie to them, he'd told her point-blank afterward he wouldn't do it again.

It was so easy for him to be self-righteous. His grandmother let him do whatever he wanted.

Mina pursed her lips at Lizzie, openly annoyed, as she explained, "We're not lying, we're—"

Michael waved the excuse away midsentence. "Yeah, I know. You're heading to the country club." He shoved the last piece of burger into his mouth, chewing and lecturing at the same time. "First of all, you know how bad Lizzie is at lying. Second, you've been burned once for doing it. Give it a break, diva."

"Thanks for keeping this B/U, Liz," Mina said flatly, shaking her head.

"Sorry," Lizzie whispered. In truth, she didn't know it was only supposed to be "between us," as in just her and Mina. Not like she ran and told their parents. She'd only told Mike. She tore at her napkin, letting the bits fall into her empty fruit cup. "It just came out as we were talking about weekend plans."

"What weekend plans?" JZ asked, placing his food tray, piled high with fries and two burgers, on the table as he sat down across from them. He threw a fry in the air and caught it deftly with his mouth.

Brian sat next to him. His plate was equally full.

They were freebie trays—extras given to the athletes if they got in the right line with the right cafeteria staff right toward the end of the lunch period.

"Nothing." Mina shook her head slightly at Michael and frowned, hoping he'd end the conversation. They could discuss it later, and she'd make him understand why she was going through all this trouble and why she wasn't worried about getting caught. But she wasn't interested in having all of her business out there in front of Brian (Mr. Suddenly Popular All-damn-ready).

Besides, the Frenzy plan was cut-and-dry. Why was everyone making it such a deal?

But Michael was on his advice-guy kick.

"Mina and them are gonna lie to Mrs. Lopez so they can hit the Frenzy next week," he tattled.

"What's the Frenzy?" Brian asked, stopping midchow. He looked from Mina to Michael.

Mina kept mum, throwing all sorts of bad karma vibes Michael's way. He worked his eyebrows, sending his own clear, "I don't care if you're mad, 'cause you're wrong" vibe.

"Football jam, next weekend. Wanna roll with me?" JZ asked.

"Hell yeah," Brian said. They knocked fists before going back to steaming through their plates, trying to finish the free grub before lunch ended.

"Mike, maybe you can go, too," Mina said, thinking maybe Michael was just envious that she and JZ had the in and he hadn't been personally invited. But he quickly squashed that theory with an exaggerated eye roll.

"I'm not 'pressed." He refused to let Mina off the hook. "So it's cool with you if Kelly gets in trouble just so you can get to the Frenzy?"

"She won't get in trouble, Mike," Mina said. She had no intention of getting into details. Not right now.

"How come you can't go?" Brian said.

Mina listened, horrified, as Michael told the truth. "Because her parents not down with her meeting this guy there."

"Oh, my God! Okay, Mike, seriously you're putting all my stuff out there," Mina said. Embarrassed, she scooped up her uneaten food and stuffed it in her book bag, flustered. The bell was going to ring in five minutes. She'd wait in the hall for it. She stood to leave when Michael stopped her.

"I'm just gonna say two words," he said.

"Don't say it," Mina warned. She knew exactly what he was going to say. She narrowed her eyes into slits, daring Michael.

He better not say it. He better not open the door to what was— at least right now—one of the most embarrassing moments of Mina's life.

"Ty DeJesus," Michael announced loudly. He said it again, louder, "Ty DeJesus!"

"Uh-oh, he brought up the 'T' word," Lizzie groaned. Her eyes skittered nervously between Mina's pinched annoyance and Michael's playful "Yeah I said it" glare.

Ty DeJesus was a sore subject. Not only had he made a complete fool of Mina, but the whole clique had almost got caught lying for her. If Lizzie had to pinpoint a time when it was obvious Mina had a severe case of boy-crazy fever, it was the summer before eighth grade.

Mina had been more than just a little doe-eyed over Ty. She was all crushed out gone over him, and she let herself (and the clique) get sucked into a web of lies and half-truths because of it.

Lizzie remembered nearly fainting when the Mooneys ran into the clique chilling by Auntie Anne's that day and saw Mina wasn't with the rest of her friends. She'd fearfully stammered her way to a realistic answer to their, "Hey, where's Mina?"

She still wasn't sure what would have been worse: if Mina had actually ridden to D.C. with Ty and his buddies that day, of all days, when the Mooneys had decided they'd do a little shopping instead of just dropping them off at the mall like they had the previous four times, or if Mina had burst around the corner, while they were still standing there, hysterical in tears the way she had after Ty dissed her.

Lucky for Lizzy and JZ, Michael was cool under pressure, and the Mooneys adored him and believed pretty much whatever he said. Because they had believed his simple, unstuttered answer of, "She ran to the bathroom." And rather than wait for Mina to come back from the "bathroom," they had continued on their way, reminding the clique to meet them at the movie's exit in two hours.

If Mina's parents had known Mina had been sneaking off with Ty, instead of chilling at the mall with the rest of them, for four weekends, she would have been grounded well into her twenties, Lizzie along with her for being an accessory to the lie. Of that, Lizzie was positive.

That was exactly why she'd broken down and told Michael about the Frenzy plans. The thought of helming the lie without him tied her stomach into knots.

JZ took a ridiculously large bite from the burger. His cheeks puffed like a chipmunk as he chuckled. "Ty DeJesus. Dude was wack."

The bell rang, and like soldiers responding to a trumpet call, everyone stood and moved. Kelly and Lizzie made their way to the cafeteria door, and Michael followed behind them.

"Jay, hold up," Mina said, jogging up behind him.

He and Brian exchanged a soul shake, tight hand grip with a pound on the back. "I'll catch up with you at practice," JZ said. He hefted his backpack on his shoulder. "What up, Mi?"

"I went to see Ms. Dunkirk before lunch about joining the paper," she said.

"Word? You Mina star reporter now?" JZ joked.

"She's making me try out," Mina said, tight-lipped, letting out another internal sigh. She pushed past the depression brought on by the thought. People shoved by them, trailing sluggishly out of the cafeteria. Mina stepped closer to a table, out of the way of traffic. She lowered her voice, forcing JZ to step closer and cock his ear to her. "I have to write a trial article. Me and Miles Stevens. The best one wins."

"You probably got it. Don't even start tripping," JZ said, looking to the door. He began easing away.

"The article has to be about Brian," Mina said, stopping him in his tracks.

She bit her lip.

JZ's brows furrowed, but he recovered quickly. "New dude Brian? Brian James?"

Mina nodded.

"How Ms. D. know about him already?" JZ asked, genuine confusion and, Mina was certain, hurt in his voice.

He put his hands, fingers locked, on top of his head. He looked like someone waiting on a pat down from the cops. His hands slowly slid down the ocean of black waves in his hair to his forehead as he absorbed Mina's words. Just as the hands reached above his eyebrows, he'd slid them back to the middle of his head.

Mina was totally on board with JZ tripping—kicking, screaming or holding his breath if he wanted. She'd had her fair share of mind tantrums today and didn't mind a little company if JZ wanted to go there.

Since JZ wasn't a fan of overt affection, she nixed the idea of hugging him or even saying something nice. Not like saying something nice would change what was, anyway.

The Freshman Phenom wasn't the feature for the first basketball article of the season.

Ouch!

But she didn't look at things like JZ did. This was definitely something to trip about, in her opinion. So instead of hugging or being flip, she simply answered his question. "Coach Ewing requested that Ms. D. cover him."

"Requested, huh?" JZ muttered.

Mina watched his shoulders heave and then click, the slide stopped.

He brought his hands down, fixed his book bag on his shoulder and put his game face back on. "Word?"

Mina peered up at him. "You alright with that?"

"I guess I gotta be," JZ said. "I'll holler later."

He took long strides to the door, quickly leaving Mina behind.

Craig Who?

"Talkin' you got a man/Okay, ma and?"
—Mya ft. Jay-Z, "Best of Me"

Mina was pretty sure the *Bugle* article was going to be a disaster.

She hadn't talked to Brian about it yet.

She had no interview questions planned.

It was Wednesday; time was flying.

She sat with the clique, at lunch, at their regular table, waiting for Brian to return. She needed to at least let him know about the article.

She took tiny spoonfuls of pudding as Michael, beside her, ate a taco salad and Kelly crunched on carrot sticks. Brian came and sat, his plate piled high with fries and a cheese steak.

"Hey, Brian, I—" Mina started when Lizzie and JZ came storming to the table.

"Liz, I froze. I'm sorry," JZ pleaded. "I know you don't believe me, but Mr. Collins . . . seriously, dude is just waiting for me to mess up."

"Well, if you'd pay more attention in class instead of daydreaming, it wouldn't matter how much Mr. Collins hates you," Lizzie spat. She sat down in a huff and nearly ripped her yogurt out of a cold pack bag.

"What's wrong?" Mina asked. She looked from JZ to Lizzie, but neither answered. Mina was sure she'd seen a silent something pass between them as JZ pleaded with his eyes, asking Lizzie for something no one else at the table understood. Lizzie's silence was what he wanted because his eyes rested when Liz said nothing.

Mina asked again, anyway. "Liz, what's wrong?"

And again, Lizzie looked up at JZ . . . For what? Permission?

And JZ worked his eyes, eyebrows twitching in a quick rise and fall.

"I don't really want to talk about it," Lizzie said quietly. She turned a spoon over and over into her yogurt. Her nose wrinkled as if the thought of eating it was suddenly the last thing she wanted to do.

Michael, instinctively knowing how to switch topics, asked Lizzie about last minute costume changes for *The Wiz*. Lizzie participated, reluctantly at first, then seemed glad to be talking about anything other than whatever she and JZ were beefing about.

Figuring she'd get the scoop later, Mina again went to address Brian about the interview, when one of the varsity players invited him and JZ to sit outside in the café with them.

JZ got up to join them so fast, he turned his chair over.

Mina saw Lizzie give him a sly (evil eye) glance without missing a beat in her convo with Mike.

Mina watched the two of them walk out to the fishbowl, their conversation wildly animated as they headed into the cold day. Annoyance tightened her eyebrows into a scowl.

Not that she hadn't expected that he and JZ would be out there with the rest of the varsity ballers eventually, but reality stung. For her, getting into the café was like wanting a present for her birthday or Chrismahannakwanza really bad. Even if in the back of her mind, she knew she'd get that present eventually—maybe not this time but at some point—her whole mind ached wanting it. And here it was, three days and Brian was already chilling in the fishbowl, literally. It was cold as sin outside. But Mina would have gladly sat out there freezing her nippers off if she'd been invited.

Right before lunch ended, JZ and Brian emerged from the fish-bowl.

Whatever squabble JZ had with Lizzie had been magically washed away by being out in the cold, apparently, because he no longer seemed apologetic.

He squeezed Mina's shoulder and asked her to let him hold her copy of *Silas Marner*.

Why not ask one of your new Upper buddies for it, she wanted to say. But instead, she snapped, "Where is yours?"

JZ had things too easy sometimes.

Envy was not a pretty look, she knew. But she couldn't help herself.

"Lost it," was JZ's succinct and nonchalant answer.

"And what collateral are you giving up to make sure I get my copy back?" Mina asked, eyebrows raised and all ready to deny him. Knowing JZ, he'd end up getting out of the fifteen-dollar fine due for lost books. But she'd never be that lucky if he lost her copy.

"You know I'm gon' give it back," JZ said, all smiles.

Mina rolled her eyes and noticed that Lizzie did, too.

"Un-ah. I need to hold something hostage," Mina said. "Or else you'll leave my book sitting somewhere or . . ."

JZ sucked his teeth. "Look how you do your boy." He pulled his Blue Devils basketball hoodie off and handed it to her. "Here."

Mina snatched it up, her smile wide, her annoyance melting. "That'll work."

The team had just gotten the customized blue hoodies at prac-tice the day before. Each had the player's jersey number (JZ was ten) emblazoned in a bright (but not eye-squinting bright) gold on the sleeve. It was as much a part of being on the team as playing the game. Mina knew JZ wouldn't let her keep it long. She slipped it over her head.

"Don't lose it," JZ warned.

"I know you're not talking." Mina laughed and flipped him her book as she and Lizzie made their way to Freshman Lit, where outside of JZ's begging gaze, Lizzie finally confided in Mina how JZ had cheated his way to a "B" on the Algebra II quiz. Telling Mina about it upset Lizzie all over again, and she asked the teacher for a pass and left Lit early to go to the health room.

Mina wasn't sure what to make of the whole thing. JZ ignored her when she brought it up. Typical. If he didn't want to talk about something, he was a champ at stonewalling.

What Mina did know was, she wasn't about to trust JZ with her book too long. On the other hand, she loved wearing his basketball hoodie the rest of the day. So many people had come up to her asking if she and JZ were dating.

Dating?

Her and JZ?

Please.

And these were people she thought would know better.

She wasn't hating on the little extra attention the hoodie got her. But, bottom line, she needed her book. So later that same night, Mina called him. "I'm coming to get my stuff, Big Head," she informed him.

Before rushing her off the phone, JZ told her he would leave the book in the kitchen because he would be outside playing ball with Michael and Brian. At the mention of Brian's name, Mina hustled herself into a coat and asked her mom to drop her off at JZ's. She was losing time and needed to get the *Bugle* article started.

By the time Mina arrived, the game was in full-swing under the bright lights of the full-sized court.

JZ waved. "Hang out for a minute," he hollered as he dribbled the ball.

Even bundled up in a down coat, hiking boots and a knit cap, Mina sat freezing on the sidelines. She blew into her gloved hands. Without thinking, her eyes followed Brian down the court, his easy gait emphasizing his athletic ability.

Mina sat riveted, watching the three boys run lithely up and down the court. Michael, who liked a pickup game of ball now and then, as long as it stayed friendly, held his own against Brian, who was taller and more muscular, and JZ, who was speedy and fast with his hands. It was an informal game of one-on-one-on-one, every man for himself, fighting for the ball and an open shot.

Brian blocked Michael's then JZ's shot, rebounded the ball both times and made four points within minutes of Mina sitting.

Like JZ had declared (over and over) Brian was good.

Even wearing only his Blue Devils sweatshirt and shorts in the brisk cold, perspiration formed a shiny gloss on Brian's face. Steam rose from his head as the heat from his face clashed with the cold air.

As good as Brian was, JZ and Michael were giving him a run for his money. Mina took pleasure in how they kept up with him, shot for shot, block for block. Her stomach flip-flopped as the game's pace picked up, each player trying to one-up the next, taking shots from farther and farther out from the three-point line.

For a moment she blocked out the numbness spreading through her butt cheeks from the frigid cold. She couldn't take her eyes off Brian. He was sinking three pointers left and right. Each time, he'd glance Mina's way. But when he'd look she'd quickly avert her eyes, pretending to be engrossed in Michael or JZ running up the court.

He headed up the court once more, running close to her sideline seat. Mina pulled her foot back just as he brushed by, nearly touching her leg. He cut his eyes toward her and winked a cocky "watch this" before stopping short and taking a perfectly aimed three-point shot.

Mina rolled her eyes behind his back. Show-off.

That was a pretty shot, though, she admitted to herself, her eyes still following as soon as he ran back up the court to play defense.

Twenty minutes into the game, butt numb, fingers frozen, Mina called, loud enough to get JZ's attention, "Jay, I'm out!"

All three guys stopped and looked her way.

"Huh?" JZ called back.

Mina stood up and began walking away. "I said I'm rolling out. It's too cold out here."

Brian called after her. "We're done." Without any effort, he shot the ball toward the hoop from midcourt and made it.

"Sweet," Michael said, giving him a pound.

JZ trotted toward Mina. "Hold up."

"Un-ah, I'll wait for y'all in the house." Mina beat a path indoors.

Minutes later the guys appeared in the kitchen, their talk about Brian's last shot, loud and excited. Mina sat at the kitchen bar. She peeled off her gloves, rubbing her hands together and blowing into them to get the blood going again. Brian stopped in front of her stool and took her hands in his.

"Your hands feel like icicles." He massaged each finger from tip to hand.

Mina was too startled to snatch her hands away. Brian's hands were surprisingly warm after having been outside so long. His semi-warmth smoothed over her frozen digits, slowly thawing them, and the heat moved from her fingers to her cheeks.

Mina slipped her hands from his, breaking the spell.

"I'm thinking my boyfriend probably wouldn't be too happy with us playing handsies," she said, mustering up what she hoped was a flirty but reprimanding voice. She was surprised at how far away her voice sounded. An itch crept up her throat, and she cleared it away, bringing herself back to the present.

Oh, God, had she called Craig her boyfriend out loud? Or had she only thought it?

The hitched-eyebrow look of surprise on both JZ's and Michael's faces answered that.

She sent a frantic telepathic message to them, praying they

wouldn't suddenly decide to break into a round of stupid boyish teasing.

Boyfriend? What boyfriend?

She held her breath.

"Boyfriend, huh? My bad." Brian laughed. He threw his hands up like a thief dropping the goods. "You have any Gatorade, Jason?"

JZ threw him a bottle. Brian caught it easily, cracked it open and chugged.

Mina finally allowed herself to breathe. She watched Brian, out of the corner of her eye, take a seat at the opposite end of the kitchen bar and tried to ignore the tingling in her hands. She cleared her throat again and spoke up. "So, Jay, what happened today?"

She knew very well what happened but wanted JZ to cop to the whole thing, once and for all.

It annoyed her when he played sly. "What?"

Mina sucked her teeth. "Why was Lizzie so hot with you?"

JZ sucked down some Gatorade, taking a long time on purpose. He swallowed completely, looked at the bottle as if it held the answer, then shrugged. "It wasn't nothing."

Mina folded her arms. "How can it be nothing when she was so mad?"

"Dag, so literally, my business is not my own?" he asked with a brittle, angry edge. "Just leave it, Mina . . . for once."

Mina felt as if she'd been smacked on the bottom and sent to the corner. Suddenly her coat felt heavy and suffocating. Brian was pretending to be really engrossed in drinking his Gatorade.

Michael poked his head in the refrigerator, making busy there.

Still, Mina felt as though everyone was waiting for her to respond. She got up off the stool and walked over to JZ. She lowered her voice, in case his parents were lurking nearby.

"Jay, she told me what happened." She turned around, as if Mr. and Mrs. Zimms had caught wind of her voice and were listening, then lowered her tone to a fierce whisper punctured with anger. "Y'all could have gotten in trouble if you were caught."

"But we didn't," was his only answer. He went back to sipping the Gatorade, taking small nips as if it were hot tea.

Mina's voice spiked. "Jay, do you know how freaked Lizzie is about this?"

"She'll get over it," JZ said, but not without wincing. Even he knew he was playing Lizzie foul, and Mina seized the moment to tell him so.

"Yeah, she will, but it doesn't mean she'll *forgive* you." She did one last check, and when she was assured the Zimms were nowhere nearby, she let him have it. "You put her in a bad spot, Jay. That's wack."

"Oh, like you getting Kelly, Lizzie and Cinny to lie for you so you can go to the Frenzy next weekend?"

"That's diff—"

"No, it's not, Mina." He sucked his teeth, rolling his eyes as he leaned against the counter, arms folded. "It's not different. How come it's all innocent and swazy when you're asking somebody to do something that could get your ass put on lockdown, but if somebody else does, you're all ready with the lecture? What's up with that?"

Michael came and stood between them. He tried to lighten the moment by blowing into an imaginary whistle.

"Come on, y'all two, chill."

"It's not me, it's her." JZ flicked his head at Mina. "She's got three people set to lie for her so she can creep to a party to see some hardhead. But I'm wrong 'cause—"

He stopped short.

"'Cause what?" Mina's mouth was set in a tight line. "Go ahead and say it."

She did another head check before she whispered, "You're wrong 'cause you made a friend help you cheat." She shook her head disapprovingly. "And it's not like you don't know the stuff, JZ. Lizzie says you know it if you'd just think about it instead of basketball for a hot minute."

JZ barked a harsh, nasty laugh. "Naw, no you didn't go there. Mina, come on . . . Mike, she ain't go there, did she?"

"Look, I'm not trying to get in the middle," Michael said. "I think—"

"Mina, okay, of all people, seriously, you don't need to take it there," JZ warned.

"I wasn't trying to be smart. I'm just saying what Lizzie said," Mina said, her voice returning to reprimanded child. She knew when it came to ammunition JZ had plenty of it. She glanced over at Brian, who looked as if he were watching a comedy skit or bad reality TV.

And in a way it was very *Laguna Beach* meets *Two-A-Days*.

"Okay, real talk?" JZ asked. But he kept talking before anyone could answer him, his jaw tight. "I'm fighting to keep my spot on the team. And I do know this algebra mess, but I froze yesterday. If I had known Liz was gon' trip like this, I wouldn't have bothered to ask for her help."

"It wasn't help she gave you; it was answers. And that's why she's sick about it," Mina said. Her lips pursed into a tight pucker. "Just make it right, Jay."

"What? Like how?" JZ eyed her suspiciously.

"You need to tell Mr. Collins you—" Mina lowered her voice dramatically—"cheated."

"It was just a fuggin' quiz!" JZ's sigh was explosive. His hands started doing that slide to the middle and front of his head. He seemed to be talking more to himself than Mina or anyone else. "It was a pop quiz . . . It's not even like something he planned. Just one more thing to screw me. I would have never asked Lizzie to do that on a real test . . ." His mouth turned down in an angry frown. "But man, Mr. Collins . . ."

He trailed off, looking off to a corner of the kitchen, seeming to debate the situation. But the debate must have ended up in a tie because he only hung his head as his hands did their slide dance.

"Dude, look, just talk to Coach and see what he can do," Brian said.

JZ took a deep breath, and his head dipped lower as he let it out. He knew he couldn't. Mr. Collins's warning to never have one of the coaches run interference for him rang clear in his ears. But he didn't bother to share that with Brian.

"You still have Friday's test, just rip it," Michael suggested. He gave JZ a soft pound on the back. "Hear me, son? Just rip that fool."

JZ cracked a weak smile.

Mina felt for him. It wasn't like JZ to cheat. He didn't have to. He was a solid "B" student. A solid "B" student in advanced classes, the farthest thing from the dumb jock stereotype. She knew how desperate he must have been to do something like this.

She tried to make peace with him. Stepping closer to him, she tugged his arm. "Can you at least just talk to Lizzie and . . . you know, get things cool between you?"

JZ nodded, but kept staring down at the floor.

Brian stood up.

"I can give y'all a ride home if you want," he said to Mina and Michael.

Mina was glad he offered. If she called her mom to pick her up, she'd end up blurting the whole Lizzie/JZ story to her, and she didn't want to share this. But sometimes when things ate at her, she found herself telling her mom just to get it off her chest. She knew this was one thing that would stay between the clique . . . unless Lizzie or JZ let it out.

Michael and Brian gave JZ a pound, and they all left him, standing in the kitchen, his back against the counter, his head down, staring a hole into the ceramic tiles as if they could help him.

It was silent inside of Brian's Explorer as they took the short ride from Dogwood to Maple Court, Michael's cul-de-sac. Brian asked Michael if they all wanted a ride in the morning and Michael said yes. Then with a fist pound, Michael was gone.

Brian waited for Michael to get inside before he pulled off.

"You alright?" He glanced over at Mina.

She nodded. Her throat was too tight to answer. She felt like bawling but refused to do it in front of Brian. As much as she liked him and as comfortable as everyone seemed around him, she felt horrible that so much clique business had been discussed in front of him. She felt naked and wondered if he was judging them.

JZ was a cheater, and she was nothing more than a two-bit schemer. Wow, who wouldn't want them for friends?

As Brian turned left into Sweet Birch, her cul-de-sac, he said in a very JZ-like "all things are cool, eventually" voice, "If Jason talks to Coach, he can probably help him work this through with that teacher."

Mina snorted softly. "Then what about Lizzie?"

Brian frowned. "What do you mean?"

"Even if JZ can get Coach Ewing to clean the slate for him, their math teacher is Lizzie's drama director . . . What about her? Mr. Collins might kick her out of Bay Dra-da."

Mina took pleasure in his silence. He didn't know everything about them. And furthermore, everything couldn't be worked out by your coach. If JZ had to learn that the hard way, so be it.

Then she felt bad. Brian was just trying to bright side it, something Mina did all the time.

She was about to say something to soften things, take some of the gloom off the situation, when it occurred to her, she still hadn't taken care of her own business.

"Oh, I keep forgetting to ask you, can we spend a little time together?"

"So, would the dude you trying to hook up with at the Frenzy like that?" Brian asked with a sly smile.

Mina frowned, then realized what she'd said. She fumbled, trying to rephrase her question. "No . . . I meant . . . I've got to write an article about you for the *Bugle*. So I need some time to interview you. Can you help me out?"

"Oh, yeah. Some dude named Miles came up to me in the hall yesterday," Brian said. "Something about he wanted to sit and watch a few practices, then talk to me."

A sliver of regret cut through Mina. Why hadn't she thought about sitting in on one of the practices? Now if she asked to do it, Brian would know she was copping Miles's style. Shoot!

"So when you wanna hook up . . . I mean, talk to me?" Brian said, grinning wickedly.

"It's due Monday." Mina shrugged. "So soon, I guess."

She didn't know why it was so hard for her to just make a solid date.

"How about you roll by practice tomorrow?" Brian suggested. "Coach let this Miles dude talk to me then. He'll probably let you, too."

Good, so Brian brought up the suggestion to attend a practice. Even if she looked like she was jocking Miles, she could always remind him she'd been invited to the practice and didn't even have to ask.

The silence filled around them again until Brian asked, "Which house is yours?"

"Sixth house on the left." Mina pointed through the darkness.

"You and Jacinta down with a ride to school tomorrow?"

"Is it a date?" Mina chuckled under her breath.

Brian squinted over at her, his face a question mark.

"Just joking," she explained before Brian labeled her a loon. "My parents don't let me ride in the car with guys."

"Aw, dag, should I drop you off right here?" Brian slowed the car down.

Mina laughed. "No. I'm pretty sure the rule is strictly for dating purposes."

"Shoot, I guess they don't know it's just as easy to hook up before school as it is on a Friday night after the movies." He laughed. "Probably easier."

"Please." Mina rolled her eyes to the car's ceiling. "I don't need them thinking about that. Then you'll need a background check just to give me a ride to school."

"I'll be sure to e-mail you my social security number in case they want to check me out."

They both laughed, and an easy comfort settled around them.

"So how do you like the DRB so far?" she asked, putting on her interviewer's cap.

His shoulders rolled up, then down slowly in an easy shrug. "It ain't nothing like the Dee dot Cee . . . but it's okay."

Mina scowled. "How come people from DC always think it's the bomb?"

"'Cause it is," he said with a conceited snort. "But I only went to school in DC. I lived in Potomac."

"So who did you roll with in the Dee dot Cee . . .?" She sniggled. "By way of Potomac?"

"It was just me and my boys, Jamie, Coop and Zeek."

"Dag, y'all didn't have any girls rolling with you?"

Brian shook his head vigorously as though the thought was ludicrous.

"Aww, see, your clique is sorry," she teased, her shrill voice vibrating in the closeness of the truck. "When it's just a bunch of hardheads, you get in too much trouble. Girls help smooth out all that nonsense."

Brian cracked a smile, an odd look on his face. "You have an opinion about everything, don't you?"

Mina was glad the clique wasn't around. She knew the answer would be a hearty, emphatic "Yes!"

"I wouldn't say that," she said, refusing to become the interviewee. These questions were about him. She quickly flipped him another.

"I guess you like girls who play dumb?" Her voice became high, and she added a ditzy twang for effect as she twisted her hair around her finger and tilted her head to the side. "Oh, Brian, you're soooo cute when you're dribbling that . . . that big orange thing. What is it called? Oh, yeah, a bas–ket ball."

"So if I'm down with that type of girl, you wouldn't be the one, huh?" Brian chuckled.

"Got that right," Mina said proudly. She knew a few girls who loved playing stupid to get guys. Her imitation wasn't that far off. Suddenly her conversation with Kelis burst into her head, and she went from interviewing to nosy. "The grapevine has you hooked up with my squad mate."

She kept her face straight as Brian glanced over, inspecting her, for what Mina didn't know. She waited for him to deny it. But instead, he said, "You talking about Kelis?"

"Whoop, so it's true." Mina hid her surprise (disappointment) with a head shake and giggle.

As Brian's car pulled up in her driveway, Mina was ready to go in for the kill and ask what he saw in Kelis. But as she tumbled words in her head, trying to find the best noncatty way to say it, he asked suddenly, "So who's your boyfriend?"

Mina's tongue tied and fell silent. He was doing it again, turning this into a conversation, getting too much info on her. She was going to have to be much quicker on the draw with questions for him. She made a big deal of zipping her coat to her neck, adjusting the top so her chin rested inside the warmth, even though the heater was blowing hot air into her face.

"Why did you stop talking?" Brian's eyes gleamed as he teased. "I thought girls like you never ran out of things to say."

"I'm saying, even if I told you his name, it's not like you'd know him," Mina said, confident in her little trick of avoidance. "You just started classes this week. I know you won't know him."

"Try me. I've met a lot of people so far." He put the car in park and rested his hands on the steering wheel. His eyes and smile teased with every word. "So, who's this boyfriend that would be ready to throw bows 'cause I was trying to do you a favor and warm your hands?"

"Oh, you were helping me out?" Mina snickered.

He nodded, looking sincere as a Boy Scout.

Mina looked toward the house. Now would be a good time for her mom to look out the window or call her cell to see if she was on her way home. But of course, buptkus. Nothing. Her mind moved a mile a minute, calculating the odds of Brian approaching Craig to ask if he and Mina were really dating. Guys didn't sit around talking about that kind of stuff like girls did.

Did they?

She gambled. Not answering would make it too obvious she was lying . . . or predicting the future as she liked to see it. Craig was going to be her boyfriend. He just wasn't yet.

"Craig Simpson," she finally answered.

Brian looked up at the ceiling of the car, as if leafing through a mental file. "Junior, plays football, kind of looks like Pharrell?" His eyes lit when Mina's jaw fell. "That's him, isn't it?"

Mina's eyebrows scrunched. "Dag, do you know what he had for breakfast today, too?"

"Told you I met a lot of people." He laughed. "I have gym with him. So that's you, huh?"

Mina didn't want to dig herself any deeper. She could hear the locker room gossip already.

Man, you mess with that girl Mina? Brian would say.

Naw, kid, we're just friends, Craig would answer back.

Mina groaned at the thought. But she couldn't think of a single question to ask that wouldn't look as if she was obviously trying to change the subject. So far, life as a reporter wasn't agreeing with her.

"So you've been in my car and not his?" Brian said, a sly smile on his face. "You know, since your parents got this little rule about you taking a cruise in a dude's whip." The grin spread across his face as Mina's eyebrows and mouth did a wordless acrobatic routine. "So you think he's cool with me giving you a ride?"

"Why wouldn't he be?" Mina lied. "Craig doesn't own me."

She grinned back, trying to match Brian's confidence even as she thought, *If guys do talk I'm gonna have some explaining to do.*

But what Brian didn't know wouldn't hurt him, like how Craig probably didn't give a rat's tail who Mina rode with (she doubted).

One thing was for sure, if Craig really was her boyfriend, Mina was basically violating all types of BF/GF rules of flirting. Because at that very moment, Brian was definitely flirting with her, and she was one hundred percent enjoying every second of it.

And it was all wrong. Not his flirting, her *liking* it.

"Alright, Miss Independent, I'll tell you what . . ." Brian leaned back, away from the steering wheel, one elbow resting on the door.

A chill tap-danced down Mina's arms as his curly lashes fluttered slowly while he took his time looking her up and down. His face was unsmiling, and Mina realized he was just as cute without showing his pearly whites.

Brian leaned closer to her, resting his arm on the middle console, gave her another of those "I'm checking you out" looks and shook his head as he said, "If I was your boyfriend, I'm not sure I'd be down with that. But I won't tell if you won't."

He winked. "See you in the morning."

The goose bumps on Mina's arms multiplied as she opened the door to step out. She shivered involuntarily, staring long after the darkness swallowed Brian's truck.

The Jedi mind trick was no joke.

What boyfriend?

May the Best Man Win

"I'm hot 'cause I'm fly/You ain't 'cause you not."
—MIMS, "This Is Why I'm Hot"

The next afternoon, Mina stood outside of the gym, willing her legs to carry her inside. She felt silly being nervous. But what if the coach kicked her out? What if he pointed out that attending a practice should have been the first thing she asked for? Why had it taken her three days? She cursed Miles for having the idea first.

If Ms. Dunkirk found out, she might think Mina wasn't reporter material. Weren't reporters supposed to instinctively know how to dig for their information?

Mina squeezed her eyes tight and gave her body a little shake to rid herself of the gnawing anxiety. Miles didn't have the market cornered on sitting in on the practice to get background for the *Pop Life* article. *It's not like he invented the idea,* she thought, taking one step closer to the door. Besides, Brian had invited her. It was his idea. Not hers. So she wasn't really taking Miles's idea.

She stood just off to the side of the doors, her panic rising and falling, so no one from inside could see her through the doors' two narrow glass panes.

Murmuring and laughter, the familiar sounds of a team warming up, seeped under the door. Mina didn't have to see this to know it. The team wouldn't be doing any joking and laughing if they were in the middle of a drill or the coach giving instructions. At least her squad wouldn't be. Coach Embry allowed ten minutes of warm-up, and if the squad even thought of talking outside of that time, laps, push-ups and what the coach called suicide cycles, which Mina thought of as suicide missions (three straight tumbling passes until your arms and legs were spaghetti), were the coach's way of saying, Shut it up.

Speaking of cheer practice . . . She glanced down at her watch. She'd told Coach Em she'd be late because of a class assignment, which was true. But she'd have hell to pay if the coach walked around the corner and saw her "hanging" around the gym, boy watching.

She took a deep breath, straightened her shoulders and pushed the gym door open. Sitting in groups of two, pulling each other forward in a hamstring stretch, every single varsity player stared at her. Mina scanned the crowd until her eyes found JZ and Brian. They were partners.

Jay threw her a head nod, and she gave him a hasty hand wave as she looked for Coach Ewing. But he'd seen her and was striding her way.

For a second, Mina mistook the etched look of sternness on his face as anger for disrupting practice. She took a few steps toward him—if he yelled at her from across the room, she may as well crawl under the bleachers and die now—and began explaining, "Hey, Coach Ewing, I . . ."

"Hey, Mina." A smile broke out on his brown face. "Here to check Brian out?"

Her shoulders sagged with relief. "If that's okay."

She could still feel the eyes of the team on her back. It felt weird being the only female in the whole gym. No matter how low she talked, her voice, high and squeaky compared to the bass of the players, echoed back off the walls.

The coach patted her shoulder, beaming. "You should have told me you were coming."

"I . . . I . . ." Mina stammered. She didn't have a good answer other than she hadn't given one kernel of thought to attending practice until Brian said Miles had already done it.

"It's okay," the coach said dismissively. "But if I had known, I would have let you use my office." He looked around the gym as he explained, "But now I have a student in there taking a test. Maybe you two can just sit at the top of the bleachers. It's about as far away from the noise as you'll get once I get the team going."

Mina followed his gaze to a corner. "That's fine. But I was kind of hoping to watch practice in progress for a few minutes before talking to him."

"No problem. Just wave him down when you're ready." The coach blew his whistle. "Alright, let's roll."

The players hustled to their feet and scrambled over to the coach. Mina scurried out of the way and stood off to the side, watching.

It was easy to see why the varsity basketball team was hands down one of the tightest teams in the school. There were only twelve of them, and after only two weeks of practice, they already shared a language of their own, playfully pushing and shoving each other as they broke into two lines for sprint drills.

Mina envied their bond.

The junior varsity cheer squad had twenty members, and they were sort of close, but not what Mina considered tight-knit. Most of the girls were former gymnasts, new to cheerleading, which made for some crazy good tumbling passages in their routine for Counties. But Mina missed the closeness she'd had with the girls on the Raiders recreation squad—most of whom had gone all-star because of their lust for competition. Counties were the only competition the high school went to. It was lame. But Mina couldn't see not cheering her school teams on, walking around in her spirit gear, leading the student body at pep rallies and being on total display in the name of Blue Devils spirit. So she'd chosen the school over an all-star cheer squad.

Well, sort of. There was also the very minor fact that her mother had said no, no and triple no to Mina's request to cheer all-star. Too much time. Too much travel. Too much money. And did she forget to mention, no?

Sadly, the closest person to Mina on the squad was Kelis. At least close in that way of being around someone long enough to have that comfortable slipper kind of thing.

"Heads up!" a yell came from the center of the court, reminding her she was in a gym full of fast-moving balls. Mina ducked and did a girly scoot away from the ball hurling toward her.

JZ came up, chasing after the ball. He snatched it up from the bottom row of the bleachers where Mina had stood seconds before.

"Did it get you?"

Mina shook her head.

After only a few minutes, JZ was already glistening with sweat. His well-toned arms shone as if oiled. He wiped his face on his shirt. "Doing your *Bugle* article?"

"Yeah." Mina looked around for the coach. But he'd disappeared. She should have known JZ wouldn't risk talking to her if he was there. She moved in closer, desperately trying to avoid the echo. "Did you and Lizzie talk?"

His eyebrows crinkled. "She won't talk to me."

In a way, Mina couldn't blame her. Even if JZ fessed up, it could mean Lizzie's starring role, not to mention being on Mr. Collins's bad side. If she had time, she would fuss JZ out again. But she didn't. And by the sound of his voice, he was majorly bummed that Lizzie was igging him. She didn't bother to share with him that Lizzie wasn't really giving him the cold shoulder. Not much. She was preoccupied with getting caught, and clamming up was how she dealt with it.

"She'll get over it," Mina said, her eyes darting over to Brian at center court, shooting free throws. She couldn't afford to get thrown off her task.

"I don't know how to make it right." JZ armed away a drop of sweat heading to his eyes. "Either way I'm dogging both of us by telling the truth."

"Can you tell Mr. Collins that you cheated and Lizzie didn't know?" Mina said hopefully, then thought of one better. "Or maybe not even mention who you cheated off of?"

"I guess," he said unconvincingly.

Mina could tell he didn't want to confess at all. He confirmed her suspicions when he scowled.

"I still don't see what me truthing up is gonna do."

Mina was no saint. She doubted she'd be that honest herself. But, it wasn't about that. Lizzie was known to be horrible at lies. And this was a lie about a grade. Mina could see this lie driving Lizzie straight out of her mind.

"It'll help Lizzie feel better," Mina reminded him. "You need to find a way to make things right with her. Maybe you can do it without truthing up." She shrugged. "I don't know."

JZ sighed heavily. He looked over at Brian and snorted. "First, I was tripping over this article you have to write. I ain't gonna lie. It should be about me." He wiped his face with his practice jersey again. "But, then I was like, shoot, as long as I get my playing time, I ain't gonna trip over no *Bugle* article. And now this . . . Mr. Collins . . . Algebra II . . . I just keep fuggin' myself up."

"Woo-woo!" Brian called, clapping his hands for the ball.

JZ chucked it at him. As if Brian's call for the ball had snapped him out of a trance, JZ's voice perked up. "Look, I got this . . . I'll work it out. You just do your thing so you can get the column. Then I expect coverage 24/7." He smacked the underside of Mina's notepad, trying to strip it out of her hand, but Mina had it snug against her stomach. JZ laughed as he ran back to the team. "Later, Mi."

Mina hoped JZ was right.

She went back to the sideline and called out to Brian.

On her third call, he finally heard her and walked over, a big smile lighting up his eyes.

Mina couldn't help smiling back. "Hey," she said softly as if in a library instead of a gym full of loud, echoing bouncing balls and rowdy guys. "Can we talk for a few minutes?"

"Anytime, Miss Reporter. Brian loves the press." He chuckled, grabbed a towel off a nearby ball rack and straddled the bottom bleacher.

Mina sat beside him, unable to stop looking at how his hair, now wet with sweat, was even more curly than normal. Her fingers itched to run through the thick mass until, okay, ew, she thought about how sweaty it was, pushing that thought far away.

"Show me what you got," Brian said. He reached over, turned on her digital recorder and began clowning. "I was born March 17, 1989, on a cold St. Patrick's Day. My mother almost named me Shane Chilly O'James."

He laughed rich and deep.

Mina smiled but refused to laugh. She had to hold on to a piece of her journalistic professionalism . . . whatever that meant when said reporter was carrying a purple notepad with pink hearts and writing with a pink pen that said, "I heart your boyfriend."

"Seriously?" she asked.

His head bobbed up and down. "Yup, my birthday is on St. Patty's Day. I'd show you my license but it's in the locker room."

"I'm gonna start calling you Shane," Mina teased.

Brian groaned. "Naw, don't do that to me, Toughie."

Mina frowned. "Toughie?"

"That's what I'm gon' start calling you 'cause you like being in charge, nahmean?" He placed a leg atop the bleacher and leaned against it, just chilling. "Am I right?"

Of course he was right. Being in charge was what she did best. But to Brian, she shrugged.

He laughed as if knowing she was full of it. "So what's up, Toughie?"

Mina put on what she hoped was a disapproving scowl, but inside she was smiling, *Aww, he has a nickname for me.*

She opened her notepad and shot off her first question. Within minutes, the questions became easier to ask, flowing faster, more smoothly. She even asked a few questions offhand when Brian would say something she found interesting enough to follow up on.

As Brian talked, Mina watched him and everything going on around them. Like how he gave her questions thought before jumping into the answers; and how when it was a question he had to really think about, he'd lean his elbows on his thighs, head turned to the side, looking up into the empty stands; or how he switched so easily from serious to joking, flipping off a few of the players who teased him, calling him "Bugle Boy," when they walked by to get a towel.

She took in every detail, scribbling vague notes whose meaning she hoped she'd remember later.

There was no question Brian didn't answer, including the one she saved for last. "So, girlfriend or no?"

She felt her chest deflate slowly, satisfied, as he said, "Nah." She laughed along when he said, "But you know, a brother is taking applications."

Mina checked her watch. A good reporter was mindful of her source's time. "Well, thanks for kicking it with me." She closed her notepad and stood up, choosing to pass on a handshake. Too corny. "I appreciate it."

It felt longer, but she'd gotten the actual interview done in fifteen minutes. And thanks to Mike, who'd suggested she bring the digital recorder, the whole thing felt more like a conversation than an interview. *Good looking out, Mike,* she thought as she tapped the recorder's off button.

"So you got all you need?" Brian asked. He sounded sincere, as if, if Mina didn't, he'd be willing to go longer. Sweet.

"I'm good. Plus, I'm already late for practice." Mina walked to the back of the gym, heading toward the gymnastics room where cheer practice was held.

Brian walked with her. "That's right. I heard y'all got Counties in two weeks."

"Yup. And since JV sucked last year, the coach is working us crazy to avoid a repeat." Mina sighed at the uphill battle of coming back from a ninth place win out of thirteen teams. "We have a lot of tumblers, though. We're hoping to be in the top four."

"So you want me to come cheer you on?" he asked, syrupy sweet. He feigned hurt feelings when Mina laughed. "Naw, I'm serious."

"Well, we can use all the help we can get." She pushed the door open, debating whether to play along with Brian's obvious flirting. She took a step out of the gym, then turned back around. "That is, if you can handle the competition. Craig will probably be there, too."

Brian laughed loud. "Ay, like they say, may the best man . . . I mean, team win."

With that he jogged back to practice.

Are You Ready for Today?

"That's how you try to treat things like, just stay hungry."
—Notorious B.I.G ft./Jay-Z, "My 1st Song"

The bad news was Mina was right.

Boy, did JZ hate those times.

He'd royally messed up not just his own biz but possibly Lizzie's. Lizzie hadn't said a word to him since lunch on Tuesday. And JZ would be lying if he said he didn't care. Lizzie was his friend, a good friend, and he didn't want to take her down if his ship sank from this Algebra II mess.

He stood outside the classroom, waiting on her. The halls ran long and deep, bleeding blue and gold. School-colored signs predicting the demise of the Sam–Well Trojans at tomorrow's game covered every wall. He cracked a smile at one with a grinning Blue Devils mascot (not prettily drawn) with a balloon coming out of its mouth that said simply, "Blue Devils Wha? Wha?"

That was one of Mina's. An artist she wasn't.

Not an inch of wall was visible behind the signs, crepe paper and spirit paraphernalia.

It was the scent of victory that had him so crazy these last few weeks. The love of the student body. The thought that he could make all of the signs on the wall come true. Beat the Trojans. Smash Sam–Well. Blue Devils #1. He could do those things by stepping on the court.

He'd done a good job of playing it off at practice. Even though he'd known there was a chance he wouldn't be anywhere near the team bench, he'd talked trash with the rest of the team about Saturday's game.

Now, today was *the* day. And the way he felt, unprepared and guilty to boot, his head wasn't exactly in a test-taking space.

Speaking absently to those going by, dapping him up and wishing him luck for tomorrow's game, JZ faced north, the direction he knew Lizzie would be coming from. Within seconds, she rounded the corner. She was back in her jeans and tee, but still had her hair out. It blew in the breeze she made as her legs picked up the pace toward the classroom.

Focused, most likely on the problems to come, she didn't see JZ until he touched her arm.

Startled, she gasped, frowning.

"Can we talk?" he asked sheepishly.

JZ saw the battle of emotions on her face, and it hurt him. Lizzie had to think about whether or not she wanted to even be near enough to talk. Still, she let herself be led a few feet away from the classroom, to a hall window that looked out on the campus.

"Liz, I'm really sorry, for real," JZ said. He leaned against the wall and started his hand dance. He did this for a few seconds, amidst her silence, then let his hands drop. "Brother is foul like a mug, huh?"

He was surprised when a small smile turned up Lizzie's lips.

"Very foul," she agreed in a soft voice.

JZ chewed on the inside of his lip as he thought. In his mind he'd gotten only as far as an apology. He still had no idea how to make things right. He'd be straight up lying if he told Lizzie he planned to confess. He knew it was the thing to do, but he wasn't convinced he was going to.

"Look . . ." He thought for a second more, then spoke from the heart. "Whatever you want me to do to make this right, I'll do it. For real."

His heart thumped hard and slow. He didn't know if he could take Lizzie saying he had to confess. But he meant what he'd said. If she told him to do it, he would. No questions, no trying to convince her of a Plan B.

Lizzie's green eyes looked worried as she stared up at him. "Are you ready for today?"

The look made JZ want to kiss her. He couldn't believe she still cared if he failed or not after how he did her.

"You know what?" He sighed, laying his head on the cold glazed concrete of the wall. "If I stop overthinking this, I will be. I just feel like I'm thinking about a million things at a time and the math problems are waaayy in the back."

"You know this stuff, Jay. Just. . . . focus," Lizzie said, hugging her books to her chest.

"Thanks." He smiled weakly. His heart was still doing its slow, loud thump. There remained that one loose end. "So what do you want me to do? I mean it, I'll do whatever."

"Let's just get through this first. Okay?" Lizzie said it as if she were talking to a small child, which was exactly how JZ felt.

I should just let her take my hand and lead me to class, he thought, shaking his head at the image.

"Thanks for looking out this week. Your tutoring helped. It really did." He nodded along as if he needed to convince both of them.

"I hope so," she said and then did tug on his sleeve, pulling him toward the classroom as the bell rang.

Whatever Happens Between Them ... Is Between Them

"It's just the cutest thing when you get to fussing."
—Ne-Yo, "When You're Mad"

Friday afternoon, Raheem carefully pulled his new car into Jacinta's aunt's, small gravel driveway. Sludge covered the roads from an unexpected chilly rain from earlier in the day and still his used emerald-shaded Acura was squeaky clean and shining. *His butt probably stood outside freezing for hours to get the whip blinging like that,* Jacinta thought, watching him from the house.

Raheem was so proud of the car. He'd saved for an entire year for it and finally purchased it a few days ago. The last few times they'd talked (and weren't arguing) the vehicle occupied his mind and conversation almost as much as sports. Jacinta wasn't sure where she ranked among his hobbies but suspected it was after the car.

As if to confirm her suspicions, Raheem gave the car one last quick admiring glance before approaching the house—clearly reluctant to part with it for even a few minutes.

They'd just seen each other last Friday, but it still felt as if she were seeing him for the first time. It always did nowadays. She watched him stroll to the door and soaked in everything about him. He hadn't bothered with a coat, instead sported a knit cap over his neat rows of braids and a Trojans hoodie. His muscular body looked heavier than usual, no doubt from wearing a few layers under the sweatshirt.

She smiled, loving the thin strip of facial hair hugging the outline of Raheem's jaw. How many girls at Sam–Well were all in that fine face on the regular, she wondered, then banished the thought. She didn't want to know.

She knew every trait of that face well. She had known Raheem since she was five and he was seven. Back then, she walked the tomboy line—ripping and running with him and Angel, hanging out like she was one of the boys, them treating her as rough.

But the first time Raheem had teased her about her new soft curves, which seemed to appear overnight when she turned ten—the little spitfire that usually gave as good as she got burst into tears. After that, she wore the baggiest clothes she could find to hide her changing body until her father refused to buy any more oversized clothes.

Like a well-tuned timer, two years later, just as she had grown comfortable in her new skin, Raheem's teasing turned to curious awe. And the games of tag turned into verbal rounds of flirtatious truth or dare. Days after her twelfth birthday, Raheem asked Jacinta to "go with him." She eagerly accepted and really believed (no matter how silly it seemed to anyone else) that they would be together always.

She saw him today through her twelve-year-old eyes, her best friend, a little boy who had fought for her when another boy called her mother a crackhead, taught her how to spin a basketball on her skinny little finger (for two seconds!) and was her first kiss.

Their two years together washed over Jacinta, filling her with a rush of sentimental affection. She hadn't felt this sappy for him in a long time. It felt good.

Everything was going to be okay between them. She could feel it.

Swinging the door open before he could knock, she spoke, her voice almost shy.

"Ay, girl, what's up?" Raheem smiled. "You ready?"

"Yeah." Jacinta yelled out to her aunt, "Aunt Jacqi, my ride is here!"

Jacqi appeared at the top of the stairs, looking every bit the fly aunt in snug jeans and a pair of UGG boots. "Hi, Raheem, come on in."

"How you doing, Ms. Jacqi?" Raheem said respectfully, stepping inside.

His gaze swept around the house and finally rested on Jacqi, who was blessed with curves on top of curves. It was no secret from Jacinta that Raheem had a crush on her aunt, had since she baby-sat him years ago.

Back in the day, Jacqi would tease him, prophetically, about being Jacinta's "little boyfriend."

Jacqi pretended to scold him. "Boy, you make me feel old. Stop with that Ms. mess!"

She hugged Jacinta and continued her motherly lecturing. "Okay, you make sure my niecy gets there in one piece."

Raheem grabbed Jacinta's bag. "Trust."

"Cin, don't forget I'll be back late Sunday," Jacqi said in full mothering mode.

"Okay. Have fun." Jacinta backed out the door, anxious to be alone with Raheem.

Not finished, Jacqi called after Jacinta. "Oh, and tell your father to call me. My car is acting up. He promised he'd look at it for me."

Already halfway to the car, Jacinta called back, "I will!"

"See you," Raheem said, walking to catch up with Jacinta.

Jacqi waved, watching the car pull away.

As Jacinta snuggled into the car's leather seats, on instinct she reached for the radio to surf stations. Raheem scowled at her, just short of smacking her hand, and turned back to the original station. "Girl, you tripping . . . touching my tunes."

"Umph, my bad!" she huffed. "Don't get all cute now that you got a whip."

"Me get cute?" His eyebrow pitched. "Naw, I'm not the one changing."

"Oh, but I am?"

Jacinta was disappointed but not surprised that the arguing had begun so soon.

Raheem cut his eyes toward her. "I don't know, are you?"

"What are you saying, Raheem? Just say whatever is on your mind, please." She folded her arms and slammed back against the seat. "I'm not for the games."

"Nothing. I ain't saying nothing."

He drove in silence for a few seconds, then changed his mind, deciding it was something. "Jacinta, look, I know you gotta do what you gotta do while you living over in The Woods. But don't *you* get cute just 'cause you changed zip codes."

Jacinta asked, "Is this about Angel and Kelly?"

"In a way, yeah," Raheem said. His usual gruff voice became surprisingly gentle. He rubbed her knee. "But it's about more than that, too. I mean, that's up to Angel how he wanna handle Kelly. But, you all concerned about it like whatever go down between them gon' cost you something. You concerned about losing Angel's friendship or Kelly's?"

His candor shocked Jacinta. When it came to relationship issues—especially ones connected to Angel, who usually found someone new to call girlfriend every week—Raheem never said much. Now he was practically campaigning for Angel.

"Why would I have to lose either one of them as friends?" She peered over at Raheem, watching him think. His eyes swept the road before glancing her way.

"If something went down wrong between them, whose side would you take?"

Jacinta huffed under her breath. "I don't know, Heem." She found herself pleading. "Look, if things go bad with them, it don't have nothing to do with me . . . with us."

Raheem's dark brown face was thoughtful, as though he wasn't so sure.

Jacinta tried to convince that look away. "And besides, if anybody's going to be doing any hurting or dogging, it's probably gonna be Angel." She laughed, then turned serious again. "Look, can we just agree that whatever happens between them is between them?"

Raheem shrugged. "Far as I'm concerned, yeah."

Jacinta searched his face for any hidden clues before asking, "Okay. Well then, if that's the case, why are we talking about this? Or are we really talking about us?"

"No. We talking about how Angel wouldn't supply your moms with drugs and how you owe him to remember that," Raheem lectured.

"I do remember." Jacinta's voice was thick with passion. "Ain't nothing changed!"

She never needed a reminder that out of respect for their friendship, Angel refused to sell her addict mother drugs. Not that her mom hadn't found them elsewhere. But Angel made sure no one from his crew was the dealer. Jacinta took consolation in his gesture. It was one of the reasons, on a growing list, why she wasn't about to choose between him and Kelly. If things went bad, they went bad. It had nothing to do with her.

Raheem kept his eye on the road, but peeked over at Jacinta. She looked cute, with her mouth all poked out.

He couldn't care less what went down between Angel and Kelly. He only wanted to see where Jacinta's loyalties were, wanted to know Jacinta was still there for them—for him. He reached out and caressed her cheek with his thumb. "We alright, baby girl?"

Jacinta nodded, but it felt as if someone were sitting on her chest.

The car's heat, warm and soothing when she stepped into the car, now scorched her face. She felt trapped, and she sensed Raheem was talking in riddles.

Was he saying that if she wasn't totally down with him and Angel, on every subject, her love for him wasn't real?

She'd begun the day looking forward to seeing Raheem, but now being with him was suffocating her.

When the car finally pulled up to her building, she was glad. Still, when Raheem reached over to kiss her, she instinctively let his lips cover hers and gave in to his soft pressing. Just like that, things were normal again. The tension and uncertainty disappeared, and she let the warmth of his kiss linger on her lips while she melted deeper into the car seat.

"We gonna hook up later?" Raheem whispered.

"You know I have to spend time with the fam." Jacinta added quickly, "But tomorrow after the game we gonna chill, right?"

"That's cool." Raheem sat upright in the seat. "Me and that fool Angel will probably cruise tonight."

"Just don't be having no chicken heads up in here!"

Raheem acted as if he had to think about her demand. "Yeah, well, you know how Angel is—"

"Oh, okay, let me find out," she warned.

"Girl, chill, ain't no girls gon' be up in here." His big grin teased her. "Go 'head in the house before Jamal be out here on my ass."

Jacinta pecked him on the lips and hopped out of the car. Her heart ached for the way it used to be as she watched him drive off.

No She Didn't!

"Say that I'm sick and I'm sprung, all of the above."
—Ne-Yo, "Sexy Love"

Piles and piles of magazines wallpapered Mina's floor. *InStyle* mingled with *Seventeen*, *Girls Life* bookmarked a page of boots in an issue of *Lucky* and a stack of *Vibe* teetered inexplicably on a small pile of *Teen Vogue*, smothering the smaller mag. In the middle of the mess, Lizzie and Mina sat. Surrounded by the latest in celeb gossip and fashion previews, music blasting sufficiently loud enough to wake the dead, the girls cut each other off as they hopped back and forth between hot gear and hot boys.

Mina yanked a copy of *Teen Vogue* from under the *Vibe* stack, causing the inevitable avalanche. Her feet slid over the magazines as she stretched her legs out and propped her back against the bed.

"This yellow string bikini is hot." Mina flipped the mag upside down and over so Lizzie could see. "That's me next summer. So what's the scoop on JZ's test? Did he pass?"

"Either Jay's not telling or Mr. Collins hasn't told him yet," Lizzie said.

Mina shook her head, chuckling. "Dag, Mr. Collins is hardcore with him. Why is he dogging Jay like that?"

"Mr. Collins is really not that bad . . ." Lizzie flipped a magazine page, then pointed out an outfit to Mina before she went on. "But he definitely has an ish with athletes."

Mina nodded in approval at the outfit as she declared, "He must have been a wannabe back in the day."

Their cackling laughter rivaled the loud music for a few seconds.

"You know . . . maybe I'll do the string with ya this year," Lizzie said thoughtfully, a sly grin on her face.

Mina slammed the mag shut, gaping. "For real?" She eyed Lizzie suspiciously. "You won't leave me hanging again?"

Lizzie crossed her heart and laughed. She'd broken the pact to convince their moms to let them wear string bikinis last summer. Mina was still salty about having to give up buying the "perfect" orange string bikini that fell just right on her small waist and booty-licious curves.

But standing in the dressing room staring at herself in the swimsuit, Lizzie had chickened out. Something about the thought of only a small, loosely tied string keeping the rest of the world from seeing her goodies froze her. The string bikini was too fashion forward for her . . . then. If she could find the right one, next summer, (read, bigger than a headband) she was willing to give it another go.

"If I can find one that's not like dental floss, I'm with you," Lizzie promised.

"Alright, bet." Mina toed a copy of *Seventeen* over to Lizzie. "Here, look at these."

Lizzie leafed through a few pages, then sat up, cross-legged. "So, I've been thinking about this whole Todd thing."

Mina dropped her magazine, grinning. Fashion was on pause if Lizzie was seriously thinking about letting Mina play matchmaker for her, especially with Todd—tall, thin, newly blond and her favorite of JZ's jock buddies.

Even as a brunette, Todd with his goofy humor and crooked pearly white grin was a cutie. But the blond, surfer-dude look was working for him. Obviously, Lizzie thought so, too.

"Yeah? You want me to talk to him?" Mina asked.

Lizzie's cheeks burned red. "Okay, slow down." She pulled off the band at the end of her hair and slowly began unraveling the braid, taking her time and talking equally as carefully as she went along. "You didn't want to hook Todd up with me just because we both hang around you and JZ and he's like—" she wrinkled her nose—"easy bait or something? Like I'm so hopeless you can only nab someone who you know will be around."

"Not at all." Mina frowned. "I think he's mad cool. A real sweetie and totally your speed." She ticked off more reasons that one of JZ's closest basketball buddies was ideal for Lizzie. "You know how crazy Todd is, always cracking jokes and stuff. Humor is very sexy . . ." She giggled. "And he thinks he's so hip-hop, which makes him sort of a dorky kind of cool."

"He's still rebounding from a summer breakup, though . . . right?" Lizzie said, still working the braid.

"Yeah. But *she* dumped *him*. I think he's ready to move on," Mina said, confidently in the know.

Todd had admitted being bummed about the breakup. Mina blamed it on his kind heart and semigoofy ways. If there was a joke to make, Todd made it. He was always mugging, joking and cracking.

It was Jen's loss. Todd was a good catch. As far as Mina was concerned, for every girl who thought Todd was too silly, there would be a girl who could appreciate his fun streak, like Lizzie. Personally, Mina loved Todd's 24/7 humor, even though it was more like 24/5 since Jen dumped him by e-mail right before school started while he was visiting fam in California.

Mina suspected some of his funk was also from missing JZ on the JV basketball team. Todd and JZ had been playing ball together since they were ten, and Todd made no secret about his near worship of JZ's ball-handling skills. As the center on the team, he'd always seen it as his job to get JZ an opening to the basket—unselfishly giving up his own points if JZ had a chance to shoot.

Mina kept it to herself that maybe if Todd were a little more selfish, he'd have moved up to varsity, too. Just her opinion.

Todd was definitely no slug on the court. His long legs were speedier than most tall players'. And he'd grown a thick skin since he was the only one of JZ's team members brave enough to tag along when JZ played street ball in The Cove.

At first, all the black players in The Cove called him, "Ay, white boy." "Ay, white boy, throw me the ball." "Ay, white boy, good game." "Ay, white boy, you coming back with JZ next time?" When they finally christened him "T," Todd was as excited as a boy on a first date.

JZ didn't have the heart to tell him that they first started calling him that because Todd was so skinny that when he held his arms straight out to his sides he looked like the letter "T". None of the Cove players even knew his name was Todd at the time.

After the boys from The Cove gave him his nickname, Todd joined JZ on a no sugar, no fast food diet to bulk up on muscle so he could play as aggressively as the Cove guys without getting bruised black and blue. While the regimen gave JZ crazy toned muscles and a six-pack, Todd ended up even skinner. But thanks to a weird growth spurt over the summer and the magic of weight lifting, he had finally grown out of that awkward skinny phase and had some meat on his lanky frame. He was looking, in Mina's opinion, hottie tottie.

Todd was perfect for Liz.

"We get along great. And he is a sweetheart," Lizzie thought aloud. She ruffled her hair, then dipped her head forward and shook the blond tendrils into submission. Her voice came back muffled from under her hair. "I don't know if I can see us dating, though . . ."

"Well, you know he'll be with us at the 'Ria tomorrow. Once basketball season starts you can't move without Todd being there. But we'll take it slow." Mina nudged Lizzie with her toe. "I'll make this happen if you want me to."

Lizzie threw her head back, letting her hair fall to her shoulders in a moppy tumble. She hugged her knees to her chest, pleased at the thought of Mina playing Cupid for her. It felt good, reinforcing that she was still the head best friend in the house.

She knew she was being silly feeling that way. It wasn't a competition between her, Kelly and Jacinta for Mina's attention. Yet it still felt good when Mina singled her out and did something best friendish, reminding the other two girls she was here first.

She had always taken comfort in the fact that neither she nor Mina was allowed to formally date until they were fifteen. Even though JZ had been enjoying solo dates since they were twelve, Lizzie always figured she and Mina would be the only two freshmen in DRB High still going out on "dates" in groups of twenty— Mina's daredevil tactics and temporary insanity with Ty DeJesus aside. But no. Now, Mina didn't just have Craig, whom she was no doubt heading to Boyfriend Town with, but there was Brian, a "crush"—whether Mina admitted it or not—that Lizzie sensed could go beyond that if Mina put her mind to it.

The whole Craig vs. Brian dilemma had Lizzie feeling slightly woozy about the dating thing. It had never mattered much to her before—she was fine crushing from afar—but she didn't want a repeat of the soc project, being left out of another new part of her best friend's life. She wanted them to go down this road together, like they had just about everything else before they started high school.

Normally, Lizzie would reject Mina's matchmaking, but not this time.

"How you'll find the time to hook me up between your two crushes is beyond me," she said finally.

"No, no. Now get it right." Mina wagged a finger at Lizzie. "I am not crushing on Brian. We're in a state of perpetual flirtation. That's it."

"I like that one." Lizzie laughed. "Perpetual flirtation."

Mina popped her collar. "I know, right, that's a good one."

A distant yell came from downstairs as Mina's mom called out, "Mina!"

"Huh?" Mina yelled back.

"Girl, don't make me yell over that music. Come here!"

Mina walked to her door and motioned for Lizzie to turn down the music. "Huh?" she called out again.

Mina heard the roll of her mom's eyes in her testy, "Jason is down here."

"Ma, can you send him up? Thanks!"

Mina headed back to her seat on the floor.

"No, I can't," Mariah Mooney said in a very "and that's that" tone.

Mina could envision her mom at the bottom of the stairs, hands on her hips, eyebrows raised, losing her patience.

"He's not alone," her mother said. "You girls come on down."

Mina and Lizzie exchanged a puzzled look before scrambling out of the room, slipping and sliding on the mess of magazines as they flew.

Mina wondered who it was. If it had been Michael, her mom would have said so. She also would have sent Michael upstairs. Technically, boys were not allowed beyond the family room or sunroom—and definitely not allowed in Mina's room.

But Michael and JZ were exceptions. Mina was never sure whether it was from some sort of parental intuition that screamed Mina had no attraction, whatsoever, to her two best boy friends and thus no danger of any funny business; or habit, since the Mooneys had known the boys since they were four and five, respectively, and had been letting them go up and play in Mina's room for the last ten years.

Whatever it was, she and the guys hung out in her room on the PC, listening to music or talking all the time. No big.

So who had JZ brought who couldn't cross her parents' invisible, but very real, boy border?

She stopped in her tracks when she saw Craig beside JZ in the sunroom.

Lizzie smashed into Mina's back.

"Ow," Lizzie said, rubbing her boob. "I smushed my . . ." Her voice went up an octave as she noticed the boys over Mina's shoulder. "Oh, hey, Jay, Craig."

"'Sup, girls?" JZ grinned.

"What's up?" Craig threw Mina a nod.

"Hey, Craig." Mina stepped into the sunroom and smacked at JZ playfully. "How come you didn't tell me you were bringing Craig?"

Never in a million years would she let anyone besides the clique see her looking a sbummy mess: dingy capri pants, the ready-for-the-trash-bin (except she loved it) tee and her hair pulled back in a messy, nestlike jumble of spiral curls. Yet, there was Craig, standing right there beside the long sectional sofa, cheesing at her as she tugged absently at the worn, holey, oversized cheer shirt that she never wore outside the house, aware that she was looking less than glam.

"Me and Jason heading over to Bo's later for a Madden tourney. He said he had to stop over here first, so I'm just tagging," Craig said when it was clear JZ wasn't going to answer. He made sad eyes. "What, you don't wanna chill with me tonight?"

Mina's grin stretched a mile long. "Oh, naw . . . I just didn't know Jay was bringing company." She turned back to JZ. "How did the test go?"

For a second JZ's happy face faltered. His eyebrows caved, and he frowned. "Don't know."

"I thought your dad wanted an answer immediately," Lizzie said.

"Yeah . . . but Mr. Collins didn't say anything to me and he hasn't called." JZ's voice took on a wishful longing. "Maybe it's all swazy. Must mean I got my "B.""

"You ineligible for the game tomorrow?" Craig asked.

"Naw, but if I don't pass this test, my pops is pulling me," JZ said, no longer tense about the truth. He pulled his knit cap off, then stuffed it in his pocket. "Probably Mr. Collins is gonna wait until a few seconds before the game to tell us. Dude wanna announce it over the loudspeaker or something."

He mimicked talking into a microphone and made his voice tight and feminine. "Mr. Zimms, I'm afraid to announce that you have . . . failed. Thank you. Please go back to your fun and games."

Everyone laughed.

Mina searched JZ's face for his real feelings.

"You're taking it well."

He was more relaxed than she'd seen him all week since the whole cheating incident.

"No other way to take it, baby girl. Dude is after me." He blew out a loud breath, reflecting. "If I passed, I passed. I can't do boo about it now . . . and neither can he." JZ stripped off his coat and rubbed his hands together. "Let's do this, Liz-O. You got me as your line boy for at least an hour."

"Let me go get the script," Lizzie said. She ran up the stairs.

"So you rehearsing, too?" Craig knocked elbows with Mina.

Mina threw a dismissive wave at JZ. "No. That's all JZ tonight."

When Lizzie came back, JZ led her by the elbow out of the room. "Alright, we're going downstairs to the family room." He turned back and winked. "Y'all kids have fun."

Mina rolled her eyes, silently thankful Craig had no way of knowing how hot her face was.

She settled on the sofa, one leg tucked beneath her. She tucked a stray strand of hair behind her ear, then giggled uncontrollably at the thought of becoming as shy and nervous as Kelly.

Craig took a seat beside her. He nudged her knee. "What's so funny?"

"My friend Kelly always tucks her hair when she's nervous, and I just did it," Mina said, still giggling. "It's just funny 'cause she does it all the time without even knowing it."

Craig leaned over, and Mina could smell minty mouthwash. "I make you nervous?"

She let the swirl of mint float around her before she answered dreamily, "Un-ah . . . I mean, not much."

He chuckled, pulling himself back upright. Mina was thrilled that he didn't scoot all the way back over. He was still close enough that their legs touched. She refused to move an inch for fear he'd put space between them.

"Now, how your boyfriend gon' make you nervous?" he asked.

Mina groaned and hid her face in her hands.

So guys did talk.

"Oh, my God," her muffled voice cried. She brought her hands down so they just covered her mouth. "Okay, let me explain . . ."

He laughed. "Yup. The grapevine saying that me and you doing that exclusive thing."

"And what member of the grapevine told you?" Mina said as if she had to ask.

"New dude, Brian." Craig's eyes crinkled, pinning Mina to her spot. She couldn't look away from his playful gaze.

"What did he say I said?" she asked as nonchalantly as possible for someone totally busted.

Craig laughed. "Ahhh see, you're telling on yourself."

"What?" Mina's eyes went wide with innocence.

A sly grin spread on Craig's face. "I never said he said *you* said anything."

Mina tried to take a new course but wasn't fast enough on her feet. "Well . . . I mean, I figured . . ."

"All he said was, 'Ay, your girl interviewed me for the *Bugle*.'" Craig's voice grew animated. "And I didn't know you wrote for the paper, so I was like, 'Yo who dat'? And he goes, 'Mina.'" He chuckled, reliving the conversation. "So I was like, 'Oh, yeah, that's me, kid.'"

"Oh," was all she could say as relief seeped from her ears. Her chest heaved slowly as she let herself breathe again. "I was actually only joking when I told him that we were going out. But I didn't think he was gonna go back and tell you."

"Oh, so you on that busted tip?" Craig rocked his leg back and forth so it knocked against Mina's knee lightly.

"Big time," Mina admitted.

They laughed.

"Good thing you got a little sexy thing going on." Craig tugged at Mina's tee shirt. "Well, maybe not tonight."

She pushed his hand away, embarrassed and tickled all at once. "That's not even right. I didn't know JZ was bringing you over."

"Oh, so you would have come out looking all fly Friday night if you had known?"

"Mos' def. I have a rep to uphold," Mina joked.

"It's cool." He leaned in so they were only inches apart, and Mina's goose bumps came back times ten. "Ever since I saw you at Jason's party in that bikini, your sexy status was sealed. I love me some cheerleaders with thick legs."

Woo-hoo, thank God for my gymnast's thighs, Mina thought.

"So, Craig," Mina's mother's voice called from the other side of the room.

Craig and Mina both jumped. Mina hurt a muscle in her neck looking up.

She swallowed hard to get her heart back in her rib cage and out of her throat.

Her mom strolled over and took a seat on the opposite side of the sectional sofa. "I recall a quickie intro at Mina's party, and Jason reintroduced you when you guys came in. But I feel like there's a more formal intro in order." She raised an eyebrow at Mina, message clear.

"Yes, ma'am," Craig said politely. He glanced over at Mina.

Mina cleared her throat. "Mom, this is Craig Simpson. He's a junior at DRB High and a varsity football player. Craig, this is my mom . . ." She hesitated, feeling silly calling her mom Mrs. Mooney to Craig. But her mom's soft smile didn't hide the seriousness in her eyes. "Go on," they said. "Mrs. Mooney," Mina finished.

Craig pushed off the couch and walked over to Mina's mom, hand extended. "Nice to meet you."

"I'm Mariah." Her eyes twinkled as she shook his hand. "You can call me Ms. Mariah, or Mrs. Mooney is fine."

Mina's heart skipped, ecstatic that Craig had passed the politeness component.

"So do I know your mom or dad?" Mina's mom nodded almost imperceptibly as Craig sat back down three feet farther from Mina than before.

Mina bit back a smile as she watched her mom watch Craig.

Ding, ding, he'd passed phase two—better known as the home-training gauge. Craig had enough home training to know he'd better back up off Mina in front of her mother. He was probably a three out of five on the home-training scale, meaning he knew how to act around adults. Good enough.

This was going as good as could be expected for a pop-in visit that Mina had no way of preparing for.

"My mom, um . . ." Craig cleared his throat. "Her name is Lynn. My dad's name is Richard."

Recognition dawned in Mariah's eyes as she went through her mental file. "Does your mom work for Krispy Kreme?"

Craig smiled, nodding vigorously.

"Okay. I have the Krispy Kreme account. Your mom is their franchise coordinator."

"Yup . . . I mean yes, ma'am, that's her." Craig and Mina exchanged a quick "oops" look.

"My mom has her own public relations firm," Mina explained. "I thought the Krispy Kreme account would mean free donuts but . . . " She shrugged.

Mariah and Craig laughed.

"I wouldn't dare think about having free donuts around. It would ruin your girlish figure," her mom teased. "That's why I keep all the free donuts at the office."

There was another round of laughter. Mina couldn't believe how well things were going. She prayed her dad wouldn't pick this time to come home from his company's Happy Hour. His Twenty Questions would be way less friendly, she was sure.

Mina's mom stood up. "Well, you see I had to introduce myself because Mina has this crazy theory that one or both of you will turn to dust if I ask any questions."

Mina popped her eyes and faked a smile. *Okay, Mom, move on,* she thought. She didn't want her mom going into joke territory. Embarrassing and stupid info bits always followed.

"Oh, Craig, did you know that Mina was potty trained by the age of two? I have pictures."

She hurried her mother along. "No. It's just until now it wasn't a big deal for you to know anything besides his name," Mina said behind a plastered grin.

Mariah put her hands on her hips. "Yes, but this is his second time visiting my home. My daughter has enough home training to know she should have come and introduced me, officially."

Mina decided to shut up. She felt an embarrassing exchange on the tip of the iceberg.

"Anyway, Craig . . ." Her mom made a "Mina's a lost cause" look before focusing back on Craig. "I'm glad to meet you, finally. Mina's talked a lot about—"

"Ma," Mina warned. She frowned, shaking her head in a firm don't-go-there motion.

"Okay, well, Mina's mentioned you once." Mariah laughed. "I'm glad you're okay with the fact that she can't go to that party with you next weekend. She swore it would be the end of the world." Mariah walked to the door leading back into the house. "But you guys can hang out here anytime."

And with that she was gone.

Mina was speechless.

No, her mom didn't just totally out the fact that she was so not allowed to go to the Frenzy.

No.

She.

Didn't!

Game Time!

"So I know that I'mma win/It's on once again."
—DJ Unk, "Walk It Out"

Mina bounced about, checking her watch every few seconds. She unwrapped her thick blue and gold spirit scarf and draped it around her shoulders. "Hurry up, Kelly," she yelled, out of patience. Her voice echoed off the high ceilings of the foyer. "You know how crowded the game is going to be, and I want a good seat!"

Kelly rushed down the stairs. "I'm coming, I'm coming!" She dashed into the kitchen and kissed her grandmother on the cheek. "Bye, Grand, I'll see you later on."

"Okay, have a good time, baby," her grandmother called out. "Adios, Amina."

"Adios, Mrs. Lopez. My mom will bring Kelly back home." Mina rewrapped the scarf quickly as she high-stepped toward the door. She pulled Kelly's arm. "Come on, girl. Don't keep Angel waiting."

Kelly shushed her as they closed the door.

"What? I thought you said your grandmoms was cool with it?" Mina asked as they hustled toward the car.

"She is. But still, I don't want her to know I'm seeing him to-night," Kelly said. It nagged at her that she was still being so secretive.

They hopped into the car, and Kelly greeted Lizzie, Michael and Mina's mom.

"How's your grandmom?" Mina's mom asked.

"She's fine," Kelly answered.

Mina's mom rolled her eyes and nodded toward her daughter. "I wanted to peek in and say hello, but Ms. Mina is rushing everyone to get to this game."

Mina cautioned them. "This is the most crowded game of the year. If we get there late, we'll be watching from outside."

"Did JZ ever find out if he's playing or what?" Lizzie asked. She was as nervous as JZ probably was about it. She wasn't sure what she wanted him to do about the cheating thing—thinking about it still made her stomach drop. But she wasn't angry anymore. She wanted him on the court tonight just as much as anyone else.

"I talked to him this morning and he still didn't know," Michael answered.

"This is the worst." Mina sucked her teeth. "I know Jay is going crazy right about now."

"Is Jason in danger of failing?" Mina's mom, alarmed, glanced at Mina, then at the others in her mirror.

They all shook their heads no, but let Mina explain the story—at least the whole story minus the cheating thing.

"I'm sure he did fine," Mina's mom assured them. "If he'd failed, I'm sure Mr. Collins would have notified his dad right away."

"I hope so." Mina's stomach felt light. She was hopped up over tonight as it was; not knowing if JZ was going to play made it worse.

When the car pulled up in front of the gym, game time was still forty minutes away. The parking lot swarmed with cars. A line snaked from the gymnasium door, out into the parking lot and to the road. Blue Devil blue and gold mingled with Trojan gold and burgundy as people decked out in their team colors streamed into the gym.

Mina hopped out of the car before it came to a full stop.

"Mina!" her mother fussed in exasperation.

"Sorry. Oh, we're going to walk home, okay?" Mina said, closing the door.

Her mom put the window down. "I thought you told Mae Bell that I was bringing Kelly back home." She scowled, a lecture at the tip of her tongue. "I don't want to go against what we told her."

Mina pleaded. "But we're going to the 'Ria afterward, Ma. We'll all walk her home, promise."

Mina's mother looked up hurriedly into her rearview mirror. Cars were piled up behind her, waiting on her to move. She eased the car forward as she lectured. "Mina, be home by eleven-thirty. Call me from Kelly's to let me know you all are on your way. Hear?"

"Yeah, okay, Ma. Bye," Mina said, already walking away from the car.

Once they pushed through the crowd Mina grabbed Lizzie's hand and dragged her toward the rally area, Michael tagging behind. The ten rows of bleachers in the middle of the home side of the gymnasium were already brimming with students in their bright blue and gold.

Mina spotted Kelis, a little spot of pecan amidst the many white faces of the DRB student-athlete body with a blue and white cheer pom sticking out of her ponytail, and led everyone to the row right above her cocaptain's seat. They busied themselves shedding their heavy bundles.

"Hey, girl," Mina said to Kelis.

"Hey, Mina!" Kelis said. "Girl, I wish we had as many people at our JV game."

"Oh, I know. But that's alright. This will be us next year." Mina high-fived Kelis.

The din in the gym grew louder, the air stuffier as more students squeezed onto the bleachers.

Mina spotted Angel in the doorway scoping out the huge crowded room. She nudged Kelly and pointed her head toward the door. "There you go."

Kelly held her breath as she checked Angel out for the first time since they met. She suddenly found herself unprepared to see him face-to-face, even though it was an awfully cute face.

His skin, a honey-roasted almond when she'd met him late summer, was now a little paler, his face clean except for a well-maintained patch of hair on his top lip. His dark brown eyes squinted into slits as they roamed the gym for her.

His close cut was faded on the sides, but lush and curly on top. Casual in jeans, a down coat and Timberland boots, he was fine as ever. He looked every bit the typical high schooler coming to root his team on until a hulking figure appeared at his side, scanning the gym. He was older, probably in his twenties.

His tall, but bulky frame was made bulkier by the thick goose-down coat he wore. His unsmiling face scrutinized the crowd. The frown lines in his forehead tripled when he took inventory of the Del Rio Bay fan side. He whispered something in Angel's ear, nodded toward the crowd, then stepped back. Kelly watched, recognizing the beefy dude as one of Angel's enforcer's from their first meeting.

Last time, there were two. Guess it was less obvious to walk around with one mean-looking dude than two.

"Wave to him, Kell," Mina commanded, watching Angel's fruitless search for them. She stood up and waved her arms. "Angel! Ang-gellll!"

Michael shook his head in amusement. "Now, you know he can't hear you in all this noise."

"Angel! Angel, it's Mina and Kelly!" Mina said louder, waving both arms high above her head. She waved him in as if she were working air traffic control when he suddenly squinted in her direction and nodded. "Kelly, stop being silly and stand up so he can see you. I know it's not me he's dying to see."

Kelly slowly stood up and waved shyly. Angel broke out in a grin as he strolled over, alone. The incredible hulk had somehow completely disappeared into the swelling crowd without Kelly noticing.

Jacinta's face broke through the crowd, and Mina did another round of hand waving. It was unnecessary because Jacinta automatically looked to the rowdies section and headed over.

Mina pumped her arms to an imaginary groove in her head. "Aw shoot, we rolling mob deep tonight."

Angel squeezed onto the crowded bleachers beside them.

"Hey, Angel," Mina sang out.

He nodded in Mina's direction. "How you doing?" He smiled warmly at Kelly and squeezed her knee. "What's up, Mami?"

"Nothing," Kelly said shyly. She leaned over and spoke directly into Angel's ear. "I didn't think you would find us in this huge crowd."

"I almost didn't. But then I saw Mina jumping up and down and it caught my eye," Angel explained.

Jacinta squeezed by everyone else to sit between Mina and Michael.

"Hey, Cinny," Lizzie greeted.

"Hey, Liz. Dag, it is packed up in this joint." Jacinta eyed the swollen bleachers on both sides of the gym. She knew this was a big game, but this was insane.

Angel snorted. "And y'all got me sitting over here with all these Del Rio Bay gray boys!"

"Oh, you just gon' have to deal with that tonight, boy—" Mina teased.

"Since everybody's manners are on vacation . . ." Michael interrupted, giving his girl friends an exasperated look. He reached his hand out to Angel for a pound. "Hey, man, I'm Michael."

"Oh, I'm sorry. Michael, this is Angel," Kelly said. "And that's Lizzie down there."

Lizzie peeked around Kelly and waved.

Angel nodded toward Lizzie. He turned to Kelly. "Y'all roll deep, huh?"

Dipping in their conversation, Mina answered for her, "Oh, trust." She sang out, "Who you wit'?"

Michael and Lizzie sang back. "Rolling wit' that clique, that Del Rio Bay clique 'cause you know we roll thick."

Kelly sat quietly, smiling as the clique stood up, dancing in place and slapping hands.

"How come you didn't answer back?" Mina nudged Jacinta.

Jacinta waved it off. "You know I gotta be for my Boo tonight."

Angel leaned up to be heard. "You got that right."

Mina gave Jacinta a "whatever" look, then started chanting. "Del Rio, Del Rio, Del Rio." Most of the rally area joined in.

"Umph, I gotta sit through this all night?" Angel muttered. He gently bumped shoulders with Kelly. "You lucky I like you, girl."

Blue Devils, Wha? Wha?

*"(And we are . . .) the coolest motherfunkers
on the planet."*
—Outkast, "So Fresh So Clean"

The crowd cheered wildly as the whistle blew, signaling the start of the game.

The announcer blandly read through the Sam–Well starting five.

The Del Rio Bay players were still nowhere to be seen, making the most of their home debut by staying well hidden in the area near the gymnastics room. The tactic worked; the crowd drowned out most of the Trojan lineup with their hoots and screams.

Mina gripped Lizzie's knee. "Oh, I hope Jay starts." She closed her eyes. "I can't look . . ." She put her hands over her ears. "I can't listen!"

Lizzie laughed, tugging at Mina's hands, trying to force her to listen, even though she could barely stand the suspense. They joined the rest of the crowd and stood, waiting for the team to be announced.

"What if he didn't pass?" Mina fretted. Her heart sank for JZ.

Michael *ssh*ed her, then added quickly, "If he'd been pulled, he'd probably be in the stands by now."

Jacinta shook her head, talking over the frenzied noise. "Maybe he went home instead of being embarrassed."

Mina groaned.

The announcer paused as a club mix blared from the speakers

and the lights went down. A white strobe bathed the dark room in speckles of dancing lights as each Del Rio Bay player was called to the center of the floor.

DRB High knew how to do it up right.

Mina and Lizzie gripped each other's hands as the music went to a low buzz and the announcer moved on to the starting five. There was a thunderous roar when Brian's name was called.

Mina was too nervous to cheer.

She felt Lizzie's hand tighten in hers and instinctively closed her eyes. There were two more players left, hidden in the shadows.

She said a silent prayer that one of them was JZ as the announcer's voice filled the gym. "And your starting shooting guard, freshman phenom, Jayyyyyyyyyyson Zimmmmmms!"

The entire clique screamed, a high-pitched collective of excitement, along with the other Rally Rowdies.

"Do your thing, dog," Michael hollered.

"Go Jay!!!!" Mina screamed.

"Thought you couldn't listen?" Lizzie teased, finally breathing again.

"I cheated." Mina laughed into her ear.

A thunderous chant of "Let's go Devils" broke out. Stomping feet filled Mina's chest with bass, and she joined in banging her feet on the wooden bleachers.

Mina reached over Lizzie and tugged Kelly's sleeve. "See, that's why I was rushing." She pointed to the last minute spectators, unable to find a seat, who spilled out of the doors and onto the edge of the court. The ref blew the whistle, warned them to step back off the court, then informed the coaches that a technical foul would be called if the fans interfered with the game.

A chorus of light booing rang out as administrators made the rounds, clearing people from the sidelines.

Five minutes into the action, the game was stopped to clear fans away from the doors. Security, off-duty policemen, manned the sidelines, ensuring only the cheerleaders remained courtside.

Once the game got rolling again, Mina yelled in Jacinta's ear, "Girl, Raheem is hot tonight."

Jacinta grinned, openly proud.

He scored nearly every time the ball was in his possession. His golden touch had quickly earned the Trojans a narrow lead. But Brian and JZ worked the floor to keep the Blue Devils in the game. Brian's aggressive style and accurate shooting coupled with JZ's finesse and fast feet forced the Trojans to double team, just to stay ahead.

With only minutes left in the second quarter, JZ pushed the ball down the court, stopped short and shot a three-pointer to put the Blue Devils back in the lead.

The crowd lost it, bringing the decibel level to an all-time (and painful) high.

"That's my boy!" Mina shouted. She chanted, "Go Jay! Go Jay! Go Jay!"

Lizzie and Michael joined her.

Jacinta rivaled Mina with her own chant. "Go Heem! Go Heem! Go Heem!" She called over to Angel. "Come on, help me out, Angel."

He shook his head, refusing. "Man, Raheem got this. I ain't worried."

Thirty exhaustive minutes later, with the score tied at halftime, people emptied the crowded, stuffy gymnasium and filtered into the hallways or trickled outdoors.

Kelly's mouth went dry when Angel grabbed her hand and said, "Come on, shorty. Let's go out for a few minutes."

She looked frantically at Mina, Jacinta and Lizzie, hoping someone would volunteer to go along or at least give her an excuse to stay in the gym. The deal was she'd spend time with Angel as long as everyone else was around.

She didn't know how to stay put. Angel would think she was crazy if she said she couldn't go.

But the clique was debating a visit to the concession stand, paying Kelly no mind. Reluctantly, she willed her legs to stand up and walk out with Angel alone.

As soon as they neared the gym door, the incredible hulk appeared at Angel's side.

"We gon' head outside for a minute," Angel informed him. "Hang back."

The hulk nodded and disappeared as fast as he had arrived.

Kelly and Angel sat outside on the concrete benches in front of the school.

"I didn't think you'd even recognize me." Kelly's teeth chattered from the cold.

"I can't forget this face." He chucked her chin softly before taking her frozen hands into his and rubbing them warm. Angel cocked his head and gave Kelly a look. Despite the cold prickling her face, Kelly's cheeks grew hot. So far Angel had been all Mr. Tender, no trash talking.

"What?" she asked, wondering if he was about to say something smart.

"So what's up with us, Mami?" he asked simply.

"Us," she repeated.

"Yeah, us. Me and you? I mean, is there a me and you?" Angel continued to roll his hands over Kelly's, never looking away from her. His intensity threw her off, and with no one to hide behind or distract them, she was forced to stare right back at him.

The only thing keeping her from looking away was the question in his eyes. She sensed that Angel was just as unsure as she was, even though he was the one always putting the straightforward questions to her.

She was scared, happy and worried at the same time and totally unsure which vibe to go with . . . so she was just as surprised as Angel when she joked, "Are you sure you know how to handle a 'good girl'?"

"Well, all the girls I date are good 'til I get to 'em." Angel laughed. He squeezed her hand. "I'm just joking. I got you, Ma. I know you not used to swinging with a shot caller."

Since Angel mentioned his hustling first, Kelly swooped in. "So who is that guy with you tonight?"

"That's Rosie."

The thought of a person that imposing being called something as delicate as Rosie was ridiculous, and Kelly couldn't help giggling.

"He got my back," Angel continued.

Kelly looked at Angel's boyish face and let his words sink in. Had his back in case of what, a fight? A shooting? Stabbing? Thoughts of Angel needing someone to have his back didn't go with his soft, playful voice and questioning eyes. Kelly wondered what more she didn't know about him.

He rubbed her face with his thumb in smooth, gentle strokes, and Kelly found it hard to conjure an image of those hands doing harm to anyone. But then, that was what Rosie the incredible hulk was for, right?

Before she realized it, Angel moved in and kissed her. His lips soft but chilly on her frozen mouth began to warm up as they moved over hers.

Angel pulled back and smiled. "I been wanting to do that since day one."

Kelly's head buzzed. She was glad she was sitting down because her legs were wet noodles. Through her haze, she heard Angel ask, "You ready to go back in?"

Kelly nodded from far away, but she stayed glued to the seat until Angel, standing, reached out to help her up. When she finally stood up, Angel kissed her again, this time wrapping his arms around her as he did. Kelly let herself be kissed, again, forgetting about the cold, anyone who happened to be looking or what would happen next.

For once she was doing instead of thinking, and it felt nice—lip-locking nice.

When Angel pulled away, the shock of the cold air hit Kelly's face and brought her back to her senses. Giddy with pleasure, she glided back inside the gym.

Bring It!

"We do it deadly/This how we keep it poppin'."
—Danity Kane, "Showstopper"

Once again, the game was in high gear. The crowd's collective roar was so loud the ref's whistle was impossible to hear. A Del Rio Bay player mistook a high-pitch sound from the crowd as the whistle and stopped right in the middle of a play. The ref charged the team for a time-out. The action stopped again when a few rowdy students, unhappy with the bad call, threw rolls of toilet paper on the court.

The refs ejected the students from the game, causing the crowd to jeer.

There was still a tie score as the game neared the fourth quarter. Mina bit at her lip, her eyes swimming between the scoreboard and the action on the floor.

Angel yelled down to her. "Uh-oh, we ready beat that ass! We gon' bring it now!"

Mina challenged with false bravado. "Shoot, bring it!"

But it was anybody's game.

"Y'all boys hanging, though. I gotta give 'em their props," Angel said.

"If we lose, Raheem gon' be pissy." Jacinta pouted.

"We?" Michael questioned.

"Sam—Well, I mean," she said.

Mina reminded her in a dead serious tone. "You're a Blue Devil now, girl."

"Naw, not tonight. Look, Mi, we cool and all but . . ." Jacinta left the obvious unsaid. The only team she was on tonight was Team Raheem.

"We'll let you off this time," Mina cautioned, with an unspoken "don't let it happen again" at the end of her sentence.

"Kelly is still with us, though, right, Kell?" Lizzie inquired.

Angel answered for her. "No girl of mine gon' be rooting for them Del Rio gray boys."

Mina raised her eyebrows at Kelly. "Oh, it's like that now?"

"Come on, you guys, it's just a game," Kelly pleaded, leaving out the fact that since coming back inside she'd barely paid much attention to the game. Instead, she was focused on how close she and Angel sat, how their legs pressed together and how he kept touching her knee, hand and face. Even the loud screams of the crowd were drowned out by her heart swooshing in her ear. Angel made it hard to concentrate.

Just then, Raheem scored a three-pointer, and Jacinta squealed.

"That's my baby!" She clapped enthusiastically.

The bucket pushed Sam–Well into the lead by two points. They dominated for two full minutes and Del Rio went scoreless.

Mina threw her hands up in frustration. "What is wrong with them?"

"Let's go, Jay!" Lizzie screamed as JZ dribbled down the court.

Within minutes, JZ's fast feet and quick thinking narrowed it to a three-point game. Coach Ewing called a time-out. There were only seven seconds left in the game, and the Blue Devils needed a three-pointer. It was only the third game of the season, but when it came to playing the Sam–Well Trojans, every meeting was do or die.

The crowd's frenzy reached a crescendo. After the time-out, the noise was deafening.

Mina, Lizzie and Michael stood up, their eyes riveted to the court. They collectively wished for their friend to pull off the improbable, but not impossible, feat of sinking a three-pointer with mere seconds left on the clock.

Jacinta stood, too, bouncing in her spot as she hoped against the shot. She knew having a pleasant night with Raheem would be out of the question if Sam–Well lost the game.

The game clock started, and JZ brought the ball in for Del Rio. Brian was in three-point range, but was double-teamed. He finally outran the two guys defending him, clapped for the ball and smoothly caught JZ's pass.

There was an audible gasp from the crowd as Brian took the shot and missed by inches.

The Blue Devils had lost.

Sam–Well fans stormed the court. Only a few points separated them from the losing score, but it was enough and sweeter because they had spanked the Blue Devils in their own house.

Mina groaned and sat down hard.

Angel yelled over the ruckus. "On the real, y'all played a good game."

"It was anybody's game, y'all," Jacinta said sympathetically to her sad-faced friends. She felt bad for them. But for reasons of her own, she was glad Sam–Well pulled it off.

"We be gunning for y'all in the regionals," Michael said, holding out hope. On his way down the stands, he gave Angel another pound. "Nice to meet you, kid."

"I'm not rolling to the 'Ria with y'all. Angel gon' give me a ride home. I'll see you Monday," Jacinta informed her friends, as she, Mina and Lizzie filed out of the bleachers behind Michael, along with the crowd.

"Have fun," Mina said.

Angel turned to Kelly. "Why don't you hang with me, Cinny and Raheem tonight? I'll bring you back home."

"I . . . I'm not sure I can. I mean, my grandmother thinks I'm with Mina and—" Kelly rambled.

Angel pressed. "What time do you need to be back home?"

"Eleven," Kelly admitted. Eleven seemed so early. She prepared herself for Angel to laugh. Instead, he nodded.

"Alright, I'll have you back in time. That gives us almost two hours together," he reasoned, making the decision for her.

Hello Subtlety, Meet Mina.

"You've so sexy/Perfect for me."
—Twista ft. R. Kelly, "So Sexy"

Nothing eased a loss like a hot slice of pie. So Mina, Michael and Lizzie walked across the school's parking lot toward Rio's 'Ria, ready to drown their misery in a freshly baked pizza pie along with the rest of the Blue Devil fans.

"So you think Jay gonna be in a good or bad mood?" Mina asked, providing her own point, counterpoint. "We lost, but he played a really good game." She laughed, a crazy-sounding cackle. "Shoot, he better be happy. He almost didn't play at all."

"Still, I say bad," Lizzie guessed. JZ was hotly competitive. Once she and Mina had beat him and Michael in a game of basketball in his swimming pool, and JZ wouldn't let them leave until they played best two out of three, which of course, he and Michael won easily.

Michael shrugged. "You know JZ. He not gon' be happy, but he'll already be thinking about beating them in regionals."

Lizzie silently agreed.

They grew quiet as a ragtag hooptie, muffler rattling, with "Do it Trojans" soaped on the window pulled alongside them. None of them uttered a word, knowing it was best to keep walking. Fights had been known to break out at the annual Sam–Well/Blue Devils game. Tonight's matchup had been peaceful, and the clique wasn't about to break the peace treaty.

A few seconds later, the car window came down, and a Trojan lunatic flashed the finger as he hooted, "Whupping Blue Devil ass since 1970. Ya heard?!"

"Bama," Michael muttered, picking up his pace.

"I know, right." Mina scowled. "Scrubs."

The car's engine revved, and the car peeled off, marking the last of the celebrating Trojans as they sped back to their side of Del Rio Bay, ensuring there would be no stray Sam–Well fans at Rio's 'Ria. The 'Ria was in Blue Devil's territory. No self-respecting Trojan would be caught dead hanging out there on a game night, even if it were the last pizza joint on earth.

A small comfort to the Blue Devils fans, many who would likely give up their rights to the 'Ria along with their right arm if it meant beating the Trojans. But for tonight, the 'Ria was their safe haven from the Trojans' gloating.

The clique waited for the light to change before crossing Main Street with two dozen other muted Blue Devil's fans. But the somber mood evaporated as they stepped through the doors of the 'Ria and into raucous Friday night banter, blaring music and people flowing between tables and the two pinball machines.

Absent from the laughter and conversation was any mention of the loss. Only hope for "next time" saturated the Blue Devils' lair. The Blue Devils had nineteen more games to prove they were the bomb.

Spotting Todd in a corner, Mina hotfooted it across the room, Michael and Lizzie on her heels. Petite and speedy, Mina squeezed behind chairs and swerved around huddled masses like a character in a video game maze.

Todd was already smothering Mina in his long arms, lifting her feet off the floor in a bear hug, when Michael and Lizzie caught up.

Michael and Todd slapped hands and touched elbows—the middle school basketball team's greeting. "What's up, kid?"

"Nothing, man." Todd gestured to the empty table for five. "I saved us a table."

"Brave man," Lizzie said, alluding to the 'Ria's well-known and strict no-saving-seats policy. She wondered aloud how Todd had managed it. "How many people did you have to fight off?"

Todd squinted, pretending to count. "About a dozen. But anything for my peeps." He bowed at the waist and pretended to kiss Lizzie's hand.

Lizzie blushed and Mina nudged her.

Mina latched on to Todd's arm. "So, T, you ready to jump back into the D game?"

She batted her eyes at him playfully.

Todd frowned. "D game?" He turned to Michael. "What's that? Defense? Help a brah out, Mike."

Michael shed his coat and shrugged as he sat down. "You on your own, playah. I don't know what that dude up to."

Mina laughed. "Why I gotta be up to something?"

Michael raised his eyebrow. "'Cause you probably are. Todd, man, I'd watch my back."

Todd craned his neck and turned in circles like a dog chasing his tail.

He sat down in the chair with a thump, pretending to be worn out. "Whew! Alright, I'm in trouble 'cause I can't watch my own back."

"I'm talking about dating," Mina said. "Are you ready to begin accepting GF applications?"

Lizzie smacked at Mina and shook her head no. She didn't want Mina to bring this up right now. Not when Todd could openly reject her. Gah! That would be horribly embarrassing, even if it was only in front of Michael.

Mina waved her off as if to say, "I got this."

Lizzie slunk over to a seat at the far end of the table, wishing she could crawl underneath it.

Her face was warm, from embarrassment and the blazing heat of the 'Ria brought on by too many bodies and baking pizza ovens. She peeled her coat off and prayed for the ceiling to cave, a tornado, anything to stop Mina before she made a total fool of them both.

She'd known Todd for as long as Mina had, and the thought of hanging out with him one-on-one gave her little flutters in her stomach. Having her first date be with a guy who was already a friend was a definite perk. But still, when Mina said she'd take care of this, Lizzie foolishly thought she meant something more low key like IM'ing Todd or talking to him without Lizzie there.

Hello, subtlety, meet Mina; Mina, meet subtlety, she thought, trying to sink into the background.

JZ came up beside Mina. "What up, y'all?"

"Jay," Lizzie practically screamed, hopping out of her seat. She hurled herself toward JZ and hugged him. "Good game tonight."

JZ hugged her back, his face confused. "Thanks. You do know we lost, right?"

Lizzie nodded, but kept her grip around JZ's waist. "Still, you were in the zone. And that means you passed, right?"

"Yup. That punk Mr. Collins didn't let us know until two hours before the game," he said.

Michael whistled. "Talk about cutting it close."

"Shoot, who you telling?" JZ seemed to flinch at the memory. "But yeah, he called my father and made up some bogus mess about having an engagement and not grading the tests 'til this morning. Anyway, I got an eighty-nine."

"I was a nervous wreck thinking you had failed," Mina said.

"Eighty-nine. Oh, my God, Jay, that's great." Lizzie squeezed him in a warm embrace.

Michael reached across the table and gave JZ a pound. "That's cool, kid. Good game, too."

Todd pounded JZ on the back. "Dude, that three-pointer you made at the buzzer was sick."

JZ nodded, uncomfortable with compliments after a loss. The coach hadn't exactly torn them all new holes, but he'd come close. No matter how good a game they played, they'd still lost and there were sprint drills and shooting marathons in the team's near future.

JZ agreed with the pending punishment. A loss by three points meant only two things—they hadn't been fast enough on rebounds and had missed one too many easy shots. Nothing Coach could do would be as bad as what JZ would put on himself. He'd be up early tomorrow, running and gunning on his own. The important thing was his slot was safe. He would live to play another day with the Blue Devils.

He looked down at Lizzie locked to his side. He had no idea what had brought this on, but he wasn't mad. The whole cheating thing seemed years ago. He was glad to get some Lizzie love. It meant things were really cool between them. "Ay, Liz?" he said.

She looked up at him. "Yeah?"

"Can I ummm . . . sit down or do you plan on holding on all night?" He teased with a straight face.

"Sorry." Lizzie let go reluctantly and sat back down.

JZ took the seat next to her.

Refusing to give Mina another opening to talk, Lizzie rushed into conversation. "Sprint drills tomorrow?"

JZ snorted. "You know it."

"You were on fire, though. You and Brian tore it up," Mina said. She took Todd by the hand. "We'll be back."

Eyes following Mina and Todd as they made their way to the front of the restaurant, Lizzie held her breath and pretended to listen as JZ and Michael began talking basketball. Full court presses, zone defense and other sporting terms went over her head as she watched Mina lead Todd to a quiet spot.

There was no such thing as a quiet corner in the 'Ria, really. There was a body in every crevice and corner of the pizza place, and between the music and loud talking, you were lucky to hear the person just a nose length away. Mina pulled Todd into the tiny foyer at the 'Ria's entrance and made the best of it.

"What's up, Mina?" He imitated Captain Kirk, gesturing and breaking off his words. "I get . . . the-feel-ing . . . you're trying to . . . tell me something."

Mina smiled. "Such a cutie." She squeezed his hand excitedly. "That's exactly why I think you guys will make a good couple."

Todd scanned the room. "Me and who?" He pointed across the room. "Is it Beth? I love big boobs."

Mina smacked him. "Eww no and that's TMI."

Todd laughed. "Okay, who?"

To avoid the crush of people still pouring in, Mina pushed herself out of the way until her back was against the wall. Todd stood inches from her, looking down, waiting.

"Okay, I need for you to keep an open mind about this," Mina warned.

Todd groaned. "Okay, she's fugly, right?" He narrowed his eyes. But even mean came off silly on Todd. "Is this a pity date?"

Mina sucked her teeth. "No and no. I'm just saying it's someone you may have never, you know, saw as GF material."

"I'm officially curious." He put his hand on Mina's shoulder and pretended to get serious. "Is it you, Mina? Are you in love with the Toddster?"

Mina laughed loudly. Todd may as well have just told his funniest joke ever.

"Dang." He made hurt puppy dog eyes. "Okay, laughing out loud in a guy's face is not good for our manly egos."

She giggled. "Sorry. But no, it's not me. It's Lizzie."

Todd instinctively looked back toward their table.

Caught eavesdropping, if you could call it that from twenty yards and no chance of hearing a word anyone was saying, Lizzie almost broke her neck trying to look in the other direction.

"Lizzie, huh? She's digging me?" Todd popped his collar.

Mina rolled her eyes but couldn't help laughing. "Alright, T, this isn't elementary school. I'm not gonna pass you a note asking you to check yes or no, will you go out with her."

"Well, how come she's never stepped to me?" Todd asked, taking another sly peek at Lizzie, who was doing a very bad job pretending not to look.

He waved to her, and she turned bright red and turned her head away.

Todd laughed. "Oh, yeah, she's digging me."

Mina tugged at his shirt, forcing him to focus on her. "Todd, look, it's not like Lizzie has been nursing some secret crush on you . . ."

"Ouch." Todd winced. "You really know how to build a guy up, Mina."

"I just meant that you're single and so is Lizzie, and I think you guys should try hanging out a bit more together . . . see if there's an exclusive hookup in your future."

"So . . . wait?" Todd frowned. "She's not digging me?"

Mina explained as if talking to a two-year-old, "Yes, she likes you, Todd. But she's an old-fashioned type of girl . . . she wants *you* to ask *her* out."

Mina watched as Todd eyed Lizzie, considering this. "Isn't she looking all fly now that she's wearing her hair out?" she said.

Todd's eyes grew wide. He snapped his fingers, then nodded. "That's it. I knew there was something different about her. She is looking hot."

Mina nodded, proud as a parent. "So, you down or what?"

Todd squinted suspiciously. "This isn't a pity date, right?"

"I already told you no." Mina rolled her eyes, Todd's silliness wearing on her just a tid.

"No. I mean are you taking pity on me since Jen kicked me to the curb?"

Mina crossed her heart. "Nope. Lizzie really would like you to ask her out. So will you?"

Todd nodded. "Alright. But I've gotta do it my way, Mi." He flipped the collar on his polo. "Let a playah do his job."

He sauntered back into the restaurant, limping in what he thought looked like a pimp daddy swagger.

Mina giggled, following. "Whatever you say, T."

She gasped when someone pulled her back by her arm.

"What . . ." She smiled when she saw it was Craig. "Oh, hey."

"Hey, where you sitting?" he asked.

Mina pointed to JZ, and Craig followed her to the table.

Everyone at the table greeted him enthusiastically.

"We need another chair," Lizzie pointed out to no one in particular. She was too embarrassed to make eye contact with Todd.

Craig turned to two girls sitting at a table behind them. His smile was genuine and warm when he said, "Ay, shorty, can we use this?"

Mina could tell the Alpha girl, the only one bold enough to look up at Craig, was about to say no until she saw who was asking for the chair. That longing, eager-to-please look on her face said she'd let Craig take her chair if he wanted. She nodded slowly, smiling as Craig pulled the chair from their table to his own.

Dang, pity the person whose seat that was, Mina thought wryly. But Craig's hot factor had that effect on girls. Heck, it had that effect on her. Feeling like the world's luckiest girl, she leaned in so she and Craig were shoulder to shoulder, enjoying the simple ease of being so near him.

His usual Bounty freshness smell competed with the scent of the 'Ria's baking dough. Mina would never be able to smell laundry and pizza together again without thinking of this very moment. She grinned as Craig whispered, "So you leaving a brother hanging next Saturday, huh?"

She lowered her voice so they wouldn't interrupt the rest of the table and their conversation about the night's highlights.

"Okay, here's the thing," Mina said, turning so her lips were almost touching Craig's ear. "Truth is, my parents squashed the Frenzy. So I was going to stay with my girl Kelly and head over there anyway."

Craig chuckled. "Aw see, I thought you were a good girl." He leaned back, giving her a once-over with his eyes. "Look at you going all rebel on me."

Mina giggled shyly. She was a good girl, but Craig made her feel like doing bad things. She kept that to herself.

"Seriously, though, you gon' sneak out?" Craig asked.

"I'm not *sneaking* out." Mina didn't even cringe at the half-truth that was slowly building into a lie. "We'll be staying over at Kelly's. Her house is huge." She laughed. "Trust me. We could be *there* and her grandmother wouldn't know it."

"Right, I hear that," Craig said. He leaned in, putting his lips near Mina's ear. Mina waited for him to say something, but instead he kissed her ear lightly, sending shivers down her back.

Oh my God, Oh my God, Oh my God.

She sank deeper into her lean and sighed contentedly when Craig put his arm around her . . . chair.

So she was corny. But the girl behind her would probably pay for every round of pizza ordered tonight to be in Mina's spot. She let herself enjoy it.

"So, Lizzie," Todd announced loudly from the opposite end of the table. "Rumor has it that you've been having dreams about getting next to all this." He gestured grandly to his tall frame.

Everybody at the table burst into laughter except Lizzie, who turned a pasty white as all the color in her face fled.

"Real smooth, T." Mina laughed.

"Playah, your game is tight." JZ laughed, jumping up to give Todd a pound.

"Right, right," Todd said. He wriggled his eyebrows at Lizzie. "So whaddya say, Liz? Wanna kick it with six feet worth of vanilla chocolate?"

"Can I die now or later?" Lizzie groaned. She didn't know whether to laugh or cringe.

Todd got up and walked over to Lizzie's seat. He got down on one knee. "Come on, Liz." He made sleepy eyes and stroked her hand playfully. "Go with me to the casbah."

"And where is that?" Lizzie played along, even though it felt as if she were on stage with the entire 'Ria as the audience. But minus a few people near them staring at Todd on his knee, no one spared a second glance.

Todd shrugged. "I don't know. But if you go with me, we'll probably find it faster." He grinned. "And if we don't find it, wanna go to a movie instead?"

Lizzie giggled as she nodded. "Sounds cool."

He kissed her hand with a loud smacking sound before standing up. He bowed.

"Thank you, milady."

"Aw man, dog, you were serious?" JZ asked.

Todd nodded. "A little birdie told me that Liz would be down with hanging out with me."

Michael snorted. "A little birdie named Mina, I bet."

Mina couldn't help smiling.

Craig squeezed her shoulder. "Cupid, huh?"

Mina nodded. "Just trying to hook up two really sweet people." She brushed her nails on her chest and blew at them. "I do good work."

"Man, I told you chicks wack," JZ warned. "Look at how Jen did your ass."

"Jay, stop blocking." Mina scowled him down.

"Gee, Jay, thanks," Lizzie said.

"Aw naw, I didn't mean you, Liz," JZ apologized, then waved Mina off. "I'm not blocking. I just don't want my boy jumping back before he's ready." He teased. "You know he's sensitive."

Todd fluttered his eyelashes. "Liz, please be gentle with me."

Lizzie laughed. "I promise."

"Seriously, what just happened here?" JZ frowned.

Mina balled up a napkin and threw it across the table at JZ. "We'll send you the cliff notes on Monday."

She laughed, but it caught in her throat when she saw Kelis and Brian out of the corner of her eye. They stood close (too close) together by the jukebox that no one ever used—music was piped in overhead and always played the latest grooves—and Kelis was smiling into his face. *Looking like a puppy waiting for a pat on the head,* Mina thought jealously.

Brian nodded every few seconds at whatever Kelis was saying. Suddenly he bent to whisper something in her ear before walking away. Mina forced her eyes away from Kelis's grinning face and turned her attention back to the table.

Ready or Not . . .

"Let me take you home."
—Terror Squad, "Take Me Home"

Angel pulled his car into the parking lot of Sam–Well High School just as Raheem emerged from the building.

Raheem jogged up to the car and slid into the backseat where Jacinta waited anxiously. "What up? What up?" he shouted, his good mood infectious. "Hey, Kelly. How you doing?"

Barely audible, she spoke. "Fine."

"Good game, Boo," Jacinta gushed.

"Y'all whipped that ass, kid," Angel said. He put his fist up over his head, toward the backseat, for a pound.

Raheem returned the gesture, touching his fist to Angel's.

"We handled our business," Raheem agreed, then added in a humble gesture, "but JZ and that dude, number 16 . . . Brian, got mad skills. If he had made that last shot—" He shook his head away from the thought of being on the other end of such a close loss.

"Won't we have to play you guys again?" Kelly asked.

Angel peered at Kelly, surprised she had spoken after being so quiet the entire ride. Jacinta had done most of the talking since they'd gotten in the car.

"Yeah, probably during regionals," Raheem crowed. "But ain't no way you gon' beat us. We on a roll."

The win had him feeling good. He sat back and put his arm around Jacinta. "So, where we heading, son?"

"Just back to the 'hood," Angel answered. "We can max at my crib for a while. I gotta get baby girl back home before eleven."

Kelly swallowed hard at the mention of Angel's apartment. She realized how little she knew about him. She had no idea what they would do at Angel's but doubted that it would be playing board games. *Just don't leave me, Cinny*, she prayed to herself.

When the car pulled up to the apartment, Angel's place seemed alive with activity. All of the lights were on, and music poured out of the apartment from every corner of the living room. Kelly half expected to see a room full of people instead of an empty apartment. She was astounded at the level of music until she noticed a speaker on a high shelf near the front of the room and another in the rear. The living room was only about ten feet across, so the speakers easily surrounded the area with sound.

She took short, hesitant steps into the living room and stood in the middle of the floor, unsure what to do or where to go.

Angel walked into the kitchen. "Make yourself comfortable. Y'all want something to drink?"

Kelly shook her head no.

"I'm good," Jacinta said.

"You want something, son?" Angel offered.

"Naw, I'm alright," Raheem answered, shedding his coat and throwing it in a chair.

"Heem, can you give me and Kelly a second?" Jacinta whispered to him, catching him before he could take a seat.

He nodded and walked into the kitchen.

Jacinta grabbed Kelly's arm and walked her over to the couch. "Are you okay?"

Kelly blurted. "Are you and Raheem staying here with me?"

Jacinta gave her a gentle smile, then shook her head no. "I can't promise that, Kell. I mean, me and Raheem don't get a lot of time together lately. You know?"

Kelly jumped up and paced in a small circle. The loud music compounded her tension as her head throbbed in tune with the booming bass.

"I shouldn't have come," she said, sitting down again.

"But you did," Jacinta said, not unkindly.

Kelly sighed. "What do I do?"

"I can't answer that, Kelly."

"What if he wants to . . ." Kelly shuddered, unable to finish.

"If he wants to what?" Jacinta asked.

Kelly's whisper was a dull scream. "Have sex!"

Jacinta laughed. "All that talking y'all been doing and you haven't talked about where the relationship is going?"

"Yeah, we have . . . sort of. But, I didn't expect to be at his apartment tonight," Kelly admitted, embarrassed. "I was going with the whole group-dating thing."

"Alright, look . . . I'll try and convince Raheem to stay here and chill with y'all. But I can't promise we will," Jacinta said, amazed at how highstrung Kelly was.

Kelly's nervousness was like a living thing. Her muscles were taut with tension, yet her hands trembled and fluttered. Jacinta could feel her friend's anxiety simply by being next to her. She placed her hand on Kelly's tense shoulder. "You'll be okay. Don't do anything you don't want. And Angel is cool—he not gon' force you to do nothing."

The words must have been a magic bullet because Kelly relaxed immediately. She prayed Angel was as easygoing as Jacinta thought. She took a deep breath and exhaled fully to dispense some of her jitters.

Either they had been listening or had a sixth sense that the girls' conversation was over, because Angel and Raheem came back into the living room seconds later. Angel walked over to Kelly, took her hand and guided her off the couch. Raheem slipped into her spot. Kelly threw a nervous glance backward at Jacinta.

"We be back," Angel said over his shoulder.

"She's scared, Heem," Jacinta said, watching as Kelly's legs disappeared up the stairs, thinking, *She on her own now.*

Raheem sucked his teeth. "She alright. He just went upstairs for some privacy. It's too cold to sit outside tonight."

"Still, Angel is used to girls practically stripping their panties off for him. Kelly probably has a lock and key on hers."

Raheem laughed, and Jacinta joined in for a second, then turned serious again. "For real, though, I hope she'll be okay."

Raheem caressed Jacinta's chin and guided her face closer to his. "She a big girl, Jacinta," he said, before closing his lips over hers.

Jacinta let Raheem's nearness distract her. The thought of Kelly's plight was far away as she snuggled in his arms.

A single blue lightbulb bathed Angel's room in serenity. The light cast strange shadows over the walls covered in posters of scantily clad models, singers and female pop groups. As Kelly's eyes adjusted to the strange lighting, she noticed stacks of shoe boxes dominating one wall of the small room.

"Are those boxes full?" she asked, counting them under her breath.

"Yeah. Gots to keep a fresh pair of kicks," Angel bragged.

Kelly took in the name-brand boxes as she perched on the edge of Angel's bed. "You must have a few thousand dollars' worth of shoes over there."

Angel shrugged and joined Kelly on the bed. "Probably. But I didn't bring you up here to talk about my good taste in shoes."

Kelly looked him in the eye. "What did you bring me up here for?"

He put his palms out in front of him and turned them over. "No

tricks up my sleeve, Ma. I just wanted some time with you alone . . .
away from your clique."

Feeling as if it were her only chance to speak before things took
a turn, Kelly blurted, "I like you, Angel, but I don't know you. Do
you live here alone or with someone else? Do you plan to be a hustler your entire life?"

She took a deep breath, surprised at her last question, but glad
she'd said it. Her stomach stopped churning, and she relaxed now
that she'd said what she had been thinking during the ride to his
place.

She waited, expecting the trash talker to make an appearance.
But Angel was smiling. His voice was patient.

"I live here with my uncle. And no, I don't plan on being in the
game my entire life. How's that for the 4-1-1?"

"Where's your uncle now?" she asked, warming up to the in-
quiry.

Angel's answer was curt. "Minding his business while I handle
mine."

Kelly persisted. "Does he deal drugs, too?"

Angel rolled his eyes, growing bored with the interview. But he
kept his tone even. "Kelly, let me be straight with you . . ." He stood
up and looked her in the eye. "Just like you don't know me, I don't
know you. So I'm not gon' sit here and put my business out there. It
ain't no secret that I hustle, but right now that's all you need to
know."

Having said his piece, he took his place on the bed, pulled Kelly
onto his lap and wrapped his arms around her waist. "Anything else
you want to know about me, I'll tell. But as far as me telling you
how I handle mine in the game . . . that's like you breaking me off
some. It ain't gon' happen. At least not tonight. Know what I mean?"

Kelly giggled. "Well, at least you know you're not getting any
play."

Angel tickled her side. "I'm not getting any tonight, key word being *tonight*." He hugged her tighter. "It's not about that, though, shorty. You make a brother want to do corny stuff like hang out at the pizza parlor and go out for ice-cream cones."

"Now, why is that corny?" Kelly asked, craning her neck to look back at him.

Angel nuzzled his face in her side. His voice was muffled as he answered. "Um-eh. It just is. But I'd do all those things with you if you asked me to."

Angel sounded like a little boy, his voice sweet and soft. She couldn't imagine him being mean or violent. At ease, her next question floated out of her mouth without a second thought. "Why do you like me, Angel?"

He answered without hesitation, his face still buried in her side. "I like how sweet you are. I like how innocent you act. When I saw you with Cinny, that first time, you looked out of place. Plus you got a little cute thing happening."

"If you knew I wasn't from around here, then how did you know I would give you my number?" she asked. "I could have been one of those snobby girls."

Angel grunted. "Shoot, it's the snobby girls who end up falling for ballers in the first place. All of y'all wanna know what it's like to be with a bad boy." In full trash talk mode, yet sounding as if he meant every word, he finished, "I wasn't worried about you turning me down."

Kelly teased, still looking back down at him. "Someone is mighty full of himself."

"Am I? Ain't you sitting here in my crib?" He lifted his head and looked up at her, eyebrow hitched. Kelly laughed, embarrassed, her joke backfiring. "I think I made my point," he said.

Angel was right. Kelly had been attracted to him from the very start—first because he was cute, then because she was curious about him. Bad boys were magnetic. *Even if your legs want to walk away, the rest of you can't,* she thought, explaining how she felt about him.

She sat on his lap, enjoying the way his voice vibrated in her back as he talked. They stayed that way for thirty minutes, talking the little details that made them interesting to each other in a city like Del Rio Bay that had only a five percent Latino population. Kelly learned that Angel was originally from the Bronx, but hadn't lived there since he was four, and that his parents were dead. He talked about his mother in the same wistful voice Kelly used when she spoke of her grandfather. It made her question even more how someone with Angel's obvious intelligence would turn to hustling drugs. But he'd made it clear he wasn't going to discuss it. So she carefully avoided asking the questions on the tip of her tongue like did he stand on a street corner and deal, did people come to the apartment, how did he get the drugs?

Her curiosity brimmed, but she held back.

"Alright, I better get you back," Angel said suddenly.

There was a pause, and Kelly asked quickly, "So are we . . . dating? I mean . . . you know, officially?"

"Is that what you want to do?" Angel snickered. "Date?"

He said the word as though it was the most amusing word he'd ever heard.

Kelly's face turned hot. She felt silly for asking the question, for assuming anything about Angel at all. She stood up, but Angel caught her around the waist and pulled her back down beside him.

There was a sheepish smile on his face as he said, "It's been a long time since I been a good boy."

Kelly laughed. "Were you ever?"

"Naw, not really," Angel said without even a hint of a smile. "But, I think I know how they supposed to act. So, I'm down for giving it a try." He leaned in and kissed her. "So, you my girl?"

Kelly nodded, then lifted her head for another kiss.

He kissed her firm and deep before forcing himself to stop. "Alright, one more like that and I can't be responsible for my mack coming down on you," Angel said, taking Kelly by the hand and leading her out of the room. He stopped in front of the bedroom next to his and knocked once. "Ay, Heem, I'm out, son. I gotta take shorty home."

A muffled voice answered. "Alright."

Kelly stared at the closed door, wondering if Cinny was behind it.

In answer, Jacinta called out, "Bye, Kelly. I'll see you later."

Kelly called out uncertainly, frowning, "Bye."

Angel read the shock on Kelly's face and snorted.

"What?" she asked, her eyes still drawn to the closed door.

"That's what I mean . . . about how innocent you are. You surprised Cinny and Raheem in there, ain't you?"

Kelly started to lie—she didn't want to *always* come off like a naïve child—but she couldn't. She was very surprised. She nodded.

Angel shook his head, chuckling. "Thought so."

"I never heard them come upstairs, that's all," Kelly retorted, trying to swallow some of her shock. "How did you know they were in there?"

Angel looked into Kelly's face to see if she was serious and saw that she was. *I guess Cinny don't tell her new friends everything, after all,* he thought. He played the whole thing with a simple, "'Cause that door was open when we first came upstairs."

"Oh," Kelly said. She looked back up the stairs at the closed bedroom door as they reached the landing and knew she wasn't ready for that.

Flirt-As-You-Go

"Well, baby, here it is/You better step to it."
—Mos Def, "Brown Sugar (Fine)"

Monday afternoon, Mina sat in the school's library daydreaming. It was her independent study period, and she usually tried to get homework done. She was putting the finishing touches on her article. It was due today. But her hand kept wandering from the keyboard to her notebook where she doodled Craig's name over and over. Craig Simpson in big letters. Craig Simpson in small letters. Craig Simpson in cursive. Craig Simpson in bubble letters.

When Mina had gone outside to wait for Kelly Saturday night, Craig had come with her. They stood outside snuggled together, talking about everything and nothing. Craig had a younger sister, two cats (funny, she saw him as a dog dude all day long) and was hoping to get a motorcycle for his seventeenth birthday. Every new nugget of information made Mina feel that much closer to him—not the Craig she'd imagined he was when she'd crushed from afar, but the real Craig whom only his closest friends knew.

Oh, my God, she was becoming a close friend: someone in his circle.

The whole thing had her head swimming, and then he'd gone and nearly exploded it by kissing her. It happened so naturally, so easily, that Mina didn't have time to do any of her fantasizing about what their first kiss would be like.

Just as she'd said, "I wonder where Kelly is? It's ten-forty," Craig nuzzled her neck, sliding his lips slowly from her shoulder blade to the bottom of her ear (and it hadn't even tickled), then slowly turned her around. Instinctively, Mina held her head up, and Craig moved in smoothly for a kiss.

Hands down, the best kiss ever. True, she'd only ever kissed Ty—and that wasn't bad at all—but Craig's kiss had her so dazed, it had taken a full three minutes to realize Angel's car was idling at the curb right next to them.

Mina now looked down at her scribbling. The paper was so saturated with pen, barely any paper was visible. As if noticing the scrawling for the first time, Mina dropped the pen as if it were on fire. She focused back onto the computer monitor and forced herself to write something other than Craig's name. Anytime she had to stop and think about her next sentence, to make sure her hands wouldn't betray her again, she raked her fingers through her hair.

After five solid minutes of reading the same paragraph, Mina gave up. The article was done; at this point she was only overthinking it. She needed to call it finished and be done. Groaning, she checked the clock on the wall in front of her to see how much longer she had. As her eyes swept upward, she caught sight of Brian sitting in a cubicle in the far right corner of the library. He had a light head nod going. Mina instinctively looked for the white wire that would confirm he was rocking to something on his iPod.

She saw a tiny piece of the wire dangling from beneath Brian's button-down shirt with the French cuffs and knew the little earpiece was well hidden in his ear farthest away from the aisle, where a passing teacher could snatch him up about it.

Debating whether to remain hidden, Mina summoned the nerve to approach him. She saved her document and popped the CD out of the drive. She would just say hello. So he liked Kelis, big deal. What did she care?

So how come her heart beat loud in her ears as she stood?

Exhaling, she reminded herself that she and Brian had a weird, kind of comfortable flirt-as-you-go type friendship. Nothing more, nothing less.

Brian gave them all a ride to school pretty much every morning. Mostly the guys talked sports or guy stuff and she and Jacinta kept to their own conversation. Occasionally they all joked together or Brian inevitably cracked on Mina, teasing, and she did her best to crack back—usually falling short of her mark, resulting in her giving him the talk-to-the hand sign.

Take that, Kelis, I spend more time with your man than you do, she thought wickedly.

Mina walked stiff-legged until she forced herself to walk normal. She relaxed her shoulders, plastered a smile on her face and in three long strides was next to Brian's chair. She tapped Brian's shoulder, giggling as he jumped, startled.

"What's up, Mina?" He clicked his iPod off.

"Hey," Mina said. "I haven't seen you in here before. Is this your free period?"

"Yeah. Last week I met with Coach to go over plays, though."

Mina's pulse began to slow down. See, normal conversation, no big deal, she coached herself.

"Sorry I'm late," a familiar voice said from behind.

Mina's throat closed, making her feel as if she were breathing through a pinhole. Her body stiffened as Brian grabbed his backpack from the floor and stood up.

"Hey, Kelis," Brian said.

Kelis expertly squeezed herself between Brian and Mina. She smiled the bright, arrogant smile of someone who was about to get a privileged look behind a secret curtain. "Hey, Mina," she chirped.

Mina's voice was barely above a whisper. "Hey, Kelis."

"Me and Kelis were going to chill together until next period. You want to hang?" Brian asked.

"N-no," Mina stuttered, then forced her voice to be louder, stronger. "No, that's okay. I just saw you sitting here and wanted to say what's up."

"Sure?"

Brian's smile was friendly, but Mina detected something behind it—a challenge? Whatever, she wasn't interested. "Positive," she snapped, not caring how harsh she sounded.

Kelis tugged at Brian's French cuff, then slid her hand into his. "Okay, Mina. See you at practice, girl," she said. "Come on, Bri."

"Later, Mina," Brian said, allowing himself to be led away.

"Bye," Mina said, then whispered in disgust, "Bri."

Hours later, two P.M. on the dot, Mina was in Ms. Dunkirk's classroom, sitting alongside Miles as the *Bugle* advisor read both of their articles.

Refusing to show any worry, next to Miles's calm demeanor, the only proof that Mina was out of her mind with fear was a little tremor in her leg. It jumped nervously, an impatient tick. She glanced at the clock. Practice was in fifteen minutes. If she got the *Pop Life* spot, being late would be worth it. If not . . . the thought of doing suicide cycles was about as appealing as eating a raw onion.

"How come you didn't do yearbook this year?" Miles asked, leaning casually into the aisle to talk to her.

"Truthfully, I was wondering the same thing about you," Mina said. She crossed her legs at the feet to keep them still.

Miles brushed a piece of brown hair out of his eyes. His hair was a messy mop, always long and unruly. "I was hoping if I got a spot on the *Bugle*, then next year I might nab a photog position with the paper."

Mina forced her eyebrows straight. They desperately wanted to scowl. If all Miles wanted to do was be a photographer, why not just go ahead and do that.

He answered the question before she could ask.

"All the slots were full this year. The paper and yearbook share photographers, and there were only five slots." He shrugged. "I wanted something to fill the time until I can do it next year."

"You know the *Pop Life* thing was my idea, right?" Mina asked, unable to stop herself from bragging.

Miles nodded. "Yeah. It's a good idea . . . perfect for you, too, Mina."

Mina suppressed an eye roll.

Her heart leapt when Ms. Dunkirk rattled the papers in front of her and walked their way.

"Good luck," Miles whispered.

"Same," Mina said.

She sat up straighter in the chair and gave herself a pep talk, except the only thing she could think to say was, *I better get this column.*

"You're both very good writers," Ms. Dunkirk said. Her face was etched with the type of pleasure only seen on a teacher's face when a student does well, a combination of pride and maybe a little wistfulness of their own talent as a teen. Ms. Dunkirk jiggled the papers in her hand lightly. "Miles, why do you want to be on the *Bugle* staff?"

Mina's heart raced. Who knew there was going to be a verbal quiz?

Miles batted absently at his hair as he answered. "I spent three years on the yearbook staff because I like telling stories." His shoulders hitched, making the bottom of his brown mop sway. "I don't care if it's with words or pictures, but it's cool seeing what pictures say about the school year."

Ms. Dunkirk nodded. Her face didn't betray whether she liked or disliked the answer.

"Mina?"

Mina's mind went blank. All her real answers to the question were definitely wrong. It was her idea. It was her idea. And umm . . . it was her idea. She took a deep inhale, but the kind where only your chest swells, so no one could see her anxiety. As she released it slowly through her nose, a better answer (and the truth) came out. "I'm obsessed with popularity . . . I mean, like what makes people popular."

She paused, and Ms. Dunkirk nodded for her to go on.

"It drives me crazy that some people are popular for no reason at all." Mina snickered. "Or popular because they say so and everyone goes along with it. I came up with *Pop Life* because I thought it would be cool to put a person's background on shine. And then maybe for people who are already popular, it explains why." Mina took a breath. "But some of the people I want to cover aren't what others would consider popular, but I think they have good stories that are interesting."

"Popularity is relative," Ms. Dunkirk said simply. She bounced the papers in her hand. "Do you think *Pop Life* is going to change how people feel about the people you cover?"

Mina frowned, thinking about it for a second. "I don't know." She shook her head. "But it might."

Ms. Dunkirk looked at the both of them. "Well, based on your writing ability, you're both even."

Mina's shoulders sagged. She kept her eyes on Ms. Dunkirk, whose face was thoughtful, as if maybe she still didn't know what name she was going to call.

"Miles, you originally applied for a photographer's slot, right?" she asked.

He nodded.

"I didn't expect your writing to be quite as sharp," the teacher admitted.

Mina's shoulders sagged more. *Just say it*, she screamed in her head.

"I'm going to give the column to Mina," Ms. Dunkirk announced suddenly.

A small breath of defeat came from Miles.

Mina's eyes popped. She knew she'd gotten the column by a slim margin over Miles. She could hear it in Ms. Dunkirk's voice, high-pitched wonder as though Ms. Dunkirk had no idea she would say Mina's name until she said it.

"Me?" Mina asked, stupidly, double checking in case Ms. Dunkirk had meant to say "iles" and not "ina."

Ms. Dunkirk had moved on with the business at hand. "Miles, I'd like to keep you as a reserve photog." The papers finally rested, no longer jiggling in her hand. "Next year the first open spot is yours. How about that?"

"Do you think I'll get any assignments as a reserve?" Miles asked eagerly. He didn't seem quite as disappointed upon hearing about the reserve position.

"I think so," Ms. Dunkirk said.

"Okay." Miles put his hand out to Mina. "Congratulations, Mina."

Mina shook his hand, grinning crazily.

"Thanks, Ms. D.," she said in a daze as her hand went up and down in Miles's gentle grip.

"I need for you to present a few people you want to cover." Ms. Dunkirk made her way back behind her desk and sat. "Give me a small graph of info on them so we can decide who we'll cover next."

Hearing Ms. Dunkirk giving out orders, all business, no time wasted, snapped Mina out of her giddy daze.

"Okay." She looked over at the clock. It was twenty after two. "Umm . . . I have to get to cheer practice."

Ms. Dunkirk waved her off. "We'll talk tomorrow."

"Thank you, Ms. D. You're gonna love *Pop Life*," Mina said. She grabbed her books and sailed out of the room.

Do It Right or Do It Again

Minutes later, Mina dumped anything unrelated to cheerleading out of her head. Schoolwork, Craig, Brian, the *Bugle*—gone. Poof.

All that existed was the lone nail hole in the wall on the opposite end of the mat. She stared a hole into the mark. *Keep your eye on that spot, keep it there,* she said to herself. Exhaling long and deep, she took three long, running strides into a back handspring and landed just short of her mark.

Shoot, dangit and hell, hell, hell!

"Look, if you all aren't going to get it right, we can call this competition off right now!" Coach Embry barked.

Mina dropped to the mat—exhausted. *Call it off, then,* she thought. They had been practicing since school let out, and it was nearly six o'clock. Weren't there laws against working them that long? Where was an administrator when a sister needed one?

"From the top! Do it right or do it again!" the coach demanded.

Mina hated the motto. She mocked under her breath. "Do it right or do it again."

"What's that, Mina?" Coach Embry asked, eyebrow raised to her hairline.

The other girls threw private, knowing looks of agreement Mina's way. They were all tired.

"I was just counting off, Coach," Mina said.

"Well, do it out loud, then. Lead the team or step to the back," Coach Embry challenged.

Mina resisted the strong urge to suck her teeth. Coach Embry had a habit of spouting clichés, phrases Mina and the squad sarcastically labeled "Embryisms." They swore the coach sat at home every night thinking up new phrases to annoy them.

A former professional cheerleader with the Del Rio Bay Buccaneers, the woman was an inexhaustible source of "motivation" or, in Mina's opinion, torture.

Mina stood in her designated spot and waited for the music to begin. Right on cue, she exploded into movement as the loud, busy music spewed from the speakers. Her face took on an animated cheerful look, and she lost herself in the frenzy of the routine.

So far, it was flawless.

Mina started her run for the back handspring, and for a second her eyes met Brian's. The brief second cost Mina. She missed her mark again.

The entire squad groaned in unison. They knew Mina missed it by mere inches, but Coach Embry was a perfectionist. Without a single word among them, the squad regrouped to their initial positions and started the routine again.

An hour later, Mina entered the gym from the locker room, moving slowly, fidgeting with her ponytail. Brian saw her, but kept talking with Michael as he watched Mina walk toward them. He absorbed her every move.

Even though she walked as if she were tired, she looked fresh and rejuvenated in a pair of black nylon track pants and a black "Baby Blue Devils" hoodie, like she'd just stepped out of a sporting goods ad. Brian didn't detect any defeat, even though he'd seen the coach fuss specifically at Mina twice, blaming her for missing some mark invisible to Brian. Her commitment had impressed him.

He felt slightly guilty because he knew for sure that at least one of those missed stunts was his fault. He'd seen Mina's eyes grow wide with surprise when their gazes met and then bam, the coach had begun yelling.

He'd wandered over to the gymnastics room only because once his own practice was over, he'd seen a few of his teammates looking through the windows. Curious, he'd joined them at the doorway, staying long enough to see the squad practice the routine three times.

To Brian, each time it looked as if they hit it perfectly. But the coach had not been pleased until the third and final run-through. Brian was surprised at Mina's athleticism; he admired her strong leg muscles during her flips and her inexhaustible energy throughout the dance.

He chuckled to himself as the word "spunky" came to mind.

She didn't look very spunky right now, though. But he'd watched her turn it on three times. She had it in her.

"You ready, Mike?" Mina asked.

Michael turned around at the sound of her voice. "Hey. I didn't know you were finished." He hopped down from the bleachers and grabbed his bag. "Yeah, we ready. Brian gon' give us a ride."

Mina nodded, glad. She was too tired to walk tonight.

"I saw you getting your cheer on. You're good," Brian said, voice laced with admiration.

Too worn out to analyze his words for sarcasm, Mina nodded a thank-you.

They reached Brian's truck, and Mina stepped toward the back door.

"You can sit up front," Michael offered.

Mina scanned the parking lot as she stepped in. "Where's JZ?"

"Headed to the 'Ria with Rachel," Michael said.

"Celebrating his celebrity with a little honey, huh?" Mina joked tiredly.

Brian and Michael laughed and started a conversation that Mina barely heard.

She laid her head back on the headrest, closed her eyes and let the conversation flow around her. The comfortable seat and the warm air from the truck's heater quickly lulled her into an easy sleep.

A few minutes later, her shoulders jumped when her brain informed her body that the car had been still for a period longer than required for a stoplight. Brian and Michael were still chatting. She lifted her head and through sleep-glazed eyes took in the familiar sight of Michael's house.

Michael noticed her stirring. "Coach Em worked y'all today, huh?"

Her eyes heavy with fatigue, Mina stretched them wide to bring herself back from the short nap. "You know it," she said, opening the car door. "I can walk from here, Brian. The cold air might wake me up."

"It's no big deal for me to drive you home. Come on," Brian coaxed.

Mina slid back into the truck. "Shoot, you don't have to ask me twice. See you, Mike."

"Bye, diva. Get some sleep," Michael said. "See you, Brian."

Brian turned to Mina. "You were knocked out."

Mina yawned, nodding. "Six A.M. to six P.M. is a long day . . . " She trailed off into a short rant. "I've been trying to get the coach to let us coordinate competition practices differently. Like maybe let us go home right after school and then do practice four to eight. But nooo."

Brian chuckled. "Y'all were working it out, though. You gonna rip it at the competition."

Mina stifled another yawn. "I hope so."

"If your squad ever wants to do a training session with the Wizard cheerleaders, just let me know," Brian offered, pulling the truck into Mina's driveway.

Mina sat up straighter, suddenly energized. "Really? How could you do that?"

"My father is the boss of the director that manages the cheerleaders. Sometimes they do minicamps with local cheer squads."

"That would be cool. Our coach used to be a Bucc'ette. That is all she talks about." Mina affected a booming nag and mocked Coach Embry. "When I was a Bucc'ette, it was about total dedication, eight-hour practices. Come hard or don't come at all."

Brian laughed. "Just let me know. I can ask my father to hook you or your coach up with the contact."

"That's right, you're an NBA brat," Mina said, recalling details from their interview. The sudden realization that she knew a lot about Brian shocked her. The idea of interviewing a boyfriend wasn't as far out as it sounded. She yawned. "By the way, thank you."

"What for?" Brian gazed curiously from his side of the truck.

"I'm officially the *Pop Life* columnist thanks to the article I did on you."

Brian held his fist out for a pound, and Mina gave it a shy bang.

"So when do I get to read it?" he asked.

"I think it will be in the next issue . . . so I guess next week," she said, opening the door to get out. "Alright, well, I might take you up on that offer with the Wizard cheerleaders. Thanks for the ride."

"Hey, Mina," Brian called.

"Hmm?"

"Here, take my e-mail address . . . That way if you want Sheila's contact info, you can e-me," he said. "You have some paper?"

Mina rummaged in her backpack and produced a notebook and pen. She handed them to Brian.

He scribbled something before handing the notebook back to her. "Alright."

Mina hopped out. "Thanks, Brian."

"Holler."

"Mina closed the door, and Brian pulled off as she walked into the house. She dropped her backpack, still holding the notebook, and went to put it into her bag when she noticed Brian's note with his e-mail and phone number.

Why not hit a brother up sometime? YES, I'm flirting with you! And I won't tell if you don't.
   -B

Guess Who's Back?

"Arguments, face up in the air like you hatin' me."
—Ghostface Killah, "Never Be the Same Again"

With JZ's spot secure on the team, every Blue Devil's game was now a must-see for the clique. So when Thursday arrived, it was expected that they'd all hop into Mina's dad's Navigator and head up to the Northern Rio Wranglers/Blue Devils game. And everyone did, except Kelly.

Sitting home, in the spacious family room, she stared moodily at the television and fast-forwarded through the channels too quickly to identify any programs. There was a time when the luxuries of her home were all she needed—all she wanted. The wide screen plasma television, the theater room and game room, the tennis courts had always been her safe haven from the snotty, clannish students at Mc-Stew Prep. Then she'd transferred to DRB High, made friends and who would ever believe, had a boyfriend.

But tonight, she was home (smells like old times), not at the game where everyone else was, but home. It tore her up inside.

It was one thing when you didn't know what fun you were missing. But knowing all of her friends were together while she was at home was unbearably frustrating, like putting the key to a jail cell inches outside of a prisoner's reach.

Not that Kelly was into sports. She played tennis, because her grandmother felt as though someone should get use of their home tennis court. But it wasn't until she started hanging out with Mina, who was very competitive and a team spirit guru, that Kelly was introduced to the excitement of team sports—spectator style. Thanks to the weekly football and now basketball games, for the first time Kelly's social calendar was full.

The fact that she had a social calendar, one not put together by her grandmother, was still new and exciting. Missing the game sucked.

Kelly had been all set to go. Then, that morning, her grandmother had informed her that she couldn't join her friends. Grand wouldn't say why, just that she needed Kelly at home. And now she was sitting there alone (what else was new?) and her grandmother was upstairs somewhere. *What is it that couldn't wait?* She fumed, feeling an unusual pang of anger at her grandmother.

Kelly's phone vibrated loudly. She jumped at the small buzzing noise it made. She'd had a cell phone since seventh grade, and until a month ago, the only person who ever called it was Grand. Now it buzzed, twittered and rang constantly. She loved the phone's busy noises and how it kept her in close contact with the girls. She flipped it open:

Miss ya Boo-Boo!

It was Mina. A smile penetrated Kelly's sullen face as she typed back:

This so sux. R we winning at least?

From Mina: Yup! Dey ain't no comp 4 da Devils! I holla ltr!

The cellie went off again. Kelly looked down at it eagerly, anxious to stay in touch with every second of the game. But this time it was Angel:

Me n u at da mall Sat?

Kelly's face lit up again. She had casually mentioned her week-end plans to meet up with the clique at the mall, knowing Angel would make his way there if she was there. She typed back:

Not sure . . . girls staying @ my house tmrw nite. Mall may-b sunday

Angel: let me n heem roll 2 ur crib n hang out w/yall

Kelly grinned. Yeah, like that was going to happen.

"Hi, baby," a voice chirped from her side, causing her to stop midway through her message.

Kelly whirled around, startled. She looked up into the smiling face of a honey-colored woman with thick, wavy chestnut hair to her shoulders. It was like looking into a mirror.

Rebecca Lopez-Narcone leaned down and hugged her daughter from behind. She smelled of Ginger Essence—a light, slightly fruity fragrance that floated around her as if it were her natural scent.

Kelly loved and hated the smell all at once. She was rigid in her mother's embrace.

Her relationship with her mother was complex. But it boiled down to one simple sentiment, resentment. Rebecca was physically away often, and when she was around, she was still somehow absent. Kelly gave up wishing for a true mother-daughter relationship long ago.

"God, you look wonderful, Kelly. You're growing into quite the little hottie," Rebecca drawled, laughing. She flipped her hair and beamed at her daughter.

Kelly's cellie buzzed anxiously as Angel sent messages inquiring if she was still out there.

Rebecca remarked, "Someone is blowing up your phone, honey. Better answer it."

Kelly's fingers flew as she typed a message to Angel:

c u sorry gotta go

She flipped the phone closed and sat back, waiting for Rebecca to explain her presence.

Although Kelly looked exactly like her mother, their similarities stopped there. Years of trying to blend in with the background had conditioned Kelly to be reluctant to speak up. Even now when she was with her friends, she observed more than she spoke.

Her mother, on the other hand, was the type of woman that breezed into a room commanding attention by the sheer flow of her nonstop conversation. There were no awkward pauses with Rebecca Lopez-Narcone—there weren't any pauses at all. She talked constantly.

"Look at you, always the quiet one. No love for your mamacita?" Rebecca teased, pouting, feigning hurt feelings.

Always the actress—always on, Kelly thought with disgust before answering with little emotion. "Hi, Mom. What are you doing in town?"

The greeting came off like "What the hell are you doing here." Usually she kept her disdain buried deep, but tonight her mother was a good target for her frustration at missing the game. Every drop of venom in her voice melted a little of her anger.

In a dramatic motion, Rebecca dropped down beside her daughter on the sofa. She flipped her hair and raked her fingers through the lush, fashionably styled 'do.

Kelly smelled ginger shampoo as her mother's hair swayed.

Rebecca threw her hands up in a fit of drama. "Well, your grandmother called me all in a tizzy. Apparently, you are now dating." At this, she beamed before continuing. "Grand is just not ready for the trials and tribulations of dating right now. So, I guess I'm the Cavalry."

Kelly grunted. "*You're* the Cavalry?"

Rebecca admonished. "Hey, watch that tone, missy. I was a teenager once. I can relate."

"I didn't hear you come in. Did you just get here? Where is Grand?" Kelly asked. She craned her neck around, looking past her mother to look up the stairs to see if Grand was nearby. But the house—she suddenly noticed—was eerily silent.

"Momma's upstairs. Phil didn't fly in with me. I'm solo tonight. You know Marques Houston is touring and Phil is helping him with his new single. Oh, Kelly, if you were a little older, honey, I swear that boy would be perfect for you—"

"Mom," Kelly blurted, interrupting her mother's mindless banter. "Why are you here? What's going on?"

With a noisy sigh, Rebecca stroked Kelly's hair as she answered. "Grand is worried about you . . . well, about this new friend you have. Angel, is it?"

"Yes. What about him?"

"He's not exactly from Folger's, is he?" Rebecca asked.

"Not at all. He's from—"

"The Cove," Rebecca finished, heavily, as if saying it made her tired. "Yes, I know. Your grandmother told me. Kelly, we need to talk."

"Grand made you come all the way home to have a talk about sex?" Kelly rolled her eyes to the ceiling. "You're a little late, Mommy. I had that talk with Grand years ago."

Rebecca chuckled. "No. That's not why I came home."

"Then, what? I'm sure Phil needs you . . . especially if Marques Houston is ready to go on tour." Kelly's words dripped with uncharacteristic sarcasm.

Rebecca threw her daughter a weary sideways glance, not used to seeing her full of so much piss and vinegar, as her father would have called it.

She hadn't seen either of her kids since right before school started. They had been unable to make it back for the Thanksgiving holiday because Phil was in marathon production sessions trying to help Trey Songz with an album. When she called to let them know, Kelly had seemed happy, though a bit put off by her parents missing the holiday. Rebecca figured she'd make up for it over the Christmas break. Today, Kelly seemed sulky and moody. Rebecca had never seen her this way. She chalked it up to teen drama and pressed on.

She looked Kelly in the eye. "There are some things I need to share with you. Things I probably should have shared sooner."

Sins of My Mother

> "Everyone has a secret/But can they keep it."
> —Maroon 5, "Secret"

Kelly and her mother were in Rebecca's wing of the house, a huge suite of rooms that met every one of Rebecca and Phil's needs. From relaxation—a spa section for his and her massages and pedicures—to fitness—a pimped-out workout room that included a state-of-the-art audio and video system that could beam Rebecca's trainer in via satellite—the Narcones' suite was a rarely used haven designed to keep Rebecca happy mind, body and soul.

As Rebecca sat at her dressing table brushing her hair, Kelly waited on the edge of an oversized chair, tense. She envied her mother's smooth confidence, eying how her mom even brushed her hair with drama—broad, sweeping strokes that made the hair sway.

Kelly always thought of her mom as gorgeous. Even though she looked very much like her, Kelly had never applied the same adjective to herself. She cleared her throat to remind her mother she was waiting, still there for the big mother-daughter talk Rebecca had made this special trip home for.

As if truly forgetting she was there, Rebecca jumped. She turned away from the mirror and graced Kelly with another of her 1000-watt smiles.

"So, Mami, what's going on? You came all the way back from Atlanta to say what? That you're happy I'm dating," Kelly proposed, her voice low and curious.

"I think it's nice that you're dating. Maybe I can meet . . . Angel," Rebecca announced, beaming, proud to have actually remembered his name.

Kelly couldn't believe her ears. Just ten days ago, in a second of weakness she'd actually wished to have her mom here to discuss Angel. And here she was all ready to have some girl talk about Kelly's new "beau." Whoever said be careful what you wish for wasn't kidding.

Rebecca began. "Kelly, you know we've never discussed your real dad much . . ."

"Not at all," Kelly interjected.

"That's fair," Rebecca acknowledged. "But I married Phil while you were still so young. I always thought you would come to think of him as your only true father."

"You guys have hardly ever been around. How can I think of him as a father when he's not here?" Kelly asked.

Her parents' constant absence had always been a sore spot, but she had never addressed it with her mother before. But if the soc project had proven anything, it was that Kelly was able to be firm and outspoken on things that really pushed her buttons. Her mother touching down to talk crushes and dating three years too late was suddenly one of them.

Sometimes her quiet passion took her by surprise. It certainly had caught Mina, Jacinta and Jessica off guard when Kelly blasted them about their immaturity during the project. It was the first time she'd raised her voice at anyone, but the girls' constant bickering and sniping had torn her last nerve to shreds, and Kelly had let them have it barrels blazing.

She was growing oddly comfortable with speaking her mind.

But her mom's answer to the observation was terse. "Kell, I'm not bucking for any mother of the year awards, okay?" Rebecca changed gears again, her voice soft, almost pleading. "You may never understand me, but I hope that you can at least respect me and the decisions I've made over the years. I felt leaving you with Grand and Poppi was best."

Kelly sucked her teeth quietly. Her anger rose, causing her words to have a heavy Spanish lilt to them. "Mami, I know you didn't come all this way to talk about leaving me with Poppi and Grand; and if you did, then consider your job done." Her body vibrated with quiet fury, and she lowered her voice as she went on. "Poppi was the only father I ever knew. But he's gone. What's the point in discussing my 'real' father now? He's dead, too."

Rebecca avoided Kelly's blazing stare as she whispered, "Because your real father isn't dead."

Kelly's stony glare chilled Rebecca. She kneeled in front of her, face drawn and full of pain.

The hurt in her mom's expression threw Kelly off. She wasn't used to seeing her mother display any other emotion except "on," a cheerful, upbeat façade that her mom once informed Kelly was simply part of "the business," her casual reference to the music industry. Still, her mother's obvious grief didn't move Kelly much.

Just Mami acting, she thought.

"Kelly, the reason Grand called me is because she's afraid you're going to get yourself in trouble . . . just like I did," Rebecca admitted.

Unwilling to play into her mother's soap opera performance, Kelly's voice dripped with venom, but with a soft edge of confusion. "My father isn't dead and Grand is afraid I'm going to end up like you. Like you how?"

She let her mother pull her gently to the floor. Kelly sat cross-legged, and her mother folded her legs beneath her, following suit. They sat there, mirror images, across from each other only inches apart.

Rubbing Kelly's hand with short, nervous strokes, Rebecca's

words rushed out. "Right after college I came back home to Del Rio Bay and worked in the publicity office of the DRB arena. One night while I was working a pro basketball game, you know, handling the three-point shoot-outs and contests they hold during time-outs . . . I met one of the contestants; a good-looking Puerto Rican guy named Rico Ramirez. Your dad."

Rebecca inhaled deeply, her eyes closed. Once composed, she exhaled and smiled as if she'd pushed some sort of internal reset button.

"I was the one in charge of making sure the person filled out the paperwork to get their prizes, and Rico and I started talking." Rebecca chuckled at the memory. "We hit it off . . . and eventually, started dating. Rico was from Del Rio Crossing . . ." She paused and glanced at Kelly, who was listening intently, curious.

Kelly filled in the short silence, pointing out. "Del Rio Crossing, the low-income housing across the bridge?"

"Yes. What we always called the projects before everyone became so politically correct." Rebecca sneered and for a second seemed to address the demons from her past more than Kelly as she declared, "I didn't care, though. Rico was nice. He was funny and fun to be around."

Kelly's mother paused, lost in the memory, and then realized she was stroking Kelly's hand. She shook her head and came back to the present. "But your grandmother wasn't crazy about him. All she talked about was how I was going to end up supporting him because I had a college degree and he, only a high school diploma. But what I never told my mother, at least not right away, was that Rico sold drugs."

Kelly gasped, then noisily cleared her throat to cover the sound. Luckily, her mother was too caught up in her memories to notice.

Rebecca's eyes wandered past Kelly, focused on invisible images of her past as she continued. "Rico was no big-time hustler, but he always felt like he made more than he would have doing construction or working at a fast food place. I knew better. It was crazy to be with him knowing what he did. But part of me called it being liberal and not looking down my nose at him. You know?" she asked Kelly, peering into her face for understanding.

Kelly nodded. She really did know.

"After about a year, I got pregnant with you, and Rico asked me to move in with him—"

"You moved to the projects?" Kelly asked, shocked. Her mother was one of the most high maintenance people ever. The thought of her moving to the projects was even more unbelievable than her being unmarried and pregnant.

"No." Rebecca chuckled. "We bought a small house. And Rico always kept his business away from the house. I really felt like we could live like that forever. Plus, I figured he would grow out of it and try to go legit one day."

"How did you hide what he was doing from Grand and Poppi?" Kelly asked, caught up in the story in spite of herself.

"Well, you were a good distraction," Rebecca replied, pushing a strand of Kelly's hair behind her ear. "Grand always did adore you. You were the reason they probably didn't outright disown me over my relationship with Rico."

Rebecca's hands fluttered to her lap. Unable to find anything to do with them, she constantly fidgeted with her hair or Kelly's. She powered forward, revealing how Kelly's grandparents disapproved of her father, how Rebecca skirted the issue of his job—never lying but never commenting when her parents asked how they managed on only her salary.

Kelly was completely lost in the story. The layers kept unfolding.

Her mom explained how she took some strange level of pride in the fact that she and Rico never asked Kelly's grandparents for money—even knowing that Rico's money came from illegal means.

Once, Rebecca paused for what felt like forever, but Kelly was afraid to break the spell of her mother's memories by prompting her to go on. She waited, four then seven minutes before her mother finally spoke. "Then Rico was busted and things went crazy."

Kelly's shoulders hiccupped as she gasped. Her mom nodded, as if she felt the same way.

"Your grandparents had no idea what he did until he went to jail. But when he did, the government froze our assets, since drug money is earned illegally. I couldn't access our bank accounts. We lost the house . . ." Rebecca shook her head, thinking back on the chaotic period. "And Poppi had to hire a good lawyer to keep my name out of the whole mess."

Just then, as if sensing something, Kelly's mom looked over at the door. Kelly followed her gaze and saw her grandmother at the door. Her face was pinched and tired looking. She shuffled away as silently as she had appeared.

Kelly looked back at her mother. "Are you saying Rico is still in jail?"

Rebecca nodded. "Business was too good," she said with a sad smile. "Rico wasn't the top man, but he was among the top. He'll get out . . . one day."

Kelly couldn't help herself; she prodded. "Do you still love him?"

Rebecca choked out a bitter laugh. "That's a loaded question, Kells. I'm afraid to tell you the truth. It could send the wrong message."

"I'm not a baby, Mami," Kelly whined.

Rebecca pushed Kelly's hair behind her ear again. "Nope, you aren't. It's been almost ten years now since Rico was sent off to prison."

Rebecca reflected on the years long gone and sighed heavily as if they were all coming down on her at that very moment. "Yes, there is a part of me that does still love him . . ." She pursed her lips, then corrected her thoughts. "At least loves what we foolishly thought we could have together. But once he was busted, your grandparents made it clear that they would help me out of the mess I created only if I promised to cut off contact with Rico. I didn't have much choice. The trial, the media, losing almost everything we had—it was all so scary. I was more than happy to go back to my nice, quiet life with my parents."

"Don't take this wrong but . . ." Kelly searched her mother's face for any sign that she was lying. "This is like a horror story you tell your kids to scare them away from opening a certain door." She shook her head, not wanting to believe. "I mean, Grand calls and tells you some guy from the projects has called me, and now . . . this," she said, the accusation clear.

Rebecca nodded. "It's a lot to process. But it's all true. I don't know Angel and I don't want to pass judgment on him. But when Grand found out Angel was from Pirates Cove . . . I think she had flashbacks." She chuckled nervously. "Horrible flashbacks of cops and lawyers and young, dumb girls." She shook her head slowly, then snorted. "She wanted to tell you the night Angel called, but she felt it was my place to tell you. You ever heard that phrase, the sins of the father?"

Kelly shook her head no.

"Well, it just means that if you don't right some wrongs, then others you love are destined to repeat those mistakes. Grand doesn't want that to happen and neither do I."

Kelly's heart thumped loud and wild. The entire time her mother was talking, she'd waited for her to reveal that she and Grand knew all about Angel hustling. But story time was over and it hadn't come up.

She was relieved but couldn't help resenting the heart-to-heart. She also resented the convenience of her mother's love story and how, just like their faces, it mirrored Kelly's own. As usual her mother's presence only added to Kelly's confusion. Arms folded, she challenged her mother. "So now that I know, what exactly is supposed to happen?"

Rebecca shook her head. "That's up to you, Kells. But, your

grandparents and I always thought that maybe if we shielded you—
put you in the best schools, the right activities—you wouldn't ever
have to deal with what I endured." She prodded, "Aren't there
plenty of nice guys at your high school?"

"Of course, Mami," Kelly said, swallowing the impulse to roll her
eyes toward the ceiling. She lectured her mother as if *she* were the
child. "But surely you aren't going to sit here and tell me to not see
Angel, especially after telling me the real story of *my* father."

"No. I'm not going to say that," Rebecca answered. She cracked
a sardonic smile. "I have to be honest. I never planned to tell you the
truth about your father. If your grandmother wasn't so worried, I
wouldn't have now. But I think she's hoping you have more sense
than I did." She laughed. "And you probably do, even at fifteen. I
was twenty-two when I met your dad, and I still didn't have enough
sense to turn the other way."

Kelly stood up, towering over her mother. "Thanks for sharing
that, Mami. Is that all?" she asked, her words clipped.

Rebecca swallowed hard over the lump forming in her throat.
She had no delusion that she and Kelly had a great relationship. But
this new icy side to her daughter hurt. Her feelings deflated, she answered, "Yes, Kelly. That's all."

Kelly walked to the door. "Great. I'll see you later . . . or are you
flying back out tomorrow?"

Rebecca's answer was a low whisper. "No . . . I, I'll be here for a
few days."

"Mmmm, okay," Kelly said. She walked away, first slowly, then
began running. She wiped at the tears streaming down her face and
tried to recall one, just one solid conversation she'd ever had with
her mother. Nothing came to mind. And now this. She found her
parents' story interesting, even moving. Her mother spoke so affec-
tionately of Rico (*hard to think of him as Daddy*) that Kelly was
touched.

But it was all too much. The confession, Grand being unable to reveal the truth, the years of thinking her dad was dead. On top of it all, the similarity of her situation and her mother's was scary. Sins of the father was a real . . . bitch. Kelly couldn't think of another word for it.

She wanted to believe she was too smart to repeat her mother's mistakes, but the truth about Rico didn't change how she felt about Angel.

She threw herself onto her bed and cried harder. If her mother's presence was supposed to make things better, help her come to her "senses" about Angel, it hadn't. Kelly was even more confused now. Her last thought, before drifting off to sleep, was an angry, *Things were going just fine without you, Mother.*

A Change of Heart

"Ooh . . . looks like another club banger."
—Akon ft. Eminem, "Smack That"

Mina awoke Saturday morning wrapped in a sense of sour regret.

She was only trying to be funny last night at the 'Ria, like sarcastic funny not ha-ha funny, when she told Brian he wasn't her type. But every time she played the sound bite back in her head it just came off bitchy sarcastic.

"Whatever, you're not even my type. I like 'em rough," Mina had said after being backed in a corner by Brian's teasing. The clique had *ooh*ed and *aw damn*ed, laughing at the exchange. But hurt had been all over Brian's handsome toffee face, and too late Mina realized she'd come off too hard. She'd only been trying to find a witty comeback. It had backfired.

The fact that Brian hadn't said another word to her the rest of the night was a pretty good clue that she'd been nastier than intended.

She really had a way with guys . . . a bad way.

Ravenous (she hadn't eaten another bite after mouthing off), she pushed herself out of bed and headed downstairs for some breakfast. Instead of thinking about the regret, she focused on the other feeling, bubbling excitement.

There were only nine hours and counting to the Frenzy, the

"lie" and the chance to rock slowly against Craig until her hormones were as frazzled and worked up as punk rockers smashing in a mosh pit.

Mina pushed the "lie" far away, telling herself it was a girls' night at Kelly's McMansion, nothing more, nothing less. She, Jacinta and Lizzie would tell Mrs. Lopez they were heading to the Folger's Country Club teen night, they would dip into the Frenzy, she'd get her quickie groove on, then one quick pit stop to the teen night for accuracy's sake and voila back at Kelly's—no harm, no foul, no parent the wiser.

She sat on the floor in front of the TV, crunching on a bowl of Cap'n Crunch. She slurped up the last bit of the milk, never taking her eyes off the TV. *Endurance* was on, and she loved the straight drama of it. The people on *Survivor* didn't have nothing on the cutthroat teens of *Endurance*.

Milk squirted out of her mouth as she laughed. "Now, how come y'all didn't see that one coming," she taunted as the green team got sent to Temple.

Her mom yelled a warning from the top of the stairs. "Mina, this crazy cell phone keeps going off. Come get this thing before I throw it out of the window."

Mina ran up the stairs. "Sorry, Ma."

She had no desire to have her mom focus on the cell phone. She'd gone over her allotted number of text messages last month and had to hear it from her mother anytime the phone buzzed or beeped.

"Mina, how do you use up two hundred text messages? What person needs more than that?" her mother had lectured, shaking the phone bill at her. "Twenty dollars extra in text messages? That's beyond unacceptable."

Mina didn't bother explaining. She knew they were rhetorical questions. What was important was if she did it again, her phone was as good as out of there. And she couldn't have that. The phone was her lifeline to everything happening in and around the DRB. She'd cut back . . . soon.

Mina flipped the phone open. It was a message from Lizzie:

Did ur rents mention da prty yet?

Mina: No. Hpflly I'll know s'mthn soon

As if on cue from stage directions, Mina's mom called out, "Hey, Boo, come here for a second."

Mina ambled into her parents' room. They were both still in the bed. She hopped on and scrambled to sit between them. Something she had always done as a little kid. "Morning, Daddy," she said, pecking his forehead. She snuggled next to her mom.

Her dad grinned. "Good morning, baby."

"Thanks again for chauffeuring us last night," Mina said, knowing it never hurt to butter them up.

"Chauffeuring? That's all I am is the hired help?" He tickled her side.

She giggled. "You know what I mean, Daddy."

Mina's mom brought them back to attention, her voice sharp. "Mina, last night Jacqi mentioned that Jacinta's boyfriend, Raheem, is having a party next Saturday." She looked over Mina's head at her husband and signaled that he should continue.

He obeyed. "She basically said something to the effect that she was wondering if it was okay if you attended. Apparently she's known Raheem since he was a kid—knows his mom, etcetera . . . and said he's a good guy."

Mina nodded. "Yeah. I've met him. He is nice."

Her mom blurted, "I don't know if I'm comfortable with this. Jacqi indicated that the party would be at Raheem's friend's house, which isn't very far from Jacinta's."

Mina nodded again, confused. She couldn't tell if her parents were gearing up to say no or yes. She sat up, cross-legged, and faced them so she could look at both of them.

"Well, yeah, you know I've been to Jacinta's before," Mina explained. "Angel lives one building away. Mr. Phillips would probably be there . . . well, not there but checking in, I mean."

Mina's mom interrupted. "Jacqi made it clear that there may not be constant adult supervision. I don't agree with that. I mean, you're getting older, but no adults and all those teenagers? That's bad news."

Mina's shoulders slumped, knowing where it was going until her dad said, "But we like Jacqi, Jamal and Jacinta. If Jamal is allowing Jacinta to go, that means he must trust her . . . and Raheem."

Mina's spirits lifted.

"Mina, we're going to let you go," her mom said. Her eyebrow was raised in a silent "but." There was definitely more. But Mina was too excited. She tackled her mom with a hug.

"Thank you, Mommy," she wailed, unable to stop grinning.

Her mom cautioned. "Wait a minute. We're going to let you go but only because Jacqi agreed that Jamal would be checking in on the party periodically throughout the night. And because we want to show we trust you."

"But trust is only as strong as your actions. If you damage that trust, you start back over from square one. Are we being clear?" her dad asked.

Mina's nod was solemn. Yikes, all this trust and she was totally sneaking behind their backs tonight. A sliver of guilt stabbed her right in the heart.

One thing at a time, Mina, she thought, pushing the thought away.

"Thank you, Daddy, Mommy," she gushed, bear hugging them before bouncing off the bed. "I need to go tell Lizzie."

"Oh, and that's the other thing," her mom called after her, stopping her in her tracks. "I know Pat and Marybeth will be calling the second Lizzie asks about going. And if they decide to let her go because we're letting you go—that's even more pressure on you girls to handle yourselves properly."

"What your mom is saying is, ruin it this time and there won't be a next time . . . for either of you," her dad warned.

"Got it. Love you guys," Mina said, scrambling away.

Her dad groaned. "Love us because you got your way."

"No, for real, love you like a play cousin," Mina teased.

Her dad threw a pillow at her, and Mina ducked out of the room laughing.

Mina's mother shook her head, wringing her hands. "Jack—"

Jackson reached over and kissed his wife on the cheek. "They'll be fine. We knew it was coming sooner or later."

Her eyes glistened. "Yeah, but I thought later was college."

Jackson laughed. "One thing at a time."

Decisions, Decisions...
Decided

Kelly's room was gloriously pimped out with enough space and features to keep a sleepover interesting. If the girls chose, they could spend hours lounging in Kelly's sitting room watching their favorite shows on the plasma screen, or launch a marathon IM session in Kelly's study decked out with both a desktop and laptop, or lie across Kelly's king-sized princess bed and gab, or sit on the window seat and choose which area of the backyard to raid, or take a relaxing dip in her whirlpool bathtub (because all four of them could fit, comfortably).

They could have a supreme sleepover without ever leaving Kelly's room.

As they cooled out in the sitting room, MTVJams blasting images of rump-shaking video chicks and iced-out thugs from the plasma, they debated doing just that.

Mina sat on the floor between Lizzie's legs, her back against the pink-and-green-striped love seat, getting her hair brushed and nodding to the video.

"So are we going tonight or what?" Jacinta asked for the fourth time. Laid back in a furry, pink rocking chair that looked more like a spaceship seat from a sci-fi movie (a very girly sci-fi movie) than a rocker, Jacinta folded her arms. She raised her eyebrow in a silent "Well?"

Mina tried to concentrate on the question, but the brushstrokes, soothing and gentle, made her eyes heavy. She gave in and allowed her lids to close. She was starting to think Cinny really wanted to go because she was the only one who kept pressing Mina to make up her mind.

Stretched out on her belly on the floor, Kelly glanced up from her *Girls Life* at Mina, curious. She felt the exact same sense of dread and exhilaration she'd felt when Angel's car finally pulled up in front of his house and she realized either she had to go in or run screaming down the street into the night.

Either they were going to take a deep breath and do this or they were going to stay hunkered in the room, all night.

It occurred to her that she was ringing up naughty girl points awfully fast. Fourteen years of good-girling-it wiped out in a month.

Kelly giggled at the thought as she looked back up at Mina, who seemed to be dozing off until her eyes fluttered open and she declared, "I shouldn't go."

Mina's eyes closed again. She continued in a dreamy, half-awake state. "The 'rents are letting me go to Raheem's party next weekend and . . . I mean, that's a big step for them."

"Huge," Lizzie echoed, petting Mina's head softly with the brush. She couldn't help rooting for NOT going to the party. As usual, her fate was tied to Mina's. If Mina was caught tonight, it would be Lizzie's misfortune, too. Just this morning, her parents had reminded her of that when they'd agreed to let her attend Raheem's party.

"Mariah and Jack have said yes . . . so we're going to let you go," her mom had said once Mina called with the good news. "But we'll have to cover the ground rules."

It was a variation on a speech the girls had heard many times. They were linked by their friendship, good or bad.

Lizzie pointed it out, hoping the reminder would help Mina decide. "If you go down tonight, we both go down. Might as well learn how to talk through smoke signals 'cause I'm pretty sure the computer, cell phone and anything else tied to the outside world is hist."

"I know that's right," Mina said, head drooping even more.

"I'm not surprised. I knew you were too straight-and-narrow for this." Jacinta chuckled.

"It's not even that," Mina said, unfazed by Jacinta's light taunt. She lifted her head slightly and peered at Cinny through the mop of hair. "But I can't lie. My parents' little A.M. speech about trust got to me. If Mrs. Lopez found out that my parents had already told me no happs with the party, then she'd think I was just using Kelly and . . ." She lifted her head all the way up as if something had pricked her. "Eww . . . then I'd be one of those girls."

Jacinta frowned. "What girls?"

"The kind of girl that makes parents say, 'I don't want you hanging out with *that* girl,'" Lizzie guessed.

Mina smiled. The best friend ESP was in effect. She put her hand up for some dap, and Lizzie slid her hand over it. Mina wriggled upright and hugged her knees to her chest. "And if I just . . ."

"Invite him to Raheem's party, you getting your way anyway, right, little princess?" Jacinta said.

Kelly's face lit up. "Hey, I was going to say that, too. Well, not the princess part."

"That's what I was ready to say, too," Mina admitted. The ESP was spreading. She loved it. She stretched and stood up. "Thanks, Liz," she yawned. "Girl was ready to fall asleep, for real."

Lizzie sat cross-legged on the love seat. "Okay, so then Operation Hot Tub Chow Down is on."

"I'm with that," Jacinta said. "If we're not going to get our groove on, we can at least get our eat on."

The Hot Tub Chow Down was Plan B or The After Party, as Mina liked to think of it—the one definite part of tonight once they were back in the house settled. Kelly's oversized whirlpool tub had been tempting her for months. So she'd sent out several reminders to make sure Lizzie and Jacinta brought their swimsuits. The plan was to gather all their favorite snacks and munch out while the tub's jets created the world's biggest bubble bath around them.

"Okay, but here's the deal," Mina said, plopping down onto the love seat. She stretched her legs over Lizzie's. "Let's still head over to the party so I can tell Craig I'm not coming."

"You know what?" Jacinta said, shaking her head. "I've been hanging around you too long 'cause that makes total sense to me."

Kelly giggled. "You're going to show up somewhere and tell him you're not coming?"

Mina smiled.

"But that's still sneaking over there." Lizzie frowned.

"Technically, yeah," Mina admitted. "But only long enough for me to tell him I'm kicking it with y'all and to invite him to Raheem's."

She dug her toes lightly into Lizzie's leg, tickling her. "Seriously, nothing more." She crossed her heart. "I promise not to dance with him no matter how fandamtastic he looks."

Lizzie nodded, but Mina saw she was still nervous. She swung her legs to the floor and pulled Lizzie up by the hand, then hugged her. "For real, Liz. In and out."

"In and out," Lizzie repeated.

"In and out," all the girls chorused.

"Okay." Lizzie fought the bad feeling welling in the pit of her stomach, discounted it as nerves and tried to joke off her worry. "Because dang, I'm just now moving to dateville with Todd. Being punished is not a good look."

"Well, let's go then," Jacinta said, jumping up from the rocker. "I'm hungry. I wanna get back and get my grub on."

"Liz, you and Todd are so cute together," Kelly said. She grabbed her coat out of the closet and slipped on a pair of woolly Steve Madden clogs.

Lizzie blushed. "Nah, I mean, it's still just a friend thing, really."

"Cute still," Kelly said.

"Friends today, lovers tomorrow," Mina sang.

Lizzie blanched. "Lovers? Woah, slow it down a few centuries."

"You know your girl is dramatic." Jacinta laughed.

Lizzie stepped into her black Birkenstocks and wrapped a scarf around her neck. "Yeah, well, 'lovers' is a way dramatic word to describe me and any guy. I'm more of a seventeenth-century, maiden-in-waiting type of gal."

Mina rolled her eyes. "Dag, Liz, could you at least move to the twentieth century?"

Lizzie shook her head vigorously. "Not for this, no. I likes 'em nice and slow."

"I likes 'em rough," Jacinta chimed in.

"Oooh, I likes 'em hot." Mina laughed.

They all looked at Kelly.

She shrugged. "I have no idea how I like 'em."

Their girlish giggling floated into the hall as they stepped out of Kelly's room and started down the grand staircase.

Frenzy Fireworks

"I shoulda seen you was trouble right from the start."
—Tupac, "Do for Love"

The community of Folger's Way was Del Rio Bay's toniest nabe. Boasting everything from corporate honchos to congressmen, the neighborhood was exclusive—a mile off the main street, gated and self-contained with its own country club, golf course and park complete with a huge man-made lake. There had never been a single crime committed along its quiet, heavily forested streets, which made it easy for the girls to walk within the dark with ease.

Houses sat far back from the sidewalks, a hundred yards or more, but plenty of streetlights dotted the way leading to Coach Banner's house on Hawk's Nest Court. Hawk's Nest was the only cul-de-sac in the entire neighborhood, marking it as the least desirable part of the community—if a neighborhood full of wealthy residents could have an undesirable section. And Folger's Way did.

Never mind that the homes on Hawk's Nest were as expensive as the others in Folger's Way, they had the misfortune of being the first homes built in the neighborhood and were thus smaller than the structures on steroids throughout the rest of the nabe. Smaller like an Expedition is smaller than a Hummer. Smaller like a hippo is smaller than an elephant. Smaller like a five-hundred-pound person losing ten.

But "the bigger, the better" was the motto of Folger's Way, and the homes on Hawk's Nest, or "the court," as neighbors called it, weren't big enough. The residents on the court weren't snubbed openly (after all, the mayor of Del Rio Bay lived there), but it was well known that they were looked at as the neighborhood's second tier.

Coach Banner holding his team's annual Blue Devil Frenzy (Boys Gone Wild) there, in a neighborhood known for its quiet elegance, didn't help the court's image much. When the girls were still one full street away, through the trees, they heard faint strains of hip-hop music that could only be coming from the Frenzy.

"Dag, they are partying some kind of hard," Jacinta said, straining to hear what song it was.

They all slowed down to listen.

Mina caught a line and began singing, "Oohhhh, round here we ride 'em slow . . ."

"Ciara," the girls sang, then laughed.

"Umph, now, who you think your man grinding next to on that one?" Jacinta joked.

"I'd like to think nobody." Mina scowled. But her heart skipped. Before she could erase it, an image of Craig swaying up against some girl's phat butt to the Ciara/Ludacris jam and its sexy slow drag settled in for a nice long visit. Worse, it was joined by visions of him dancing with somebody who could slink her body like Ciara in the video. Mina's stomach dropped two inches.

Please, please, please let there be a Madden tournament occupying his mind instead of some freak bumping against him.

Seeing Mina's mind whirling a mile a minute behind worried eyes, Kelly rubbed her arm. "He's probably hanging out with a bunch of his teammates . . . playing pool or something."

Mina nodded absently. She hoped so. She still wanted to believe that Coach Banner was around somewhere keeping his football team in check. But hearing the music, however faintly, from a street away was not a good sign.

"Kelly, Kelly, Kelly," Jacinta clucked. "Okay, I hate being *that* girl opening up the real world for you. But . . ." She shook her head. "It's a party. Probably no supervision. I guarantee somebody up in there bumping naked."

Kelly tried not to, but her eyes popped in surprise involuntarily. The thought of a teacher letting students have sex in his home just didn't compute. She felt more than innocent; she felt flat-out dumb, because the thought had never crossed her mind.

"Dag, thanks, Cinny," Mina muttered. She picked up the pace, racing toward the music, which grew louder with every step.

"Mina, it doesn't mean Craig is doing anything but having a good time," Lizzie said. She nudged Jacinta as they raced to match Mina's pace. "Right, Cinny?"

"Mi, I didn't mean Craig," Jacinta said. "I was just saying . . . you know, the team probably in there getting a little buck wild . . ." She added quickly, "The ones *without* girlfriends."

Jacinta made an "I'm sorry" face to Lizzie as they jogged behind Mina down Coach Banner's driveway. Lizzie bit at her lip. Her stomach was a big knot, even more than it had been back at the house. The anxiety on Mina's face, and the fact that they were nearing a dead sprint toward the loud music, added up to trouble. She wasn't sure why. It just felt wrong.

About thirty people were outside in the yard. Some stood in small circles talking, large red plastic cups in their hands. Lizzie wanted to believe they were all drinking Coke or Sprite, but the pinch in her stomach as her gut clinched more told her otherwise. A group nearest the street were huddled smoking cigarettes in the cold, and a few couples were cuddled up near the shadows of the side yard making their own heat. It could have been worse. It could have definitely been worse. Lizzie had been expecting a serious *Old School,* Will Ferrell, let's-go-streaking raunchy romp. This wasn't it.

But still . . .

"Mina," Lizzie called out. "Wait for us."

Mina stopped just short of the door and let the girls catch up.

Why did Jacinta have to say something about Craig nasty dancing with some chick, searing the image in Mina's mind? She had to find him, had to see for herself he was just here kicking it cool with his boys.

Out of breath, Lizzie whispered, "Okay, so we find Craig and then we're out, right?"

Mina smiled weakly, then went to turn the door handle. "Right. In and out."

Lizzie grabbed her by the shoulder, stopping her before she could go in. "Mina, seriously. I'm not convinced. Are you going to see Craig and want to stay?"

Mina shook her head no, already stepping into the foyer, the girls close behind her. They peered through the darkness, letting their eyes adjust.

Kelly resisted the urge to cover her ears. Now she knew exactly why they had been able to hear the music a street away.

The calm, quiet group outdoors must have been taking a break, needing an escape from the hot, stuffy, chaotic scene inside. To the right of the foyer was the club, pitch-black except for a strobe light set on "annoy the hell out of everyone" with its ultrafast blinking and a small table lamp set on the DJ's table. In front of the DJ's table, which was set up against the back wall, was an empty spot no more than two feet wide and across as everyone obeyed the "no bumping the DJ table" rule. The rest of the room was packed with writhing, shaking bodies so close they looked as if they were attempting a mad science experiment to become one.

"There is no way we're finding him in here," Jacinta screamed in Mina's ear. She took baby steps, creeping along the hallway behind Mina, taking in the sights. "I didn't think it was gonna be packed like this."

"Me either," Mina hollered back, searching the dance floor for Craig and feeling instant relief that she hadn't found him there so far. She jumped, startled, when Lizzie tapped her shoulder and pointed straight ahead.

"There's JZ," Lizzie yelled. She took Mina's head in her hands and moved it in the direction she was pointing.

The girls walked to the back of the house and ended up in a large kitchen that led to a concrete patio, running over with people, most of them coupled off. One lone lightbulb lit the patio. Most of the bodies fell outside of its range.

JZ sat on a counter near the door leading outside. He slid off the counter, arms open wide for a hug.

"'Sup, ladies," he shouted, a lopsided grin on his face.

"What's up, Jay?" Mina asked, cautiously, squinting up at him.

What was up with him wanting to hug anybody?

JZ pulled them all into an awkward, sloppy embrace. "Ay, my girls here, y'all," he yelled to the room. But no one answered him. Only a few bothered to look his way. "Y'all my girls, right?"

Mina pulled away and looked into JZ's face more closely. His eyes were red rimmed as if he'd been up all night. "Jay, are you drunk?"

He laughed. "Man, naw, I'm . . ."

"Drunk." Lizzie nodded.

"You seen Craig?" Jacinta asked, looking around the kitchen. People were sitting on countertops and at the kitchen bar. Two guys and three girls played Texas Hold 'Em at the kitchen table. The girls had on bras and miniskirts; the guys were fully clothed.

Lizzie went to open the patio door, and JZ leaned up against it. He wagged his finger in her face. "Un-ah, what's the password?"

Lizzie looked over at Mina as if she'd know, then shrugged. "What password?"

"Since I'm gon' be a rookie on varsity next year, they making me work. Ain't that a bitch?" JZ said, arms swinging wildly as he explained. He suddenly kicked his heels, then saluted them. "Official guardian of Fort Knock'em Boots, reporting for duty. So I need a password. Y'all my girls and all, but this my job." He looked beyond the kitchen, over their heads, then turned to look out the French door before leaning in so they could all hear. "Alright, bet, if you'n know it, since Liz my girl and all . . ." He looked to one side of the room, then the other, then waved Lizzie in closer. He did one of those whispers where he thought he was whispering but was still talking as loud as before. "I'll let you out there for one kiss." He pursed his lips. "Come on, Liz-O, give me some."

Mina pushed his pursed-lip face away. "Jay, you're acting like a straight-up fool."

"Naw, okay . . ." He put his arm around Mina. "Mina, you can have one, too. But I don't want your boy getting mad and shit," he said, looking around the room again.

"Where is Craig, anyway?" Mina asked.

"Craig? Oh, naw, I meant Brian," JZ said.

"Man, he is drunk," Jacinta snickered.

"Alright, I ain't gon' be too many drunks up in here," he fussed. He stood up straight, stumbled, then steadied himself by holding the counter. "I been having a good time. I'm not drunk, just flowing."

"Yeah, well, that flow gon' have you feeling all messed up to-morrow," Mina said, trying to peer around him to the patio, but JZ's frame took up most of the French door, and it was too dark to see much from inside the house.

"Jay, I'm surprised at you, drinking during basketball season," Lizzie lectured, wrinkling her nose at him.

"For real, y'all came here to give a brother a lecture?" He frowned.

"No, just so Mina could tell Craig she not coming," Jacinta said.

"But she here." JZ's frowned deepened.

"That I'm not staying." Mina sucked her teeth.

"Lizzie, give him a kiss so we can get out there," Jacinta ordered.

Lizzie's eyes grew two times bigger. She ducked as JZ moved in to give her a kiss and fussed at Jacinta. "Cinny, don't encourage him."

Jacinta laughed. "I'm saying we wasting time messing with his drunk ass."

"Not drunk," JZ sang. "Ay, there he go. There go your man, Mina."

The girls all turned at once, to see Brian walking their way.

Mina whispered loudly, "That is not my man."

Her heart did a quick step as Brian stopped near their huddle.

"What's up, y'all?" Brian said.

"Are you drunk, too?" Jacinta asked, rolling her eyes.

Brian grinned. "Naw, I ain't drunk."

"Good. Can you get JZ away from the door, then?" Jacinta asked, exasperated.

Too scared to say anything, Mina only nodded in agreement.

She was tired of playing around with JZ, too. She'd seen him sneak a beer before. But Lizzie was right; normally JZ was a straight arrow during any sport season. Still, him being drunk wasn't the problem tonight. It was annoying, and he was ten times sillier than normal, but she was too distracted to be bothered by all of that. She just wanted to find Craig and go. For a second the thought "My mother was right" crossed her mind, and she kicked it out swiftly, refusing to go there.

"Why you let your boy get like this?" Jacinta asked Brian, hands on her hips.

Brian put his hands up as if to ward off a lecture. "I'm not his mother." He gave JZ a pound. "You alright, dog?"

JZ nodded. "Oh, damn, this my jam." He pulled Lizzie's arm. "Dance with me, girl."

"Well, we've gone beyond in and out," Kelly said, watching Lizzie stumble over her feet, trying to keep up as JZ dragged her into the front room.

Brian shook his head, chuckling. "I'm driving. So he cool."

With the sentry gone to get his groove on, Mina opened the French door leading outside. Brian took her hand in his and pulled her back inside.

Forgetting that she'd offended him last night, she scowled. "What are you doing?"

She frowned down at his hand.

He let go quickly and threw up the "my bad" hands again. "Just . . . before you go out there. Can I talk to you for a second?"

Now what?

Once JZ was gone from the door, her concern about Brian's previous silent treatment had waned quickly. She had no idea why she thought Craig was on the patio. Hopefully he wasn't since that was obviously the make-out point. Still, she had to make sure.

"We'll go look for him for you," Jacinta assured her. "Come on, Kell."

Brian motioned for Mina to follow him. He entered a door off the kitchen, and Mina found herself in a laundry room. It was dark and surprisingly quiet. Her eyes automatically squeezed shut when Brian clicked on the light. She blinked them rapidly until they adjusted to the brightness.

"What's up?" she asked, arms folded, leaning against the washer.

"Umph, that's right, Toughie all about the business," Brian teased.

Mina didn't crack a smile. She was glad Brian wasn't mad at her. But that had quickly become second on her list of things she wanted tonight.

Any other time she would have probably been happy to be in the mix of this party. Glad to be invited to see all her classmates getting dumb. But at that very second, all she really wanted was to find Craig and be out. If she messed up and got caught, then Raheem's party would be off-limits, and she'd never get her Craig time.

Brian leaned up against the door. "Why you dog me out like that last night?"

"I didn't mean to be so . . . nasty," Mina admitted. "My bad."

"I'm saying, okay, I thought we had a little vibe going." A tiny grin stayed hidden on Brian's face. But his eyes, as always, were smiling.

Mina was surprised at how serious he was. Her urgency to find

Craig took a dip and was replaced by uncertainty. Why was Brian saying this? Why did he care? She had Craig and he had Kelis. She could live with becoming a good friend of Brian's as long as he never asked her to double date with him and Kelis. That she couldn't live with.

"We're cool," she answered finally.

He smiled. "So I could be your type, then?"

"Hello, I have a boyfriend and you have a . . ." Mina shrugged. "Whatever Kelis is to you."

"Not my girlfriend," he said tightly, as if he was tired of explaining. "Look, I'm just trying give you a heads-up."

"A heads-up about what?" Mina scowled, growing antsy again. She didn't feel like playing a riddle game.

"Kelis been all up on Craig for the last hour," Brian said.

Mina's head reared back as if it had been pushed.

Kelis and Craig?

Then it all came to her at once, like being hit over the head with a hammer. She was being played.

All the flirty exchanges with Brian and his constant "I won't tell if you won'ts" all made sense now. She'd almost let his flirting lure her in. How dumb was she thinking Brian really liked her, when it was so obvious, now, that she was just the game piece.

If she had actually been dumb enough to choose Brian over Craig . . .

She could see it now, Brian bragging about how he'd played her and Craig against each other as he moved on to the next chick.

No wonder he was always teasing her about her "boyfriend." Every time she flirted back was another point for Brian.

Like how every time she rode in the car with him (eight times so far) or spent any time with Brian (not counting rides to school, three times) she had one more thing Kelis didn't.

Score so far, Mina eleven, Kelis two.

She chuckled and shook her head. Guess they were playing each other.

"You hear me?" Brian asked, staring at her as if she was crazy.

"Yeah, I heard you," Mina said, her face blank. Maybe she'd played along at first, but now Brian was going to play without her.

"And you don't care?" His right eyebrow arched high.

"I said I heard you; it doesn't mean I believe you," Mina said. "Ever since I told you Craig was my boyfriend, it's like you've been working to get me on your team."

Brian sucked his teeth. "Word?" He folded his hands together and took a deep, exaggerated bow at the waist. "Come on, school me on my master plan, oh, wise one."

"Whatever, Brian. You always saying you won't tell Craig if I don't, like we were in on something together." Her voice went up a notch in its anger. "I guess I didn't fall for you fast enough, so now you dogging Craig out, trying to turn me against him."

"I'm the mufuggin' man, then, because somehow my magical powers also hooked your boyfriend up with another chick, too." He applauded and took a stage bow.

Mina rolled her eyes. "Well, guess what, if you don't mind your girl getting her groove on with Craig—if they even are—why should I?"

She felt amazingly calm, even more so when Brian shook his head and opened the door, then stepped back so she could walk out first.

"Alright, Toughie, I was trying help *you* out," he said, then added before she was out of earshot, "And I told you she *not* my girl."

He watched her walk outside to the patio, head high and self-assured, knowing the only way she was going to walk out of there the same way was if she was one Grade A actress. Counting down in his head, he waited for it . . . five, four, three, two, one . . .

"Fight! Fight!" echoed from the patio into the house.

Love Sux

"It's time to be a big girl now."
—Fergie, "Big Girls Don't Cry"

If Mina knew half as much as she thought she did, she wouldn't be sitting on Kelly's bathroom floor hugging the toilet, waiting for the next lurch of her stomach. If she was as good at reading the "signs" as she believed she was, she would have known Brian had been real with her all along. If she really knew all the rules of engagement, she'd be schooling her girlfriends on how to walk out on top, even after you've just been played, and how to blow off what the grapevine was bound to swear happened tonight. But she didn't.

She rested her head against the cool toilet, not once concerned with how gross having her face near a toilet was. Jacinta, Lizzie and Kelly were nearby somewhere, whispering in the semidark and ready to hold her head the next time the thought of seeing Kelis with her tongue down Craig's throat . . .

There it was.

She quickly moved her head over the bowl and heaved, letting the last of her now-empty stomach come to rest in the toilet.

"Mina, it's okay."

That was Lizzie.

"Oh, my God, if you want, I will so stomp that bitch on Monday, girl."

Cinny . . . of course.

"Mina, do you want another cold washcloth?"

Kelly.

Lizzie. Jacinta. Kelly.

As bad as she felt, having them there saying all the right things soothed her. They understood when she didn't answer any of them, just moved back across the room and sat on the floor in front of the big tub, waiting for her to get herself together.

Mina flushed, then sat back on the floor against the toilet. She rested her head on it and closed her eyes, trying to piece it all together.

What the hell had happened?

All she remembered was Brian, weird smirk as he tried convincing her it wasn't all good and that Craig and Kelis were . . . then going outside where Jacinta and Kelly nearly bulldozed her trying to get her to go back into the house because Craig and Kelis were . . . She recalled Jacinta and Kelly babbling, talking at the same time. She'd only caught a few words: "He's not out here, Mi." "Hey, let's look back on the dance floor." But Mina had seen him, sitting on the far right of the patio. She was sure it was him. His back was to her, and there were shadows from the one lightbulb, so she couldn't say one hundred percent. But she'd recognize that cute, olive-shaped head anywhere. It was him. Except . . . no, maybe it wasn't him because there was a girl in his lap. Jacinta and Kelly were right; he wasn't out here. She'd turned to go back inside when the girl on Olive-head's lap laughed. The laugh was loud and wrong. Even with the thumping music, Mina could hear it. She knew that laugh. She stopped, couldn't move. She watched as the girl whispered something in the guy's ear and got up. The guy pulled her back down onto his lap, and they made out for a full twenty seconds. Then he let the girl pull him up from the chair, and they headed Mina's way . . .

It was a serious blur from there.

Tiny flashes of action popped into Mina's head, and she tried to put them in order.

Craig looking dumbfounded.

Kelis giggling, "Hey, girl," as if it were the most natural thing on earth for her to be holding the hand of Mina's boyfriend.

At some point, she'd heard JZ's voice say, "Aw, man, that's foul."

Somehow Lizzie was standing next to her, holding Mina's hand, tugging . . .

Then Jacinta had slapped Kelis. That Mina remembered because that was when somebody had shouted, "Fight. Fight." And everyone outside had scrambled around them, waiting for more.

But there wasn't any more. Just that one slap and the girls pulling Mina behind them as they left. She didn't remember the walk home. Hardly remembered Mrs. Lopez asking what was wrong.

Did remember wondering, What was wrong with who?

Until . . .

"She's crying," another woman, chic in a pair of Baby Phat jeans and high-heel boots, had said. "Why is she crying?"

It wasn't until Kelly called her Mom, that Mina realized who she was. She'd met Kelly's mother for only the briefest second earlier that night. Kelly had made it clear with the quickie intro, "Guys, this is my mom, Mrs. Narcone. Mami, this is Mina, Jacinta and Lizzie," that warm and fuzzy wasn't how she and her mom rolled.

The girls had whisked her up the stairs, surrounding her like worker ants trying to get their queen back to the nest, as Kelly made up some story about Mina's boyfriend breaking up with her over the phone while they had been at the teen night.

Mina remembered that because she remembered thinking, *Man, Kelly is getting scary good at this lying thing.*

They had been in Kelly's room only seconds when Mina felt the first nauseating pull that signaled any and everything she'd had to eat that day was about to be sacrificed to the porcelain god.

Feeling as if someone was watching her now, Mina opened her eyes. Kelly hovered over her, staring into her face.

"Sorry," Kelly whispered. "I didn't know if you were sleeping."

Mina shook her head.

Kelly sat beside her. Then Jacinta and Lizzie moved in. They sat clustered near the toilet, quiet, no one sure what to say.

Finally, Lizzie said, "You know, he was drunk, Mina. Maybe he . . ." She shrugged. "Didn't realize . . ."

"That his tongue was tangled in Kelis's?" Jacinta asked, dripping sarcasm by the liter.

"No, I just meant sometimes people do stupid stuff when they drink," Lizzie said lamely. She wanted to pull best friend rank, remind Jacinta that she'd been the one who'd had to endure Mina's ubercrush on Craig for the last year. She was the one who'd sat in the 'Ria over the summer and listened to Mina fantasize about being Mrs. Craig Simpson, Girlfriend Extraordinaire. Mina had the hots for this guy in a major way. And he'd done something majorly stupid tonight. But if Mina wanted to forgive him . . . well, Lizzie didn't agree but would understand. She didn't want Mina feeling any pressure to end the brief relationship just because the four of them were now the founding members of the I Hate Craig Simpson club. At least for this very second, they were. Tomorrow? Who knew. She forced herself to speak up. "Mina, what Craig did tonight sucked—"

"Big-time," Kelly chimed in.

Lizzie made a face, and Kelly took the hint to back off. "I just want you to know that if after all this, by Monday, you want to hear him out and give him another chance, I'm with you."

Jacinta frowned. "What? Why would she give him . . ."

Lizzie sighed heavily. She wasn't entirely comfortable going toe-to-toe with Jacinta. But if they were all going to be real friends, arguments were part of the package. She was going to have to speak her mind, no matter how intimidating Jacinta's tone could be (and it was very).

"Cinny, Mina's had a crush on Craig forever," Lizzie explained.

"And there are other cute dudes at Del Rio High besides him,"

Jacinta countered. She lowered her voice, as if talking to a baby. "Mina, I know you digging him. But don't be dumb for him. Drunk or not, he was wrong."

"You guys," Kelly whispered forcefully, silencing them. "Let's just . . . you know, be here for Mina."

The uncertain tension crept back in.

Mina lifted her head and stared straight ahead. She inhaled, then exhaled deeply. Inhaled, exhaled. The images tumbled in her mind, confusing her. Which things happened and which things had she imagined?

Craig dancing with Kelis to Ciara's "Oh". Real?

She honestly couldn't keep it straight.

"Let me ask you guys something," she said, seeing their faces around her, outlined in the dark.

No one answered. They just scooted in and waited for her to continue. After a few seconds she did. "I really did see Craig pull Kelis back onto his lap and then . . . french her. Right? I mean, I didn't make that up, right?"

She looked first at Lizzie, then Jacinta, then Kelly. Even in the darkened room she could see their faces were blank. No one nodded in confirmation or shook her head in denial. No one made a sound or moved a muscle, and Mina knew. She drew her legs to her chest and cried into her lap, shaking with silent tears.

Life Goes On...at the Mall

"Don't wanna think about it/Don't wanna talk about it."
—Justin Timberlake, "What Goes Around . . .
Comes Around"

It didn't seem right for life to go on after such a nasty scrape with reality. But it did. As planned, the girls went to the mall Sunday afternoon. They tried their best to avoid talking about what everybody really wanted to talk about, even though once a topic was off-limits, it was deliciously tempting to utter. They spent the first half of the day figuring out how to carry on a conversation without certain words: party, Craig, cheerleading, Ciara, dancing or kiss. Because anytime they did, Mina sank into a deeper funk.

But Kelly knew what would cheer her up. As they sat in the food court, sharing a bucket of fries, she teased out her ace card. "Oh, I forgot to tell you guys, my mom got me tickets to the Jingle Jam." There was a huge suck in of air as the girls gasped collectively. Kelly finished quickly. "And she arranged a private meet and greet for me, and I can bring anyone I want."

"Meet and greet who?" Jacinta asked, munching on a fry.

Kelly kept her eye on Mina. "Chris Brown." She was pleased when Mina not only perked up, but screamed, causing a nearby mother with an infant in her arms to jump out of her seat.

"OH, my GAWD!!!! Aaaagggghhhhhhhh!!!!" Mina yelled. "Oh, my God, tell me you are not kidding, Kelly. Are you serious?"

Kelly shook her head, grinning, glad to be the reason Mina, at least momentarily, had forgotten all about last night. Thank God a Chris Brown song hadn't been playing when she'd seen Craig. Jingle Jam would have definitely been a bummer.

"Kelly, for real?" Jacinta said. "You know everybody gon' be hating on us after this, right?"

"Let 'em hate," Mina said, already wondering what she'd wear. What did you wear to meet your future husband?

"Yup, Chris is coming by the studio when he's in town for the Jingle Jam, and my mom hooked up a little get-together." Kelly beamed. It was her mother's way of waving the truce flag. Kelly would accept it, but she wasn't talking total forgiveness just yet. There was still the little matter of that whole "your father is dead" lie that she planned to hold over Rebecca's head. At least for now.

Mina's hand fluttered over her chest dramatically. "Kelly! Don't play. For real?" She shook Kelly's shoulders. "Don't play. You know I love me some Chris."

Lizzie nodded. "Me, too. *Love* him."

"No joke. All of you guys are invited. And the guys, too . . . if they care about that sort of thing," Kelly said. She dipped a fry into ketchup and took a dainty bite off the tip.

"And don't y'all get mad when Chris be trying to get with me, alright," Mina said, pretending to elbow Jacinta and Lizzie back.

Jacinta snorted. "Yeah, right. You mean with me."

"Oh, like he wouldn't like me?" Lizzie said.

"Girls, girls, please," Kelly said, holding up her hands for silence. "Since he's coming to my house, I get Chris."

"Aw, dag, she straight pulled rank on us," Jacinta laughed. "I thought you were gonna say something serious."

"I did. He's mine," Kelly said, setting off a new round of laughter.

"*Love* Chris Brown. Kelly, you're so lucky," Lizzie said wistfully. There was dead silence.

Lizzie looked around at the girls. "What did I say?"

"Kelly's just sensitive about people saying she's lucky about getting hooked up with stuff like this," Mina said. She didn't expect Lizzie to know. It was another thing she and Cinny had learned during the soc project.

Kelly shook her head. "It's not really that. But I hate when people say I'm lucky when my life's just as messed up as anyone else's. You know?" She knew they didn't—she could see it on their faces. "Just because I get to meet Chris Brown, it's not like my life is perfect."

"Sorry," Lizzie said, uncertain what else to say. She stuffed a few fries in her mouth and decided to keep mum.

"Messed up?" Jacinta frowned. "I don't know about all that. Yeah, you just got a moms who not around. So do I." Jacinta shrugged. "But you live in a phat crib, got a grandmoms who love you and your family got money coming out the pie hole."

Mina nudged Jacinta. Jacinta didn't always hear how abrasive she came off. Mina didn't mind reminding her. She didn't want an argument to break out.

"What? I'm just saying," Jacinta said.

"Okay, how's this for messed up?" Kelly paused dramatically, then said, "I just found out my real father isn't dead but in jail. He was a drug dealer from Del Rio Crossing who my mom basically shacked up with."

"Dang . . . okay, yeah that's messed up," Jacinta agreed.

There was a low grade buzz as the girls cautiously pressed Kelly for more information. Kelly brought them up-to-date. She left out her worries about how she and Angel fit into the whole picture. She didn't have to. Lizzie brought it up for her.

Lizzie raised her hand as if she were in class.

"Yes, Lizzie," Kelly played along.

"Am I the only one who sees the, um . . . irony in this? You know, the whole Angel thing." Lizzie nervously glanced around the table to see if anyone else agreed. "Or should I just shut up now?"

She was relieved when Mina wrapped her arms around her and laid her head on Lizzie's shoulder.

"You're good," Mina said, glad to be talking about anything else but last night. "But that is a mad weird coincidence, Kell. Worse than my parents laying on the whole trust thing yesterday morning like they knew I was going to do wrong."

There was an awkward silence as everyone waited for Mina to cry or get sad at any mention of Saturday. They'd worked hard to act like Saturday didn't exist. But Mina sat up and sipped on her soda, seemingly okay.

"Well, it's official. Kelly is a hood rat, y'all," Jacinta teased.

Kelly rolled her eyes. "See, that would be funny if . . ." She paused, pretended to think and then declared, "No, it's not funny."

"I'm just playing, girl," Jacinta said. She gave Kelly a shoulder push.

"Everything happens for a reason, though," Mina said. "Maybe you met Angel to help him get on the right track before it leads to him getting busted."

"Not a bad point," Lizzie said. "Except . . ." She hesitated. She'd never given Jacinta or Kelly advice, and she was afraid to now. It felt odd to give her two cents on a serious matter; like it wasn't her place. She went on, apologetically. "Look, I'm not trying to offend you or Cinny, since Angel's her friend . . . but Angel knows what he's doing. It's not your job to save him from himself, Kelly."

"Who said Angel needed saving?" Jacinta sniffed.

Lizzie's body went rigid. She'd seen that look on Jacinta's face twice before. Last night and the time Lizzie had said Raheem looked mean. But she pushed herself, again, to speak her mind. "Cinny, I didn't mean he needed saving," Lizzie said cautiously. "But what he does is wrong. And it's not like he can do it forever, either. What happens when he's eighteen and gets caught and ends up like Kelly's real dad?"

"All I'm saying is, not everybody that does something bad is a bad person . . . my opinion," Jacinta said, the edge in her voice mellowed. "And even though this is more y'all butterfly and starfish viewpoint than mine, why *can't* it be that Kelly might be the person that helps Angel get out of the game?"

"She could be. But I wouldn't want that pressure," Lizzie said, noticing the big worry crease in Kelly's forehead. "I don't think it's Kelly's place to do that."

Worried she'd already said too much, Lizzie took it down a notch. "Look, that's just me. I don't have anything against you for liking him, Kell."

"So, like I'm the last person who should be giving dating advice right now," Mina said. She smiled as the girls chuckled nervously. "But, to me, why not make all the mistakes now? You know, while we have parents and friends to bail us out." She shrugged and gnawed on her straw as she said, "I think I'm pulling my weight in that department." This time they all laughed openly. "I think seeing Angel or not is up to Kelly." Mina reached across the table and gave Kelly a girly pound. "And if it goes bad, you know we got your back."

Kelly smiled back gratefully.

"Alright, enough of this Destiny's Child 'I'm your girl, you're my girl' stuff," Jacinta said, standing up and stretching. "Let's walk the mall."

"Well, Angel meets my grandmother later tonight," Kelly announced as they walked. "So either everything is about to hit the fan or . . ." She thought about the or. Or she and Angel were about to pull off the best acting job this side of the Academy Awards.

"Or your grandmother will say you can see him?" Lizzie prompted.

"I guess," Kelly admitted. "I like Angel, but if he doesn't pass the Mae Bell Lopez test, I'm only fooling myself thinking I can see him." She chuckled. "And I'm not bold enough to keep sneaking around with him. I'm a basket case as it is."

Mina smiled wryly at the sneak reference. Not like she was very good at it herself.

"Ay, Liz, there's Todd." Jacinta pointed behind them across the aisle at the Electronic Boutique.

"Oh, let's go speak, guys," Lizzie said, turning that way. She took a few steps, then stopped when she realized no one was behind her. "What's wrong?"

"Liz, will you think I'm the world's worst best friend if I said I just can't take seeing a happy couple right now?" Mina said. She hung her head a little, feeling bad for being so shallow. But seeing Liz and Todd happy, right now, was just too much.

"Mi, we're not a couple," Liz said. "It's just Todd."

"I know but . . ."

"I'll roll with you," Jacinta said. "Come on."

"I'm sorry," Mina said.

Lizzie gave her a quick hug. "It's okay. I'll tell him you said hey." Mina mustered a smile and watched them walk off.

She and Kelly walked on for a while until Kelly stopped to look at a music box in a window. Just as she did, Angel tipped up beside her and signaled to Mina to keep quiet.

"That's so cute," Kelly said, raising back up. "I like—" She jumped as she backed into Angel, who grabbed her in a hug.

He whispered in her ear, "What's up, Ma?"

Kelly gasped. "Oh, my God, you scared me."

Angel kissed her on the ear. "Now, who else would be all up on you like that?"

Raheem walked over. "Ay, y'all. Where's Cinny?"

"Back there with Lizzie." Mina gestured to the food court far behind them.

Great. She couldn't bear to see Lizzie speak to Todd, and now Raheem and Angel were here. She was now officially in couples hell. This was so not her weekend.

Raheem scowled. "Lizzie? Y'all white friend?"

The girls nodded.

Raheem stared toward the food court and reluctantly started walking along with the group in the opposite direction.

"So, y'all coming to our jam?" Angel asked, putting his arm around Kelly's waist.

"Yeah," Mina said, trying to forget that she'd be going solo now. Well, unless Craig had a really, really . . . really good explanation for last night. Her heart jumped at the prospect of forgiving him.

"If everything goes well tonight, I will," Kelly reminded him.

"Stop worrying, Kelly. I'm gon' be on my best behavior," Angel promised, giving her side an assuring squeeze.

"You know Cinny invited Brian, Michael and JZ, right?" Mina asked.

"Yeah, that's cool," Raheem said, turning to look behind him for the fifth time. "So, Cinny's back that way, right?"

Mina nodded. "I'm sure they're not too far behind us. Lizzie wanted to speak to T. You know him, right?"

"White boy, come play ball over The Cove with your boy, JZ?" Raheem confirmed.

"Ohhh, White Boy," Angel said. "Yeah, we know dude."

"Why she back there with them?" Raheem asked, mystified. He kept staring behind him as if expecting Jacinta to appear any second. Without waiting for an answer, he said, "I'll catch up with you, Angel. I'm gon' go see if I can find her."

Mina looked after him. "Is he alright?"

Angel chuckled. "Yeah. Just pressed."

They arrived at the center court, a large open area in the shape of a circle used for the mall's special events. The court was overrun with people. Mothers carefully watched their little ones run around the center of the circle, and teenagers lounged on the benches, some watching the little kids in amusement, others ignoring the pealing laughter of the youngsters altogether.

Angel took a seat on a top step and pulled Kelly down beside him. They sat close, with him whispering in her ear. Feeling the tears building, Mina excused herself. "I'm gonna run into Macy's real quick, Kell. I'll be back," she said, taking long strides away from Kelly and Angel's affection. Just one Friday ago she'd been cuddled up with Craig like that in front of the 'Ria and now . . . She got to the Macy's bathroom as soon as the first tear ran.

"Then, What Does It Matter?"

"Now I'm all confused 'cause for you I have
deeper feelings."
—Musiq, "Half Crazy"

As Kelly sat with Angel, she noticed how good he was at making her feel like they were the only people in the room. It was the way he spoke low so she had to concentrate on his voice to hear; how he always touched some part of her body, a hand, leg or put his arm around her. Now, they sat on the top step in the center court without one inch of space between them. Angel had Kelly's hand in his and was stroking it.

He had her wrapped in his world. The screaming kids running themselves silly in a circle and the buzz of mall traffic were growing louder, but seemed off in the distance to Kelly. All she saw was Angel's eyes on her. All she felt was Angel's hands on hers. All she heard was a voice inside screaming, *We should cancel tonight.*

Because tonight, Angel was going to meet Grand—not because Kelly wanted, but because Grand insisted, and it was the only way she'd give Kelly permission to go to Raheem and Angel's party.

"Of course I expect to meet your new *friend,* Kellita," Grand had said sternly when Kelly's eyes popped in surprise Friday night at the request.

Grand and Kelly's mom had been sitting in Grand's room, obviously talking about what they should "do" about Kelly's new friend.

But when Kelly arrived (at their request) they made it seem as if it were a simple temperature check. You know? *So how ya feeling now that you know your father isn't dead and was a drug dealer to boot?*

Great, thank you!

When they'd found out Kelly wasn't going to be jumping out of any windows over the "information," as Grand called it, Grand had eased in the request (demand) to meet Angel.

Kelly's mom, a woman who never sat still, instinctively tucked at her hair, which was swept into a tight chignon, and chirped, "Oh, I'd love to meet him, too, Kell."

But Kelly was fast on her feet this time, making sure they weren't going to drop any new bombs on her. No long lost siblings out there, right? She wasn't adopted, right? Couldn't be, she and Rebecca looked like twins—except one was thirty-six and one was fifteen.

With no more secrets to discover, Kelly didn't have to think long to answer the question, *Do I want my mom there to meet Angel?*

Nope, no and no thanks.

She didn't need her mom being all smiley-faced flittery around Angel, asking him enough questions to put a small police investigation to shame: "So where in New York did you live?" "How old were you when your parents passed?" "Oh, it must be tough being raised by your uncle. What's his name by the way?" Or worse, what if her mom detected that Angel was a hustler as soon as he swaggered through the door?

It made no sense, but Kelly was nearly convinced her mom had some sort of internal radar. Maybe Grand wouldn't notice. But Rebecca would. Kelly was certain.

No worries now. Rebecca was heading back to L.A. as Kelly sat there in center court, her hand warm and tingly in Angel's. And Kelly took a little satisfaction in that.

With one simple question, "So, Mami, when do you fly back?"

Kelly had ensured Rebecca wouldn't be around (like her not being there would be new).

When her mom said Sunday morning, Kelly had quickly announced, "I'm going to ask Angel if he can stop by Sunday evening."

Kelly knew it hurt her mom's feelings to be excluded. Her face had crumbled, and her hands had flown, birdlike, back up to her chignon, smoothing it out nervously. Kelly had pretended not to see her mom wince. It didn't escape her mom that she'd purposely proposed the meeting date only after asking when she'd be leaving.

Rebecca hadn't even tried to counter by suggesting Saturday.

Which Kelly was prepared for, anyway. The sleepover with the girls was her excuse if her mom had suggested that.

But Rebecca hadn't. And that was really the whole point of Kelly not wanting her there anyway. A real mother would have insisted that, of course, she meet her daughter's first boyfriend (even if Kelly never officially called Angel that around her mom and Grand). But, her mom hadn't.

Part of Kelly almost wanted her to, even though she had her counter answer ready.

But her mom hadn't.

She hadn't asked.

Typical.

Kelly was sure she was more than happy to run back to Phil and his plans for Marques Houston's tour. She was better at playing Phil's assistant than she was at playing Kelly's mother. So Kelly was only helping her out.

Now, ensured her mom would be nowhere near for the visit, Kelly fretted about what her grandmother would think about Angel.

What if that whole radar thing was genetic?

She looked at him in a pair of loose-fitting but not oversized jeans, black boots, a long-sleeved rugby and a black Dallas Cowboys knit cap he kept pulled almost to his eyes. Clean-cut prep he wasn't. But he also wasn't tatted down (well, Kelly had no idea if he had tattoos; she'd never seen his bare arms), didn't have on his grille today (and she'd remind him not to wear it tonight . . . duh!) or have on any blinding, tacky jewelry.

He looked *normal* enough. Still, she found herself saying softly, "Maybe we should cancel tonight."

"You said you couldn't come to the party unless I met your abuela, right?" Angel said.

Kelly nodded.

"If I gotta do the whole meet-the-Cosbys thing to get you back over to my crib, then that's what I gotta do." He chuckled.

"The Cosbys?" Kelly said, frowning in confusion.

He laughed again. Not mean, but as though everything Kelly said amused him. He knocked his leg against Kelly's softly. "I'm just saying, if I gotta get all formal and meet your fam so we can still kick it, it's cool."

"I know you said that you don't want to talk about—" she cleared her throat—"your involvement in the game . . ." She took one nervous look around the court as if a swarm of cops would come pouring in if she said it too loud. Her voice went even lower as she continued. "But, at some point . . . I mean, we need to talk about it."

"Why?" Angel stared at her, gripping her with his eyes.

"Because . . ." Kelly paused, unable to look away as she tried to think of an answer. *Because . . . what?* Because she was very much treading into repeating-the-sins-of-her-mother territory. Treading and starting to sink.

Was that good enough? she wondered.

But she didn't say that to Angel. To him she said, "Because, I don't see how I can separate you from the whole hustling thing."

"If Jacinta hadn't told you, would you even know about it, Kelly?"

Rosie flashed in her mind, and she wanted to be sarcastic. "Uhhh . . . yeah!"

But, being honest with herself, except for Rosie's strange presence—she was sure he was there in the mall somewhere lurking nearby—she couldn't say she'd know Angel was a drug dealer. She admitted as much with a shake of her head.

"So, then, what does it matter?" Angel challenged.

"Because I do know and it just does," Kelly said, a sense of urgency in her voice. She snorted. "At some point I'm going to stop being caught up in how cute you are."

Angel kissed her on the cheek. "No, you won't. And if you do, I have other tricks up my sleeve that will keep you sprung."

Angel interlaced his fingers with hers. "I tell you what, let's just get tonight over with before we start planning out my future."

Kelly stuttered. "I . . . I . . . wasn't trying to plan your future. I just . . ."

"Can't let it go?" Angel asked, smiling into her eyes. "Look, I'll be a good boy tonight. Your grandmoms will love me, and we'll keep kicking it, no worries style. You wit' it?"

Kelly nodded slowly. What other choice did she have now? She had to keep treading or risk drowning.

Change, Not So Good

"We try to take it slow/But we're still losin' control."
—Black Eyed Peas, "Shut Up"

"Alright, Lizzie, let's roll," Jacinta said, sounding like a mom ending her kid's play date.

"Aw, come on," Todd whined, adding to the whole mom/kid effect. "The game's almost over."

"No, you're killing me," Lizzie said, gladly giving up the controller to an anxious freckle-faced boy behind her. She and Todd had spent the last fifteen minutes playing NBA Live at the EB Games. If you could call Todd mercilessly beating Lizzie's team, playing. She had no idea how to play the game, was only pushing buttons. She and Mina never got involved with the sports stuff when JZ and Michael played. Mina liked driving games, and Lizzie liked anything that involved only moving the controller buttons left, right, up or down. But she had faked her way to ten points somehow, anyway.

Spotting Raheem walking toward the EB Games store, Jacinta gushed, "There goes my Boo."

Todd craned his neck around. "That's right, you're dating Raheem Patterson," he said, appropriately in awe of the man who had nearly single-handedly beat the Blue Devils at last week's game. "Dude is fire on the court."

Jacinta waved and called out to Raheem.

He strolled over. "What's up?"

"Hi, Raheem," Lizzie said.

He nodded a hello.

Jacinta said, "Raheem, this is Todd. Todd this—"

"I know T," Raheem said as he and Todd exchanged a soul shake, slapping hands and grasping fingers lightly at the end.

"What's up, man?" Todd asked.

"Nothin', son, it's your world," Raheem said.

"Naw, kid, it's yours. Good game last week," Todd said sincerely.

"Thanks. So you ain't on varsity?" Raheem asked.

Todd grinned, his cheeks crimson. "Not yet."

"Right. They could have used you out there last week," Raheem said.

Todd beamed at the compliment and ran his fingers through his hair in a nervous gesture.

There was an awkward silence as the talk of basketball, their only common bond, ran its course. Todd broke it first.

"So, Liz, since I beat up on you a little bit, I at least owe you a milkshake or something," he said, taking a hammy bow.

"I won't turn down a free shake," Lizzie said. "Cinny, just come get me before you head to find Mina and Kelly. See you, Raheem."

Raheem cracked a small, phony smile. He threw a head nod Todd's way as the two walked over to the food court.

Watching Lizzie and Todd be silly, nudging and shoving each other as they walked, Jacinta made fun of her friends with a motherly cluck. "These girls fall so easy." She hugged Raheem around the waist. "You been here long?"

He shrugged.

Jacinta looked past him in the direction he had originally come. "Where's Angel?"

"He with Kelly," Raheem snapped.

Jacinta chewed at the inside of her cheek. The tension between them was thick. Raheem was too quiet and wasn't hugging her back. *What have I done now?* she thought, more nervous than annoyed.

She took the plunge and asked, "What's wrong?"

"Nothing," he said, looking over her head into EB Games. He pretended to be engrossed in the demo of the NBA Live game, then glanced over at Lizzie and Todd. They were talking, laughing and enjoying each other. Raheem imagined Jacinta at ease with them, spending more time with them than she did him. His jealousy took over. He blurted, "So, now you playing matchmaker for the white girl?"

Jacinta pushed her lips out as she exhaled. She fought to keep her voice even as a tight ball of tension moved from her head to her chest.

Not here, not now. She didn't want to argue today.

She spoke through clenched teeth. "Raheem, the 'white girl' is my friend, and I just walked over here to speak to White Chocolate . . . I mean, Todd, 'cause Mina going through some drama and didn't want to roll with her."

His eyes widened. "Your *friend?*" he asked, his voice wet with disgust.

"Yes. My friend," Jacinta spat. "What's wrong with that?"

"You know what, Jacinta, I didn't come out here to waste my time running after you while you run behind . . ." He made a face as he searched his memory for the right name before giving up and rolling his eyes.

"Lizzie. Her name is Lizzie," Jacinta spat. She threw her hands up and dropped them hard at her sides, stinging her legs. "This is played out, seriously. Now every other time we're together we're going to argue about something?"

Raheem snickered. "I'm not arguing."

His well-acted serenity pissed Jacinta off even more. She ramped up the argument. "Yeah, alright. I'm missing exactly why it should bother you that I'm standing here talking with friends. Shoot, you know Todd better than I do probably."

Raheem chuckled, mean and bitter. "Your friends, huh? Ain't this something? Funny, 'cause a year ago you would have probably looked at somebody like . . . Lizzie and thought she was corny."

The truth in his words hurt her like a physical blow. Jacinta kept her game face on, but anger tore through her, making her eyes water and her lips tremble. Just because she was starting to open herself to new people, Raheem was upset with her. And it kept snowballing. First, he was upset that she might be growing away from him. Now, he just didn't want her to have a life or enjoy herself at all unless he said it was okay.

If she was still calling him, saying how miserable she was at Del Rio High—like she had nearly every night her first month there—it would be all good.

Raheem glared at her, waiting for her to respond. She matched his glare with a steely stare of her own, determined not to back down.

Her voice was forceful and determined when she finally spoke. "You right. A year ago I felt different about a lot of things . . . including us."

She left him standing there as she walked over to the food court.

Mr. Tender Meets Grand

"See brotha got this complex occupation."
—Erykah Badu, "Other Side of the Game"

Later that evening, Kelly stared into the pitch-black evening from the kitchen. *Hurry up,* she thought, trying to will Angel to appear. She'd told Angel to come over at 6:30 P.M. and it was 6:25 P.M. Her grandmother was a stickler for punctuality, and Angel would automatically have a strike against him if he was late.

She was nervous, terrified and seriously ready to call the whole thing off when Angel's black Honda Accord finally pulled into the large, circular driveway. Kelly eyed it carefully, trying to see it through her grandmother's eyes.

For the most part it was a simple car, nothing brand-new or overpriced. Kelly knew the irony of the whole thing was that if Angel were from Folger's Way, the car would be pricey. Half the kids from Folger's drove big SUVs or older (like one year older than the current model, not ten years older) model BMWs.

But Angel wasn't from Folger's. If he rolled up in an expensive ride, it would send sirens blaring in Grand's head. Reflecting on the soc class for a second, Kelly wondered how prejudiced it was to judge somebody by what type of car they drove. Until her gaze fell on the rims of the Honda, the flashiest part of the car. They definitely stood out and they sparkled. Even in the darkness Kelly could see them shining.

Kelly knew from Jacinta that each rim had cost Angel six hundred dollars, which meant he had spent twenty-four hundred for the entire car. What teenager could afford that, much less one from the projects?

God, they scream hustler, Kelly thought, spiraling into full panic again.

She took a deep breath and let it out noisily, trying to gain control of herself. At least Rosie wasn't with him. She nearly burst into a fit of giggles at the thought of Angel bursting into the house with his enforcer in tow.

It was funny in a just-crazy-enough-to-happen way.

She imagined introducing her prim, proper, tiny grandmother to the tall, menacing-looking Rosie.

"Grand, this is Angel and his bodyguard, Rosie."

She giggled nervously, close to losing her grip. She clenched her hands to calm the nervous tittering.

After one last look at the car, she assured herself it was fine. Her grandmother probably had no idea how much rims cost or even what rims were as far as a status symbol thing. Kelly certainly hadn't given it much thought until Jacinta and the other girls pointed them out.

She scolded herself for overreacting.

The doorbell rang, and seconds later Kelly heard Kevin say, "Hi. Yeah, she's right here."

Angel's head popped around the corner. He had changed clothes. Now he wore a Washington Bullets throwback jersey, jeans and a pair of Iversons. Kelly knew the jersey alone probably cost a few hundred dollars, not to mention the shoes. But, thankfully, he looked like any other boy off the street.

His pants weren't sagging (*thank God*). He didn't have on a hat (*so I don't have to remind him not to wear it in the house*) and no gaudy jewelry (*not sure I've ever seen him wear that anyway*).

Kelly knew she was obsessing and stereotyping, but she didn't care. The face-to-face with her grandmother had come way earlier than she intended. Not that she had ever intended to have Angel over, if she was being honest with herself.

"What's up, Kelly?" he asked, teeth gleaming white.

His soft voice and warm smile relaxed Kelly a little.

"Hey," she said shyly.

"Your rims are tight, man," Kevin said.

Kelly looked at Kevin open-mouthed. Even her little brother was more hip than she was.

"Thanks, son," Angel said, giving Kevin a pound. "My name's Angel."

"Kevin."

"I'll take you for a ride one day."

"Really? Cool," Kevin said.

"Kev, can you go tell Grand Angel is here, for me?" Kelly asked.

Kevin nodded. "Nice meeting you, man," he said, giving Angel a soul shake.

"Same here, kid." Angel watched Kevin walk away. "Little dude is cool."

"Cooler than I ever thought," Kelly admitted.

Angel leaned in quickly and kissed her on the lips. Kelly glanced nervously toward the stairs to see if Grand was coming. But Kevin was only to the top landing. She relaxed and returned the kiss with a small peck of her own.

Angel stepped back. "So, you nervous?"

"Very nervous!" Kelly blurted.

He smiled devilishly. "Don't even know what you got yourself into, do you?"

"I'm beginning to see," Kelly answered wearily.

She took Angel's hand and led him down the long hallway toward their family room. She knew Grand would prefer to sit in the more formal living room. But Kelly felt uncomfortable enough. Sitting on the proper, hard furniture in the living room would push her over the edge. She felt it in her bones. She could see herself now so tense and nervous she'd fall into an uncontrollable fit of laughter, and they'd have to haul her off to the mental ward.

So, definitely not the living room.

Kelly pointed to the middle of the sectional sofa and, in an un-characteristically bossy tone, directed. "You sit here."

She chose the end of the sofa nearest the stairs for herself, certain that her grandmother would choose the easy chair nearest her. From Kelly's seat, she would be able to look at both Angel and Grand directly.

Her grandmother's voice floated into the room. "Hello. Kelly, you know I prefer to entertain in the living room."

Kelly fought to keep her voice from trembling. "Oh, I know, Grand. But I thought we'd be more comfortable down here."

Mae Bell walked over to the sofa toward Angel. He stood up.

"Hi, Angel. I'm Mae Bell Lopez, Kelly's grandmother." She extended her hand, and Angel shook it firmly.

"Hello, Mrs. Lopez. It's nice to meet you," Angel said formally, in Spanish.

Mae Bell nodded approvingly. "You, too. It's always nice to meet Kelly's friends. Please, sit down."

Kelly relaxed a little. Hearing Angel speak in Spanish put her at ease because it reminded Kelly of her grandfather, made him feel nearby. *Papi, please help me through this*, she prayed silently.

Mae Bell sat in the easy chair, as Kelly knew she would, her feet crossed casually. The chair rocked slightly.

"Is Angel your given name?" she asked curiously.

Angel chuckled. "No, ma'am. It's a nickname that was given to me by my mother. My given name is Anthony."

A pang of shame went through Kelly as she realized she hadn't known that. All she had ever heard anyone call him was Angel, and it never occurred to her that it wasn't his real name. *Okay, that's not good,* she thought pensively.

"That's a nice name," Mae Bell said, then jumped right to business. "Kelly tells me that you're having a party next week."

"Yes, ma'am," Angel answered. "My friend Raheem and I are celebrating 'cau . . . because Sam—Well is having a good season so far."

Mae Bell nodded. "That's nice. Will your parents be there?"

"My parents died when I was six." Angel kept a respectful level of eye contact with Mrs. Lopez.

"I'm sorry to hear that," Mae Bell said, nodding. "Kelly and I lost her grandfather five years ago. I understand how painful it is to lose someone so close."

"Yes, ma'am. Kelly told me a lot about Mr. Lopez," Angel said.

Kelly grinned. She saw the light in her grandmother's eyes at that. She let herself breathe. Angel was pretty good at this being a good boy stuff.

Without a tremor or shake in his voice, Angel seemed oddly comfortable as he explained. "My uncle, Eduardo, raised me. But yes, ma'am, he'll be at the party. Also, Ja . . . " Kelly could see Angel mentally correcting himself before he spoke it. "Mr. Phillips will be next door."

"Yes, Jacinta's father?" Mae Bell asked.

"Yes, ma'am."

Mae Bell quizzed him. "Angel, you're aware that Kelly is fourteen, correct?"

"Yes, ma'am."

"How old are you?" she asked.

"Seventeen. I'll be eighteen this summer."

"So, you're graduating from high school this year? Do you have plans for college?" Mae Bell asked smoothly.

Kelly swallowed hard. She was helpless to jump in once the question was out there. Her body drooped as she dreaded to hear the answer. What did a young hustler do after graduation?

"I'm not sure about college. My uncle was hurt real bad three years ago and was out of work for a long time. I've always had to work to help out," Angel admitted. Mae Bell raised her eyebrows slightly.

Kelly's heart pounded. Work? Yikes. Why was Angel going there?

Angel continued. "He's back on his feet now. But I still feel like I owe him for raising me. And school would be expensive."

"Don't you think the best way to help your uncle is to pursue a higher education?" Mae Bell asked gently, ever the schoolteacher. "What better way to help than to put yourself on a solid career path?"

Kelly's head turned from Grand to Angel as they spoke, as if she were watching a tennis match.

Angel cleared his throat, for the first time on unsure ground. "Yes, ma'am. I mean, I hear you, but . . . my grades are not really scholarship worthy." He shrugged. "I've thought about community college. But, it's like . . . whatever my uncle can afford."

Mae Bell nodded respectfully.

Kelly exhaled loudly, causing both her grandmother and Angel to look over at her. She bowed her head slightly.

"What happened to your uncle?" Mae Bell added quickly, "If I'm not prying."

"He worked construction and was hurt on the job. He was out of work for two years, so I took on part-time jobs to help out."

Part-time jobs?

Kelly was torn between laughing out loud and screaming from the pressure of the truth building up in her head. But the conversation went on around her without incident.

"So that would have made you what . . . fourteen at the time?" Mae Bell asked. She clucked. "That's quite a burden for a fourteen-year-old."

"Yes, ma'am. But you know, everyone does what they have to sometimes."

Mae Bell sighed softly. "That's certainly true." She paused for a moment, lost in thought, then pushed herself out of the chair. "Well, I'll let you two visit. I just felt it was appropriate that I meet you before your party."

Angel jumped to his feet. "Yes, ma'am. It was nice to meet you, Mrs. Lopez."

Mae Bell gave Angel a warm hug as she said in Spanish, "It was nice meeting you, too. Don't be a stranger. Now that we've met, I expect to see you around now and then as long as you and Kelly are friends."

"Yes, ma'am."

Angel and Kelly watched Mae Bell disappear down the hall.

When she was gone, Kelly slumped down into her seat, exhausted by the short but intense meeting.

Angel laughed softly. "It wasn't that bad."

"Says you," Kelly shot back. She moved to sit closer to Angel on the sofa. "You know what's embarrassing?"

"What?" he asked.

"I didn't know your first name was Anthony."

He winked at her, bragging. "Too sprung by my good looks to care."

Kelly shook her head, wringing her hands. "You're joking, but what other excuse do I have for not knowing that? How can I seriously say you're my boyfriend and I don't even know your first name?"

"I told you, just ask and I'll tell you whatever you want to know," Angel said gently.

"Okay." She took a deep breath, then lowered her voice into an urgent whisper. "How come you never told me about your uncle getting hurt?"

"I don't know. I mean, is it important to you how I got in the game in the first place?" he asked, frowning into her eyes.

"Yes," Kelly whispered. "I mean, it explains it . . . kind of."

"When my uncle got hurt he was doing a side hustle. I was too young to work construction, so he set me up with his connect." He threw his hands up. "He just got back on his feet this year. So I'm still trying to hold things down."

"So then you can stop," Kelly said, eager hope in her voice. "You're obviously smart . . . go to college, get a job."

Angel shook his head. He took Kelly's hand in his and rubbed it absently with his thumb. He talked in that "you're so amusing" voice again. "Like I said, let's just get through tonight."

Kelly continued whispering. "Angel, I told you about my father. You don't want to end up like him."

"I won't—"

Kelly interrupted him, her whisper a near shriek. "Don't you think my father felt the same way?"

Angel kissed her cheek. "You just have to trust me for right now. Come on, walk me to the car," he said, getting up.

Why I Should Stay With Heem...

"Every time I try to leave, something keeps pulling
me back."
—Chingy ft. Tyrese, "Pullin' Me Back"

Jacinta was out of ideas on how to deal with the growing distance between her and Raheem. She looked at a blank piece of paper. Her last resort, a list of pros and cons for staying with Raheem. It felt very Mina-ish, and Jacinta would have laughed if the importance of how the list ended up was the least bit funny.

It wasn't. She dived into the pros first, smiling as she thought about why she loved Raheem. But when it came to the cons, she wrote each one furiously—the pen nearly ripping the paper. She was so hot with him for making a scene at the mall, she felt like screaming.

Every bone in her body said to break it off and tell Raheem it wasn't working anymore. Then, as soon as she was positive that was the answer, a cool streak of memory would rush through her, making her want to call Raheem and plead with him to help make things work.

She glanced over the list:

Why I should stay with Heem

Pros	Cons
I love him	He makes me feel bad for making new friends, trying new things, etc...
He's always protected me like family	Every time we talk I feel like he's testing my loyalty
Been dating for almost two years	Starting to feel like he doesn't trust me (just waiting on the accusation that I'm creeping on him)
Known him forever	I think I'm outgrowing him!
He can be fun	
I feel safe with him	
He's stuck by me through ugly times (Mom's issues!!!)	
I can tell him anything	
Never gotten this close with anyone before (my first!)	

Jacinta sighed. There were more pros. Wasn't that simple enough? When you weighed the pros and cons and one list was longer, it won. *Right?*

She stared at the list. The last con pierced through her. Her hand had shaken when she wrote the words. Seeing it on paper, in black and white, made her eyes tear up. *I don't want to outgrow him. I love him*, she thought stubbornly.

The shrill ring of the cordless phone startled her. Jacinta eyed it as if it were a snake ready to strike. She answered it wearily. "Hello."

"Hey . . . it's Heem."

"Hey," Jacinta said, the usual excitement in her voice missing. Anger slowly bubbled.

"So what's up, Ma?"

Jacinta snapped. "Raheem, you went off on me at the mall. What do you think is up?"

His voice remained even and casual with a sure confidence that Jacinta would forgive him. "Slow down, Ma. I was wrong. I know. My bad."

The admission caught Jacinta off guard. Had he just apologized? She wasn't sure how to answer, and there was an awkward pause.

Raheem filled the silence. "I know I punked out going off like that. It's just, I can't get used to not seeing you when I want. And when we do spend time together, usually your whole clique is there or around somewhere. That's just . . . new for me."

As tears of frustration and relief welled in her eyes, Jacinta's anger dissolved. She looked down guiltily at the list and pushed it away as if it were on fire.

"I hate how little time we have together, too . . . but my father not gonna let me come home every weekend. So seeing you at the mall with my friends is all we have some weekends," she explained.

"I know," Raheem admitted sheepishly. "I'm sorry, hear?"

Jacinta answered softly. "Yeah. Okay. But we can't keep arguing like this. It's starting to . . ." She stopped, unwilling to share her true feelings.

Raheem pressed. "Starting to what?"

"To cloud how I feel about you," she answered vaguely.

"Well, what does that mean?" he asked, and Jacinta was glad to hear that he sounded more confused than angry.

The words flowed out of her mouth in a torrent. "When we fight like this I get so hot with you. It's like you don't understand how hard it is for me to be away, to have to make new friends, to be in a new school. You say it's hard on you, but *I'm* the one living it,

Raheem!" Anger pulsed through the last few words. "And when I get mad I start thinking that . . ." She stopped short of admitting wanting to break it off and said simply, "I just start thinking, that's all."

She could hear his shallow breathing and wondered if she had gone too far. She braced for the backlash. But Raheem's voice was calm when he spoke.

"You right. But sometimes it don't *look* like it's so hard on you. You have new friends, and you defending them and hooking 'em up with each other and shit . . . It's mad crazy for me to see you like that," he admitted. "You've always been more to yourself. You different now."

Jacinta sighed. "Yeah. But me being different doesn't have to be a bad thing. Does it?"

Raheem was silent. Jacinta held her breath, waiting for him to answer.

He spoke finally. "No. It don't have to . . . but it feels like it will be."

Jacinta put her hand over the phone and exhaled loudly, relief coursing through her veins. She had come so close to cutting him out. His apology meant more than she wanted it to, but she took the chance to set up a few ground rules. "Look, we have to stop worrying about how my being over here in the 'burbs will change our relationship. When I'm home with you that's all I'm focused on. But you keep bringing up that I'm not there all the time . . . I can't change that, and I'm just tired of going over the same old, same old."

"Alright. I'm gonna try harder. I mean that," Raheem said.

Jacinta lay back, smiling. "Okay. Raheem?"

"Yeah?"

"I love you."

"I love you, too," he said.

Jacinta's face hurt from grinning so hard. She closed her eyes and let his voice take her back to when things were less confusing.

Da Straight Truth

"Are some things better left unsaid?"
—Lyfe ft. Fantasia, "Hypothetically"

Mina didn't hate being an only child. For every sibling she didn't have, she had a close friend to fill the void. But the number one con of being a lonely only was not having sibs doing dumber stuff than her to distract her parents from the dumb stuff she did. And not just the dumb stuff. Despite her parents working long hours, they were current on everything in Mina's life. A blessing and curse, for sure.

Everything she did was an event to her parents. The shrine of photos and certificates that plastered their family room capturing her at every age, milestone and accomplishment proved that. Even the small stuff mattered to her parents. So, she knew the obligatory "How'd the sleepover go?" loomed. And she couldn't be held responsible for what she revealed once it was out there.

Her mother had the power to elicit truth from Mina with a simple eyebrow hitch.

Mina debated meeting the conversation head-on, forcing a chipper face and declaring it was the best night of her life before disappearing into her room the rest of the night. But her body betrayed her. Chilling at the mall alone while Kelly, Lizzie and Jacinta had someone had taken a lot of energy.

Pulling on a pair of the most comfortable gear she could find, she climbed on top of her bed and lay there in a heap, singing silently along to the slowest, saddest songs on her playlist.

The house was too quiet. Devoid of mindless girl chatter to keep Mina's mind occupied, even the thought of hanging out with Chris Brown couldn't help her shake reality.

To her mom's credit, she waited two full hours after Mina had gotten home from the mall before knocking on her bedroom door.

"Hey, Boo," her mom said, walking in and taking a seat on Mina's bed.

From her newly appointed position as rag doll model, Mina didn't bother to get up. She hugged a pillow to her and scooted over to make room.

"Did you girls have fun last night?" Mariah asked casually.

"Um-hmm," Mina said.

Mina's mom let the silence fall between them long enough to catch the faint but constant noise of instant messages—song bites, bells, dings, doors slamming. She shook her head. "You're worse than I was at your age with the phone." She walked over to the screen and watched as the messages came pouring in. "Who is Bluedevils33?"

"Craig," Mina said woodenly.

"Umph. He's sent you fifteen different messages. Must be love." Her mom chuckled.

"Pssh, not," Mina said, her voice flat and angry at the same time.

Mariah sat back on the bed. She tugged at Mina's sloppy, lop-sided ponytail. "Okay, what's up? You're lying here like you lost your best friend. You're wearing these . . ." She pulled playfully at Mina's sweatpants. She hadn't seen Mina wear sweats in two years. "Are you and Liz fighting again?"

Mina shook her head no. She wasn't about to go all baby and confess her deepest sins and fears. Nope. Must resist the urge to vent. She was not going to . . .

"Craig totally played me," she blurted.

"Aw, sweetie, I'm sorry," Mariah said, pulling her into an embrace.

Mina let the tears flow, unashamed at how good it felt. The story came out no holds barred—the sneaking, the lying, the total embarrassment. Her mother listened, wordless, until Mina's final, "Of all people he had to go and hook up with."

"So, it wouldn't have hurt you if it were someone else?" Mariah asked, a smile playing behind her questioning gaze.

"No," Mina claimed, letting the warmth of her mom calm her. "I mean, I don't know. I guess."

"So you lied to us?" her mother said.

At the reminder that she'd told the whole truth and nothing but the truth, Mina threw herself back onto the bed. She should have known better than to let it *all* come out. She could have said someone told her about Craig. But no, she was Ms. Distraught and Honest. She didn't even have the energy to beg for her life (or forgiveness).

She let her mom pull her back upright by the arms.

"Well?" her mom said, waiting.

"Yes," Mina mumbled. "But, honestly, we only went so I could tell Craig I wasn't staying."

"Karma's a real trip, isn't it?" her mother said.

Mina snorted. "Yup."

"I won't tell you that I told you so." Her mom's eyebrows flexed like she wanted to. But wouldn't. "That I told you a party like that wasn't a place to hang out with a guy you're just starting to see exclusively," her mom said. She kissed Mina's forehead, then stood up. "And I won't bother to remind you that nothing good ever comes from a lie. Because I bet, right about now . . ." She walked to the door and turned back around. "You know all of that already." She winked. "Feel better, baby girl. Life goes on."

"Ma," Mina called out as her mother went to close the door. Her mom's face poked back inside. "Can I still go to Raheem's party Saturday?"

Mariah chuckled. "Now, what do you think?"

She closed the door quietly behind her.

"You set yourself up for that one," Mina muttered to herself. She went to lie back down, but the lure of the IM was too strong. Mina dragged herself over to the computer, sat at her desk and scrolled through the messages, many of them from Craig. She deleted them all, except for Michael's and JZ's.

Mike-Man: Hey Deev, WTH happened last nite?
BubbliMi: asking myself the same ???
Mike-Man: J said there was DRAMA. spill
BubbliMi: Craig is an azz period
Mike-Man: ouch could u be more specific tho

Mina typed up the short version, then switched to JZ.

Jizdaman: Mina u there?
BubbliMi: 'sup?
Jizdaman: u alright?
BubbliMi: r U alright Mr. Official Guard of Fort Knock 'em Boots?
Jizdaman: LOL I'm cool. Seriously tho . . . what's up?
BubbliMi: ::sigh:: Y guys b doggin?!
Jizdaman: he was drunk, Mi
BubbliMi: he wasn't that drunk
Jizdaman: it was foul fo sho . . . but . . . man I don't know what to say . . .
BubbliMi: did u know he was w/her? is that Y u didn't let us out there?
Jizdaman: NO NO NO I would never do u grimy like dat Mi 4 real

Relief flooded her heart. It didn't make what Craig did any less foul, but she was glad JZ wasn't covering for him.

Jizdaman: he keep pinging me, u know I'm not down w/that cupid ish but he said tell u he wuz sorry

BubbliMi: w/e
Jizdaman: thought so . . . I'm not passing no more msgs
BubbliMi: good c u
Jizdaman: u mad at me?

Mina took a few seconds to think about it. She didn't feel like lecturing JZ about how silly he was the night before.

Jizdaman: Mi? dam u taking a long time is that a yes?
BubbliMi: not at u . . . u was trippin last night not cool . . . but naw, not mad
Jizdaman: cuz u know u my girl right?
BubbliMi: yeah yeah me and all ur other hooches
Jizdaman: don't trip. U know u my girl 4 real. We cool?
BubbliMi: we cool
Jizdaman: Peace baby girl

Mina rubbed at her eyes. They were heavy, itchy and tired from crying most of the night. She knew the only way to ignore the PC was to sign off. And right now she needed a nap or at least time away from the computer—the white background was irritating her eyes even more.

She went to sign off when a message popped up.

Bluedevils33: I know u mad but talk 2 me pls!!!!!!!!!

She stared at it, her hand ready to delete.

Bluedevils33: eb allowed one fug up . . . right?

Yes, but why did you have to go and do it in front of so many people, Mina thought. She reluctantly responded.

BubbliMi: u made me look like a straight up fool

Bluedevils33: didn't mean 2 hurt u

BubbliMi: I gotta cheer w/her Craig!

Bluedevils33: sorry it was stupid

BubbliMi: Y

Bluedevils33: cuz I was wrong

BubbliMi: No Y wuz u all up on her

Bluedevils33: almost 2 hours go by u didn't show up thought u wasn't coming, started drinking, tripping

BubbliMi: oh so w/o me there u was gon just move on 2 da nex chick?

Bluedevils33: not like that. Her and Brian got in argument, she was upset, I was just talking 2 her, trying 2 b nice . . . went 2 far

She and Brian were arguing? About what? Mina's fingers itched to ask. But instead she wrote . . .

BubbliMi: w/e

Bluedevils33: that's da straight truth

BubbliMi: I gotta go

Bluedevils33: talk tmrrow?

BubbliMi: c u

She logged off in a hurry. Even if what Craig said was true, it didn't change that he and Kelis . . . It didn't change anything.

Wait ... What Just Happened Here?

"You know they gon' blame it on the drinks."
—Jamie Foxx ft. Kanye West, "Extravaganza"

Here's how a day goes from bad to worse:

Six-thirty A.M. Sitting in the car with Brian, Jacinta, Michael and JZ. Awkward, awkward silence. No banter. No witty stories, just everyone trying to avoid talking about the one thing that everybody wants to talk about until Michael, the only person who wasn't at the already infamous Frenzy of '05, says, "Can I bright side it for y'all?" General consensus, sure, go ahead and try. "Well," Michael says, as if he's really thought this out. "Since Brian's chick hooked up with your man, why don't y'all just hook up? Even stevens swap. Everybody's happy." Awkward, awkward silence.

Seven-fifteen A.M. Waiting for the second bell to ring, sitting in first period, sociology, with Kelly and Jacinta STILL trying to avoid talking about the one thing that everybody wants to talk about. Jessica, second in command of the bitchiest clique to ever walk the face of the earth, stands in front of Mina's desk, smirks, flips her weavilicious 'do and says, "Oh, my God, so everybody was wondering how you ever got with Craig anyway. But now that he's hooked up with Kelis, too, it's pretty obvious he just has a thing for nobody wannabes. No girl from the pop side will want him now." Hair swish, hair swish, evil laugh, walk away.

Eight-thirty A.M. Complete and total breakdown in the second-floor girls' bathroom. Debate, call mother and claim a sick day to avoid more ridicule and the inevitable cheer practice with evil, boyfriend-stealing slut-nugget cocaptain OR suck it up; it could be worse (that whole weekend over at Jessica's comes to mind). Realize that having bamboo shoots up fingernails is better than a weekend at Jessica's, so this whole Craig and Kelis thing is practically a birthday party, until . . .

Ten A.M. The entire student body officially now knows. Find out who her real friends on the squad are because they come up in the hall and give their condolences, admit they always thought Kelis was an evil, boyfriend-stealing slut nugget. Together wonder, Is stealing a squad mate's boyfriend grounds for getting kicked off? Hmm . . . it's a thought. So far five of the twenty JV members have weighed in. Not bad. Day not too horrible until . . .

Eleven-fifteen A.M. Get cool hellos and phony waves from three JV cheerleaders who would normally stop and gab. Ha, so Kelis has allies. This is not looking good for that whole team-bonding thing.

By eleven-thirty that morning, Mina was feeling the weight of the whispers and sneaky stares. If she ever needed any proof that the DRB High grapevine was powerfully fast, her misery was it. And while thoughts of the day getting worse had crossed her mind, she'd almost convinced herself that the stares were no worse than the time she'd been forced to wear an ugly, neon electric blue tee shirt the entire day for soc. And that hadn't been the worst part, close . . . but, the worst part had been playing second-class citizen to anyone from soc who got to wear a dark, not nearly as ugly, crimson tee shirt. She'd spent an entire day carrying the books of Reds, and only speaking when one of them had spoken to her. She'd survived (barely) unscarred. Sure, she couldn't look at any neon color anymore without gagging. But, she had it in her to withstand the staring of her peers; was (unfortunately) becoming an old pro at it.

Standing at her locker, she told herself that the road to ultra-popularity was paved with a few embarrassing mishaps. So, she was obviously well on her way.

"So, you alright?" Brian asked, suddenly beside her.

She'd been so proud, reflecting on her new philosophical out-look, she hadn't seen Brian standing next to her. He was sporting the athletic thug look in an Under Armour top gripping his biceps and chest, a pair of oversized black jeans and steel-toe black boots.

Startled, Mina's shoulders hitched. She shuffled things in her locker, unable to look at him directly. Speaking of embarrassing mishaps.

Hello, guy I thought was playing me who watched me get played.

She quickly reminded herself, *The road to ultrapopularity is paved with a few embarrassing mishaps.*

"I'm okay," she said finally, her quiet voice echoing in the hollow locker. She wished she could crawl inside.

Brian moved in, lowered his voice. "Your girls got you up out of there fast. But now I guess you see that I wasn't—" he snorted— "trying to get you on my team and that your boy is wack."

Mina threw the last of her books in the locker and faced him. "Look, thanks for looking out."

Brian shrugged. "You cool with me, Toughie. Even though you were tripping hard Saturday." He put his fist out for a pound. "I for-give you, though."

Mina closed her locker and gave Brian's fist a light tap with her own. She waited for the person next to her to leave before she leaned her back against the door. "Can I ask you something?"

Brian nodded.

"What were you and Kelis arguing about?"

He rolled his eyes. "How you know we were arguing? Your boy tell you that?"

Mina shrugged. She didn't feel like getting into all that.

"You heading to lunch?" Brian asked.

Mina nodded.

He started walking. "Alright, come on."

They walked slowly down the hall, people breezing by as they ran against the impending bell.

"It wasn't an argument. She came there with a friend, saw me dancing with somebody else and caught a 'tude." Brian smirked as if the whole thing was a silly game he had no time for. "Me and Kelis were just kicking it from the start. It wasn't exclusive or anything. But you know she wasn't trying to hear that." He shrugged it off. "Then she started going off about how I must be feeling somebody else, asking who it was and whatnot." He chuckled bitterly. "Chick started throwing out names of who it could be, and I was like 'No, it's not like that. I'm swinging solo, shorty.' Then she called out your name, and I guess I didn't answer fast enough." He threw his hands up like "And that was it."

Mina stopped in her tracks. "Hold up, so she thought you were digging me and that's why she went after Craig?"

"I guess," Brian said.

"All this because you didn't say no to my name fast enough?" Mina asked, quickly putting the pieces together.

"Something like that," Brian said.

"That's messed up," Mina said more to herself than Brian. Her head ticked slowly side to side as she put this new information into the picture. Kelis was mad at Brian. Mad at her, too. Craig saw she was upset and was just trying to help her out. So Craig hadn't been lying. Kelis had been playing him, trying to get back at her and Brian.

"But your boy wasn't all innocent either," Brian said, rudely reaching into her thoughts.

Mina sputtered, trying to recover. "What? I . . . I didn't say he was."

Brian rolled his eyes. "Pssh, yeah, but that's what you're thinking, ain't it?"

Before Mina could answer, her name was called from the other end of the hall. She and Brian turned to see Craig jogging toward them.

"Mina, wait up," he said.

"You're gonna be late," she warned just as the second bell rang.

"No big deal," Craig said.

He gave Brian a curt head nod. Brian did the same.

"Can we talk, real quick?" Craig asked.

"I have to get to lunch," Mina said, glancing over at Brian from the corner of her eye. She did want to talk to Craig, but didn't want to admit it in front of Brian, who obviously already could feel her caving, wanting to forgive Craig.

So she really was that transparent.

"Come on, shorty, five minutes," Craig said. He stepped closer so he was standing between Mina and Brian. He looked over his shoulder. "Scuse me, playah. Damn, can a brother get a minute?"

Brian snorted, but didn't step back. The three of them stood sandwiched in the middle of the empty hall.

"Craig, just holler at me later," Mina said quickly. Sensing the ego game about to play out, her nerves tingled.

"Where you going with him?" Craig nodded his head back toward Brian. "I saw the *Bugle* article today. What's this, another *interview*?"

"We have lunch together. He was just . . . walking me," Mina said.

"Yeah, alright," Craig said. He laid his arms across Mina's shoulders so they were almost head to head. "I know what I did was wack. But I was just helping shorty out 'cause dude here dogged her out. And—"

"Dog, you don't need to bring me in this," Brian said.

Craig turned around to face him. "Looks like you brought yourself in it, walking my girl to lunch and shit."

"Y'all, we're gonna get in trouble," Mina whispered loudly, as she glanced up and down the hall, expecting a teacher to snatch them all up at any moment.

"So, what, you want to go?" Brian said, stepping to Craig.

"Oh, my God, don't do this," Mina said, her whisper a whiny screech. She grabbed Craig's arm and forced him to turn to her. "Craig, let's just talk later. Alright?"

"Naw, let's talk now," he said. "I'm trying to be real and let you know what happened. But if you gon' listen to this punk, I can stop wasting my time."

Mina felt both their gazes on her, waiting for her to choose a side. If the floor opened up to swallow her, life would be good. She lowered her voice, as if it would really shield Brian from hearing. "I'm not listening to him . . ." she found herself saying, hating the desperate tone of her voice. "We were just walking to lunch."

"Look, I ain't stutting him." Craig frowned. "I'm saying, though, you been sweating me for a while. Who you gonna believe? Me or him?"

Mina couldn't believe he went there. It was as though what she saw with her own eyes at the party meant nothing. Craig wanted forgiveness now? Like this? He flashes a smile and she says, "Okay, Boo, we're cool"?

All she asked was for him to call her later. Now he was going all *Deal or No Deal* on her.

Her eyes skittered over to Brian's frowning face. As if he'd been waiting for that very cue, he said, "I'm out, Mina," and walked off.

"Brian, hold up . . ." Mina said and was relieved when he stopped. She lowered her voice so only Craig could hear. "Just call me later, please." She pleaded with her eyes.

There it went again, her begging him. Somehow the tables had reversed, and she was pleading for him to call her. She didn't have time to think about how it ended up there. All she knew was she wasn't going to forgive Craig on the spot. She didn't know if she was going to forgive him at all. But standing in the middle of the hall while classes were being conducted on either side of them was not the place to debate it. That much she was sticking to. "Please?" she added once more.

Craig curled his upper and lower lip in and shook his head as though he couldn't believe what he was hearing. "What, you trying to play both of us?"

"No, it's not—"

"Man, this shit is wack." Craig called out to Brian, "Ay, dude, you can have her. She ain't nothing but a jock ho anyway. See who she dumps you for when basketball season ends."

Leaving Mina in the middle of the hall shell-shocked, Craig walked off singing loudly, "She's a ho, you know she's a ho. How do you know, 'cause Craig told you so."

Mina could still hear him laughing as he turned the corner.

What just happened here?

Jock Hos and Slut Nuggets

"Because to you it's just a game."
—JoJo, "Too Little Too Late"

Craig's little rap and nasty laugh still rang in Mina's ears as she stretched, later that day, at cheer practice. She'd sat through lunch silent, not saying a word to anyone, causing Michael to ask if she needed a doctor. But she wasn't in the mood for joking. Eventually Brian, equally as quiet, joined the ballers in the café, and the clique talked around Mina, giving her space.

Now, sitting in the gymnastics room on the floor, alone, she spread her legs, stretched forward and grabbed on to her heels. She'd come to practice early, just to enjoy the quiet of the room before Coach Embry started barking, the girls started giggling and the music started its race-for-the-finish-line pace.

"Oh, good, you're already here," Kelis said from the doorway.

Mina didn't bother to look up. She stretched farther, forcing her hamstrings more than she should have. The extra pull made her wince, but she stayed down, unable to look at Kelis yet. Half expecting a sappy soap opera soundtrack to begin playing overhead, she didn't know how to play this portion of the dramedy.

Was she the pissed-off played chick who should smack Kelis?

Oh, wait, Jacinta had taken care of that for her.

Was she BubbliMi, captain and all-around bigger person who was not going to let this interfere with their cheer vibe?

Or just plain old Mina whose (ex) boyfriend had actually called her a ho three hours ago because of something this chick had caused?

So, anxious, knowing this moment was coming all day, her fingers trembled, and she gripped tighter on to her heel until their tips were white.

Kelis dropped in front of her and mirrored the stretch.

"You're pissed, right?" Kelis said, pulling her hair back into a pony before diving forward to grab her heels.

"Nah, I fully expected to come to the party and see you giving Craig CPR," Mina said in a high, shaking voice. She breathed slowly through her nose to calm herself. When she felt normal again, she rolled out of the stretch, back up to an upright sitting position, and waited for Kelis to roll up. For the first time Mina looked her square in the eye as she asked, "That's what you were doing, right?"

Lie, go ahead and lie, Mina thought. Because once she did Mina was going to fly across the mat and . . .

"Mina, I didn't really mean to . . . get caught," Kelis admitted.

Mina laughed bitterly. It was just like Kelis to be honest at a time when Mina wanted to smack the spit out of her for being a backstabbing liar. When she wanted to scream that she'd known Kelis would do something grimy to her one day. She'd just always thought it would be something like accidentally tripping Mina so she'd break a leg or arm.

Who said cheerleaders were peppy? Shoot, Mina had seen her share of cutthroat squad mates, and that was during recreation cheerleading.

Kelis scooted up and put her feet up against Mina's. She extended her hands and waited for Mina to grab them so they could switch off tugging each other forward for an extra stretch. Mina had to admit, the girl had a set of cojones the size of watermelons. It was hard for Mina to throw a tantrum with Kelis acting so . . . normal. For a second she wondered if Saturday had been a bad *Punk'd* episode, bad dream or bad trip on a drug she didn't know she'd taken.

Unbelievably, she found herself putting her arms out and letting Kelis tug her forward, just like any other practice. Boyfriend stealing, helping a teammate stretch . . . la, la, la, la, laa . . . all in a day's work for Kelis Henderson.

"I don't even like Craig like that. I was just trying to make Brian mad with his fine self," Kelis said with a snort. "And I honestly didn't think you were even coming to the party. So . . . I flirted with him to piss Brian off."

Mina came back up, then pulled lightly on Kelis's arm until she was lowered in her stretch. "You did more than flirt," Mina snapped. "And how are you gonna play your teammate like that just to piss off some dude?"

"It's not like it worked anyway." Kelis pouted. "What was up with your girl smacking me?"

Mina snorted. "She had my back. Apparently me and you haven't been teammates long enough for you to grasp the concept."

"She's lucky I didn't have all my girls with me . . ." Kelis said, trailing off.

Mina rolled her eyes. Kelis had one or two good friends, and not one of them was bold enough to buck up in Cinny's face. But she was fine letting Kelis hold on to the fantasy of actually stepping to Jacinta for payback. They both knew it was as likely as snow in July.

"I know we've never been close friends," Kelis said when she was upright once more.

She dropped Mina's hands, and they sat facing each other, still foot to foot. "But we're not enemies either . . ." She raised an eyebrow in question, but went on when Mina didn't confirm or deny. "I wasn't gunning for you when I was wildin' out. Honest."

"And you think we're gonna be cool now?" Mina asked, folding her arms and crossing her legs. "Everybody just thinks I'm Bobo the Fool today, huh?"

"I didn't say all that, Mina. I'm just trying to be . . . straight with you," Kelis said, tightening her pony. "I'm not quitting the team. And I know you're not. So . . ." She shrugged.

The team filtered in. Their loud talking saved Mina from answering. As their teammates joined them on the mat, surrounding them, Mina and Kelis left the unsaid, unsaid. As far as Mina was concerned, their relationship wasn't much different from the start.

Mourning Over in 5...4...3...2...1

"I can have another you by tomorrow."
—Beyonce, "Irreplaceable"

Five things you feel when the guy you've had a mega crush on calls you a ho:

5. You talking to me?
4. This dude is tripping!
3. Seriously, I must have heard him wrong.
2. If I kick him in the nuts, is that premeditated assault?
And the number one thing you feel when the guy you've had a
    mega crush on calls you a ho is . . . am I?

Mina sat in her darkened room, PC off, cell phone off, everything off except her brain, and it wouldn't stop asking the question, "Am I? Am I a jock ho?"

Yeah, she liked athletic guys. But could you be a ho when you'd never even had a serious boyfriend before? And she'd kissed only two guys in her life—Ty and Craig. If she was a ho, she was the world's worst.

Her stomach burbled, reminding her that it had no idea if she was or not, but it did know that she was on day two without food. The last real thing she'd eaten was a French fry at the mall, when she'd had a momentary lapse of Frenzy amnesia after discovering that in approximately two weeks she'd be near enough to Chris Brown to faint into his lap.

She considered going downstairs to have a bowl of cereal. Her stomach liked the idea, but her mind was unwilling to cooperate. So she stayed in a heap on her bed, burning up her slow jam playlist, refusing to be a part of the rest of the world. Going to school and cheer practice was it. Her room had become a fortress of solitude once she'd turned off everything connecting her to the outside.

She'd participated at lunch today only because the clique had forced her to talk. Brian had, once more, retreated to the café, choosing to sit out in the cold with the basketball team rather than be near her. At least that was how Mina saw it. He wasn't being mean to her, just indifferent since Craig had basically "given" her to him because she was . . . a jock ho.

Her door swung open, and the bright lights from the hallway attacked her eyes.

Mina threw a cover over her head, peeking out only when she heard Michael say, "Mi, come on. This is drama, even for you."

He flipped her light on and sat on the bed, JZ and Lizzie trailing behind him.

"I'm not bothering anybody. Let me be dramatic," Mina said, wrapping herself in the blanket and pushing herself to the top of the bed to make room for Lizzie, who had plopped on the other side of her.

"Diva," Michael wrinkled his nose. "I know you don't have on sweatpants."

Mina covered her legs. Michael snatched the cover back and clucked in disapproval. "Okay, not talking and not eating is one thing. But no dude should ever get you that depressed." He plucked at the pants as if they would burn him if he touched them too long.

JZ sat on the floor against the door, his long legs hunched to his chest. "I have to admit, I miss your nagging, Mi," he teased.

"He said I was a ho," Mina said, unable to stop the tears from falling. She sighed in disgust. She was tired of crying. She'd thought the tears had dried up for good Sunday night. But everything else had turned against her, why not her tear ducts, too?

Michael put his arm around her. "So what? Craig's just a hard-head who's mad 'cause he got caught." He cracked a smile, giving her a squeeze. "We know you're not like that. And everybody knows that all the *official* hos are listed in alphabetical order in the boys' bathroom."

JZ and Lizzie chuckled.

Mina laughed through the tears. "It's y'all job to love me. But now Craig hates me. You know how I hate being hated," she whined.

"He's a jerk," Lizzie said angrily. "And he has nerve calling you names when he was the one acting like a drunken he-ho Saturday."

Mina sniffled, laughing again. Warm comfort spread to her toes. She was starting to feel better whether she wanted to or not. The clique was not going to let her mourn a second longer, and she loved them for it. "Lizzie, you totally just made that up."

"I know. But he was." Lizzie grinned.

"I can't help it if all the guys I end up crushing on are jocks," Mina explained, her needle still stuck on the topic.

"Mina, you're not a ho, stop tripping." JZ frowned. "I already told Craig he ain't have to go there."

Mina's head snapped toward JZ in surprise. "Jay, I don't want you and Craig beefing. Y'all gotta play ball together next fall."

"We're not beefing. I just told him he was wrong and that you were my girl and I knew you better than that," JZ said nonchalantly, as if it were every day that he defended a girl's honor.

Mina rushed him with a hug. She was surprised when he didn't shrug it off, just let her tag him with the embrace. "Thank you, Big Head." She pecked his cheek.

JZ made a production of wiping the kiss away. "See, now there you go tripping."

But Mina heard the smile in his voice. She stayed on the floor, cross-legged, huddled next to him.

"Man, this year is not going at all like I planned. Instead of gaining popularity points, I'm losing 'em," Mina said, shaking her head, thinking this was either the world's worst freshman semester or she had to seriously rethink her priorities. For now, it felt like the world's worst and she outlined why, aloud. "First, I end up in Jess's soc group and she brands me a wannabe for life." Mina rolled her eyes to the ceiling. "God only knows what she's been spreading about me to other Uppers." She sighed. "Then I get dissed by one of the most popular dudes in school. Seriously, I have issues."

"And yet, we still risk our social status by hanging with you," Michael said, a big grin on his face.

Mina nodded. "You're joking. But I'm like popularity kryptonite right about now. Run now, save yourselves." She chuckled and laid her head on JZ's arm.

He lifted his arm around her, then gripped her in a light headlock. It was classic JZ, affection without the sappiness, and one of the best hugs Mina had had in a long time.

I'm Not a Jock, Ho

"Aint no mistaking, playing, or faking."
—Chris Brown, "Poppin'"

The next morning, Mina watched as Brian's car pulled into the driveway. Brian had never come to pick her up before. Lately, the routine was, she and Cinny met at Michael's where Brian, along with JZ, would pick them up.

What is he doing here? she thought.

She checked her watch—maybe she was running late.

No, still fifteen minutes to get to Michael's.

She ran around gathering the rest of her things. Her stupid biology book was M.I.A.

Mina anxiously lifted papers, looking under chairs, searching for it, her anxiety rising.

"Ma!"

"Mina, I told you, I have no idea where your book is," her mother called from her bedroom. "How would I know where your things are when I'm not the one using them?"

Mina exhaled in noisy exasperation. She ran into the family room and as a last ditch effort looked under the sofa. The book was there. *I'm not even going to try to remember how it got there,* Mina thought, relieved and annoyed.

She ran back out to the sunroom and gasped as Brian knocked

on one of the sliding glass doors. "Hey," she called out, turning to put the bio book in her backpack as she opened the door.

"'Sup," Brian replied politely.

"I thought I was running behind. I was getting ready to walk down to Michael's," Mina babbled, then called out to her parents, "Ma, Daddy, Brian is here to give me a ride. I'm gone!"

"Okay. Bye, honey. Hi, Brian," her mom called.

"Good morning, Mrs. Mooney, Mr. Mooney," Brian called out in the direction of her voice.

"Morning, Brian. Have a good day, guys," Jackson called out.

Mina tried peering into his truck, looking for the others as she walked toward the backseat, her usual place in the mornings.

"Naw, sit up front. I still have to pick up everybody else," Brian said. He teased her, "Don't try sitting back there like I'm your chauffer."

"Where is everybody?" Mina looked around as if they were going to jump from behind trees.

"I wanted to talk to you alone for a minute. That's cool, right?"

"Oh, yeah, it's cool," Mina said, almost believing herself even as she thought, *No, it can't be cool. You haven't said a word to me since Monday because you probably think I'm a ho.* Her legs felt as if they were full of water as she lifted them to step into the Explorer.

All she could think was that Brian wanted to once and for all distance himself from the whole mess. Probably make it clear that as gracious as it was for Craig to hand her over, he was going to have to make this the last time he gave her a ride for fear people would think they were friends.

They sat in the front of the truck, silent, a slight buzz coming from the radio.

Mina fidgeted in the seat. What was he waiting for? Was she supposed to say something first? He was the one who came to get her.

She cleared her throat, staring straight ahead. Hot air from the heater had her face blazing. She thought about putting the window down but decided against it.

Unable to take the silence a second longer, Mina blurted, "I'm not a jock ho."

Brian frowned. "Who said all that?"

"Craig . . . on Monday. But I'm not like that," Mina rambled. "I've never even had a long-term boyfriend . . . short-term either." She snickered nervously. "I'm lucky my parents let me ride to school with you, much less anybody else. I just—"

"Mina, chill," Brian said, cutting off her tumbling confession. He laughed softly, shaking his head from the overload. "That's not why I wanted to talk."

Mina's ears burned with embarrassment. Making a fool of herself was coming way too easy. Brian stared at her, making her want to smooth her hair or pick at her nose to make sure it was clean. *Shut up and let him talk,* she told herself.

"I can't figure you out, Toughie," Brian said finally, searching Mina's confused face.

"Figure out what?" Mina ventured, unable to stop herself from asking.

"I can't tell if you digging me or what. It's like . . . we met. I thought we were vibin'; then you said you had a boyfriend." He laughed. "But then you were clocking my time, hard, letting me know you peeping me with other chicks. So you definitely been watching me."

Mina's mouth fell open slightly.

"Watching you?" she said, realizing she sounded like a parrot. But she didn't know what else to say.

"Alright, look, I have laid my best mack down on you, and you hit me with the 'I gotta boyfriend' thing twice," Brian said, imitating a girl's voice. He chuckled softly, as though the thought of Mina spurning him was the cutest little joke ever. "Either I'm losing my touch or you prefer wack dudes who be playing you." He looked her dead in the eye as he said, "I'm asking you straight out—are you digging me? 'Cause I'm feeling you."

Brian's honesty was like *woah*. Mina could only stare at him. His eyes had that usual glint of playfulness in them, and his pretty smile was boyish. Yet his words were serious. He didn't seem self-conscious or embarrassed that he was putting it out there, even though Mina could have said, "Are you crazy, I already told you I don't like you like that."

But Mina had a feeling that Brian, confident without an ounce of arrogance this morning, knew she wasn't going to say that. She really, really had to work on being less transparent. Everybody was reading her like a book.

Brian's eyebrows raised. "Are you thinking about it?"

"Oh, no . . . ," Mina said, goosed into answering. "I mean, not no I'm not digging you, no I'm not thinking about it. I mean . . . yeah." She took a deep breath and started over slowly. "Okay, wait . . . I like you. But, well, I thought maybe you and Kelis—"

"Hold up," Brian interrupted her. "Forget about Kelis and Craig and whoever else. I'm saying just me and you, we're cool, right?"

Mina nodded.

"You and Craig hist, right?"

"Definitely," she muttered.

"So, then you wouldn't mind if we kicked it?"

Her head bobbed up and down, then shook side to side, confused as to what the right motion was. So she finally said, "I'd like that."

Did that sound weird?

She was relieved when Brian's face lit up.

Mina flirted, her calm returning slowly. "Are you asking me on a date, Brian James?"

He started the car. "If I am, I better spell it out, 'cause you a little slow sometimes, Toughie."

He laughed, hunching away from Mina's smack at his arm.

"Wait, I did spell it out for you," he said, as if it just hit him. "Brother gives you all his info—the digits, the e-mail . . . and nothing." He pretended to be offended. "A player has his pride. I wasn't gonna mention it again."

"Then how come you picked me up this morning?" Mina teased.

"For real, you wanna know?" He looked over at her as they came to the stop sign at the top of her cul-de-sac.

"For real, I wanna know," Mina said. Brian had every reason to run as far away from her as he could. Plus, she figured Craig had spread the word about her to half the guys at DRB High. Either they believed him and were going to shun her, or she was going to start getting a lot of phone calls from jocks.

"I thought you was gone, swept up, when dude was all up on you in the hall Monday. I figured you believed him and that was that," Brian said with a shrug. "But when I walked away you called me back."

Mina waited for more, but Brian pulled off without another word.

"I called you back?" she repeated, going Polly Parrot again.

He nodded.

"And if I hadn't?" she asked, genuinely curious, staring at Brian the entire time to see his full reaction.

"Then I'd be picking you up from Michael's this morning," he answered without a trace of sarcasm.

Brian pulled the truck into Michael's driveway and blew the horn.

"How come you didn't say anything earlier?" Mina asked. "I thought you were mad at me."

"I was waiting to see if you and dude were going to hook back up or what . . . figured if you were going to it would have happened by now."

Automatically they fell silent as Jacinta and Michael got into the truck.

Surprised to see Mina, they gave each other questioning looks.

"Well, good morning, princess," Jacinta said, her "what's up with that" face on. "Got picked up at your door, I see."

Mina beamed and snuck a glance at her from around the seat. Jacinta smiled back and mouthed, "Go, girl."

Truthing Up

"Go ahead and free yourself."
—Fantasia, "Free Yourself"

Later that afternoon JZ stood in front of Mr. Collins's desk.

Man up! Man up! he chanted to himself as Mr. Collins peered up at him. The mantra was the only thing keeping him from shaking. He hated feeling afraid of Mr. Collins. JZ was taller and no doubt stronger than Mr. Collins, even though the teacher was a grown man. It felt stupid to look into Mr. Collins's unblinking brown eyes and feel actual fear.

But he did.

Worse, Mr. Collins was a nerd's nerd. He was bean-pole thin, pale as the snow, had neatly cut light brown hair that never seemed to grow any longer than what it was, nor did it ever seem to be cut any shorter—same length every day, all day—and of course, that thick, 'stache that moved on its own when Mr. Collins was excited.

JZ tried to imagine a woman wanting to kiss his teacher's hairy lip, and the thought made his stomach sour. He almost winced, but instead focused on the ugly 'stache.

Today, it frogged as normal, going up and down as Mr. Collins mulled his fate.

JZ had come clean about cheating on the exam. He hadn't told anyone he was going to do it. He'd never checked in with Lizzie to ask how she wanted him to fix things. He'd just confessed on his own because he owed Lizzie that much.

He'd passed the test on his own. That felt good. But he wasn't going to spend the entire season sweating that stupid pop quiz. A stupid, last minute, uncalled-for, never-should-have-been-meant-to-be quiz. So he'd confessed. It was in the open. If this was the end of his basketball season . . . well, that was out of his hands.

"Mr. Zimms, you're telling me that you did not earn that "B" on your own?" Mr. Collins asked.

JZ took a deep internal breath. He'd already answered that question three times!

The second time, Mr. Collins had asked how he'd gotten the answers, and JZ had answered simply, "I looked at somebody else's paper." Mr. Collins had gotten up, scurried across the hallway to an office, then came back, just as quickly.

"And whose paper did you cheat from?" Mr. Collins's eyes danced. He was taking pleasure in having JZ on the hot seat.

JZ tried to ignore the glee he saw in the man's eyes. He'd never wanted to hit a teacher before as much as he did this very second. He swallowed hard, and it seemed to take the spit forever to navigate the lump forming in his throat.

This wasn't about ratting Lizzie out. It was about making it right. But he could see Mr. Collins expected an answer. "Lizzie O'Reilly," he said reluctantly.

At that moment, Lizzie walked in. And JZ could have sworn he heard Mr. Collins chuckle under his breath.

"Ahhh, Elizabeth. Sorry to pull you from rehearsal," Mr. Collins said. But he didn't look very sorry. He looked as though he'd been trying to catch JZ off guard and was very, very happy to pull Lizzie from rehearsal.

Lizzie's eyes crinkled into a worried squint as she walked in uneasily.

"Mr. Zimms has confessed to cheating on his exam . . . from

your paper." Mr. Collins announced the last part dramatically. As if he'd pulled a sheet off a table revealing the smoking gun. Ah-ha!

Lizzie, scared to death, was unable to say anything.

Hoping to prevent Lizzie from nodding or blurting a confession, JZ spoke up hurriedly. "She didn't know I cheated off her." His voice was much calmer than his jangled nerves let on. "I read her paper upside down."

He side-glanced at Lizzie frantically.

Lizzie, shut up, shut up, don't confess, he thought to himself, trying to send the message to her. Mina always swore there was a best friend ESP. If there was, now would be a great time for it to kick in between him and Liz.

This time Mr. Collins did chuckle. "Ha, ha, ha. Is that right?" His eyes scanned JZ's face, obviously looking for the lie. But any conflict JZ had with his words was hidden beneath his handsome brown face, smooth with calm. Finally, the teacher sighed dramatically. "So, Elizabeth, were you aware? Did you suspect something was awry that day?"

Lizzie shook her head no, too afraid to speak. She wasn't that good of an actress. Her voice was caught in her throat and would have come out a squeak, she was sure.

"I don't understand you athletes . . . jocks," Mr. Collins sneered. "And you, Mr. Zimms, are one of the few intelligent of your kind."

JZ felt like grabbing Mr. Collins by the head and shoving him into the chalkboard. His hands twitched, and he jammed them in his pockets before they did something stupid.

Mr. Collins ranted on. "Am I to believe now that you passed last Friday's test by your own mathematical prowess?" He looked down his nose at JZ as if to be clear he believed no such thing.

"I passed it honestly," JZ said. His voice rocked with honest fury. He breathed in and out through his nose to calm himself down, then continued, "It was stupid to cheat off of Lizzie. I froze. My father is expecting every grade to be a "B" or higher the rest of this season . . . and the quiz threw me off. I was nervous. It was stupid."

"Stupid, yes. You can be kicked off the team for this," Mr. Collins said, nodding knowingly. "I'm not sure what to believe. You and Elizabeth . . . are you friends outside of the classroom?"

He looked from Lizzie to JZ. Neither seemed willing to answer, afraid of the consequences if they admitted yes.

Mr. Collins took their nonanswer for an answer. "Yes, well, you can see why this leaves many doubts in my mind." His mustache frogged as he gave them each a look. "Elizabeth, this would not bode well for your future with Bay Dra—"

"She had no idea," JZ said, his fury rising again. Mr. Collins's eyes popped at the venom in JZ's voice, and JZ backed down, his voice calm, but firm as he said, "This was all me." JZ looked at Lizzie, the message in his eyes and voice. "All me."

"Then I suppose you owe Ms. O'Reilly an apology," Mr. Collins said. JZ detected annoyance or defeat. He obviously didn't believe Lizzie was innocent. Either that or he hated JZ enough that he didn't believe a word JZ said. JZ didn't care which as long as Lizzie didn't get punished.

"I'm sorry, Lizzie," JZ said sincerely. "I didn't mean to get you involved."

"Needless to say, I'll be separating the two of you. You'll have new seats tomorrow," Mr. Collins said. He rocked back in his chair. "Mr. Zimms, you will now retake the test, right here, right now. If you did not cheat, you'll have no problem replicating your success."

JZ nodded. He walked over to an empty table and tried to get his heart out of his mouth.

"You may go back to rehearsal, Elizabeth." Mr. Collins rooted in his desk for the test paper. "Oh, please let Ms. Jessamay know that I'll likely not make rehearsal until near the end."

"Okay," was Lizzie's soft answer as she gave JZ a sorrowful look, then scampered out the door.

Craig Whatshisname

"From the day to the night we ride, we ride, we ride."
—Mary J. Blige, "We Ride (I See the Future)"

Whether it was Brian's admission that he had a crush on her or the clique's late evening intervention, when Thursday night rolled around, Mina's mood was 180 degrees better. There had been a few vulgar jokes and snickers from the jocks in Craig's clique, but Mina ignored them, chanting her mantra, "The road to ultrapopularity is paved with embarrassing mishaps," until the feeling to crawl under the school through the holidays passed.

Practice with Kelis was bearable thanks to Kelis's ability to act as if it were perfectly normal to use a teammate's (ex) boyfriend in a game of revenge and then still gossip together. Mina had done her best to give Kelis the cold shoulder, but the girl was immune to it.

On Wednesday, when they were in the locker room changing into practice clothes, Kelis sat next to Mina, tying her shoe. "Girl, guess who is trying to holler at me?" she asked, as if the weekend's madness were old news.

Mina stared at her, scowling, wanting to say, "Like I care." But she was too polite. Polite as in, she hated conflict with a passion and took weird comfort in the fact that things between she and Kelis were love/hate as usual. Having Craig walk by her as if she were invisible was hard enough. No matter how many times she reminded himself *he* was the jackass, her brown sugar cheeks blazed whenever they passed in the halls without as much as a glance each other's way.

So she'd muttered, "Who?" to Kelis and let her ramble on about how Bo (one of Mina's past crushes, a few shared IMs, nothing more) had called her the night before. Mina had tuned her out by the time they hit the mat to stretch.

Now, feeling as close to normal as she'd felt all week, the thick scent of garlic and baking cheese made her stomach gurgle loudly. She had some serious making up to do in the eating department. Setting plates on the table, she inhaled the yummy smells and hummed.

"So, is it a coincidence that you're suddenly happy again after that little A.M. visit from Brian?" her mom asked. She was carrying a hot pan of lasagna to the table.

"Brian?" Mina's dad came up behind her and goosed her neck. "Wait a minute. So two weeks ago I had to keep you and your mother from throwing bows over you not getting to go to this party with . . ." He squinted, trying to access his memory. Then clicked his fingers. "Craig What'shisname. And now, he's already been laid to rest?"

He bowed his head in mock reverence.

Mina snorted. Laid to rest? That was a good way to put it.

"Do I need a score card to follow this game?" he teased.

Mina winced. She knew her dad was joking, but it hit too close to home. "Daddy, it's not like that. Me and Brian are just friends anyway."

"Oh, I know. It better be," he said, giving her a stern eyebrow arch. "No dating until . . ."

"I'm fifteen," Mina sang. She took a seat at the table. "Can I have a definition of what dating *is* allowed until next September?"

Mariah chuckled, sitting down. "Maybe it's easier if we tell you what's not."

"Okay." Mina nodded. Her way wasn't working very well. She may as well try her parents'.

Jackson Mooney sat down. He led them in a prayer, then dug into the tray of lasagna as he said, "Well, lying certainly isn't." He frowned at Mina, passing her the spatula. "If you have to lie to be around any guy . . . pretty good sign that's on the not allowed side. Just use common sense, baby girl. That's the only rule I want you to follow."

Mina pretended to be focused on scooping a square of lasagna onto her plate. She waited for her mom to add on. When she looked up, Mariah was staring at her with an odd smile on her golden brown face.

Mina looked down guiltily, thinking of how she'd given her mom the cold shoulder for days after they'd (she'd) squashed her Frenzy plans. Bickering with her mother was like breathing; they did it all the time. But it never stopped Mina from feeling bad when she knew she had been especially bratty. This time karma had come back and kicked her in the teeth for it. She waited for her mother to give her a hard time. Instead, her mom got up and stood behind Mina's chair. She wrapped her arms around Mina's neck, smushing their faces together.

"Just ease us into all this, Mina," her mom whispered. "I know you're not a baby anymore. But you're still our baby."

Mina swallowed over the lump in her throat and tried to get the small bite of lasagna down. She felt her eyes getting itchy. Tears were near.

Her father blew out an exaggerated breath. "Aww, come on. Not over dinner." He shook his head. "Man, what I wouldn't give for a little more testosterone in this house."

Mariah went over and shoved his shoulder. She swiped at her eyes as she laughed and sat back down. "Oh, don't act like you won't be crying the blues when some knucklehead finally takes her off our hands for good."

Jackson munched on his lasagna. "Shoot, no, I won't either." He rolled his big hazel eyes playfully. "Then all her expensive habits will be *his* problem."

Just then the sounds of Dem Franchise Boys, "Lean wit it, Rock wit it," came from Mina's room. Mina's shoulders straightened as she looked toward the stairs from where the sound came.

"Why are your speakers so loud?" Her father scowled.

"Like you need to ask. Obviously she was waiting for somebody specific to log on." Mariah smiled.

"Well, we're eating," Jackson Mooney said, playing the role of stern dad, even though he was the official softy in the house.

Mina quickly took a few more forkfuls of lasagna and salad. "I'm full," she said, meaning it. After a few days off from eating regularly, her stomach was already straining from the half square of pasta.

"When was the last time Daddy and I were both home in time for dinner, Amina?" her mother asked wistfully, anticipating Mina's request to leave the table.

Mina picked at her plate. "I know. I didn't ask to be excused."

"But you want to," her mom said, taking a dainty bite.

"No. I'm fine," Mina said.

Her dad chuckled. "Go on, Mina."

Mina jumped up, gave her dad then her mom a kiss, then ran up the stairs, two at a time.

"Jack," Mariah fussed.

"It was my turn to play good cop," he teased.

"It's always your turn," Mina heard her mom say right before she threw herself into her chair and quickly read Brian's IM.

BJB-boy: What up girl? Did u ever find out if u can go to the jam this wkend?

BubbliMi: Hey. I doubt it 2 scared 2 bring it up 2 the 'rents again

BJB-boy: right, right

Mina bit nervously at her lip. New week, new guy, new party—same issue. It was going to be awfully hard to date anyone if she couldn't go outside of her house. Her fingers hovered over the keyboard as she worked up the courage to ask Brian to chill with her instead of going to the party. She took a deep breath and . . . chickened out, only asking:

BubbliMi: so u still going?
BJB-boy: I was just going cuz u was going

Mina grinned. She tugged at one of her spiral curls, typing one-handed.

BubbliMi: word?
BJB-boy: word. U punished or can u have co.?
BubbliMi: not sure. I'll ask tho. Y? Would u come chill w/a sistah?
BJB-boy: No doubt

Mina was smiling so hard her face hurt.

BJB-boy: u still want me 2 come 2 ur competition?
BubbliMi: mos' def
BJB-boy: alright. Cuz JZ and Michael said they'd ride w/me
BubbliMi: cool
BJB-boy: Look, I gotta bounce. Jus came on 2 see what wuz up for the wkend. I told my boys I'd roll up their way 2 see 'em play 2nite
BubbliMi: So, you gon' be seeing any old GFs 2night?
BJB-boy: Now that's my bidness Sike! Naw, it's just the fellas. Plus, I'm already trying 2 get w/dis lil honey from around the way, u know?

Mina was glad they weren't on the phone or Brian would have definitely heard the grin in her voice. She played along:

BubbliMi: Oh, right, right. Is she cute?
BJB-boy: She alright
BubbliMi: Just alright?! ☹
BJB-boy: I'm not trying 2 blow ur head up.
BubbliMi: LOL. It's alright, I have a date 2night 2.
BJB-boy: Anybody I know?
BubbliMi: Yup my girls. Standing date every Thurs
BJB-boy: Say nice things bout me.
BubbliMi: Hmm . . . I'll try.
BJB-boy: Alright, ltr, Toughie.
BubbliMi: cu

Mina sighed happily, unable to wipe the cheesy grin from her face. The thought of missing Raheem's party had fallen off her radar. Cooling out with Brian, away from a big crowd, was fine with her. And as long as they did it under the watchful eyes of her parents, she was pretty sure the get-together fell under the newly defined Mooney rules of dating.

A set of blaring horns sounded. Her girls were on already for their Thursday night chat.

Liz-e-O: Hey girl. What u know good?
CinnyBon: It's all good in da hood
BubbliMi: But don't forget the 'burbs baby!!! LOL!
K-Lo: Hey girlies
Liz-e-O: ROLL CALL
BubbliMi: Brian is going 2 chill over here on Sat w/me while y'all off getting ur groove on. I'm sad . . . but not too sad.☺
CinnyBon: Raheem called and apologized Sunday night. I'm in love again. :::cheesing:::

K-Lo: My grandmother thinks Angel is a nice young man from
a troubled background. He'll be accepting his Academy
Award next month. :::giggling wildly:::::

Liz-e-O: Todd and I are just friends . . . but he's fun 2 talk 2.
Sorry, guess my news is a yawner.

BubbliMi: Lightning round. Kelly, how far can u go w/Angel b4
ur grandmother finds out his troubled bkground is really his
troubled present?

K-Lo: taking it 1 day @ a time. It's all I can do. Lizzie, has Todd
tried 2 kiss u yet? If so, dish. If not . . . r u gonna let him when
he does or keep playing the friend card?

Liz-e-O: he hasn't tried. I told u guys I'm 17th century dating.
n since whenever Todd's mouth is moving a joke is coming out
of it he's just my speed. We'll prbly kiss sometime in the next
milleny. Ok MY turn. Cinny, how come u keep giving Raheem
2nd chances even tho every time u guys get together ur fighting? Do u really think u guys will stay together?

CinnyBon: ouch Liz hitting hard in da light'n round. I want it 2
work. sometimes I feel like I'm the only one who does tho.
Ok. Mina, if Craig hadn't been straight fool would u have
given up da goodies?

BubbliMi: LOL :::blushing::: Dag Cinny!

Liz-e-O: Mi, u know u gotta answr.

BubbliMi: let's just say I thought about it

K-Lo: Liz, guess me n' u r rolling in the 17th century 2gether

Liz-e-O: welcome fellow sister of the perpetual courtship

CinnyBon: LMAO that makes us the bad girls Mi

BubbliMi: nah I'm still a good girl . . . but good girls might if
the right dude comes along.

CinnyBon: I know dat's right

BubbliMi: So that's the low down. Alright girlies, I've got 2 go.
Mina's outtie.

CinnyBon: That was a good round. Good night stuck-up sisters of soul . . . yes, even u Lizzie O'Reilly.

K-Lo: See u guys tomorrow @ school.

Liz-e-O: Bye guys.

Party On: Take Two

Friday night, just when Mina had decided missing Raheem's party wasn't the end of the world, her parents did what parents did best—dropped a bomb on her. She could go to Raheem's party, but there were some rules she and Lizzie both would have to endure. Mina had quickly agreed (yeah, yeah, anything you want) and texted Brian that she could go after all.

Saturday morning was a blur of e-mails, IMs and text messages from the girls about what to wear and where to meet. Mina raced around the house, gathering sleepover must-haves: pony holders and a bandana for her hair, minibottle of mouthwash to ward off the morning stank and a fresh batch of newly updated songs to her iPod—it helped her sleep.

Twice, Lizzie went nutso on her and tried to back out of the party. First, there was a text from her worried she'd be the only white person in The Cove and people would stare. Mina dismissed that out of hand, reminding Lizzie there were white players on Sam–Well's team, Todd would be there and, most importantly, that Mina would come to her house and drag her to the party if necessary.

At noon, Lizzie said her stomach was crampy and she thought her period was ready to start. Mina promised to bring some ibuprofen and warned Lizzie not to text her any more unless it was to inform her she'd died.

Still, she understood Lizzie's sudden bout with jitters. Mina had been the same way her first time in The Cove. Mina had never seen Lizzie so uptight. She could practically hear Lizzie worrying through the text messages. She called to give her some BFF support.

"Hey, it's me," Mina said. "Is everything alright?"

"Huh? Yeah, of course. Why?" Lizzie asked, her voice high and nervous.

Mina rolled her eyes and took a patient, controlled breath. "Because your messages are getting bizarre. The Cove really isn't all that bad, Liz. I promise you'll be fine."

"Yeah, I know," Lizzie said, her heart skipping. Easy for Mina to say, she'd been there before. Lizzie was having serious second, third and fourth thoughts about it. What were her parents thinking letting her go?

Better to back out now out of Cinny's earshot. Lizzie didn't want to offend her.

"I promise I will not leave you," Mina said.

Lizzie snorted a laugh. "Yeah, right. You mean until Brian flashes one of those cutie smiles."

Mina was dead serious. "No, I mean it. You're my girl. By your side all night 'til you're comfortable."

"Serious?" Lizzie asked, breathing better.

"Serious. Now, stop tripping. I'll see you tonight, right?" Mina said, making it obvious she expected a yes.

"Okay." Lizzie obliged. "Yes, Mother!"

Mina giggled. "Bye, girl."

When party time arrived, Mina was jumpy with anticipation.

She double-checked her bag (for the fourth time) to make sure she had everything to stay over at Jacinta's before fussing in front of the mirror to comb her already flawless hair. She glanced nervously over at the clock. It was already seven-thirty. She texted Lizzie, determined to stay on her:

Where r u?!

From Lizzie: Almost @ ur hse—rlx!

Mina toted her bag down the stairs. "Ma, Daddy, are y'all ready? The O'Reillys are only a few seconds away!"

"Yes, stop shouting," her mom answered.

Mina admired her mom's outfit. "Ooh, you look nice, Mommy. Where are you guys going?"

"Some Japanese restaurant in D.C. that your dad's been raving about."

A horn blew, and Mina grabbed her jacket and dashed to the door. "They're here."

Her mom laughed. "Come on, Jackson. Mina's so anxious, I think she could convince Patrick to drive off without us."

Mina giggled, unable to hide her excitement. She would have never in a million years thought the week would have ended up like this. On Monday, she'd prepared herself for a chunky-monkey, love-talking slow jams weekend cuddled up with her iPod in sweatpants. Now she was back on the party circuit. Sweet.

Mina and her parents hopped into Patrick O'Reilly's Suburban and greeted their close friends warmly.

Mina appraised Lizzie's outfit approvingly. As she and Michael had recommended, Lizzie wore an orange satin mini, an orange, brown, blue and white striped mock turtleneck and high brown boots. They were going for a 1970s go-go look, and Lizzie's hair was swept into a high, tight ponytail, which grazed the nape of her neck, to top it off. "You look so cute, Lizzie. It's so retro," Mina squealed.

Lizzie's dad's lecturing interrupted the girls' chatter.

"Girls, do we need to go over the rules?" his stern voice asked.

Lizzie and Mina gave each other an exasperated look, rolling their eyes. "No," they chimed.

Patrick O'Reilly was a tall man, muscular, who kept his dark hair low, a near crew cut. Even from the backseat, Mina could see the look of seriousness on his face. The ruddy complexion that often made him look as if he'd just come from a workout was even more flushed tonight as he looked in his rearview eying the girls.

Mina's dad said, "Okay, good. Rule number one—"

Mina protested. "Daddy, we said no!"

"I know, which is exactly why we need to go over them," her father insisted.

Mina and Lizzie sighed.

Lizzie's mom said, "I know you've heard them a million times before, but this is a big step. It's your first house party without us." She turned and gave the girls the evil eye. "I mean, your first party with our permission."

The girls stifled a giggle.

"And we're trusting you," Mina's mom reminded them.

"So, rule number one—stay together," Mina's dad called out as the girls lip-synced along.

Lizzie's dad fixed them with another look in his mirror. "Rule number two—do not leave the party unless you're going right to Jacinta's house. And if you do, leave together."

"Rule number three—absolutely no drinking," Mina's dad said. "I don't believe Jamal would allow minors to be around alcohol, but I know how teenagers can be. If there is alcohol or drugs there, just say no."

Lizzie and Mina muffled their giggles. Mina was glad the Suburban was big. She and Lizzie were too far in the back for their fathers to see they were making faces and laughing in the darkness.

Lizzie's father said, "Rule number four—watch out for one another."

"Rule number five—keep your legs closed," Mina's dad said.

Lizzie's father added a short, solemn nod in agreement.

Horrified, Mina screamed, "Daddy! That was not one of the rules."

"I know. I just made that one up," her dad replied.

Mina's mom hit him on the shoulder. "Jack, the girls know how to carry themselves."

Lizzie's dad replied, "Hey, we just threw it in for extra measure."

Lizzie's mom sighed. "Girls, your fathers just mean dance and enjoy hanging out with your friends. But don't feel pressured to . . . do anything you'll regret, just to have fun."

Mina shook her head. Thank goodness, they were almost there and running out of time to make up more rules.

"Orange and Mint Chocolate Chip"

"Adrenaline rush like wooh."
—Lloyd, "Hey Young Girl"

Mina jumped out of the truck as soon as it stopped, throwing her parents a quick, cheerful, "See you tomorrow."

Jacinta saw her coming and opened the door wide. She looked fashionably understated, yet very put together in a pair of tight, very low waist jeans, a pair of black heel boots, a very girly top that clung to her curves and Raheem's Trojans jacket. "Hey, girls," Jacinta sang. She eyed Lizzie's outfit. "Liz, good look, girl."

"Thanks." Lizzie blushed.

Before Mina could say anything, Jacinta raised an eyebrow. "Don't even start about the jacket."

Mina did a snort chuckle and raised her hands in surrender. "I wasn't gonna say a thing . . . I mean, we're in Trojan country, so I guess it's cool." She pinched a corner of the jacket between her fingers as if it would burn her. "Better keep it on this side of the DRB, though."

Jacinta swatted Mina's hands away as they laughed.

Mr. Phillips spoke as he walked by to speak to Lizzie's and Mina's parents. The girls chorused a hello before running off to the room Jacinta shared with her eleven-year-old sister, Jamila.

"As soon as Kelly gets here, we can bounce," Jacinta said.

"Are we sleeping downstairs tonight?" Mina asked.

"Um-huh, but you can leave your stuff up here for now. I've been over to Angel's twice already; the party's in full swing," Jacinta informed them.

"Already? Dag," Mina said, disappointed. She hadn't wanted to miss a second.

Jacinta went over the lowdown on curfew. "Okay, we have to be back in the house by twelve-thirty. My dad knows half the crowd have provisional licenses and need to leave by midnight anyway. But, he said we could help Angel clean up if we wanted. That's why twelve-thirty."

"Twelve-thirty is later than my normal curfew," Lizzie admitted.

Mina laughed. "You know it's later than mine."

"Believe me, my father will be there around eleven-thirtyish anyway. So if you gon' do wrong, do it before eleven-thirty," Jacinta joked.

"Hello?" Kelly's quiet voice called out from downstairs.

"There she is, let's go," Jacinta said, already heading to the door and bounding down the stairs before the girls could throw their bags in a corner.

Mina was close behind her. "Just drop your bags in the corner, Kell. We're missing out."

Kelly teased, "Umph, pressed much?"

"Daddy, we're gone," Jacinta yelled.

Her father appeared from the kitchen. "Okay. I'll be in and out. Have fun and be good. I mean it, girls, I'll be checking in every now and then. And when my face is in the place, I expect everybody to be accounted for."

"Yes, Mr. Phillips," the girls chorused, the picture of innocence as they filtered out of the house.

Mina heard the music well before they actually reached Angel's apartment. She hoped that all of his neighbors either were invited to come or weren't home. The dead couldn't sleep through all of the thumping caused by the bass.

People spilled out of Angel's two-level apartment, scattered throughout the small yard, on the curb and on the front stoop. The cold didn't seem to bother anyone, and Mina soon realized why. It was scorching inside of the small apartment.

As the girls entered, curious heads turned to eye them up and down.

Jacinta strode through the crowd, waving to a few folks who weren't there the last time she stopped by.

The girls stepped into a living room that was wall-to-wall bodies. The room was empty of all furniture to ensure maximum dance space, except for the DJ's area. He took up one entire wall with his equipment, one big speaker next to him blaring toward the door and another behind him, facing the kitchen area. The setup blanketed the entire house with music.

People flowed out into the kitchen clear into the backyard.

The girls walked single file behind Jacinta, sticking close together partly out of a lack of space and partly because they didn't recognize anyone else in the house and needed one another for comfort.

Raheem plucked Jacinta out of the line and pulled her into the middle of the swelling crowd, leaving Kelly in the front of the line. She stopped short and yelled back to Mina, "Where should we go?"

Mina shrugged and yelled back, "Let's just keep going forward until we find Angel."

Kelly walked a few more inches through the bouncing, gyrating bodies before she saw Angel walking toward her (trying to) from the kitchen.

When he reached them, he yelled over the music, "What's up, Ma?" He made eye contact with Mina and nodded. She waved back.

"Hi," Kelly said warmly. "Good turnout, huh?"

Angel smiled and pulled her toward the center of the room. "Oh, your boy know how to throw a party. Come on."

Kelly gave Mina an apologetic shrug as she let herself be dragged off.

Mina turned her head to yell back to Lizzie. "I guess it's me and you, chick."

She grabbed Lizzie's hand and tried pushing her way toward the back door. It was hot and close in the room, and the prospect of fresh air drew her to the backyard. She'd made it to the kitchen when Lizzie's hand slipped out of hers. Startled, she looked back in time to see JZ pulling Lizzie toward the dancing mob.

Her heart fluttered when she saw Brian standing next to him. He spoke with a nod, and motioned for Mina to come back.

She did an about-face and headed back, glad it was crowded because it slowed her pace. If the path was clear, he would see she was practically running to him.

When she finally reached him, she asked, "Y'all just getting here?"

"Sort of. We saw y'all get dropped off, but I couldn't find a parking space, so we had to ride around for a bit," Brian answered.

Mina nodded. She let the music bounce over her head and moved in sync to the beat despite the crowd. She and Brian found a comfortable rhythm as they both lost themselves in the booming bass. The DJ shouted out to the different neighborhoods represented by the party-goers.

"Somebody told me the Woods reppin' tonight!" the DJ called out. "Holler if you hear me!!!"

Mina, JZ and Brian shouted in response, pumping their arms.

Brian pulled Mina close to him and started a slow, suggestive grind. Mina's cheeks and ears burned, but she moved in time to the music, matching his grind with a roll of her hips. He moved his hands along her sides and held on to her hips. *I really could die happy right now*, Mina thought. *Craig who?*

Lizzie's voice, yelling in her ear, brought her back to the present. "Hey, Todd's here. We're going out back to sit down. Michael is out front. He told Todd to tell you to come holler when you get a minute."

Mina nodded, never missing a step.

She and Brian danced to song after song. When the DJ finally played a slow song, Brian took her hand and walked toward the front door. She was disappointed that he didn't want to slow dance with her.

The cool air hit Mina in the face, and she breathed in the crisp scent of the night. Brian was still holding her hand. Her stomach did little flip-flops as she savored how her hand felt in his. His hands were squeezably soft, and Mina focused on how her small palm fit just right into his larger palm.

"Come on, walk to the car with me," he said.

Mina looked for Michael as they crossed the tiny patch of grass serving as the front yard, but didn't see him. When they cleared the screaming blare of the music, Mina asked, "So, what's in the car?"

"Nothing. I just wanted some air and didn't feel like sitting out in the yard," Brian answered.

"You didn't want to slow dance?" Mina asked, peeking up at his face from the corner of her eye. His eyes crinkled as he chuckled.

"We could have. You want to go back in and dance?"

"No. I mean . . . you know, if you want," Mina said.

She didn't feel the same confidence around Brian that she'd felt when they first met and she had "boyfriend" to fall back on. But she also didn't feel as tongue-tied as she thought she would. She was a little wound up, felt as though she'd had too much caffeine. But otherwise, she felt comfortable with him.

"It was just hot, that's all," Brian said. "We have all night, right?"

His voice was so tender, as if he was asking her approval, it made Mina smile. "Right."

They reached the truck, and Brian slid in, popping the lock on Mina's door as he did. He cracked his window, and Mina did the same. The inside of the truck was deathly silent compared to the blasting music from the party. Mina could hear them both breathing.

"Did I ever say thanks for the interview?" she said, avoiding the silence. "I think people really liked *Pop Life*."

"Yeah, I've heard people talking about it." He pursed his lips as though thinking. "I don't think you ever thanked me, though."

Mina chuckled. "Well, thank—"

She held her breath as Brian moved his face closer to hers and kissed her, his lips so soft they felt like warm liquid. *Okay, wait . . . now I can die happy*, she thought, slithering into the seat.

His lips remained on Mina's for a few more seconds before he moved back to his side of the truck. He smiled as he flirted, "Should we go through a few weeks of what's your favorite color and favorite ice cream first? Or can we skip that part since you've already formally interviewed me?"

His brown eyes penetrated Mina's as if he were trying to see inside her head. The direct attention flustered her, and she tried to joke it off. "Ummm . . . the second one."

He moved in and kissed Mina again.

"Orange and mint chocolate chip," Mina said softly when he'd pulled back.

Brian's thick eyebrows knitted in confusion.

"My favorite color is orange, and my favorite ice cream is mint chocolate chip," Mina explained, smiling.

Brian's lips grazed hers again as he said, "We should head back."

"Head back where?" Mina asked, dazed.

Brian opened his door. "The party. JZ told me about your parents' rules. If Jacinta's father shows up there for a body check, you should be there. Right?"

Mina blinked hard and focused in on his words. "Oh, yeah, right. Just one more thing."

"What?" Brian asked, turning around.

"This," Mina said, leaning over and kissing him full and slow. She pulled away. A modest smile played on her lips as she hopped out of the car, laughing at the shock on Brian's face.

That's a Wrap

Kelly held on to Angel's hand tightly as they wove through the crowd to the staircase. When they reached the bottom landing, Angel darkened the already dim lighting. A roar of approval went up from the dancing crowd.

Kelly could barely see an inch in front of her. She took hesitant, short steps up the stairway, aware that there were people sitting on a few of the steps. She breathed a sigh of relief when they reached Angel's room, which was only slightly more well lit than the cave-like atmosphere of the living room.

The vibration from the music below made the bedroom floor shake, tickling Kelly's feet.

Angel closed the door.

Kelly walked over to the window to look out into the backyard, the only part of the party with bright light. People were scattered everywhere.

Angel joined her at the window. "You having fun?"

"Um-hmm."

He kissed her on the back of her neck, and Kelly's insides went soft at his touch. She turned around, head raised so Angel could kiss her.

"You look hot tonight," he whispered as he led her over to the bed.

"Thank you." Kelly's stomach was a ball of nerves. She couldn't stop giggling. "Thanking you sounds silly," she rambled on, until Angel pressed his mouth against hers.

Kelly leaned back onto the bed and closed her eyes. Angel's lips pressed against her face and neck.

When cool air hit her belly, she jumped, realizing that Angel's hands had slid up her shirt.

His kisses came faster, and Kelly breathlessly tried to keep up with his lips and hands. But he seemed to be everywhere all at once. She gave in and sank deeper into the bed.

Suddenly, Angel's whisper of, "You alright with this?" hit Kelly like the sting of cold water. She bolted upright, almost knocking heads with Angel, but he jumped out of the way in time.

"No. I can't do this," Kelly said, breathing heavy. So much for seventeenth-century courting, she thought. "I want to, though," she admitted, then confided, "If you hadn't asked . . ."

Angel smirked. "Me and my big mouth."

Kelly sat up, smoothing out her clothes. A wave of shamed nausea overcame her as she realized how close she had come to getting in completely over her head. If Angel hadn't stopped . . . She shuddered.

But he had. He'd asked permission, and that was what snapped her out of it.

"No, I'm glad you asked," she said, combing her fingers through her chestnut waves. "I mean . . . it's why I like you. You come off so hardcore, but you're not. At least not with me."

Angel ran his hands through his short, wavy hair and shook his head. "I could lose my player card for this."

Kelly teased, "I promise not to tell."

She brushed at her hair as she talked, trying to erase any sign that she had been lying down. Her ears were on fire just thinking about Jacinta's father catching her in Angel's bedroom.

She walked back over to the window, looking at the couples in the shadows. It reminded her of the Frenzy until she spied Rosie standing near the other beefy bodyguard, talking. It amazed her that every time she felt as though there wasn't much difference in her life at DRB High and Angel's at Sam–Well, something smacked her back to reality.

"I can't do this, Angel," she said quietly.

"That's why I stopped," he said, hugging her from behind. He kissed her neck.

She shook her head. "No, I mean . . . act like I can separate you from the hustling." Kelly's shoulder hitched, then slumped. "Or act like I can keep lying to my grandmother. I like you. But this is the first time ever I've lied to Grand like this and . . ." She looked around the dark room. "I'm definitely not ready for sex."

"So what do you want me to do, Kelly?" Angel said, raising his voice for the first time in anger. "It's not like quitting a job at the mall."

"You said your uncle is back on his feet. How come he can't—" Kelly stopped. Since Angel wouldn't go into details, she had no idea what to suggest. All she knew was her relationship with Angel felt like a game of pretend. But she wasn't sure anymore if she was pretending to be in his world or if he was pretending to be in hers.

Being at the mall together, she could handle.

Hanging out at the game, easy.

Being at a party with him, dancing—yeah.

But things were moving too fast, and thanks to her mother's "information," now whenever she was with Angel, all Kelly could see was the door being kicked in by cops busting up their game of pretend. But she couldn't explain any of that to Angel because he didn't want to talk about it.

It.

What he did, whatever he did that required two beefy meatheads to have his back.

It hurt her head to think about it anymore.

Finally, she sighed, shook her head. "Never mind, Angel."

Kelly walked around him and went to the door.

"So, what, it's like that?" he asked. "You just gon' step?"

His voice was an odd mix of Trash Talker and Mr. Tender.

Kelly wanted to turn around, get Angel to make promises she knew he couldn't or wouldn't keep. She imagined her twenty-something-year-old mother making the same type of decision with Rico (dad), except her mother hadn't walked out.

Kelly and her mother looked alike.

But they weren't alike.

"I'm sorry," Kelly said. She opened the door and raised her voice over the music that poured in. "I'm sorry, I can't."

The large, barren square that served as Angel's backyard was ripe with couples. Someone had turned out the yard's bright spotlights, making the people milling outdoors living shadows.

Jacinta and Raheem walked out, scoping a place to sit. The air was cold, but Jacinta preferred the cool to the stifling, crowded house. She peered into the darkness of the night and spotted Todd and Lizzie sitting on top of a wooden picnic table. She walked toward them, Raheem in tow.

"Hey, y'all. Can we share your table?" Jacinta asked.

Todd spoke too loud, immediately ready to clown around. "What's up, Jacinta?" He gave Raheem a pound. "'Sup, man?"

Raheem threw him a head nod. Todd was cool on the court and all, but Raheem wasn't trying to be boys with him.

Todd teased Jacinta. "So, what's up, girlfriend?"

She rolled her eyes, pretending to be annoyed. "Nothing, white boy . . . my bad, White Chocolate. You getting your player on?"

Todd laughed. "You'll have to ask Lizzie that. Am I pimpin', Liz?"

Lizzie chuckled. "He's trying."

"Ouch, now there's nothing worse than thinking you're big pimpin' and a girl says you're trying," Todd said to Raheem.

Lizzie nudged him. She liked Todd's silliness, but she knew some people found his constant need to joke annoying. Raheem seemed like one of those people. Even in the blackness, she could see his dark brown face was stoic. Lizzie tugged at Todd's arm. "Come on, let's see your moves."

Todd bounced around and then broke into a pop lock. He pulled Lizzie toward the house. "Uh-oh, you're in for a treat, Liz."

Jacinta shook her head as she yelled after them. "Don't hurt her, Todd."

"Man, he corny as hell," Raheem muttered.

Jacinta chuckled. "Yeah, but he's nice."

Raheem snorted and gave Jacinta a look. "See, that's what I don't get. He alright. But you act like some of the stuff some of your friends do or say is so funny." His voice was gruff and bitter. "Man, the stuff is straight cornball."

"He just playing around, Heem," Jacinta pointed out.

"Whatever, it's still corny," he said, dismissing her opinion.

Jacinta held her breath until she didn't feel like screaming. Defending Todd, or anyone for that matter, would only be cause for an argument. What *could* they talk about?

The awkward silence between them pressed down on Jacinta. She gazed around the yard and realized most of the people outside weren't talking at all. In one corner of the yard, near the edge of the patio, a group played craps by flashlight. And a sweet, acrid scent drifted by from another corner.

Raheem spoke up finally. "Looks like all your girls found a hookup."

Jacinta nodded, pleased. She held on to the opening, determined to keep things nice between them. Then Raheem ruined the moment. "Speaking of hooking up . . . what's up tonight with me and you?"

"Is that all our weekends together are about?" Jacinta blurted, unable to take it back once it was out. She hadn't meant it to, but it came out as an accusation.

As expected, he became defensive. "Naw, Jacinta, that's not what they about. But the weekends that we have I don't remember having to force you."

Jacinta scooted closer to him and lowered her voice. "I didn't mean it like that. But it feels like we either arguing or sexing. Isn't there an in between?"

Raheem sucked his teeth and stood up. "Yeah, not talking at all." He walked off.

"Raheem," she whispered hoarsely, embarrassed. But he walked inside without turning around, making it halfway through the house when Charice, a girl who liked both him and Angel, pulled him up. She swooped in, grabbed his arm in a viselike grip and tugged him toward the crowded floor. "You not getting away without dancing with me, Raheem Patterson."

Raheem tried to pull away, but her tugging was insistent, so he relented and followed. She smiled up into his face as they danced. They were smashed closer and closer by the pressing crowd. "I figured your girl wouldn't mind if I stole you for one dance," Charice purred, rubbing against him.

"She be alright, I guess," Raheem said, watching as Jacinta walked in through the kitchen, looking for him. Jacinta scanned the dark room. The living room was too dark for her to see him, but he saw her perfectly.

"I figured since Jacinta moved over to The Woods, you might cut her loose. You know, have a more convenient girlfriend," Charice suggested.

Raheem smirked. "And if I did?"

Eager, she asked, "Well, you haven't cut her loose, have you?"

"No, but if I did?"

She pushed herself closer to Raheem. "Well, how 'bout we handle that business when we get there."

Raheem never took his eye off Jacinta walking by, heading toward the front door.

Jacinta walked by JZ sitting on the front stoop, talking to some girl in a pair of tight, painted-on jeans. Jacinta wondered how the girl was sitting on the cold stoop as if it were ninety degrees out. Lizzie and Todd sat on the opposite side of the step, talking.

She ran into Michael near the sidewalk.

"What's up, Cinny?"

"Hey, Mike." Jacinta looked around, distracted. "Where have you been?"

"I have some family around here. I just been tipping in and out, visiting and whatnot. I'm waiting on this dude, Rob. He rolling with me to the Players social."

Jacinta nodded, not paying attention.

"You okay?" He looked around, following her distracted gaze. "Where's Mina? I haven't seen her."

"Somewhere off with Brian, I guess." She and Michael walked back to the stoop.

He chuckled. "They already broke rule number one of their parents' rules, huh?"

Jacinta's laugh was hollow. She walked back inside just as Mina emerged from the house. Her hair was slightly frizzed from the house's humidity. She dropped down onto the step, big smile across her face. "Brian is trying to kill me in there, making me dance to every cut."

Brian stood behind her. His toffee-colored face glistened with sweat. "Who? That was you who wouldn't let *me* stop dancing."

Mina hugged Michael. "Hey, Boo. Your friend Rob here yet?"

Michael nodded. "Yeah, he's in there somewhere. We're ready to bounce soon, though. So do I get a dance?"

"Umph, when you're a sister with moves, your job is never done," Mina said. She stood up to head back in the house. "Let's roll."

Michael asked Brian, "Can I steal her for a second, son?"

"Do your thing, man," Brian said, taking Michael's place on the step.

"Jay, what happened, man?" Todd asked when the girl in tight jeans got up and walked inside.

"She going to get something to drink," JZ said.

Todd laughed. "Naw, man. I heard you got suspended for next week's game."

JZ's face cracked for an instant; then he got it together. "Yeah, I'm out for the next two games."

He looked over at Lizzie, and they exchanged a meaningful look.

"Dude, we need you out there," Todd exclaimed dramatically.

"We be cool 'til you get back," Brian said, giving JZ a pound.

"Is it your grades?" Todd pressed.

"Something like that," JZ said, quietly closing the matter by standing up and going inside.

Todd frowned.

"Long story," Lizzie said.

"Secret?" Todd asked.

"Something like that." Lizzie laughed when Todd wrinkled his face in exaggerated disgust.

Just then, Jacinta's voice rose over the thumping music. "I don't need this, Raheem!"

She stormed out of the house, Raheem close on her heels.

The door burst open, nearly slamming Lizzie in the back.

Raheem yelled, "Just wait, Jacinta! Hold up."

"Should we go after her?" Lizzie asked Todd and Brian, looking after Jacinta, then back at the shocked guys, unsure what to do.

The music still blared, but people trickled out of the house to see the blowup.

Michael and Mina dashed out of the house. Mina went to follow Jacinta, but Brian grabbed her arm.

She pulled away. "What are you doing?"

He had a firm grip on her arm.

"I think you need to let her handle her business."

"Why? She's upset. I—we should go after her."

"What happened in there?" Lizzie asked.

"Cinny bumped into Raheem as he was kissing another girl." Mina stated the obvious. "This is not good."

Kelly came outside, scanning the yard before realizing they were all standing on the stoop. "What happened? Who was yelling? Is there a fight?"

Angel appeared beside her. He looked beyond them to the street where Jacinta and Raheem were still yelling at each other.

"Cinny and Raheem are arguing," Mina said. She watched as Jacinta's figure disappeared down the street. She looked at Kelly and Lizzie. "We need to go . . . yeah, we should go."

Lizzie nodded.

Mina turned to Brian and shrugged an apology. "Sorry. We might be back . . . I don't know."

"I'll holler at you later," Brian assured her.

As Kelly went to follow Mina, Angel grabbed her arm.

"So, what's up?" he whispered.

Kelly watched as Lizzie and Mina quickly covered the distance from the door to the end of Angel's yard. She wanted to catch up. She didn't know what else to say to Angel. "I don't know," she answered truthfully. "I've gotta go, Angel."

He let her arm go, and she hesitated a second, as if she had something else to say. Angel's jaw was tight. His eyes sad and angry at the same time. Finally Kelly ran off to catch up with the girls.

They scurried along the road to Jacinta's, stopping in their tracks when they came within a few feet of Jacinta and Raheem arguing under a streetlight. Unsure what to do, they waited for the two to finish.

"See, that's some bullshit right there, Raheem," Jacinta spat. Her arms were tight against her body. She was crying. "And save all that you was just trying to make me jealous mess. You was just being ignorant and got caught!"

"Maybe I need somebody who more worried about me than their clique," Raheem growled.

Jacinta snorted. "Oh, well, when I was hanging with you and Angel, it was okay for everything to be about us three. But now I have other friends, so that's a bad thing, right?"

Raheem looked disgusted. "I just don't feel like always having to deal with your white friends and your wannabe white friends. Can't we just hang out one weekend without them or without you talking about them?"

Jacinta rolled her eyes. "This not about that. Not all your friends at Sam–Well are black. Shit, Angel not even black." She did a high-pitched, sarcastic laugh. "This about you disrespecting me and kissing all up on some other girl while I'm five feet away, Raheem." Her voice broke when she said his name, then grew stronger. "Next time just spit in my face—you'll get the same results."

Raheem lowered his voice to an angry whisper. "I was just pissed off, that's all. Trying to make you mad."

"Now, exactly how can you make me mad if I never saw you? Y'all were all the way back in a corner near the DJ." Jacinta's arms flailed as she yelled. "I just happened to see you because I was going to ask the DJ for his mic to call you up front."

"Somebody would have told you about it. I wasn't trying to hide," Raheem countered.

Jacinta scowled, unable to believe what she just heard. Agitated, her voice rose with each sentence. "Please tell me you have a better excuse than that! It's so stupid I can't believe it's coming out of your mouth! Are you talking English? 'Cause nothing you saying right now makes any sense!"

"Oh, so now I'm stupid? I guess those smart cats over at Del Rio High would never treat you like this?" Raheem shot at her.

Jacinta looked at him, eyes full of hurt. Her voice was soft. "I have no idea how they would treat me. But I never thought you'd do me greasy like this." She turned her nose up in disgust. "It's one thing to be mad at me, but it's just foul to sit up in a party full of people we both know and stick your tongue down some other girl's throat."

Raheem lowered his voice, trying to calm things down. "Cinny, I'm sorry. What I did was wack."

He rubbed his hand back and forth over his cornrowed head as he spoke. "Yeah, I was hot with you and I wanted to make you hot, too. Charice was just an easy way to do that. I was dead wrong."

Jacinta's face became calm, but her words had a shrill edge to them, like someone working hard to hold on to the last of their cool. "Congratulations. For all the work you put into pissing me off, you get a brand-new *ex*-girlfriend!"

Tears streamed down her face as she turned on her heels and ran toward her house.

In her head, she thought ending it this way was wrong. It shouldn't end like this.

But over was over.

Lizzie, Mina and Kelly ran to catch up with her. At the edge of her yard, they circled around her.

"We heard y'all breaking up. I'm so sorry," Mina said, close to tears. She felt awful for Jacinta.

Jacinta tried to sniff back tears. Her body heaved as she spoke. "Y'all didn't . . . have to . . . leave the party because of me."

"Yes, we did. We came together. We leave together," Kelly said.

Everyone nodded.

"Is it really over, Jacinta?" Lizzie asked.

Jacinta looked up and over Lizzie's shoulder. She saw Raheem shake his head once, as though he was trying to clear it of her, before walking back to Angel's.

He didn't even try and come after me, she thought, wounded.

She nodded and let the tears run down her face. "Yeah. Yeah, it's really over."

The girls moved over to the curb and sat down, forming a strange huddle of hunched-over bodies, their heads leaning on one another as they hugged. They tightened the circle around Jacinta and consoled her.

Jacinta let their words and touch soothe her fractured feelings. She knew Raheem believed that she was just angry, that she would get over it. In a few days he would probably call and try to make up, thinking Jacinta had broken up out of spite.

Jacinta's heart split further. She cried harder as she thought about having to confront Raheem with the true reason she wanted out of their relationship. She'd outgrown him. This was real. They were through. It was over. Her heart told her so.

Epilogue

"You let go, and I'll let go, too."
—Lauryn Hill, "Ex Factor"

Mina stood in front of the mirror and used the curling iron to put one last curl in her hair. The door downstairs shut as her parents went to load the truck. She quickened her pace, expertly brushing her hair into a tight ponytail and topping it off with the blue-and-gold hair poms the squad had made especially for today's competition. Satisfied that the ponytail curled neatly and the poms were straight, Mina broke into a huge smile and winked at her image in the mirror. Game time!

Mina cleared her head and tried focusing on the routine one last time. But images from Saturday (another disastrous party) flashed in her head like scenes from a movie. Seemed like one minute, she was dancing with Brian, and then in a quick blur, she was near tears trying to help Cinny make sense of the pain from breaking up with Raheem, very publicly, in front of half the teen population of Pirates Cove. Mina knew how she felt and knew there weren't any words that made it better . . . not right away.

The phone rang, bombarding the house's silence with a shrill bleeping. Mina checked the caller ID. It was Jacinta.

She picked up on the second ring. "Hello."

Jacinta's voice was sad and heavy. "Hey, it's Cinny."

"Hey." Mina immediately jumped into sympathy mode. "Are you ready? We're on our way to pick you up."

Jacinta hesitated for a beat before answering, "Mi . . . I'm not going. I'm just not up to it."

Mina coaxed, "Everyone will be there, Cinny. And I think being with Lizzie, JZ, Kelly and Michael will be good for you." Mina wasn't sure if she should say it . . . Misery loved company but didn't necessarily want it thrown in their face. She was trying to make Jacinta feel . . . not so lonely. So she said it. "And you know, Kelly could use a little support after her and Angel . . . you know . . . broke up."

She held her breath. She hadn't meant to compare Jacinta and Raheem's two years with Kelly and Angel's two weeks. But . . .

Cinny went on, obviously not minding the comparison.

"I know, but—I'm just . . . I don't feel like it . . . I don't mean to disappoint you," she rambled. "I'm just too—"

"Look, this isn't about supporting me," Mina jumped in. "It's about being around people that support you. I've never broken up with anyone . . . I mean, we won't count Craig because we were only together for a minute." She and Jacinta shared a hollow laugh as Mina rambled on. "So I won't say I know how you feel, exactly. But I do know that being around your friends will help. That much I know for sure."

Jacinta sighed, giving Mina a chance to press as if talking to a baby. "Me and my parents will be down there to get you in a few minutes. Okay?"

"Alright," Jacinta answered, her voice uncharacteristically de-flated.

Mina hung up and took a deep breath. The last few days had been challenging. This was going to be the weirdest Christmas holiday ever. Kelly was upset (not sad, just constantly perplexed) about her and Angel. And Jacinta's depression was like a blanket, covering the circle of friends' every move. No one wanted to be too happy around her, fearing they would seem insensitive to her sadness. Counties was the official kickoff to the holiday break, no more school until January. Mina didn't want Cinny so sad over the long break.

She found it especially hard to keep her priorities straight. She wanted to talk about Brian every second. But she toned down her happiness around Jacinta and Kelly. But especially Jacinta. She tried not to be too clingy on the ride into school. As bad as she wanted to think about him 24/7, Mina felt obligated to help Jacinta through the breakup.

"Mina!" Brian called out from the sunroom.

Mina grinned at the sound of his voice. "Yeah?"

"Your parents sent me in here to get you, girl. What are you doing?"

"Sorry." Mina headed down the stairs. "Cinny called, and I had to convince her to come with us."

Brian nodded. He eyed Mina in her cheer outfit. "Can I see what's under that little skirt?"

He looked back to make sure no adults were around and tugged playfully at Mina's skirt.

Mina batted his hands away, laughing. "Be good, boy."

"Okay, so me and the fellas are going to follow your parents in my truck." Brian's all-about-the-business voice reminded Mina of her father. They'd obviously been talking, going over the details of the trip to Baltimore. "We'll see y'all at the Convention Center."

Mina nodded as she closed the blinds and double-checked the sliders were locked.

Brian leaned down and pecked her on the lips. "Good luck."

"Thanks." Mina grinned, watching Brian walk out to the truck. She looked on as he said something to her father, which made the two of them laugh.

Lizzie, JZ, Michael and Kelly stood by her dad's Navigator, big bundles of talking and laughing coats. Her mom was already in the truck, waiting patiently for everyone to load up.

Seeing everyone in a good mood gave Mina energy. She hoped it would do the same for Jacinta. She locked the door behind her and hurried toward the truck. Everyone scrambled to their respective vehicle.

Her dad exclaimed, "Finally. Thank you for joining us, Your Highness." He poked Mina's side as she passed by him.

"Game time!" Mina yelled.

"Game ti-yime," JZ hollered back. He hopped into Brian's Explorer.

Mina's dad backed the truck out of the driveway and waited for Brian to pull up next to him. He put his window down and provided Brian with last minute instructions on his route, and his and Mariah's cell phone number, in case they were separated along the way. Mina was sure Brian had heard the speech a million times in the last fifteen minutes.

From her seat, she watched as Brian nodded respectfully and laughed in the right places.

Once her father was finished and not looking, Brian threw Mina a quick, conspiratorial wink. She grinned and sank into the truck's leather seating.

Jackson reviewed the crew in his truck, then eyed Mina in his mirror. "Alright, you ready for this, baby girl?"

Still looking at Brian, Mina nodded. "Most definitely."

Most definitely!

DON'T GET IT TWISTED

A Del Rio Bay Clique Novel

PAULA CHASE

ABOUT THIS GUIDE

The following questions are intended to
enhance your group's reading of
DON'T GET IT TWISTED
by Paula Chase

DISCUSSION QUESTIONS

1. The overlying theme in *Don't Get It Twisted* is loyalty and how fragile it can be, even among friends. How important is loyalty to you? And what does being loyal mean?

2. Is there a certain line you should draw when it comes to being loyal to a friend?

3. Some people take neighborhood ties very seriously. Was Jacinta being disloyal to Raheem and The Cove simply for being comfortable around and becoming true friends with Mina and the rest of the 'burb clique? If you say yes, why?

4. At one point, the narrator reveals: *Mina still had a hard time getting used to the fact Jacinta had had the same boyfriend since she was twelve. She couldn't imagine having any boyfriend at twelve years old.* What do you think about "serious" relationships for middle-school-aged tweens? Debate the pros and cons of both sides: Why is being "just friends" not enough? Or, what's so wrong with having a boyfriend in middle school?

5. Even though Kelly risked being caught in a lie to be with Angel, in the end she chooses to remain loyal to her values by breaking it off. Do you agree with her decision? Can you be friends with or date someone who is a) doing something you don't believe is

right or b) involved in illegal activity? If you say yes, how do you separate the person from their behavior?

6. JZ tests Lizzie's loyalty by asking her to let him cheat from her paper. If you were Lizzie, how would you have handled this situation?

7. Even though Craig gets caught being disloyal to Mina, she flirts with Brian throughout the entire book and only feels mildly bad about it at the time. Which of them was more disloyal? Is Craig's behavior worse because he went beyond flirting? If Craig had ever caught Mina flirting with Brian, would he have been right to be upset or even break up with her? Why or why not?

8. Kelis and Mina are classic frenemies—not exactly friends but have learned to tolerate each other. Would you be able to remain squad mates and work side-by-side with someone who betrayed you the way Kelis did Mina? Why or why not?

9. Mina's parents say no official dating until she turns fifteen, but they still allow some form of dating. Is there a difference in formal dating and just hanging out with a guy you like? Is there a perfect age to begin dating someone one-on-one? If so, what is it and why that age?

10. The clique rallies around Mina after Craig disses her. Share with the group a time when your friends really came through for you.

Enhance your book club:

1. Contact the author and arrange for a virtual visit (via chat session or teleconference) through her website www.paulachasehyman.com

2. Choose one of the above questions that you think will generate the best discussion and invite the moms of book club members to a special Mother/Daughter Anything Goes session.

No license?
No problem!
Catch up with the DRB clique as
they go road tripping in . . .

That's What's Up!

Where there's cliquin', there's drama.

Waking the Sleeping Giant

Jessica Johnson glowered.

She stood mannequin still in the school's long hallway at the floor-to-ceiling glass panes surrounding the fishbowl, the café—Del Rio Bay High's outdoor beautiful-people-only section of the cafeteria. Her eyes, focused like hazel laser beams, made the glare catlike on her coffee-bean-complexioned face.

She couldn't take them off the scene outside.

About forty people milled around the square, no larger than two average-sized bedrooms. Some huddled around the five tall bistro tables—sometimes six people deep. Others stood atop the sandy-colored concrete benches that anchored the corners, while others still were content leaning against one of the two brick walls that enclosed the area. So used to being gawked at from the windows, no one paid her much mind. Everyone was enjoying the budding warmth of the early spring—many going jacketless in the fifty degree Maryland day.

Winter had been short but fierce. Two ice storms had walloped the area, closing school for a total of seven days in February and nearly sending everyone stir crazy from cabin fever. The fifty degrees was almost hot in comparison, and the open air, addicting.

The thick glass made it impossible for Jess to distinguish any conversation, but she could almost feel the buzz of the various rowdy discussions. Now and then a loud laugh or exclamation would erupt from one of the hubs. Jess assumed it was loud. It had to be if she could hear it from inside. She imagined that the talk was of the Extreme Beach Nationals, the big cheerleading competition taking place in a few weeks: who was heading down with who, which hotel people were staying at and what madness they could get into with their parents lingering nearby.

Typical day in the café, the school's powers discussing who and what was important in DRB High land in their own version of politicking and strategizing.

The café, twenty feet wide, twenty feet across, and accessible by a single door at the far end of the cafeteria, was nothing more than an island of concrete surrounded by a patch of grass just wide enough to be a pain for the maintenance crew to cut. But it was the students' slice of heaven. No teachers patrolled it. And nobodies stayed away from its door, choosing instead to a) act as if the café didn't exist or matter, or b) gaze inside from the windows, like Jess was doing now.

Only she wasn't a nobody. Jess was a café regular, an Upper whose right it was to lounge in the café at her leisure during lunch.

And until that very second, the café had been Jessica's safe haven from wannabes and nobodies, specifically the one wannabe nobody who annoyed her more than anyone in the world . . . Mina Mooney.

Jessica's eyes squeezed into slits, piercing Mina from the shadows of the hall as Mina's head bobbed up and down excitedly, deep in conversation with Kim, the varsity cheer captain, and Sarah, Jessica's twin.

Seeing Mina there, all smiles and grins, enjoying life in the fishbowl, shouldn't have jolted Jessica. But the flash of heat she felt boiling in her chest was anger—pure and powerful. It grew as she remembered how lightly Sarah had mentioned Mina's new "status."

"I was telling Mina that we're gonna kill it at the Extreme," Sarah had said, bubbling with a mix of anxiety and excitement at the thought of Nationals.

"Look, I know you two cheer together now, but I'm way over hearing you talk about *her*," Jessica snapped. She tossed her hair, a well-kept straight weave that hung just below her shoulders, and fixed her twin with a defiant stare.

Sarah's light cocoa-complexioned cheeks darkened slightly as the crimson spread through her face. But her voice was neutral as she answered, "I know you guys don't get along." She hesitated for a second, considering asking Jess for a truce at least through Nationals. The steely glare and Jessica's tight jaw were answer enough. She swallowed a sigh before finishing. "Nothing I say will matter, will it? You love to hate Mina."

Jessica laughed, her dark face brightening at Sarah's truthful declaration. "Yup. I do."

"Well . . . you know Kim and I invited her to sit in the café, right?" Sarah cleared her throat as if admitting it out loud had dried her mouth.

Jessica's smile quickly turned into a sour lemon scowl, and Sarah's mouth did dry out. Her tongue stuck to the roof of her mouth as she quickly added, "We have a lot of cheer strategy to go over. So you know . . . I mean, you knew Mina was going to get the call to the café eventually, Jess. She's the JV cheer captain . . . she . . ."

"Is a total wannabe, Sarah," Jessica huffed. Her finger wagged in Sarah's face as though she was lecturing a young child. Something she did often when it came to social etiquette, since Sarah, a total softie, insisted on befriending every stray and underdog in her path. "I know you like hanging out with any and everybody. But Mina is . . . the way she rolls with her—" Jessica rolled her eyes and sneered— "clique." She shook her head as if warding off some sort of bad word cooties. "Like they're running things at DRB High." Her next words were thick with venom. "I hate how she thinks her little Miss *Nice-Nice* act is going to make everyone like her."

Sarah giggled. "So let me get this right. You hate her because she's *nice*?"

She was used to Jessica's rants against Mina. The two had a history, mostly bad, going back to the seventh grade. Sitting in the café didn't mean much to Sarah. The whole social hierarchy thing didn't either. But Jessica rolled with the Glams, the snotty, mostly rich kids. She took her status as a member of the ruling class serious, deadly serious, and Mina had always, for some reason, been a threat to Jessica. Jessica had even tried to get her schedule switched around so she'd have the same lunch as Mina this semester, solely to keep Mina on the outside of the fishbowl. None of it made any sense to Sarah. But a small part of her felt that if she played mediator long enough, at some point Jess and Mina could peacefully coexist in the same circles at DRB High.

Surprisingly enough, it felt good to admit that she'd been the one to invite Mina to the café. She'd been hiding it for weeks, knowing once Jessica found out, it would be an ugly scene. But Jess was taking it pretty good, in Sarah's opinion. Now that it was out, Jess could get over it. Move on to choosing a new "wannabe" to hate. And she told Jess as much. "Look at it this way." Sarah draped her arm around Jess's shoulder and tried to ignore that, as usual, Jess tensed at the affection. "At least you don't have lunch with her anymore. You won't have to actually *see* her in your precious café."

The truth in Sarah's words taunted Jessica now. Knowing Mina sat in the café was one thing. And knowing was bad enough. Seeing her sitting there was another.

Just then, Brian James walked over to the table where Mina sat. He was cute with a capital "C," his toffee complexion smooth, eyebrows thick, soft brown eyes accented by thick lashes and a head full of hair so black and curly it made Jess's fingers squirm at the thought of touching it. He stood behind Mina's chair, his six-foot frame towering easily over the three-foot-high wrought-iron bar chairs, and wrapped his arms around her waist.

Jess averted her eyes from Mina's insanely idiotic grin and focused on Brian. He was telling a joke, she guessed, because all the cheerleaders at the table giggled and Sarah gave him a high-five. Just as quickly as he came, he whispered something in Mina's ear (more insane teeth-grinding grinning) and sauntered over to a table where a few gaming geeks happily welcomed him into their conversation.

Jess closed her eyes and tried to block out the image of that wide, "I'm such a lucky girl" grin on Mina's face. She tried to force the one word that kept coming up, to describe Mina, back into the far reaches of her mind.

It couldn't be.

Mina was not, could not be . . . an Upper.

No!

True, she was sitting in the café and was dating one of the school's hottest guys. It was definitely a ridiculous level of freshman beginner's luck. But it didn't make her an Upper, necessarily. Far as Jess was concerned, Mina was popular by association, and Jess was being generous by admitting that much.

No, Mina wasn't officially an Upper yet. And if Jessica had anything to do with it, Mina would never be . . . not while they roamed the halls of DRB High together, anyway.

If Mina wanted popularity, she'd have to go through Jess first.

Popularity had a cost, and Jess was going to make sure Mina paid dearly.